Here With Me

A SUGARLAND CREEK NOVEL

BROOKE MONTGOMERY

Here With Me
Sugarland Creek, #1

Cover designer: Wildheart Graphics
Cover photographer: Regina Wamba
Cover models: Trey and Meg Valdez
Editor: Lawrence Editing
Proofer: Editing4Indies

For Anna AKA That Blonde Bookworm

Thank you for inspiring me to write an ex-boyfriend's dad romance. I had a blast (with some emotional scars) writing *Here With Me*, and I hope Fisher is the book boyfriend Daddy of your dreams!

Quote

Take my own life just to save yours
Drink it all down just to throw it up
I got a reputation that I can't deny

-Reputation, Post Malone

Playlist

Listen to the full *Here With Me* playlist on Spotify

In the Stars | Benson Boone
Last Night | Morgan Wallen
Work Song | Hozier
Once in a Lifetime | Landon Austin
Wait | Maroon 5, feat. A Boogie Wit da Hoodie
All Of The Girls You Loved Before | Taylor Swift
Wanted | Hunter Hayes
Rock and A Hard Place | Bailey Zimmerman
Trouble | Jose Ross
Heartfirst | Kelsea Ballerini
Speechless | Dan + Shay
My Type | The Chainsmokers
Stand By Me | Lil Durk, Morgan Wallen
Exile | Taylor Swift, Bon Iver
Reputation | Post Malone
So Good | Halsey
We Got History | Mitchell Tenpenny

Acknowledgments

To Echo Grayce, Charity Ferrell, Morgan Achtermeier, Britt Johnson, and Tiara Cobillas:

This story would not exist without the help, guidance, reassurance, and sisterhood from these five woman who not only showed up for me, but read each chapter as I wrote them, sent me snacks, and gave me daily encouragement to keep writing Noah & Fisher's romance. ***Here With Me*** was a labor of love and a team effort to properly tell their story, and I'm so grateful to have these women in my life. Thank you from the bottom of my heart for being by my side. I'm so lucky and beyond grateful to have you in my life and on my team!

To the readers, old and new: thank you for picking up this book and giving me a chance as Brooke Montgomery. I hope you enjoy this new world as much as I enjoyed creating it.

Welcome to

SUGARLAND CREEK

RANCH AND EQUINE RETREAT

SUGARLAND CREEK, TN

~Welcome to Sugarland Creek Ranch and Equine Retreat~

The town of Sugarland Creek is home to over two thousand residents and is surrounded by the beautiful Appalachian Mountains. We're only fifteen minutes from the downtown area, where you can shop at local boutiques, grab a latte, catch a movie, or simply enjoy the views.

We're an all-inclusive ranch. While we provide rustic lodging, each cabin is handicapped-accessible with ramps and smooth walking trails. If you need assistance with traveling between activities, we'll provide you with a staff member to pick you up in one of our handicapped-accessible vehicles at any time. Please request at the front desk or dial '0' on your room phone. We're here to help in any way we can.

To make your stay here the best experience, meet the family and learn about everything we have to offer at the retreat to ensure you have the vacation of a lifetime!

Meet the Hollis family:

Garrett & Dena Hollis

Mr. and Mrs. Hollis have been married for over thirty years and have five children. The Sugarland Creek Ranch has been home to over three Hollis generations. When the family officially took over twenty years ago, they added on the retreat to share their love of horses and the outdoors with the public.

Wilder and Waylon
Twin boys, the oldest

Landen
The middle child

Tripp
Youngest of the boys

Noah
The only girl and baby of the family

Whether you're here to relax and enjoy the views or you're ready to get your hands dirty, we have a variety of activities on the ranch for you to enjoy:

Horseback trail riding & tours
(10:00 a.m. and 4:00 p.m.)
Hiking, mountain biking, & fishing
(Maps available at The Lodge)
Family Game Nights
(Sundays and Wednesdays)
Karaoke & Square Dancing
(Friday and Saturday nights)
Kids Game Room
(Open 24/7)
Swimming
(Pool open 9:00 a.m. to 9:00 p.m. each day)
Bonfires with s'mores
(Fridays)
...and much more depending on the season!

The Lodge building is staffed 24 hours a day. It's home to our reception & guest services, The Sugarland Restaurant & Saloon, and activities sign-up.

Find all of our current information at sugarlandcreekranch.com.

We pride ourselves on serving authentic Southern food, so please let us know if you have any dietary restrictions or needs to better serve you. We offer brunch from 8:00 a.m. to 1:00 p.m. The restaurant is open for dinner from 5:00 p.m. to 9:00 p.m. If you wish to dine or find other activities off the ranch, we're less than an hour from Gatlinburg and are happy to provide you with suggestions.

Thank you so much for visiting us.
We hope you have the best time!

-The Hollis Family & Team Sugarland

See map on the next page!

A	The Lodge/ Guest Services	D	Pool House & Swimming Area
B	Ranch Hand Quarters	E	Trail Horse Barn & Pasture
C	Guest Cabins	F	Riding Horse Corral

G	Hollis Fishing Pond & Hut
H	Bonfire Area
I	Family Game Nights Area
J	Gift Shop

Author's Note:

Here With Me is a stand-alone novel in the Sugarland Creek series and recommended for ages 18+ for mature content. The following triggers are mentioned or showed on page in the prologue: suicide attempt, loss of a child, grief, and depression. Please read with caution. If any of these make you uncomfortable, please skip to chapter one. You don't need to read the prologue to understand the rest of the story as it'll be talked about briefly in other parts of the book.

Prologue

Fisher

TEN YEARS AGO

I haven't slept in three weeks, not since I buried my daughter, and everyone—including my wife and son—blames me for her death.

Not that I fault them.

I blame myself, too.

Lyla was my little adventurer. At only ten years old, she was eager to do anything with me that involved hiking, horseback riding, biking, climbing, and any type of water sport. As a former bull rider, I loved that about her. Always willing to try something new and had a blast while doing it.

My fourteen-year-old son, Jase, is the complete opposite.

He prefers to stay indoors. After years of trying to get him to go camping and fishing with me, I gave up asking.

Now, he'll grow up without his little sister because of me.

This pain is unlike anything I've ever experienced. Its searing grief gnaws at me every second of every day. Memories of that day haunt me to the point of throwing up.

I can't take it anymore.

As I held my little angel in my arms, covered in blood and

lifeless, I begged whatever higher power existed to take me instead.

"Not her!" I screamed. "Take me! I'll live in hell for eternity if you save her. She's innocent!"

She was my whole world.

I even resorted to begging any evil force to kill me so I can stop reliving it every time I close my eyes. When that didn't work, I pleaded for something to happen. Finding relief in getting struck by lightning, a semi crashing into me, or a wild animal eating me alive.

I deserve to suffer because being alive makes my family suffer.

There's nothing left for me to do but find a way to end it.

I'm hollow, my heart aches nonstop, and there's no point living in a world where my daughter doesn't exist. My family hates me so much, they can't even look at me.

Dark clouds hover above, and rain unleashes around me. The pounding echoes through the cab of my truck as if it knows what my life has become.

I called my childhood friend to meet me here. When headlights appear in front of me, I'm relieved he showed up. It's almost time.

"What's goin' on?" Damien calls out when we both exit our trucks and stand underneath a tree to avoid getting drenched.

"I need a favor," I call out, reaching behind my back and grabbing my gun.

"The hell're ya doin', Fisher? Gimme that." His eyes narrow in on it as he reaches for it.

"Get yours out," I tell him.

Damien's been a cop turned detective since he was twenty-one, so I know he's packing. If anyone can do this right for me, it's him.

"What?" He steps closer.

I release the safety, then point the barrel toward him. "I'm threatenin' your life, so when ya kill me, ya can say it was self-defense."

"Fisher, what the fuck are ya talkin' about? Put it down!"

"No! I can't kill myself, or my family won't get my life insurance. This way, they'll get all my benefits."

"Ya can't do this," he begs. "What about Jase? And Mariah? They need you."

"Trust me, they don't. They can barely look at me."

"This isn't the way, man. Let me get ya some help."

"I simply cannot exist in a world where my daughter doesn't." My voice cracks as a lump forms in my throat. "I'm the reason she's gone."

"It was a freak accident!" he repeats words he's told me dozens of times.

"Doesn't matter! I shoulda protected her," I shout. "Please! I need you to end this pain. A life for a life!"

"You need help. Talk to someone. Let me take ya someplace safe. Don't go down this path." He inches closer, but I step back.

"She's not alive, and I shouldn't be either."

"I know you're hurtin', but this would bring more pain to your family."

"Trust me, they don't want me."

"They're hurtin' too, man. Come with me, Fisher. I'll take ya to a hospital."

I shake my head fiercely. "If you won't do it, I'll find another way. I'll stand in the middle of the town square with a gun and wait for an officer to shoot me."

"So they can watch it play over and over on the local news? Goddammit, Fisher! Get in my fuckin' truck. Please!" He tries to reach for me, but I back away.

"Do it for me now, privately, and no one else risks gettin' hurt."

I'm a selfish fuck. I'm putting Damien in the worst possible situation because I know he won't risk innocent lives.

I raise my gun higher, and he freezes. "Take yours out. *Now*."

After a stare down, he finally does.

"In the head, Damien." I point the barrel to my temple. "Right after I shoot at you, do it. Don't waste time."

They'll test my clothing for gunpowder residue to confirm I shot at him first and he was only firing at me in defense.

His jaw sets. "Fine."

My heart races as I look my best friend in the eyes. They're filled with anger and tension. He might hate me for this, but he loves me and my family enough to know they'd need my insurance money to pay off the house and expenses.

"Please tell Mariah to look underneath my seat in the truck. I taped a note there for her and Jase."

Even though they hate me, I want them to know how much I love them and how sorry I am for ruining their lives by taking Lyla from them.

"This is gonna destroy them, Fisher. Are ya sure?"

I ignore his question and continue with my instructions. "Next, tell Mariah everythin' she'll need is in my fireproof safe in the shed. All the insurance and homeowner's papers. And whatever she does, make sure she burns my letter after reading."

I can't risk the police finding it and questioning my death.

Then I aim my gun at something behind him and pull the trigger.

"Fuck," he hisses when it whizzes past him.

"Do it!" I shout, keeping my gun raised.

Damien shakes his head, points it at me, then shoots.

Chapter One

Noah

PRESENT DAY

"Goddamn, I love me some cowboys in tight Wranglers. 'Tis the rodeo season for fine asses," my childhood best friend, Magnolia, blurts way too loudly. A woman ahead of us glances over her shoulder with a scowl.

I burst out laughing, nudging my elbow into Magnolia's side as we walk into the arena. Not that her big mouth should even surprise me.

"Me too," my little cousin singsongs next to me.

"Mallory, shush your mouth. You're too young to be lookin'," I tell her.

"I'm twelve!"

"Exactly. Close your eyes." I attempt to cover them for her, but she shoves me away.

Magnolia snickers as we make our way up the ramp and into the arena. It smells like leather, dirt, and sweat. People in cowboy hats and boots walk around looking for a place to sit. The Franklin Rodeo is the heart of Southern rodeo in Tennessee. Every June, my family and I make the four-hour drive to watch the shows, eat lots of food, and listen to the live bands.

As a professional horse trainer on my family's ranch, I work with many clients for events like these. Barrel racing is one of my favorites to watch because I love that adrenaline high while anticipating them making it around the barrels without knocking them over. The excitement of each horse crossing the finish line gets me fired up every time.

One of my clients, Ellie, competes today. I've had butterflies in my stomach for the past week waiting for this. I live for the satisfaction of witnessing how the time I put in pays off. I also love showing my support when I can. I've worked with Ellie and her quarter horse for the past year, though she's been doing it a lot longer than that.

As we walk through to find a place to sit, I notice a few trainers glare at me and whisper to each other. I'm not surprised, considering it happens each time I'm at a competition, but it doesn't hurt any less. Most of them are in their forties and think I'm too young to have the success I do. I hear the rumors about how I only got here because of my last name and parents' money. On top of my being too young, the male trainers don't think I'm strong enough to train difficult breeds and like to degrade my skills to "good enough for a girl." But the truth is, I wouldn't keep my clients or get new ones if I couldn't back up my promises with talent.

"Don't look at them." Magnolia nudges me. "They're envious pricks with small dicks."

I snort, avert my gaze, and stay focused on maneuvering around people.

"And that's why they didn't get an invite to the Hollis fundraiser event of the decade," I gloat with a snarky smirk.

"Damn right. They could only wish to be good enough to be personally invited by *the* Noah Hollis."

I've been a trainer for years, but I've had to work at it every day since I was a teenager. My parents' money and ranch for me to practice on helped advance my skill, but my drive to learn and improve brought me to this level. Still, that makes me unlikable in this professional industry.

Six months ago, I proposed an idea to host a fundraising competition that'd benefit injured or rescued horses. I invited local trainers to bring their best clients to change the public's misperceptions of me and give them a chance to know the real me. Not only is it beneficial to the charity and community but it's a way for us to network as professionals.

My family's been all hands on deck in securing everything we need for it, and the first annual event will take place on our ranch in only a few weeks.

When we find seats, Mallory spots some friends she met at camp and asks to sit by them a few rows over.

"Don't leave the buildin' without me," I remind her before she wanders off. She's still close, so I can keep an eye on her. She moved in with my family a couple of years ago after my aunt and uncle passed away and has become a little sister to me. Although she drives me nuts sometimes, I'm super protective of her.

My parents and four older brothers are here somewhere. We venture off to different things, and since we brought three campers to sleep in, we come and go as we please. As an honorary family member, Magnolia tags along to most of our outings.

After ten minutes of waiting, the emcee announces Ellie's division.

"I'm gonna get closer."

"Well, shit. Don't leave me here." Magnolia follows me down the steps. You're not supposed to stand in the front and block others' views, but I'll only be a few minutes.

A few riders run, and one barrel tips over, making us wait for them to reset it.

"A hot guy in the row above ours is checkin' ya out," Magnolia whispers.

Turning slightly, I see the man she's talking about. Shoulder-length brown hair. Sharp jawline covered in dark scruff and a matching mustache the perfect length for inner thigh scratching.

His biceps look like they'll rip through his rolled-up shirtsleeves if he moves another inch.

My eyes widen as I return my gaze to Magnolia's smug expression.

"Told ya. He's bangin'."

That's an understatement.

I shrug so I don't give away how my heart pounds with how attractive and out of my league he is. "He looks too old."

More like twice my age.

At twenty-two, the oldest man I've dated was Jase Underwood, and he's only two years older than me.

"So what? You don't have to have Daddy issues to sample a finer cuisine."

I roll my eyes at her choice of words. Sneaking another glance, I notice his gaze remains fixated on me. He's rugged like a cowboy, which isn't much of a surprise at a place like this.

"He's probably glarin' at me for blockin' his view."

"No, babe. You *are* his view. That's a look of lust, trust me." She flips her long dark hair and steals another look.

"You'd know that look, wouldn't ya?" I snort.

"The look of thinkin' dirty things. I bet he's undressed ya in his mind three times and envisioned your boots wrapped around his neck."

I roll my eyes. "Doubtful. Wouldn't be surprised if he came down here and scolded me."

"Maybe he'll punish you with spankings..." She waggles her brow, and we get lost in a fit of giggles.

Clinging to the railing, I keep my attention ahead so I don't miss Ellie's entrance now that they've restarted.

Finally, Ellie and Ranger race into the arena. She's decked out in sparkly pink, including her cowboy hat, which I helped pick. She's not dubbed the Rodeo Princess for nothing.

"Yeah! Go, Ellie!" I cup my mouth and scream as she clears the first barrel.

Leaning as far over the railing as possible, I shout louder.

"Want me to lift ya up so you can be in there with her?" Magnolia mocks.

"Too bad I didn't make a sign."

She laughs but eventually gets into the spirit and cheers with me.

Ellie's posture is perfect as she rounds the second barrel and rushes for the third.

"C'mon, Ranger! Go, go, go!" I jump up and down at how flawlessly she's performing.

When Ellie rounds the final barrel, I nearly lose my mind. They race toward the finish line, and everyone goes wild.

"Fifteen point seven six eight," the emcee announces, then repeats it over the crowd.

"Holy shit!" I cover my mouth after I realize how loud I am.

"That should put her in first place, no problem," Magnolia points out.

"Her fastest barely cleared fifteen point nine. I can't believe how much time she shaved off."

"Probably all that cheerin' ya did. Encouraged them even more." She nudges me with a cheeky grin.

"Ha ha. But I bet you're right. Maybe I should add that into my trainin'. Sideline of me screamin' at you." I cackle.

"Speakin' of *screamin'*. Go celebrate by talkin' to the sexy cowboy. Maybe he'll have ya screamin' later for a different reason." Magnolia pushes me toward the stairs, and if I weren't living on this adrenaline high, I'd run in the other direction.

I don't mind taking risks. In fact, I thrive off the excitement of trying new things. But when it comes to dating and guys in general, I say things that get me in trouble.

"Good thing I'm wearin' my lucky cowboy boots." And my favorite white floral sundress that makes my boobs look awesome. It's the beginning of summer, and the temp is already in the low eighties, so I wasn't about to sweat my ass off being outside most of the day.

Magnolia smirks and urges me to go.

I walk up to his row, excuse myself as I shift my body in front of a few people, then sit next to him.

"Hi." I angle my body toward him as he takes a swig of his Budweiser.

He chokes when he realizes I'm speaking to him.

"Hi," he coughs out.

"You don't mind if I sit here, do ya? I saw you kept lookin' at me and thought maybe I was in your way." I flash him a mischievous smile, then pretend to look in the same direction as I was standing. Tilting my head to where I stood, I add, "But now that I'm here, I don't see how I coulda blocked your view."

I return my gaze to his as a half smirk forms across his face. "No, I could see just fine."

His deep timbre has a shiver rippling down my spine. I'm eager to hear it again.

"Oh, good. So ya musta been glarin' at me for another reason." Our knees are almost touching, and I'm tempted to inch closer until they do.

He stares at me as if he's contemplating his words. "I wasn't glarin'."

"Coulda fooled me. You were definitely starin' awfully hard, then." I lick my lips and wait for him to elaborate on why he fixated on me. When the awkward silence drags on, I continue, "Anyway...since you seem as comfortable as a cat in cold water with me sittin' here, I'll go back to my friend. You're free to join me. The view is great."

"Not as great as mine was."

I stare at him—half shocked and half giddy at his words. "A-are you hittin' on me?"

"Maybe I am."

Crossing my legs, I wave him on. "Well then, just go on and ask me."

He tilts his head as wrinkles form between his brows. "Ask you what?"

"For my number."

"I don't even know your name."

"It's Noah. What's yours?"

"Fisher."

"I like that. So now that we know each other, do ya want my number or not?"

He brings his bottle back to his tempting lips and watches me over the neck while he takes a sip. "You're very blunt."

"And why shouldn't I be?" I ask, keeping our gazes locked. "Are you used to shy women? Is that what ya prefer? If I'm not your type, you can just say so. It won't hurt my feelings."

"That's not it."

I shrug and say, "Okay," as if his lack of eagerness didn't bruise my ego. "If ya change your mind, I'm bartendin' at the Cantina lounge tonight. First beer's on me."

I've been a volunteer for the past few years since my family's ranch is a sponsor. My brothers pitch in too, but they don't do it for the charity proceeds. They're only after single girls' numbers, which is exactly why they'll need a babysitter at the fundraiser.

Before Fisher can respond, I sashay myself out of his row and back toward Magnolia.

Her eyes are wide, and her mouth is agape. "Where the hell did that side of you just come from?"

I link my arm through hers as I lead us to where Mallory sits.

"I channeled my inner Magnolia. Figured I'd never see him again anyway, so why'd it matter if I make a fool outta myself?"

"Jesus. By the way your bodies were leanin' into each other and the intense eye contact, y'all were turnin' me on for a minute." She makes a show of fanning herself.

We laugh as we take our seats in front of my little cousin, who's busy gossiping with her friend. I resist the urge to glance up to see if he's looking at me again but decide to play it cool as if I don't care either way. So much for going up there and giving him my number. Instead, I'm kicking myself and panicking about what a fool I am. Now I wish the ground would open up and save me from the humiliation.

Once all the racers have run, Ellie's declared the winner, and we shoot to our feet, clapping and letting out piercing whistles. I couldn't be more proud of her focus and determination. Even when she had bad training days, she'd get back up and work harder.

"Isn't that Craig Sanders?" Magnolia whispers in my ear as we watch the team roping event.

My eyes follow as she points in his direction, and my lip curls. "Unfortunately."

I'm not surprised to see him here as a trainer himself, but he's local to Sugarland Creek. He's probably trying to find clients or steal them from others.

He's a snake like that.

"Oh shit, he's comin' over." My back stiffens as he makes a beeline for us.

"Howdy." He tips his hat, and I cringe. "Congrats on the win."

"Thanks," I say. Although it's Ellie's win, he's bitter she came to me after she fired him last year.

"She was a little slow on that second barrel. Might wanna help her fix that so she doesn't have such a narrow win next time. Would hate to see her slip into second."

Magnolia shoots him a murderous glare as I force a grin. "I'll keep that in mind. Thanks so much for your valuable input."

His jaw twitches as if it's full of tobacco chew. Gross.

Mallory's clueless about what's happening and chimes in, "Which racer was yours?"

Magnolia stifles a laugh as I bite back a smile.

"Mine ain't here," he tells her in a forced drawl.

Craig can't keep clients because he has a shitty attitude and no patience.

"How come?" Mallory asks, ignorant of the irritation covering Craig's face.

Instead of answering, he gives me a nod. "See ya 'round, Noah."

"God, I hope not," I mutter.

He's another one who thinks he should be more successful than me because he's older. He also blames me when his clients leave and hire me instead.

Once the events are over for the evening, Magnolia takes Mallory to our camper while I head to the lounge for my shift. She promises to stop in later, but considering my brother Tripp is here, I doubt she will.

She's crushed on him since middle school, but he's never returned the feelings or been the settling-down type. He's only two years older than me, so I can't blame him. Eventually, though, she'll move on from her crush, and he'll be too late.

As I hand out drinks and chat with customers, my mind wanders to Fisher. Every time someone approaches, my heart skips a beat at the thought of it being him. I'm not sure he'll show up, but I want to be ready if he does. I grab a napkin and write down my number. This way, if he chickens out and doesn't ask me, I'll just casually hand it to him. He can decide whether he wants to use it.

Grabbing another napkin, an idea hits, and I jot down my ex's number. If he asks for it and the vibes are off, I'll give him Jase's instead, and he'll be none the wiser.

Chapter Two

Fisher

As soon as I walk into the lounge, I'm tempted to walk right back out.

What the fuck am I doing?

Noah's gorgeous and charming and at least twenty years younger than me. I shouldn't have been staring at her, but I couldn't help it. The moment my eyes landed on her, she consumed me.

She exuded so much energy and excitement it was impossible not to notice her. The way she cheered for her friend and got everyone excited brought me back to my bull-riding days when competing was my life and the crowds would go wild. Watching her had adrenaline roaring through my body, and I wasn't even the one in the arena.

When she sat next to me, my heart seized at our proximity. I nearly swallowed my tongue when she spoke to me.

Why the hell would she be interested in a guy twice her age?

Once the initial shock of her coming up to me wore off, it was too late. She'd already walked away with an invitation to meet her for a drink. After my long day, I wasn't planning to stop at the bar, but the thought of seeing her again was too intriguing not to go.

It took me two hours to talk myself into going in the first place, and now that I've found her, I can't keep my eyes off her.

She smiles and laughs while chatting with customers and the other bartenders. She hands out drinks and sways to the live music. Scrubbing my sweaty palms down my jeans, I walk over and hope she's as happy to see me as I am to see her.

As soon as her gaze finds me, her lips split into a wide grin, and she walks over with a Budweiser.

"You came." Her face lights up as she sets down a napkin and the bottle in front of me. "But now the question is, did ya come for my number or the free beer?"

"I came to see you. The drink's just a bonus." After taking a seat, I take a sip. The liquid helps cool me down as her flirty inspection heats my body.

Her brows rise as she digs into her pocket and pulls out two napkins. She looks between them before settling on one and shoving the other back. "In that case, I'll give you this."

When I look down at it, I grin when I read her number. "How'd ya know I'd come?"

"I didn't, but I was optimistic." She shrugs, resting her elbows on the bar and inching closer. "I figured if ya hadn't shown up by the end of the night, I'd give it to the next best-lookin' guy."

My muscles flex as I lean toward her and continue to give her my full attention. "The next best, huh? Who woulda that been?"

"See that guy over there..." She nods toward a man chatting in the corner holding a glass of dark liquor. "His name is Hunter. Thirty-two. He's a publicist for one of the big-shot bull riders. Used to ride, too."

Taking a drink, I size up the guy and force myself to keep breathing. He's not that impressive. In my heydays of being a rider, I bet I could've run circles around him.

Noah twirls a loose piece of her golden blond hair. "Suit and tie ain't really my type, but he seems cocky enough to at least give good oral. But if I had to guess, you'd be better at it."

Choking on my beer at her sudden outburst, I cough until it clears down my throat. *Jesus Christ. She's trying to kill me.*

"You alright? You choke a lot." She hands me a fresh napkin, and I take it to wipe my mouth.

"You keep takin' me by surprise." My voice is full of gravel as I try to choke down the lump of nerves.

Her hands go to her hips as her cherry-red lips curve into a grin. "You're not used to women hittin' on ya? That seems unlikely."

I love how bold and free she is. Noah's unlike anyone I've met before, and the urge to claim her mouth is stronger than anything I've ever felt.

Blunt, beautiful, and unapologetically herself.

And way too goddamn young.

Shaking my head, I position my hand to hide my smile.

"Are you...blushin'?" she taunts, tilting her head to get a better look at my face.

Straightening my spine, I move my hand down to my aching cock. "No. I don't blush."

Noah's lips curl up into an amused smirk as her own cheeks tint pink. "You, cowboy...are *blushin'*."

My pulse jumps, and I grip the Budweiser like it's my lifeline. "Between the two of us, you're the one who looks hot and aroused."

Her eyelashes brush her cheek before she sweeps her gaze up to meet mine. There's a wild and chaotic flicker behind her hooded eyes as she licks her bottom lip and reveals a secret smile.

I'd like to pull that lush lip between my teeth and explore every inch of her mouth with my tongue.

"I—" She pauses, inhaling a deep breath. When her dress stretches tight against her chest, hard nipples appear as her breasts rise and fall.

"Have I rendered you speechless?" I keep my eyes on hers as I tip the bottle of my beer up and drain it. Thank God the other bartenders are taking care of the customers because I like having her full attention.

A wild, possessive staking roars up inside me to claim more than just that.

"If ya wanted to force me to be quiet, there are more fun ways to keep my mouth busy that'll benefit both of us." A slight lift of her shoulders tells me exactly what she's implying.

"Jesus Christ."

My cock heard that one.

She catches me adjusting myself and smirks. "Need another?"

I hand her my empty bottle. I shouldn't have too many since I drank whiskey straight from the bottle to give me enough liquid courage to show up here.

"Depends. How late are ya workin'?"

"We close in less than an hour. You have plans?"

"For you? Yes."

She inches closer. "Go on..."

"I'd like to find out if you're a screamer or a moaner."

When her lips form into a tight smile, I worry I've crossed the line. People move and talk all around us. The music's too loud for anyone to eavesdrop, but by her silent intrigue, she's not worried about being heard.

She hands me another bottle, and when I grab it, she doesn't release her grip. Our fingers brush, and we're in a silent war of who's going to let go first.

"If you're doin' it right, I'm both."

My brain flatlines.

Before I can respond, Hunter and a couple of guys walk up. He purposely picked her since another bartender nearby has no customers.

Hunter smacks the bar top, stealing her attention. "Hey, gorgeous. Think ya can hook us up with another round?"

I tightly grip the beer bottle while waiting for this asshat to get lost.

"Sure thing." Noah whips her hair over her shoulder as she

turns to open the cooler. She bends, and my eyes narrow in on her ass since her sundress barely covers it. When I glance over, I notice Hunter's doing the same thing.

Fuck me. I'm no better than this douche.

Noah sets three bottles down and tells him the total. He holds out a twenty but doesn't release his hold when she goes to take it.

"What's it gonna take for me to get your number?" He flashes a cocky grin that I'm tempted to punch off his face.

"Now what would ya do with my number?" Noah holds still as she waits for him to release the money.

"A professional bull rider and the best show horse trainer in the state..." He sticks out his tongue and slowly licks his lips like a hungry hippo. "I'm sure your imagination can fill in the blanks."

So she's a horse trainer. *Impressive.*

Noah plasters on a smile even I can tell is fake as hell. "You tryin' to get off in eight seconds?"

I snort, holding back laughter.

Hunter turns and scowls but then quickly realizes I'm twice as big as him and returns his gaze to Noah.

"Let's make this easy," she says to him. "You pay for your drinks, give me a *hefty* tip, and I won't embarrass ya in front of your friends."

He stares at her uncomfortably before letting go of the cash.

"Don't forget the tip jar..." she singsongs, putting the money into the register.

Hunter frowns, digging more out of his wallet and aggressively shoving it into the canister.

As soon as they walk away, I stare at her, impressed. "That's how you manage to get the big tips, huh?"

"A girl's gotta do what a girl's gotta do in this economy."

I chuckle. She's funny as hell, and damn, those smart-ass comments are hot.

"Thank God I was here to rescue you from your second-best choice. He seemed a little eager to get into your pants," my words tumble out.

"They all are until it's game time, and then they're fumblin' on the field like a bunch of third-stringers."

An animalistic groan releases from my throat at the desire to show her exactly what she's missing.

"Is that why you're switchin' to older men? Because we can do it better?" I drain my second beer.

I swear I witness her whole body shudder. Without asking, she hands me another bottle.

"Honestly, I wouldn't know from personal experience, but I'm all about givin' the elderly an equal opportunity."

I clutch my chest as if her words gave me a stroke because they might as well have. "You're brutal, ya know that? Actin' like I'm shufflin' around with a walker."

"Everythin' shuts down at eleven. You better get a head start now so we don't have to push ya out in a wheelchair."

"I'm startin' to think you gave me your number so you can get on my AARP plan."

Wrinkles form between her brows as if she's contemplating what that is. "I'm pretty sure my dad has that."

I scowl, and my gaze darkens as she bursts out in laughter.

The sound of it softens my heart. I could listen to it for hours. And do whatever it takes to keep her laughing.

"So I'm curious. What was on the other napkin you pulled out?"

"I can't tell ya that." She shrugs with a playful smile.

I lean over the bar with my arms crossed, lowering my voice. "And why's that?"

She inches closer as if she's going to tell me. "Because then I'd have to kill ya."

I arch a brow, amused. "That so?"

She shrugs helplessly. "It's girl code. Can't share our secrets."

"What if I promise to tell you one of my secrets? Will ya tell me, then?"

"Hmm. That's very temptin'." She taps her lips that I'm itching to taste.

"I'll make it worth it."

"Alright, then." Her lips tilt up in a victorious grin as she reaches for her pocket and pulls out the second folded napkin. She holds it between us.

I'm close to grabbing it before she yanks it out of my reach.

"In case I changed my mind about givin' you my number, I wrote down my ex-boyfriend's."

The hand that was close to stealing it backs away. "Didn't know women did that."

"After a couple dozen times of tellin' boys no, we got smart. Usually pissed off our exes, too, so it was a win-win for us."

"Clever."

She crinkles up the napkin and throws it away. "I'm still friends with mine, so I wouldn't actually wanna do that to him. But it'd be a funny prank."

Customers pull her away as the music changes to an upbeat country song, and people file onto the dance floor. If she weren't working, I'd take her out there with me and use any excuse to touch her. My hands wouldn't leave her body until I was forced to.

That thought shakes me to my core.

My wife and I loved going out on the weekends before our daughter passed. We'd dance and drink until closing. Tonight's the first time in a decade I've even thought about dancing with another woman, and it only took two conversations.

I haven't had a woman in my bed since I was married. I've gone on dates and kissed them good night, but that's where it ended. The desire to have someone like Noah underneath me should terrify me. But it doesn't.

We have an unexplainable spark, and I won't waste time questioning it. I've spent years punishing myself for my past and how I handled things, but I don't want to deprive myself of potential happiness.

Noah hurled herself into my life for a reason. For the first time in only God knows how long, I want to follow my heart and see where it takes me.

Checking my phone, I realize the bar closes in less than twenty minutes. It's not as busy as it was when I first arrived, but now I'm anxious for the evening to end. I want more time with her. Preferably alone.

Ten minutes later, the band announces their final song and the last call for drinks. People flood the bar, pushing me out of my spot. Standing back, I keep my eye on Noah as I finish my third Budweiser.

Remembering I have her number on the napkin, I program it into my phone, then send her a text.

FISHER

I'll wait for you outside, and if you stay with me at my camper tonight, I promise to have you screaming within eight seconds.

My phone vibrates just as the bar empties and people file out, me included.

NOAH

It takes more than eight seconds to impress me, cowboy.

Smirking, I type out another message.

FISHER

So what would impress you?

NOAH

You'll have to wait and find out...if you can keep up with me.

Her words have my cock twitching as dirty thoughts swirl in my mind. I've never wanted someone I just met as much as I want her. I should leave her alone, but I can't find the strength to walk away. It's too late now. I'm all in.

FISHER

You're playing with fire, Noah. I'm gonna make you eat those words.

NOAH

I didn't earn the nickname AJ in high school for nothing. So if I'm gonna die from taking a risk, then it might as well be death by orgasm.

AJ? I type out a text to ask what that means, but then it hits me.

Adrenaline junkie.

That fits her.

I swallow down the lump stuck in my throat as I reread her text.

Death by orgasm. *Fucking Christ.*

This girl is bold.

Then she sends another text before I can respond.

NOAH

Assuming you can actually give me one. Don't wanna make your pacemaker flatline.

Goddamn. *She's brutal.*

And I can't say I've ever craved anything more.

FISHER

Your pussy's already aching for me, sweetheart. You'll be begging me to let you come, and maybe if you're a good girl, I'll give you exactly what you need.

More people fill the sidewalk as they leave the bar, and the doors lock for the night. I'm not sure how long it takes for them to close, but I'd wait here all night for her.

When my phone vibrates a couple of minutes later, it's a photo of Noah's white panties. She's holding them up on display, and I immediately worry about the other bartenders seeing them.

NOAH

I'm always a good girl.

FISHER

Put those away.

NOAH

You don't like them?

She follows her message with a sad face emoji.

FISHER

You're going to make me lose my mind if I think about another man seeing those.

NOAH

If you're not a fan of voyeurism, I suggest meeting me behind the building where we can be alone.

People linger on the sidewalks and in the parking lots, so it's definitely a better idea not to let them see what I'm about to do to her. She has no clue what she does to me.

FISHER

Keep those off. I'll be there.

Chapter Three

Noah

I shove my panties into my bag and say goodbye to the other bartenders. They were oblivious to what I was doing since I snuck into the bathroom to freshen up.

Once I go out the front doors, I walk around the building where food trucks park overnight. My nerves are in overdrive as I wipe my sweaty palms down my sundress.

I've never met a man before where the chemistry is so intense and immediate.

And hell, he hasn't even touched me yet.

I've also never had a one-night stand.

I played it cool, but my heart raced as we talked. When he texted, asking to see me after my shift, excitement ran through my body at the thought of us being alone together.

Magnolia was right. I need to get out and experience life instead of only focusing on work. Although, I'm not sure she was referring to this. She'll flip when I tell her it's with the guy from the arena.

I hardly know Fisher, and it should be concerning I'm about to go hook up with him. But this mystery man makes me throw all logic out the window. After being embarrassed when he didn't immediately jump to ask for my number, I was enthusiastic when he showed up at the bar. He was more calm and chatty than our first conversation, which helped me relax and not be so nervous.

The more we talked and flirted, the more I craved his attention. I haven't slept with a man since Jase—two years ago—and I'm ready to break my dry spell. There was one guy after him named Dylan, but it never went all the way. I stopped it before we could go further because I felt guilty as hell, like I was somehow cheating even though Jase and I were over. We've remained friends, so that's a part of it, but it's been long enough now. I need to get laid without worrying it'll somehow affect my ex.

I kept watching Fisher's calloused palms—a sign he most likely does manual labor or works outside—and it made me want to find out what else those hands could do. My vibrator is soul-snatching worthy, but a girl can only go solo for so long before it's not enough.

I miss the physical contact and the emotional release that comes with having a partner.

If I'm going to have a random hookup, it might as well be with a guy who looks like he knows what he's doing. Even with a bar between us, his deep voice and dark gaze had goose bumps covering my skin.

It doesn't hurt that he's too hot for his own good and much more experienced than me. He kept up with our conversation and then again when things escalated to sexting, so it'd be no surprise to learn he's just what I like in bed, too.

"Excuse me, cowboy. You waitin' for someone?" I ask as soon as he comes into view.

Fisher turns, and a deviant smirk plays over his scruffy face. He's pulled his hair back into a low messy bun, but I'm already fantasizing about threading my fingers through it. His jeans cling to his muscular thighs, and he's so much broader up close with a barrel chest and thick arms.

"I was gettin' worried you weren't gonna show up." He walks toward me with his hands in his pockets, and an appreciative, heavy gaze roams down my body.

"I think I'm worth waitin' for, don't ya?" I inch closer and realize the full length of him is at least a foot taller than my five-foot-four.

"Absolutely. I've been dyin' to try somethin'."

Before I can ask, he leans down and closes the gap between us. But I stop him before his mouth meets mine.

"You're not gonna murder me, are ya?" My words blurt out before I can stop them. I suddenly came to the realization that we're in a very narrow-looking alley with dumpsters and bad lighting. All that's missing are the constant stream of sirens blasting in the distance.

"Does it look like I wanna kill you?" He takes my hand and pushes it against his erection, proving just how much he wants me. Considering he's wearing jeans, and I can still feel how hard he is, I should be terrified of how thick his bulge is.

I swallow hard, and when he releases his grip on me, I stand taller. "I mean, isn't this the start of every true crime podcast episode? Guy fucks girl before stranglin' her and dumpin' her body?"

He blinks as if he's waiting for the punchline. But I've watched enough *Dateline* to reconsider how stupid I was to meet him back here.

Magnolia will kill me if I let a sexy cowboy who finally cleared out my pussy cobwebs murder me.

Maybe I shouldn't have given him the idea of dying by orgasm.

"Noah, if I were gonna kill ya, I wouldn't have been seen with you at a bar with dozens of witnesses."

Valid point.

"So you can promise I'm not gonna die within your presence?"

His lips tighten as if he's holding back a laugh, then he scrubs a hand along his scruffy jawline.

"Yes, I promise. But..." He cups my chin, bringing our mouths dangerously close. His breath on my flushed skin heats every inch of my aching body. "You'll be ready to by the time I allow you to come."

Did he just say...*allow me to come*?

He closes the space between us and captures my mouth before I can think of a response. I inhale his woodsy cologne that might not be on at all. He's the type of guy who naturally smells like that from getting his hands dirty. Hell, I don't even know what he does for a living, but I don't care. I don't want to get in my head anymore tonight. Not when I'm with him.

I need this.

I think he does too.

The warmth of his body is all-encompassing as his tongue slips between my lips. Butterflies invade my stomach at how good it feels, and I need more. Frantically, I grip his T-shirt, and a deep moan escapes my throat when his hardness pushes into me. His hand skates up my back and settles around my neck, holding me in place as he steals my breath.

"Fuck, Noah."

His mouth moves to my jawline and neck. The way he sucks and licks my skin permanently inks my soul. My breasts swell in anticipation of his touch, and my thighs squeeze at the intensity of his mouth. It's unlike anything I've ever felt, but when he leaves a trail of bite marks, a sharp gasp echoes between us.

"You liked that," he rasps and then captures my lips again.

My heart pulses uncontrollably as if it can't keep up with the sensations taking over. When he releases a deep growl, I know he's just as eager as I am.

"We should go," I breathe out when his hand slides under my dress and cups my bare ass. "Before we get arrested for indecent exposure."

When he digs his fingertips into my flesh, I grind harder into him. I love that I'm the reason he's this turned on.

"You shoulda thought about that before doin' this to me," he murmurs and then brings his mouth back to mine as I rock against his erection. "Since I owe you a secret, here's mine. I can't walk away from you now."

"Thank God." I look around, making sure we're truly alone,

and decide to live up to my nickname. Grabbing his hand, I lead him toward one of the food trucks. It's closed for the night, but the doorknob looks easy enough to pick. Digging into my bag, I pull out a couple of bobby pins and stretch them out.

"What're ya doin'?" He presses against my back as I shove both pins into the lock and twist them in opposite directions. "How do ya know how to do that?"

"My four older brothers taught me all kinds of shit just because they could." I chuckle because if Fisher knew half the things I did to keep up with them when I was younger, he'd run in the other direction.

"I'm gonna need more of an explanation than that," he says when I get it unlocked. It took me under thirty seconds in near pitch-black. My brothers would be so proud.

Maybe not if they knew I was using this skill for trespassing, but that's on a need-to-know basis.

I shove the pins back into my bag and walk inside. "It's not like we're stealin' anythin'. C'mon."

He follows me, closing the door behind him. As soon as he does, I drop my bag and fall to my knees.

"Noah..." He looks around, but everything's covered in shadows. "You shouldn't be on this dirty floor."

I chuckle that he's worried about *that* right now. "I can take it. I live and work on a horse ranch, and trust me, I've sat in worse."

I lower his zipper, unbutton his jeans, and then shove them and his briefs to his ankles. He inhales sharply between his teeth as I wrap my hand around his thick shaft and stroke him.

When he lifts his shirt and removes it completely, I'm greeted with solid muscles. From what I can see, dark hair lines his abdomen and chest.

How is this man single?

"Fuck me. That feels too good already." His voice is gruffer than before as he grabs my jaw, forcing me to look up at him. "You didn't have to do this for me, Noah. I coulda waited."

I shrug with a smirk. "I couldn't."

Before he responds, I wrap my lips around him and swirl my tongue along the tip. Fisher curses as he holds on to the counter with one hand and tangles his other in my hair. As I continue licking and stroking, he moans and tightens his grip against my scalp, nearly yanking the strands out. I repeat the motions a few times before deep throating as far as I can.

"*Shit.* You do that so well."

He helps guide my head up and down his shaft until I gag on his length. Not only is he bigger than I've ever had, but his girth makes my pussy wet in anticipation. He's going to stretch me wide until my legs give out, and I can't wait.

Sloppy wet noises echo throughout the small space. His balls tighten as I massage them in my palm, and when he whispers my name, followed by a throaty grunt, I know he's close.

"Such a good girl you are," he praises, rocking his hips to my movements. "I'm goin' fuckin' insane with that hot mouth of yours."

Gagging at how deep he is, I hollow my cheeks to suck him harder. His hold on me is secure and possessive, but I want to give him everything.

"I'm almost there if you want me to pull out."

Desperately, I shake my head. I didn't get on my knees in a dirty food truck I broke into just for him to come in his hand.

When his fingers tighten in my hair and pull my scalp, I brace for it.

Fisher releases a low and rich growl as his back straightens. His stomach tenses as I continue stroking and sucking until he's completely sated and finished.

Rapid breathing echoes between us as I swallow hard and savor his taste.

"Fuck, Noah. I can't believe you did that."

He looks at me in lust and shock when I swipe my finger over my bottom lip to make sure I've captured everything.

"We're not leavin' yet." He pulls up his jeans and tucks himself back into his briefs.

After I wipe my chin and smooth down my hair, he effortlessly pulls me to my feet as if I'm weightless. I'm not petite by any standards, but he makes me feel that way by how he manhandles me.

He palms my cheeks while his tongue invades my mouth, and our bodies collide.

One of his hands slides between my thighs, and I spread them wider as he thrusts a finger inside.

"Is this wet pussy for me?" he whispers against my ear, and a shiver radiates down my spine.

"Mm-hmm." My head falls back as the pad of his thumb circles my clit. He's hardly touched me, and I'm already breathing like I ran a marathon in the desert.

"Tell me."

"Yes, I'm *so, so, so* wet. Please don't stop."

"Are ya gonna let me taste this sweet cunt?" He spears a second finger inside. I gasp at the tightness but desperately need more.

"Right here?" I ask.

He chuckles against my ear. "Don't get shy on me now, *AJ*. You started this. Let me finish it."

The way he seductively drawls out my old nickname has me close to the edge and surrendering to his command.

Fisher kneels, lifts my sundress, and swipes his tongue along my aching slit. "Should we see if I can get ya there in eight seconds?"

"Oh my God." My eyelashes flutter closed as I brace myself against his shoulder and the counter behind me.

After a few moments of him sucking my clit and licking my pussy, he grabs my thigh and lifts it over his shoulder.

"Hang on so I can worship this cunt like the goddess you are. Start countin'."

I barely have time to register his words before he shoves his whole face between my folds. The way he devours me is unlike anything I've ever experienced. I'm already aware of how addicted I could get to this.

I dig my nails into his thick hair. The roughness of his facial hair scratching against my skin is everything I imagined it'd be. My clit pulses against his tongue as a fresh wave of electricity hits me.

"Fisher, that's so...*holy shit.*" Erratic breathing and moaning are all that follow my words as my ability to speak vanishes.

He works my pussy with his fingers, tongue, and mouth like an expert painter creating another masterpiece. His attention and ability to have me wanting to crumple to my knees is like nothing I've experienced before.

"Fuck, I'm close."

He lifts my leg higher, nearly making my unbalanced ass fall, but his hold on me is tight and secure. Fisher controls every inch of my body while bursts of pleasure shoot down my spine.

"Count the seconds, baby." The rough edge of his voice has me melting into a puddle.

"One, two, three..." My eyes roll to the back of my head, unable to continue. "Four, five."

As I teeter toward the edge, nearly falling right off the cliff, Fisher pulls back and releases my clit.

A strangled whine escapes my throat I hadn't meant for him to hear, but Fisher smirks up at me as if he's impressed.

"I can't fuckin' get enough. You taste so sweet."

"Then why'd ya stop? I was almost there!"

Three more seconds.

"Trust me." He winks before sinking his fingers back inside me.

My eyes roll to the back of my head as his lips find my clit again, and I feel that intense sensation take hold once more.

"Yes, don't stop. *Please.*"

"Six." The intense buildup nearly takes over all my senses. I brace for impact just as Fisher pulls away again.

"No!" I nearly cry at the loss. "Stop doin' that!"

His nose brushes along my bare thigh, and his scruffy chin scratches my skin. "Almost, sweetheart."

"Stop teasin' me," I say, remembering his earlier words. He warned me I'd be begging for it and that I'd be ready to die by the time he lets me come. "If I have to do it myself because you're incompetent, then I will."

"You put your fingers anywhere near your pussy, I'll tie your wrists back and leave ya in here."

"You wouldn't dare."

"I said I wouldn't *murder* you. Never said I wouldn't leave you orgasm-starved."

"At that point, just end my misery and strangle me."

He shakes his head, chuckling with amusement. "Be a good girl, and I'll give you exactly what ya need."

Fisher sets my foot down and then stands. "Turn around and brace yourself on the counter. Then widen those legs for me."

I obey like the desperate sex-starved woman I am. As soon as I'm in position, he drops to his knees and spreads my ass cheeks, exposing me in a way I'd normally feel embarrassed. But with Fisher, I don't care what he sees or does to me as long as he finally gives me the release I need.

"Please, Fisher," I say, not in the least bit ashamed to beg.

With my body leaned over as far as I can go, he dives back between my thighs and scratches every sensitive area his mouth touches. I can hardly take it as I focus on the sensations and the movements of his tongue.

"Seven."

His nose presses into me, adding to the friction.

He moans against my skin as he holds my clit hostage between his lips. Between the sensations of his tongue and the friction of his face rubbing against me, I soar off the cliff and scream as I ride the electric waves that take me to a place I've never been before.

"Eight."

Heaving breaths release from my chest as I try to take hold of myself.

"Fuck, Noah. You came so hard. You're shaking." Fisher soothes his hands down my legs as if he knows I need comforting.

My heart hammers to the erratic sounds of my breathing, and even when I try to get it under control, I can't. I've never been pushed toward the edge and pulled back like the way he did. By the time he let me fall, my body was so worked up, it's taking everything in me to come back down.

Fisher spins me around and pulls me to his chest, wrapping his muscular arms around me. "Are ya okay?"

I chuckle at how silly this is. "Yeah. I think so."

"You've never come like that before," he says, but his tone isn't judgmental. It's filled with kindness and understanding.

"Not to that...extent. And not for a lack of trying."

"I'm glad I got to give that to you." He presses a kiss to my forehead like a tender lover. "Whoever you've been with in the past clearly didn't provide what you needed."

"You've ruined me for all other men now. I hope you're happy." My tone is firm but not serious. Though it's true. No way will a guy my age have that level of skill. *And have me counting the seconds during it.*

"I won't apologize for that."

I laugh, but it dies off when he brings his mouth down on mine. "See how good you taste? You're the one who's ruined *me* for a lifetime."

He kisses me again, and we're lost in each other until sirens blast in the air, causing us to frantically break apart.

"Holy shit." I gasp. "It's security."

Fisher quickly locks the door. Instinctively, I drop to the floor. He follows suit but then pulls me into his lap and wraps his arms around me. Although they aren't legit police officers, they could still call us in for trespassing.

"Someone probably heard ya screamin'," he whispers in my ear, and I fight the urge to laugh at the irony. "Probably thought someone was bein' murdered out here instead of gettin' their cunt devoured."

He huffs when I elbow him in the gut.

"That's not funny," I whisper-hiss. "My parents *will* murder me if I have to call them after midnight to bail me out of jail."

Considering the times I've *not* ended up in jail, you'd think they'd give me a pass for the one time I did, but I sincerely doubt it.

Luckily, the large window used for taking orders and serving food is closed, but the windshield is exposed. If the officer peeks through it, we're doomed.

"Stay calm," he tells me when I shiver in his arms. "I'm sure he's just doin' a routine check and will leave soon."

"Then why did he turn on his sirens?" I keep my voice low.

"He probably heard somethin' and thought it'd chase off whoever was out here," he says.

My heart is about to beat right out of my chest, and then I won't have to worry about getting caught because I'll be dead.

The doorknob jiggling makes me jump, and Fisher covers my mouth.

He moves his lips against my ear. "Shh."

This is it.

How I get a record and get sent to jail.

Breaking and entering private property and violating a million kitchen health codes.

At least I got a mind-blowing orgasm before I had to trade in my cowboy boots for an orange jumpsuit.

The doorknob stops moving, and I blow out a relieved breath.

We sit in silence, waiting, and then a flash of light beams through the windshield. Oh God. They're going to see us sitting here and put me in cuffs.

Stupid, stupid, stupid.

All for oral.

Really good oral.

Still, I'm never going to hear the end of this. As soon as my parents are called, my brothers, Magnolia, and everyone in Sugarland Creek will hear what I did.

And worse, my clients might find out too.

Who's going to hire a horse trainer with a criminal record?

"Anyone in there?" a man calls out, and when the light beams across my face, my heart sinks into my stomach.

Here we go.

"Don't. Move," Fisher warns in a voice so low, I almost don't hear him.

Everything around me disappears as I try to sit as still as possible.

The bright flashlight dances around the truck, and I hold my breath until it finally goes dark again.

After a few silent minutes, I exhale.

"I think he left," I say.

"We should go." Fisher stands, holding out his hand for me. When I take it and get to my feet, I fix my dress, smooth my hair, and grab my bag.

"Do ya think we messed up anythin' in here?" I quickly look around. Nothing seems out of place, but there's not much time to consider that.

"Looks fine to me. C'mon." Fisher unlocks the door and holds it open for me to step out.

As soon as I do, a light blinds me.

Fuck.

Chapter Four

Fisher

The door slams behind me, and Noah freezes when a guard stands in front of us with his flashlight in our faces.

"Think ya can lower that?" There's no need to fucking blind us.

Once he does, I see a scrawny kid no older than my son.

"Noah..." The guy laughs, and my heart pounds harder than before.

This guy knows her?

"Ian?" She steps toward him, and he beams a familiar grin that immediately pisses me off. "You asshole! You scared me to death!"

He laughs as Noah playfully smacks his arm, and he tries to pull her into a hug, but she retreats before he can.

"I saw it was you and knew you had to come out eventually." He shrugs, wearing a smug smile as he puts away his flashlight. "Magnolia called when she couldn't get ahold of you, and I told her I'd go look for ya."

"Oh my God!" Noah groans, smacking her forehead. "I forgot to text her after my shift. I can't believe she contacted you to find me. I wasn't even gone that long."

"I ran into her earlier and reminded her she had my number.

Didn't expect the first time she'd use it would be to hunt you down, but I think she just wanted any excuse to text me."

Resisting the urge to laugh, I stand behind Noah with my arms crossed and wait for him to get lost.

Ian's gaze flashes to me briefly, sizing me up. With a flicker of his eyes, his attention goes back to Noah.

Noah glances at me before turning back to Ian. "As much as I appreciate ya lookin' out for me, I'm fine."

Ian matches my pose as his skinny arms cross his chest. "So should I tell her you were shackin' up with a random guy in a food truck? How'd ya get in there anyway?"

"No, I'll tell her myself," Noah insists. "I trust you won't rat me out for this little *mishap*?"

"You mean the B&E or indecent exposure?"

I scoff, interrupting their ridiculous conversation. There was no indecent exposure, and he knows it.

"Let's go, Noah." I take her hand.

"You're not free to leave," he says, stepping in front of me. "I'm gonna need to see some identification first."

Looking down, I have a good foot and fifty pounds on him. "Or what?"

"One of you broke into that truck, and the owner may wanna press charges," he says with his full chest.

Amused, I laugh. "Go ahead."

Instead of waiting for him to respond, I lead Noah around him and walk away. I'd like to see him try to stop me.

"*Noah Hollis*, I know where your camper is! I'll stop by tomorrow to discuss this!" Ian yells, and my entire body goes rigid at the sound of her last name.

We hadn't exchanged full names.

She's a *Hollis*.

And she's already mentioned she's a horse trainer, so it's likely her family owns the same ranch I just took over for Mr. Ryan. I did my apprenticeship with him after I finished my certification. He retired after forty years and referred me to a chunk of his clients, one of them being the Hollises. There's no world in which her parents would be okay with me sleeping with their much-too-young daughter.

"He's never lettin' me live that down," Noah grumbles as we take the route to the camping area.

"Who is that guy anyway?"

"My family and I come every summer, and he's worked security for the past five events. Magnolia and I got into some trouble a few years ago, and he's chased her ever since. She's not interested, though."

"She seems way too good for him anyway," I say earnestly.

Noah chuckles and nods. "She's too busy being in a toxic relationship with her ex to give anyone else a chance. Well, except my brother. He's too young and immature to have anything serious." She looks up at me and exhales sharply. "God, sorry. I didn't mean to blurt all that out. We never discussed anything beyond tonight, so you probably don't care."

Tightening my grip on her, I stop walking and pull her to my chest. She juts out her chin as I pinch it between my thumb and finger, hovering my mouth above hers. "I do when it involves you."

Her breath hitches before I press my lips to hers, and our tongues tangle together in a battle of lust-filled desire. Threading my fingers through her hair, I deepen our kiss until she gasps.

I break away from her mouth and move down her neck, then whisper in her ear, "Stay the night with me."

A moan escapes from her throat as her head falls back. "Okay."

"And you can be as loud as ya want, sweetheart." The corner of my lips curves up when she shivers against me.

"If that's your idea of foreplay, it's workin'."

Chuckling, I take her hand and practically sprint us to my trailer.

It's eerily dark and quiet as we make our way to the campsite.

As Noah's hand stays secure in mine, all I can think about is the events that led up to this.

I'm living in a fever dream because I never thought I'd have a chance with a woman like Noah, but I'm not taking it for granted.

Tonight, she's mine.

As soon as I unlock the door, Noah walks in, and I follow.

"Oh, crap. I better text Magnolia before she sends the real cops out on my ass." She grabs her phone from her bag and starts typing.

"What're ya tellin' her?"

"Thanks for sendin' Ian out to find me, you cockblocker. You nearly cost me an orgasm. I'm spendin' the night with Fisher so he can give me more than eight seconds of pleasure. No need to send the troops out lookin' for me, well...unless I go missin' and you don't hear from me in the next twelve hours." She glances at me with a mischievous grin before continuing. "At that point, you better send all of Tennessee out on a rescue mission because even though he's really hot and is great with his tongue, I doubt he can put me into an orgasm coma for that long. Either way, I'll tell you all about it later." With a smirk, she presses the send button. "That'll keep her off my back for a while."

I swallow hard. "Well, at least for the next twelve hours."

"Magnolia wouldn't wait that long, so I'd give it until breakfast before she came lookin' for me."

The whiskey and shot glass are still on the counter from earlier, so I pour one and then offer it to her. "Shot?"

"You tryin' to get me drunk?" She reaches for it, then shoots it down.

"Should be askin' you that. You kept servin' me."

"Yeah, *Budweiser*." She snorts. "No one gets drunk off beer."

Chuckling, I shake my head as I pour another shot and take it myself.

"Ya know, that Hunter kid, I was a lot like him when I was his age," I blurt out.

"Is that so?"

"I'm a former bull rider. Lived that life for many years before quittin'."

She walks around me before coming to my side and taking the whiskey to pour herself another shot. "Interesting. I didn't peg ya as the type."

"Spent my twenties travelin' all around the country, livin' that same adrenaline junkie life as you seem to be." I smirk when she throws her head back and chugs the liquid.

"Trainin' horses is hardly a rush, but it is fun. I've done some trick ridin' on one of my own. He'll probably kill me one day, but at least I'd go out doin' what I love."

Wrapping an arm around her waist, I pull her to my chest and tilt up her chin. "I had that same mindset until it almost did."

"Is that why you quit?" she whispers.

"No, but I got injured more times than I can count. My wife and kids never knew if I'd come home alive or in a body bag."

Her brows rise, and her ocean-blue eyes widen.

"I'm not married anymore," I quickly say. "We divorced a decade ago."

"Oh." She sucks in her lower lip. "Why're ya tellin' me this?"

I scrub a hand over my jaw and blow out a breath. "Not sure. I guess because I see how comfortable you are around me and worry the next guy you feel that way with will have the wrong intentions."

One side of her mouth curves up as she bites her lip. "And you have the *right* ones?"

I press my thumb to her bottom lip and pluck it from between her teeth. "Chasin' that adrenaline high can sometimes get us in trouble, and I'd hate to see ya make the same mistakes I did. Or regret."

"The only thing I'm gonna regret is if you don't finish what you started. I can't go back to Magnolia with no juicy details beyond what I sent her."

I cup the back of her neck, pulling her closer until our mouths are an inch apart. "So for her sake, I better give you a night ya won't forget." *And mine.*

"Yes, *please*."

Pressing my forehead to hers, I groan. "Fuck. Hearin' you beg makes my dick harder."

"Good. Then we can skip that step."

Chuckling, I close the gap between us and glide my tongue between her lips. Noah responds instantly, moaning and humming as I slide my hands underneath her dress. Her heart pounds against my chest, mimicking mine, and although I can feel she wants this, I need to hear her say it.

"Noah." I pant, moving a hand between her thighs and swiping a finger through her slit. "Are you sure you want this?"

She leans back with an arch brow. "Don't go soft on me now, cowboy," she says, lowering her eyes to my groin. "I wouldn't be here if I didn't, so whatever you need to hear from me to validate what you're about to do to me, I'll say."

Amused, I arch a brow and wait.

"You have my full consent to fuck me against every surface of this place. I give you consent to put your hands, tongue, and mouth all over my body. Hell, do ya want it in writing?"

My head falls back with laughter because Noah is unlike any woman I've ever met. Her boldness and bluntness took me off guard at first, but now I'm finding it turns me on.

"Verbal consent is good enough for me," I taunt, sinking a finger deep into her pussy.

"Thank God." Her eyes flutter closed as she exposes her neck, and I gravitate toward the soft skin, sucking under her ear.

"This dress needs to come off." I pull on the fabric, but she stops me before I can lower it.

"Pull it above my head. No rippin' my favorite dress like a caveman."

"I thought women liked that," I tease, playing with the straps.

She snorts. "In romance novels."

"You read those?"

"Before bed usually. Mostly Viking and monster smut."

My brow quirks up. "I'm not even gonna ask what that is."

"Best for your ego not to."

I don't tell her that I'm well aware of romance novels. My wife read them day and night and then realized how much I lacked in the husband department. Couldn't blame her, though. I was never around.

She lifts her arms, and I yank it over her head, leaving her in nothing but a low-cut bra. I lift her foot and remove one cowboy boot before going to the other and repeating the process.

"If you tell me, maybe we could reenact one."

"You're either gonna have to gain a hundred pounds of muscle and stretch another foot taller or grow a second penis really quick to do that."

Standing, I blink, and she laughs at my expression. "Hey, you offered."

"Figured you'd read western novels about cowboys and stuff."

"My brothers act like wannabe Clint Eastwoods, so the last thing I'm readin' is anythin' remotely similar to them." She shivers in disgust, and I chuckle.

A reminder of her having four brothers confirms she's from the same family I'll be working for. Mr. Ryan told me the Hollises have five kids.

But I can't stop now.

Nor do I want to.

"Alright, so no cowboys. What about forbidden romances?" I remove my shirt and kick off my boots. If anything were to happen between us after tonight, we wouldn't be able to go public with it. Not with me being twice her age and working for her family.

"*That* is my kryptonite. I love it when two people who aren't supposed to be together fight their way to make it work."

A low groan deep in my throat releases at her words.

As her gaze focuses on my chest, I unbutton my jeans. Before

I can remove them, she takes over, slowly gliding them down and off my feet.

Leaving me in my briefs, she stands and wraps her hands behind herself. She unclasps her bra and then tosses it aside. Her breasts rise and fall as I take in all of her.

Holy shit. "Your nipples are pierced."

She looks down. "Oh, wouldn't ya know. That they are."

I smirk and then palm one. My thumb softly caresses her smooth skin, but I have the urge to bite down on her breast. "Will it hurt if I touch it?"

"Nope." She proves herself by pinching the other nipple and moaning.

When I press my lips against hers, her hand drops, and mine palms her ass cheek. "Stunning, Noah. You're fuckin' stunning."

My lips find her neck again as she wraps her arms around me, pushing my erection into her stomach. "I need you inside me, Fisher. *Please.*"

"How do you want it?" I whisper and bite her earlobe.

"Fast. Hard. Deep. All-consuming. Slow. Painfully slow. And then deep and hard again."

I chuckle at her detailed list but adore how she knows exactly what she wants.

My mouth finds hers, and I brush my tongue along her bottom lip. "Is that eight separate times or all before I let ya come?"

"You tell me. You're the one who likes the number eight." Her teasing tone has my aching cock throbbing harder against her. As much as I want to sink into her for hours, it's been too damn long since I've been with a woman. The first time she orgasms with me inside her might do me in, but I'm not letting that derail me. We have all night.

"I don't plan to stop at one," I tell her, lowering my hand to her clit.

Her breathing picks up as soon as I touch her. Noah's so responsive, it won't be long before she's coming on my tongue.

Kneeling, I spread her wide and brush my nose along the seam of her thigh. She lifts her leg for me. I hitch it over my shoulder, dive in, and work every inch of her pussy with my mouth.

After a few minutes of her clawing at my hair and moaning out my name, she squeezes my fingers and cries out through her release. I lick up her juices, then flick her swollen clit a few times before setting her leg down.

I stand and cup her face, then slide my tongue between her lips so she can taste her sweetness.

"That was intense," she whispers.

"That was only one." I give her ass a little smack. "Now on the bed, *baby*."

Chapter Five

Noah

F*uck, where is my bra?*

After Fisher took off my dress, I flung my bra somewhere. I'm not about to leave without it since it's the only one I packed. I don't need my piercings blinding my family.

As I lower to my hands and knees, crawling around with my ass straight up, I find it underneath his jeans.

Thank God.

Next, I dig in my bag for my panties.

It's one thing to make the walk of shame at seven in the morning, but it's *shameful* to do it commando.

And I am a classy Southern lady, after all.

With the exception of last night.

Once I'm dressed and slide on my boots, I grab the rest of my things. Fisher hasn't stirred once since I climbed over his naked body and slid out of his bed. I'm half tempted to check his neck for a pulse.

That'd be my luck.

Best sex of my life leads to him dying afterward.

I know he's older, but he's not *that* old.

When I see his wallet on the counter, I contemplate taking a peek at his license to see his birth year. Amid our grinding against each other make-out session, I asked if he had a condom, and he told me to grab one from his wallet, which was in the back pocket of his jeans. Once I grabbed it, I tossed the leather aside.

Glancing once more at Fisher to make sure he's still in a sleep coma, I open his wallet and look at his ID.

He's forty-four.

Exactly twice my age.

Okay, so it's not that bad.

He doesn't even look forty.

It could be worse. *He could be fifty.*

But then I blink, reread his full name, and it does. It gets so much worse.

Fisher Underwood.

It can't be. My throat tightens as I choke down the surprise I never expected.

I need to get the hell out of here before he wakes up.

God, I hope this is a hangover dream.

More like a nightmare.

All the air gets sucked out of my lungs at the realization.

I just slept with my ex-boyfriend's dad.

The sun blinds me all the way back to my camper as the heat pierces my face. It's one of those rare early summer mornings when it feels like a hundred degrees, but it should only be in the midseventies at this hour.

No such thing as global warming, my ass.

Tell that to my vagina lips that are currently glued together.

I dig my keys out of my bag and quietly unlock the door before creeping inside. Mallory sleeps on the top bunk since it's smaller and has less space. Magnolia and I share the bed beneath her, which is only a full size and nearly has us on top of each other just to fit. At least she got it to herself last night.

Deciding to shower later, I crawl in next to her and lean my body against hers.

"Get your nasty sex sweat off me," she groans, trying to wiggle closer to the wall.

I snort. "Don't ya even wanna hear the juicy details?"

"Unfortunately, yes. But after I've had coffee and you no longer smell like a dirty hoof."

Lifting my arm, I smell underneath it. "I do not. Leather maybe. That's what he smelled like. And something else manly."

She scoffs, turning to face me. "I can't believe you finally got laid. The two-year dry spell is over! How do ya feel?"

"A little sore, actually." My cheeky tone has her playfully smacking my shoulder.

"Besides that. Emotionally, mentally...how'd it compare to Jase?"

My eyes widen at the nausea rising up from my stomach, and I swear I'm going to vomit all over her right this minute.

"Mags, I need you to never repeat that sentence again." I roll to the edge of the bed and sit, then rub my temples.

"Oh shit. What happened?" She gets to her feet and then kneels in front of me. "Did ya scream Jase's name by accident?"

"God, no. Though it wouldn't have been as much of a shock after finding out something this mornin'..."

"Spit it out, woman. What'd ya find out? His age? Is he like forty-five or somethin'?"

I wince because I *wish* that were the issue. "Pretty damn close, but that's not the problem..."

She stands as I keep my gaze on the floor. "You're freakin' me out. Just say it."

Blowing out a breath, I blurt out as my shoulders sag, "He's Jase's dad."

Silence lingers between us, and when I finally look up, her mouth is agape, and her eyes glassed over.

"Mags?"

"I'm gonna need you to repeat that." She swallows hard. "Because there is no freakin' way..."

"I saw his license. Fisher *Underwood*."

"That could be an uncle. Or a long-lost relative. Maybe a second cousin. How do you know it's his dad?"

"After everything he told me, I put the pieces together. He was married, like ten years ago, talked about how he had kids, and was a former bull rider. Plus, the age difference makes sense. Jase is twenty-four, and his dad is forty-four. Jase said his parents had him young. That would've made Fisher twenty."

"Jase never told you his dad's name?"

"No, he rarely spoke about him. All he'd ever say is that they had a strained relationship ever since his sister passed and he moved away for work."

It dawns on me that Fisher's lost a child.

Jase and I broke up a couple of years ago, but we've remained friends. We don't talk as much because he's busy working in real estate, and I spend every free minute training.

"If Fisher's back in Jase's life, he hasn't mentioned it to me," I say. "Then again, we only text a few times a month."

"Wow...I mean...holy shit." She sits next to me.

"Ditto." I rub my temples again. "I didn't even ask what he did for a livin'. He talked about his early bull ridin' days, and then well, we got distracted."

She nudges me. "I bet y'all did."

Groaning, I fall back on the bed and cover my face. I don't usually get hangovers, but I feel a headache coming.

"I take it you left while he was still asleep?"

"Yes, but to be fair, I'm not even a hundred percent sure he was alive. Either he's dead or he sleeps like it."

"Oh my God. You literally fucked him into a coma. Thatta girl." She bursts out laughing, then slaps my bare leg.

"This is humiliating, Mags. How am I ever gonna speak to Jase again without confessing what I did?"

"First rule, you don't tell your ex. Second rule, you find yourself a rebound lay and forget it ever happened."

"And what if Jase brings him to the ranch or somethin'? Or I run into them in town?"

"Well, you've gone this far without doin' so. I'm sure you'll be fine. Even if his dad is around, he probably won't remember what ya look like without your legs around his head."

"Hilarious!" I sit up and push her off the bed, then laugh when her ass bounces off the floor. "That's whatcha get."

"I still wanna hear the juicy details. Don't think you're gettin' outta that." She gets to her feet, and I laugh.

"Don't worry, you'll get them as soon as I hear about what *you* did last night."

"I-I hung out with Mallory." She shrugs, but the way she avoids eye contact tells me otherwise.

"Uh-huh." I cross my arms. "We'll see about that when I get her side of the story."

Magnolia lingers around the kitchen as she grabs a couple of K-cups and then adds water to the Keurig. "Go ahead."

She knows I won't wake her, so I'll have to wait until she's up for the day. Mallory's no snitch, though. She thinks of Magnolia as a sister too, but I'm good at reading people. I'll know whether she's lying for her.

"I'm gonna shower, and then we can meet up with the fam for breakfast."

I dig out my phone from my bag and scroll through my texts until I see Tripp's name and type out a message.

"Who are ya talkin' to already?"

"Gonna see what my brother's version of events from last night is…" I hit send before she can stop me.

"Why would you assume he knows anythin'?"

"Because you didn't visit me at the bar like you promised, which means y'all were unsupervised for several hours…"

She shoots me a glare. "I'm not a child. I don't need to be *supervised*."

"No?" I raise my brows because around Tripp, she's not herself. "Are we still talkin' to the ex?"

"Ugh, why'd you have to bring him up? Gonna throw up my breakfast before I've even had any."

Chuckling, I grab my shower stuff from my duffel bag and then walk to the bathroom. Before I shut the door all the way, I peek my head out. "You need to work on your poker face. I know you're lyin', and I'm gonna get to the bottom of it."

Before she can move toward me, I shut the door and lock it.

"You're a twat, Noah." She bangs her fist on the other side. "Don't ask Tripp about me, please! He's gonna think I was talkin' about him or somethin'."

"Then ya need to stop pinin' after men who don't want you back! It's for your own good. You need to move on!" I've told her this before, but sometimes Magnolia needs a swift kick of tough love.

Tripp has avoided Magnolia for most of his life, yet she can't kick her schoolgirl crush.

It's what made her date Travis in the first place. She thought making Tripp jealous would be enough to see what he was missing, but it only put her in a toxic on-and-off relationship. Magnolia has way too much to offer to settle down for anything less than unwavering love. She just needs to see it for herself.

"*Fine*. I'll never talk or look at Tripp again if you promise you won't bring my name up to him!" Her pathetic begging has me opening the door. "I'm a loser. I know."

I pull her in for a hug. "If it makes ya feel better, we both are."

She snorts, pushing against me. "You're supposed to say '*No, you're not. You're totally normal*!'"

"Well, I could, but this unrequited crush you have is *not* normal. We gotta find you a real man who'll appreciate everythin' about you."

I love my brother, but he's too ignorant to see what's right in front of him. It'd be one thing if he didn't see her that way, and it was a case of one-sided feelings, but Tripp's played with her emotions since high school. He gives her a little attention, gets her excited that he's interested, but then gets skittish like a horse who stepped on a snake. I'd smack him if I knew he wouldn't send Momma after me.

"Hmm. Think Fisher has a brother?" She waggles her brows.

I roll my eyes at her sneaky way to bring up his name again. "He might. Jase has an uncle, but I'm not sure from which side of the family. I'll be sure to ask him when I'm dyin' of humiliation after he finds out what I did."

"*Who* you did." She snickers.

"Shush your mouth. Now go make us coffee."

She wraps an arm around me and pulls me in for a hug. "For what it's worth, I'm proud of you for goin' after someone you liked. I know gettin' over Jase was tough and bein' vulnerable with another man couldn't have been easy."

I give her a tight smile and shrug.

"I hadn't expected you to get over him by ridin' his dad, but who am I to judge?"

"Oh my God, I hate you." I shove her backward so I can close the bathroom door. She knows damn well I've been over Jase, but it's not easy dating in a small town where we all know each other's business. The pool of single men is like a kiddie pool of emotionally unavailable boys.

"Love you too!" she shouts on the other side.

Once I'm under the hot stream, I contemplate my next move. Fisher will realize I bailed on him as soon as he rolls over to an empty bed, which I hadn't intended to do when I first got up. I planned to leave him a note or text to explain why I had to leave and offer to talk later. I was so freaked out by his last name, I couldn't even think of an excuse before hightailing it out of there.

Today's the last day of the rodeo, so we could still run into each other, but if he calls, I'm not sure I'll have the courage to tell him the truth.

The reason I can never see him again.

Chapter Six

Fisher

"Well, look at the two most handsome men in Sugarland Creek gracing my presence this mornin'," Vicky gushes as soon as she hands us menus.

Jase takes one before sliding the other toward me. "You say that to everyone."

"But I only mean it about half the time." She winks, then pours coffee into our mugs. "Y'all ready to order?"

"Yes, please." I close my menu, then motion for Jase to go first. Once he's done, I tell her mine, and then she's gone.

"So anythin' new happenin'?" I ask after a moment of silence.

I rest my arms on the table, leaning forward to engage in a conversation, but Jase occupies himself on his phone. Moving back to Sugarland Creek to reconnect with my son is something I should've done years ago. When I told him I was interested in buying a house, he was excited to be my real estate agent, and I was eager to spend time with him.

"Not really," he mutters, focusing on the screen.

"When's your next open house?"

"Sunday. Why?" His head pops up. "You lookin' to buy another place?"

I give him a tight-lipped smile, sitting back in the booth. "Nah. One is plenty for me."

His fingers go back to typing something, and I blow out a frustrated breath. Jase doesn't owe me anything, but it'd be nice to get his attention for a few minutes when we're having breakfast together. Milly's Diner is a staple in town, and one we used to frequent as a family when he and Lyla were kids. Memories flood in as I look around at the old leather tan booths and inhale the familiar smells of coffee and grits. The wall behind the cashier covered in kids' artwork from the children's menus brings me back to when they'd color as we waited for our food. Lyla would purposely steal the best colors and leave Jase with brown and black.

"How's your mom doin'? And Braxton?" She remarried when Jase was fifteen, and as far as I'm aware, they have a decent relationship. Braxton raised Jase like his own, which is something I'll always be grateful for, but the thought of them being close leaves me with even more regret.

One shoulder lifts as his attention stays glued to his texting conversation. "Fine. They're takin' a trip to Hawaii soon."

"Good for them. I hear it's beautiful this time of year."

"Yeah," he replies.

Sipping my drink, I wait for him to make conversation or bring up something we can both engage in. It's on the tip of my tongue to ask questions about the Sugarland Creek ranch, but I know I'll just get more one-word responses. When they opened the equine retreat twenty years ago, I was in the prime of my bull-riding career and didn't bother meeting them even after I retired and became a farrier.

There's nothing I can do that'll fix the damage I caused my son by leaving him, but I can try like hell to be the father I should've been. Even if he won't make it easy.

By the time I was out of recovery, my marriage was over, and Jase hardly recognized the man I'd turned into. I wanted to be the parent he deserved, but he resented me—for his sister's death and for not being strong enough to stay.

No matter how hard I tried, he refused to see me. It didn't help that by the time I was ready to go back to work, all my clients moved on, and the only way to find work was outside of Sugarland Creek.

I traveled across Tennessee, Georgia, and Alabama but never stayed anywhere long enough to lay roots. Taking over for Mr. Ryan was my ticket to moving home, and damn, it feels good being back.

Since Jase is a licensed real estate agent and I was looking to buy a new house, I was able to use that as a wedge and find something to connect over, but how much he lets me in is up to him.

"You missed a good rodeo last week." As soon as I say the words, my heart gallops at the reminder of Noah and finding my camper empty the morning after we shared the greatest night of my life. Since my texts went unanswered and my calls were sent to voicemail, I got the hint.

He curls his lip, finally looking at me. His deadpan expression makes me bark out a laugh.

"That's more up your alley, ain't it?"

Even before our family broke apart and I was traveling for bull-riding competitions, Jase was never interested. I brought him to practices and competitions, tried to get him involved, but he hated every minute of it. When I retired and got certified to be a farrier, he still had no interest in being around horses or ranches. Lyla loved tagging along and talking to the horses when I worked on them. Spending time together is what made us grow so close and why her death hit me as hard as it did.

"You might like it if you actually came and saw for yourself," I say harsher than I meant to.

"A bunch of grown men actin' like idiots on dangerous animals sounds foolish and lame to me."

"They had Wisconsin cheese curds, your favorites," I taunt as a way to lighten the mood, but he ignores me. Guess that won't be our bonding subject. He used to beg for greasy food when we'd go to the state fair. That and the go-cart rides are the only reasons he'd want to go. He'd ride with his mom, and then Lyla and I would team up and race against them for hours.

"Sorry to keep y'all waitin'. Bobby Ray lost your ticket, and I made him put a rush on it. Damn kid." She sets down our plates, then steps away to grab the pot of coffee.

"Thanks, Vicky," I say once she's warmed up our mugs.

"Anythin' else I can getcha?"

Shaking my head, I grab a piece of crispy bacon and take a bite. Jase cuts into his sausage before slathering it in gravy.

"You wanna come over tonight after work? We can drink a few beers while you help me unpack," I offer with amusement. My house came with five acres of land, just enough to have a large shed for all my work supplies and no nosy neighbors.

"I'll be workin' late. Meetin' a client for dinner and then doin' some paperwork. Maybe in a few days."

I nod, focusing on my plate. "Sure, sounds good."

The rest of our meal goes much the same. I bring up topics to talk about, and he gives me short responses. But I won't push him. No matter what, I'm here for the long haul.

The anticipation of running into Noah has me driving extra slow down the ranch's entrance so I can look out my window at the people wandering around.

I park near the barn where Garrett told me to meet him and hop out of my truck. As I approach the door, a man stops and asks if I'm lost.

"I'm lookin' for Mr. Hollis. I have a meetin' with him at ten."

"And you are?"

I cross my arms and exhale. "Fisher Underwood. The new farrier."

He looks me up and down and then nods. "I'm Ayden Carson. The boardin' operations manager."

"Nice to meet ya."

"Follow me. He should be in the office."

As we walk down the center aisle, I notice how clean and organized it is, unlike most of the ranches I've worked on. At least two dozen custom Tuscany stalls occupy the space, and by the looks of it, all of them are filled with boarders. This barn is twice the size of what I was expecting.

Horses peek their heads over their doors as I go by, and one jerks his nose up, trying to nibble on my sleeve.

"That's Nibbler. Got that name for a reason." Ayden chuckles when I stop to pet him, and the horse tries to eat my shirt again. He's going to be a fun one to work on. Most experienced horses don't mind their hooves being cleaned, but some get anxious and feisty, biting at my clothes and making it harder to focus when they attempt to undress me.

Brushing a hand down my arm to wipe off his slobber, Nibbler releases a loud sigh when I step out of his reach.

When Ayden and I approach the office, the door swings open, and out walks a woman. My heart pounds in anticipation of seeing Noah, but it's not her.

"Hey." She lowers her gaze down my body and then meets my eyes with a flirty smirk.

"Ruby, this is the new farrier, Mr. Underwood," Ayden says.

Her clothes are worn and dirty like most ranch hands, so it's obvious she works here. "About time. You got your work cut out for ya." She playfully pats my bicep as she walks past me.

Glancing at Ayden, he barks out a laugh. "She's harmless but doesn't sugarcoat it. Mr. Ryan was supposed to be here six weeks ago, and that was a delay from his usual appointment three weeks before that."

"Sorry I couldn't get here sooner." I was still contracted for jobs on the other side of the state when Mr. Ryan reached out, and he must've left sooner than he told me. That means it's been at least nine weeks since their last hoof clean.

Ayden motions for me to enter the office, and when I do, a tall and barrel-chested man stands from behind a desk.

"You must be Fisher." He reaches for my hand, and then we shake.

"It's a pleasure to meet you."

"Sit, sit. Lots to go over before my team puts you to work."

Between Ruby's warning and Ayden's comment, I have a feeling this ranch is about to become my second home.

Chapter Seven

Noah

"New eye candy alert," Ruby singsongs as soon as I walk into the stables.

"Who?" I lead Buttercup into one of the grooming stalls and securely crosstie him in place.

"New farrier. He's in the office with your dad. But goddamn, I nearly tripped over my boots gettin' a good look. Might've squeezed his bicep when I walked past him, too."

I snort as I remove the saddle and set it on the stand. "Didn't you and Nash just celebrate your eighteen-month anniversary?"

She holds up her left hand and wiggles her bare ring finger. "I can still appreciate the view when he looks like a souped-up cowboy who walked right out of *Yellowstone*."

Magnolia and I have binged that show more times than I can count, so now she has my undivided attention.

"Tell me more." I grab a brush and begin grooming Buttercup. We had a long training session this morning since he's scheduled to leave tomorrow. The owner bought him on a whim without realizing he wasn't professionally trained, and he bucked her off within thirty seconds of getting on him. After four months of daily cross-training, Buttercup's time has come to an end. But since I'm a perfectionist and my own worst enemy, I can't let my boarders leave without one final session to ensure they're ready. Mrs. Clark came twice a week to ride him under my guidance so she's as prepared as she possibly can be when I'm no longer around.

"He's basically a Luke Grimes dupe. Maybe a smidge older. Dark hair to his shoulders. Scruffy jawline. Brown eyes with wrinkles around the creases. Tall and muscular. My soon-to-be *Daddy*."

Staying focused on Buttercup's grooming, my heart pitter-patters as her description matches Fisher's. There's no way he'd just show up and apply for a job here because I ignored his calls. *Would he?* He knows my last name, and it wouldn't take much internet research to find out where I live and work, considering Sugarland Creek's population is just over two thousand people.

That'd be some next-level stalker shit only considered sexy in romance novels.

"So basically, what wet dreams are made of?" Ayden barks out an amused laugh.

"You know it." Ruby chuckles.

They continue chatting as my brain freezes, wondering if there's any coincidence the new farrier is a Fisher-doppelgänger.

"Hello, earth to Noah?" Ruby snaps her fingers in my face.

I shake my head and turn toward her. "What?"

"You okay? You launched to Mars for a minute there."

I shake my head and force a tight smile. "Yeah, fine. Just thinkin' of my never-endin' to-do list."

"Want me to tack up Nibbler for ya?"

"That'd be great. Thanks."

She leaves to get his saddle, and I continue brushing Buttercup.

"While you're out with Nibbler, I'm gonna clean his stall. Think you'll be gone for a bit?" Ayden asks. He's seven years older and has worked on the ranch for over a decade, so he's more of an older brother to me. Although he's the stables manager, I do all the training, so he runs the schedule through me.

"Mm-hmm. He needs a good run today."

And I need to clear my head of any thoughts about Fisher.

I bring Buttercup back to his stall and give him a few forehead rubs before closing the door. Ruby already has Nibbler ready for me, and when I step toward them, I hear the office door open.

"There's my daughter," my dad says. "Noah, come meet the new farrier."

Swallowing hard, I turn around and am greeted by a man I never thought I'd see again.

Fisher narrows his eyes as they walk closer, and I immediately panic. He doesn't look half as shocked to see me as I am to see him. *Could my life get any worse?*

I take a couple of steps backward as they approach me, feeling the urge to run and fake amnesia.

"Comin' through," Ayden calls out behind me. I need time to compose myself but am nearly face-to-face with my dad and Fisher.

This can't be happening. He shouldn't be here. He *can't* be here.

"Noah, hold on. Wanna introduce y'all." My dad's voice gets louder.

"Noah?" Ayden's behind me.

When I turn toward him, I nearly fall into a wheelbarrow full of horse shit.

"Excuse me. I'm goin' into Nibbler's stall, and you're blockin' the entrance..." Ayden drawls out, arching a brow when I freeze.

Clearing the fog in my brain, I nod and step to the side. "Yeah. Sorry."

"Noah, this is Fisher," my dad's booming voice echoes behind me. "He took over for Mr. Ryan."

Unfortunately for me, I spin around on my heels too fast and stumble on the front of my boot. While trying to catch myself, I fall backward. The weight of my body catches the edge of the wheelbarrow, and within seconds, it goes down, tipping its entire contents on top of me.

I'm literally covered in horse shit.

The answer is *yes*. My life *could* get worse.

"Noah!" Everyone shouts my name at the same time, but all I want is for the ground to open up and swallow me down to my grave.

RIP Noah Hollis. Died of humiliation while covered in horse shit in front of her one-night stand who turned out to be her ex's dad and is twice her age. And now the new farrier on her family's ranch.

It'd make for an epic tombstone.

A hand finds mine and pulls me up. The moment I went down, I instinctively closed my eyes and mouth, and as soon as I sit up, I blow out a breath.

"You okay?" Fisher kneels in front of me, his hand still squeezing mine, and I quickly yank it out of his.

Glancing up, I find everyone staring at me. Ayden's mouth is agape while Ruby struggles not to laugh.

"I'm so sorry, Noah. I tried to warn ya, and then...I dunno. You went down so fast. I couldn't catch you in time." Ayden's voice is full of sincerity, and I should accept his apology, considering it's not his fault, but right now, all I want to do is run away.

"Let's get you to your feet, sweetheart." Dad grabs my hand and helps me to stand.

I avoid Fisher's death stare as I wipe the shit off my clothes.

"You alright?" my dad asks, helping me brush my shoulders and arms.

Ruby comes over and fusses with my hair.

"Physically, yes." When I inhale a sharp breath, I immediately regret it. That smell is coming from *me*. "If you'll excuse me—" My gaze shoots to Fisher's before meeting my father's eyes. "I'm gonna go home and shower. I'll be back within the hour."

"Sure, sweetie. I'll have Ayden show Mr. Underwood around, and you can take over when you're back."

My back goes ramrod straight at the thought of being alone with Fisher.

"I'm already behind on my trainin' schedule and will be even more now. Can't Ruby give him the grand tour?" I argue. Besides the fact I don't want to talk to him, I don't like falling behind.

"Oh, I'd totally do that!" Ruby squeals. "I'd be happy to show Mr. Underwood 'round the ranch."

Relief floods my veins when my dad takes the bait, and I excuse myself to leave.

No amount of soap will wash away the embarrassment I feel right now.

As soon as I walk in the door of my cottage, I get a FaceTime call from Magnolia.

"What in the fresh horse shit happened to you?"

I scowl as I walk through the kitchen and make a beeline for the bathroom. Before I got in my truck, I removed my boots, jeans, and shirt, and then tossed them in the bed. I'd rather drive half naked than stink up my truck.

"Ruby text you?"

"She told me ya took a stumble and to check on you." She chews on her bottom lip. "And then said somethin' about a super-hot farrier that you were avoidin'. On a scale of one to Henry Cavill, how hot are we talkin'?"

Goddammit, Ruby.

"It's not what you think." I set my phone down on the vanity and wrinkle my nose at the reflection in the mirror. Then I pull the ponytail holder out, and my hair falls around my shoulders. "Aren't ya supposed to be at work?"

"I took a mental health day."

I thread my fingers through my knotted hair and smirk. Magnolia's worked at Main Street Café for the past three years and has complained about it for just as long. "Mrs. Blanche let ya do that? She's gonna fire you soon. You know that, right?"

"I'd like to see her try." She scoffs. "If she'd listen to my fun drink ideas and branch out with new pastries, we could expand our customer base. Instead, I'm stuck makin' coffee for the senior citizen crowd. How am I ever gonna meet my future husband if the only male population I talk to are ones with dentures and bifocals?"

"You think your froufrou drinks are gonna bring in men our age? You'd be better off askin' to change the uniform to crop tops and booty shorts if that's your angle."

"Of course not, but I have an idea. The drinks would attract a younger crowd. Women in their twenties and thirties. See where I'm goin' with this?" She taps her temple like she's a genius.

Laughing, I nod. "Yeah…guys will start to flock in to meet the women. And of course, one will fall in love with you, and the rest will be history."

"Exactly!" she emphasizes. "My plan is foolproof. But thanks to my boss, I'll die an old maid just like her."

"You could always apply to work at the ranch," I remind her. "There are plenty of male ranch hands here."

"Have ya met me? You might not care about fallin' into a pile of horse shit, but I'd literally die if that happened to me."

"You're so dramatic. But who knows, you could meet someone at the fundraiser. Could be the start of your cowboy era."

"Oh yay, arrogant men in tight jeans who think they're God's gift to the world. Sign me up."

I laugh at her deadpan expression. "Guess that means Tripp's off your radar, huh?"

She scoffs. "He was never on it."

I roll my eyes at her blatant lie, and then lift my phone and grab some towels.

"Are you only in your bra and underwear?"

"Yes. I need to get in the shower, so I'll call ya later."

"I don't think so. You need to tell me what's goin' on."

"You wanna shower with me or what? I need to get back to work."

"It wouldn't be the first time." She waggles her brows, and I choke out a laugh at the numerous memories of us getting into the type of trouble that required joint showers.

"Fine, whatever." I turn on the shower until it's as hot as I can take. "No peeking. Eyes up here."

She snorts. "It ain't nothin' I haven't seen before, Noah. I went with you to your first pap smear and taught ya how to insert a tampon, remember? I've seen your cervix."

"Jesus, you're so weird." I move my phone to the shelf that won't get hit with water, then remove my bra and underwear.

"Hey, I offered to show you mine in return. You're the one who nearly fainted and got all frazzled."

I tip my head back and wet my hair. "Because you asked me to bring a handheld mirror so you could see it yourself. The gynecologist was ready to kick us out."

"Sue me for wantin' to know what it looks like." Her Southern drawl emphasizing each word has me rolling my eyes and biting back a smile. Magnolia Sutherland is the definition of a wild child who has never been told *no* a day in her life.

"Yeah, curiosity killed the cat, and I had to find a different doctor. I've already signed paperwork to make sure you aren't in the room when I give birth," I tease, lathering my palms with soap and rubbing it over every inch of my body.

"You're a liar, and we both know it. You want me sittin' right behind you, chanting *push, push, push!*"

"Please, God. No." I groan at the thought. "My husband will be lucky if he's allowed to witness the birth of his child, thanks to being scarred by you."

"Speakin' of husband. You need to talk about this farrier dude. What got ya so worked up you ended up in a pile of horse shit?"

As I work the shampoo through my thick hair, I blow out a breath in anticipation of her reaction.

"The farrier is Fisher."

"Who?"

My fingers massage my scalp, and I wait as it clicks in her brain.

"Wait. Fisher from the rodeo? The *one-night stand* Fisher?"

I wipe water out of my eyes and look at her shell-shocked face on the screen.

"Yes. Also, *my ex's dad,* Fisher. And now, the new farrier."

Her jaw drops. "Oh. My. God."

"My thoughts exactly."

"How the hell did that happen?"

"I have the same question."

Next, I move on to the conditioner, and while my ends soak, I grab my razor.

"What're ya shavin' for?" She arches a brow.

"I missed a spot on my leg, you perv."

"Mm-hmm, sure. Daddy Fisher likes it smooth, I bet."

"Do *not* call him that," I scold. This situation is fucked up as it is without those words being engrained in my head.

"Why not? He's someone's daddy."

"Jase is too old to call him that, so shush."

"Speakin' of that, ya think he knows you nailed his dad?"

"*Christ.* All of Sugarland Creek is gonna know if you're any louder." I rinse my hair, ready to get dressed and smell human again. "And I dunno. Assuming they're even talkin', it might not be long before it comes up in a conversation of who I am to Jase."

I need to text him and find out why he didn't tell me his dad moved back here. Even during our "off" moments, we still talked and told each other everything. Well, *almost* everything.

"So you don't think Fisher knows?"

"He didn't look that surprised to see me, so I think he knew I lived and worked here. Not sure on the other thing where I'm his son's ex."

"Ooh, a stealthy stalker. We love to see it."

"No, we don't. Only in your de-lulu-brain."

"A man who gets a job just to see you after ghostin' them is romantic as fuck."

"You'd be that person who gets abducted, then ask them to live out your captive fantasy."

"Don't knock it till ya try it. Travis and I did it once."

"Your psycho ex? Seems fittin' for him." I scoff at the thought of how he treated my best friend and how long she put up with it.

I turn off the water and grab my hair towel. "Doubt he even had to *act* the part."

"Let's just say it consisted of handcuffs, rope, and a lot of hair pullin'."

"What, no hand necklaces?" I giggle, wrapping a larger towel around my body before stepping onto the mat.

"He tried, but he couldn't figure out how *not* to choke me to death while doin' it, so I made him stop."

"Yeah, I bet that was his problem..." I dramatically roll my eyes in front of the screen.

"We're not supposed to be talkin' about him anyway. How did seein' Fisher end up with you in a pile of horse shit?"

As I get dressed and brush my hair, I replay the humiliating moment that led me here. She doesn't hold back her laughter either.

"That is the most *me* thing I've ever heard. I can't believe you froze like that."

I grab my makeup bag and put on concealer and lip gloss. She rambles about how I need to explain to Fisher why I ignored his calls and texts so we can live out a forbidden fantasy.

"That's not gonna happen, Mags. Besides the obvious reasons of awkwardness, there's a no employee fraternizin' rule."

"Oh, ya know your parents only set that in place because of Wilder sleepin' with the receptionist and then makin' Waylon break up with her as him."

I hold back a laugh as I put on mascara and focus on not smudging it. The memories of my older twin brothers getting into trouble are nothing new. The receptionist was so heartbroken she caused a scene and threw everything she could find around The Lodge. One of the guests filmed it and uploaded it to social media, where it got three million views in a week. I've never seen my parents want to kill my brother more. After that, there was a no employees dating employees rule set in place.

"Doesn't matter, it's still the rule," I remind her.

She shrugs with a mischievous glimmer in her eyes. "No one has to know."

Chapter Eight
Fisher

Well, shit. *Literally.*

I knew she'd be surprised to see me, but I didn't anticipate her falling into a wheelbarrow of horse shit to avoid me.

Now I'm stuck with Ruby, who's taking her sweet time showing me every inch of the ranch.

We've been inside every barn, storage shed, hay loft, and pasture.

I've also pictured a dozen places to sneak around with Noah if she'd give me a chance to explain why I'm here.

Assuming she'll even want to talk to me.

"If you want the retreat tour, you'll have to get it from Noah or one of the boys. I've gotta get back to stall duty before Ayden covers me in shit next." She laughs as she drives us back to the stables.

"Does it matter where I start?" I ask as she parks next to my truck.

"You'll have to ask Noah. She's kinda the boss when it comes to the schedule."

I open my door and hop out. "I thought Ayden was the boarding operations manager?"

"He is, but Noah trains most of the boarders, which means the schedule depends on her and what she has to do. No one really understands her madness, so we just roll with it. Best you do, too."

"Duly noted."

"You'll need to back up your truck on the other side of the barn and set up away from this entrance. Noah brings out the horses on this end, and you'll just be in her way."

"Alright, sure." I don't need to give Noah more reasons to hate me by pissing her off at work.

"She just texted she's leavin' her house and should be here in a few minutes. She'll let ya know where to begin."

I head to my truck and then drive to the south side. Once I've backed in close enough to the concrete block, I unlock the back of my rig where all my tools and machines are kept. Instead of a cub trailer, I opted to get a built-in shoeing rig so I could still pull a trailer when I moved locations. Now it's a nice convenience to have.

I clip my leather apron into place over my jeans and then grab my hoof stand and tool kit from the back seat of my truck. Mr. Hollis printed out the shoeing cards of each horse from Mr. Ryan's last visit. It tells me their toe length, angle of the foot, and what size shoe they use. Each horse will vary on their specific activities, but it's still useful to have ahead of time. Some of the horses are new since the last time Mr. Ryan was here, so I'll have to spend a bit more time on them.

It'll take a few weeks to get caught up and then maintain a routine between Noah's training schedule and the trail horses' daily riding.

Unsure of where to begin, I fuss with my equipment and supplies while I wait for Noah.

When her truck appears and she parks next to mine, she stares at me through the windshield. With a shake of her head, she opens her door and walks toward me.

My heart falls to the pit of my stomach at being face-to-face again. It's only been a week since our night together, and I haven't stopped thinking about her. Even if she left the morning after and hasn't responded to my calls or messages, I'm still happy to see her.

"You stalkin' me?" Her voice is coated in irritation.

I ignore her accusation and take a step. "Are you okay?"

"From fallin' in horse shit or because you miraculously showed up on my ranch?" She crosses her arms.

"Pretty sure I should be the pissed one here." I mimic her stance. "If you'd bothered to respond, I could've told you I was the new farrier, and you wouldn't have been so shocked to see me that you'd fall into a pile of horse shit."

She drops her arms and narrows her eyes. "You knew?"

"Not at first, but I put two and two together once I learned your last name. I figured we'd talk later, and I'd tell ya then. But since you couldn't return a text, I reckoned ya could find out the hard way."

She shoots me a death glare. "So you knew before we slept together?"

I swallow hard and answer honestly, "Yes."

"That woulda been nice to know." She walks around me, and I follow.

"Would it have mattered?"

She ignores my question as she grabs a lead rope, then opens one of the horse's doors. "This is Buttercup. He leaves tomorrow, so you'll start with him. Then I'll note which ones are a priority on your sheet. After you do the boarders, you'll move to the trail horses, and then finally, our personal horses. I assume Ruby showed you their locations?"

"She did."

She brings Buttercup out, and after sniffing me, he lets out a whine.

"He doesn't like men," she states flatly. "I'll have to stay with him so he doesn't try to kill ya."

"I can't tell if you're bein' serious or not."

She holds up the rope. "Take him and find out if you don't believe me."

"I'd rather not risk it. I've been kicked enough to last me a lifetime. But I do wanna see him walk first."

"I can tell you anythin' about this horse ya need to know. Level heel. Thick frogs. No fungus. Size four shoe."

"Unless you wanna do *my* job, I need to witness his walk."

"Fine." She pinches her lips together as if she doesn't want to cause a scene with Ayden and Ruby nearby. "Go to the end of the aisle."

I go to the doors and then turn around just as Noah leads him toward me. Buttercup has a steady walk, and his hooves land at a good distance apart. His shoulders move freely, which means he's maintaining his balance as his neck moves up and down in time with the rest of his body.

"Now turn around and walk away from me for a few seconds."

With a huff of irritation, she does as I say. If I didn't know any better, Noah Hollis isn't used to taking orders, and she's not a fan of it either.

Once they walk ten feet, she turns him around and comes back toward me.

"Well?" she asks as she approaches.

"He looks good and healthy. Nice gait."

"Told ya. I've trained him for the past four months."

"And you've done a great job, but in order to do *my* job, I need to assess each horse properly before I work on them."

"You'll have to get someone else to walk them for ya, then because I'm either in the corral, at the trainin' center, or workin' on the fundraiser," she says, following me back outside.

"What fundraiser?" I ask, intrigued.

Her shoulders relax. "It's in a couple weeks. I'm raisin' money for a charity that helps rescued and injured horses. It'll be like a mini rodeo with barrel racin', mutton bustin', show jumpin', and more."

Wow, impressive. That's a big undertaking, but I don't say that. She's being snippy with me, and I'm not about to go soft on her now.

There's a post to secure the rope, and once he's clipped in, I rub my hand over his back and let him sniff me.

"My clipboard's on my rig if you wanna mark which order I have to go in, and then I won't bother you again till I need ya."

I avoid looking at her face when I dismiss her, but by the way she scuffs her boots on the ground, she's not any happier with me than she was before.

"It's okay. I won't hurt ya," I tell Buttercup when he stomps his back foot, almost as if he's mocking Noah's actions. I resist the urge to laugh while dragging my hand down his leg to check his hoof.

"Before I forget to tell you, Shelby and Taylor Alison Swift's stalls are next to each other, and they don't like being apart too long. So you'll wanna let them say goodbye and give them a couple minutes together before you switch them out."

I snap my head up, wondering if she's fucking with me. "*Excuse me*?"

"Yeah, I know dependency can be bad, but they've been next to each other for two years. Taylor Alison Swift is Mallory's horse —my little cousin—so she's not goin' anywhere since Mallory lives here. Shelby's been here for a few years and is a full-time boarder since their owner lives in the city. We let them stay together since neither will be leavin'."

Standing, I meet her eyes. "You have a horse named *Taylor Alison Swift*?"

She blows out a deep breath. "Yes. We call her Miss Swift if ya must know."

"So you're a *Swiftie*?"

"We're not doin' this..." She points at me, then motions between us. "Business talk only."

"Said who?" I grab my toolbox kit and wheel it to Buttercup's front leg.

"*Me*. You're a ranch employee, and I'm a professional horse trainer on said family's ranch. The only reason we'd need to talk is to discuss the horses."

I get into position, then situate Buttercup's hoof between my legs and squeeze my thighs to keep it in place. He nudges my head and nips at me, pulling a chunk of hair before Noah notices and scolds him.

"Guess ya weren't lyin'." I laugh, grabbing my buffer and hammer to raise the clenches.

"Nope." She stands next to me, then hands me my shoe pullers once I'm done.

"Thanks," I say, changing out the tools and then going around the shoe until I can effortlessly pry it off. "I take it his owner is a female?"

"Yes." She hands me my hoof knife.

I bite back my laughter as she keeps Buttercup calm while handing me tools as if she's memorized every step of my process. As I remove the excess dirt and scrape away the dead sole, she rubs his head and, eventually, hands me my loop knife.

"You sing to all your horses?" I taunt when I catch her humming a Taylor Swift song.

"You gonna tease me about the one thing that's keepin' this horse from kickin' you? Pretty bold, Mr. Underwood."

"*Mr. Underwood*?" I scoff, shedding the frog until it's a nice V-shape. "Does that mean I should call you Miss Hollis?"

She lowers her gaze and glares while handing me my rasp.

"I'd prefer ya didn't."

I double-check for any flakey sole and inspect for defects or infections before I smooth and flatten the entire bottom. Then I flip the rasp over and run it over the hoof again.

"You hand Mr. Ryan all of his tools or am I just special?"

"Don't get excited. I'm only helpin' to make sure you're doin' it right."

"Oh, now you're supervisin' me?" I ask, using my hoof knife again to scrape more of the sole until it feels waxy.

"These horses are very important to me and the ranch, so yes, I wanna make sure you're qualified before lettin' you run wild with them," she states, handing me my nippers.

"You think your dad would hire me if I wasn't?" I ask, trimming around the hoof wall and making sure the toe isn't too thick.

"He was desperate. He woulda hired anyone."

I scratch my cheek. "Ouch."

"Prove yourself to be good, and it won't be an issue."

"Have you forgotten who I am?" I grab the rasp again and smooth everything down.

"No. Sadly, I haven't gotten amnesia."

"I rode bulls for a livin' and have worked with horses for years. Are you really gonna question my ability to trim their hooves?"

"It's not personal."

I finish up with my tools and then set his hoof down so I can look at it.

"It feels that way to me, Noah. I'd never question your ability to train a horse even though you're young, a little self-absorbed, and overconfident. I'd give you the chance to do your job before I questioned your abilities."

"Did you just—" Her jaw drops as she shakes her head. "I'm not self-absorbed. I'm great at what I do. One of the best 'round here, actually. It's why I book a year in advance and make twice as much as any other professional trainer within a hundred-mile radius. I've donated hours of my time to organize this fundraiser! I'm already not taken seriously in this industry, and I don't need any more *men* tellin' me how I'm overconfident."

"Oh, excuse me, I shoulda added..." I smirk at her after I've taken a second look at Buttercup's hoof and set it back down. "It's not *personal*."

Without waiting for a response, I walk to my rig and turn on the forge machine. It runs on propane, so it needs a few minutes to heat. Normally, I'd trim all their hooves first and then put on the shoes, but since she wants to witness my process, she gets to see it from start to finish now. Maybe then she'll be satisfied enough to stop doubting me.

While we wait, I grab the size four shoe and return to Buttercup's hoof to see how it'll fit. It needs to be bent in at the top a little, so I grab my hammer and pound it a few times.

"That was uncalled for, and you know it." Noah's bitter tone has me holding back an amused laugh.

"If you can't take criticism, then don't dish it out."

"I didn't criticize you."

"You told me to prove myself, Noah. Same damn thing. You think since Mr. Ryan retired and referred me to his clients, I didn't have to interview for this job? I was out here a month ago to show your father exactly what I could do."

"You were?"

"Yeah, I didn't see ya then. I swear I had no idea who you were until that Ian kid said your last name. At that point, it was too late. You and I both wanted that night to happen, so I won't apologize for not tellin' ya sooner. As far as you ignorin' my calls, well, that's on you. I wasn't gonna have an important conversation with your voicemail."

"You coulda texted and said it was urgent or somethin'..." She bites down on her lower lip as if she's trying to find a way to blame this on me. "If I'd known it was important, I woulda picked up."

Grabbing my tongs, I place the shoe inside the forge, then close the door. Once I go back to Buttercup, I set his hoof on the stand so I can clean and smooth over the top. As I do, I check for flares, hairline cracks, or bruising.

"Are ya ignorin' me now?" she asks when I stay quiet.

"When I'm done puttin' on his shoe, you can leave. Buttercup and I will be just fine without your presence."

"What? Why?"

"Because I don't need a babysitter. You can watch me to ensure I'm good enough, but after that, go back to your job so I can do mine."

"Fisher..."

"It's Mr. Underwood." I glance up just in time to catch her

rolling her eyes. With one hand on her hip, she shakes her head as if she's not used to someone defying her. Or annoyed that I am. Honestly, it's kinda hot. Full pouty lips draw my eyes to her face, and I wish I could lean in and kiss them.

"Fine, I'm sorry."

I walk around her to the machine and check if the shoe is ready. After inspecting it, I set it inside for a few more minutes.

"Did ya hear me?" she asks my back.

"Yes, loud as a donkey."

"Aren't you gonna say anythin'?"

I turn around with only a few inches between us. It'd be so easy to lean down and taste her sorry lips.

"What for, Noah? Snoopin' through my wallet when I was asleep? Or for ditchin' me without so much as a goodbye? Perhaps for ghostin' me, which even havin' to say that word at my age should be a felony. Possibly for insultin' my credibility as a farrier?" Instead of inching closer like my dick wants, I widen my stance and cross my arms over my broad chest. "So which one are you sorry for?"

She grinds down on her teeth, clearly unhappy about being called out. Her eyes flicker to the ground as if she's contemplating her next move and her leg twitches. For a second, I'm worried she might knee me in the nuts. She's definitely close enough to cause substantial damage.

"Okay, first...I wasn't snoopin' through your wallet." Her gaze moves up and finds mine. "I just wanted to see your ID so I knew how old you were."

"Is that what scared you off? My age?"

"No, not really. I figured you were about twice my age. Maybe not quite, but it wasn't the problem."

So something ran her off...

I lower my arms, but I have to interrupt our conversation to finish Buttercup's shoe. Once I grab my tongs and take the shoe out of the forge, I mold and smooth it down.

"Can you bring me a bucket of water, please?" I ask when I realize I forgot to grab one.

Without responding, Noah walks into the barn, and I proceed to test the shoe against Buttercup's hoof. It burns against it as I place it on and off a few times. Some of the edging needs to be adjusted, so I go back to my rig and put it in the forge so I can hammer it down again.

Once Noah returns, I take it out and tweak it. Then I check it against Buttercup's hoof and decide it's nearly perfect. Before nailing it in, I place it in the bucket of water to cool it down.

While I wait, I continue our conversation. "Tell me what the problem was. Maybe I can fix it?"

She inhales sharply through her nose and pinches her lips before exhaling slowly. "You can't. It's not somethin' that can be undone."

"If it's not my age, then you gotta give me somethin' else here. You didn't know I was workin' here, so I know that ain't it. What else is there?"

It's on the tip of my tongue to ask if it was something we did that turned her off, something *I* did, but by her moaning and screaming that almost made me go deaf, I doubt that was the issue. We shared a strong and intense connection that night. From the way she was begging me not to stop, it wasn't one-sided. Even now, seeing her again and being close enough to touch, a spark lingers between us that she's trying to pretend doesn't exist.

The pulse in her throat moves as she swallows hard as if she can't physically get the words out. My heart hammers at the idea of there being something so wrong about us being together that I won't be able to fix or change.

She shakes her head. "I-I don't think we should be havin' this conversation here. Or ever. It was just one night. There's no reason we can't be professionals and work on the same ranch."

My brows furrow at her quick dismissal of us.

"Noah, tell me." I step closer until we're nearly touching, until our arms brush, and I can smell her floral shampoo. "*Please.*" Tipping up her chin, I lean in and test how far she'll allow me to go. Even with her jabs, I can't stop thinking about tasting her lips again.

Her shallow breathing comes to a stop when my mouth breaches hers, but then she slams her eyes closed and blurts out, "Your son!"

I rear back, nearly falling on my ass because those are the last two words I expected to hear.

"What about my son?"

Finally, she looks at me and her expression forms into one of distress. "We used to date. It's been a while, but we were together on and off for most of my high school years and up until I was twenty."

"*Jase*? You...and...Jase?" I point at her and an imaginary shadow of my son next to her.

Her lips stay sealed as she nods.

I brush a hand through my hair, trying to wrap my mind around the fact that I not only slept with a woman twenty-two years younger than me, but she's my son's girlfriend.

Well...ex-girlfriend.

But I don't think technicalities matter much anyway. The two of them dated. They have a history. One I wasn't a part of because I only tried to reconnect with my son a few months ago. Long after they were dating and broken up. Long after he would've told her what a piece of shit father he had.

"Jesus Christ..." Those are the only words I can form. Of all the reasons I imagined she ditched me, this was never on the fucking radar of possibilities.

Instead of continuing to stand like a shell-shocked idiot, I retrieve the shoe that's plenty cooled down and finish the job. I make sure it fits properly and then hammer in the four nails. After that, I place his hoof back on the stand and do one final filing with my rasp.

Once that's completed, I set it down and then watch Buttercup stomp a few times to ensure it looks right.

"When did ya realize?" I finally ask her, moving my tool kit to the horse's other front hoof. I drag my hand over his back and down his leg so he doesn't get spooked.

"When I saw your ID," she says, standing next to Buttercup and rubbing her palm over his nose to keep him calm. "There aren't many Underwoods in Sugarland Creek. I figured with your ages that you were probably related. The more I thought about it, the more similarities I saw between y'all. Then I remembered you talkin' about how often you used to travel, and it just made sense from what Jase had told me."

"Why didn't you just tell me? It woulda been a much nicer blow to my ego if I'd known the truth." Though it wouldn't have made it any easier knowing the one woman I wanted was strictly off-limits.

"I never expected to see you again, so what was the point in tellin' ya?"

"You didn't think we'd run into each other with me livin' in Sugarland Creek?"

"I figured it was a possibility, but it didn't mean anythin' would happen. Had I known you worked here, I woulda handled this differently. But I was embarrassed about the whole thing."

"About what?"

"About havin' a one-night stand with my ex's dad. I'd never even had one before and when I actually do, it's with the one man I shouldn't have slept with in the first place. Also, I was nervous you'd tell Jase. He'd never forgive me if he found out."

"So he doesn't know?"

She shakes her head. "No, we've remained friends, but I haven't talked to him in a few weeks. I was surprised to find out you were here because I thought for sure he woulda told me."

Damn, that hurts.

It also makes me wonder how close they've remained if she's concerned this secret getting back to him would ruin their friendship. Most exes don't stay friends. But I don't know enough about my son's past to even have an opinion on how he is with other people. He's quiet with me but could be different around those who didn't abandon him.

"Yeah, we've had a rocky relationship, so I'm not surprised he hasn't told anyone about me. That's my fault, not his."

"He's told me," she admits. "Well, his side of the story anyway."

Sadly, his side *is* the only truth he knows. I never told him what I tried to make Damien do, and I hope he'll never find out.

"I'd really appreciate it if you wouldn't tell him, Noah. I'm here to rebuild my relationship with my son, and it's still very rocky. I—"

"I wasn't plannin' to," she reassures me. "No one knows except for Magnolia."

I blow out a breath. "Great."

She chuckles. "Yeah, I told her while I went home to shower, so don't plan on it being a secret for long."

"Any chance I can bribe her to keep her mouth shut?" I ask, half teasing, half serious. If Jase finds out, he'll never talk to me again. His one- and two-word responses will dwindle to complete silence.

"That's a good question..." She snorts, then shakes her head. "Nah, she knows whatever secrets I share she takes to the grave."

I nod in appreciation. I've done a lot of shitty things as a father when I was at my lowest point in life, but this would be irreversible. Even if I don't know a lot about Jase's high school and post-graduation life, I'm pretty certain hooking up with any of his exes would put me on his permanent shit list.

Chapter Nine

Noah

"Heard ya ate shit for lunch. How'd that taste?" Wilder howls in laughter before I get the chance to respond or flip him off.

"Jen was at your house last night, so why don't you tell me?" I ask, lunging Millie in the corral before I take her into the training center.

"Nice one, sis!" Waylon gives me an air high five as he makes his way into the barn.

It only took a couple of hours for the news of my embarrassment to get around the ranch. Surprised it took that long, honestly. But two can play that game. Everyone knows Wilder has a hookup routine and no one likes Jen—for good reason—but that's never stopped him.

The oldest boys of the family are the twins, Wilder and Waylon. There are six years between us, but you wouldn't know it by how immature they act. Waylon is usually the reasonable one, but they still feed off each other and act like fools most of the time. They live in one of the duplexes at the ranch hand quarters where they throw parties almost every weekend. If they weren't so good at guiding the trail horse rides and staying on top of their ranch duties, our parents would've already booted them, especially after the whole receptionist thing.

"Aren't ya too old to be gettin' flustered over a hot guy?" Wilder continues, stepping up on the fence post and giving me a better view of his smug-ass expression.

"Who said it was over a hot guy?"

"Ruby."

Ugh, I'm gonna kill her.

"*She* was the flustered one," I argue, then internally chastise myself for that stupid response. "What do you want anyway besides to annoy me?"

"I heard the *hot guy* is Jase's dad?"

"He's the *farrier,*" I drawl out. "No one said he was hot."

I put on my best deadpan expression so he doesn't see right through my lie.

"That mean your lover boy is gonna come 'round again?" he asks in a cruel, taunting voice. Wilder's never been a fan of Jase for no other reason than he was my boyfriend.

Not like my playboy brother has room to talk. At twenty-eight, he's dated most of Sugarland Creek's eligible women and some of the not-so-single older women.

"What're ya, twelve?" I glare at him, and he barks out a laugh. "We're just friends. Don't you have work to do?"

"I'm waitin' on Landen to come with the hay trailer so we can stock up the loft."

"Go wait somewhere else."

He chuckles as he hops off the fence. I watch as he makes his way into the barn. He's talking so loudly, I can hear him from all the way inside.

Thirty minutes later, Fisher tells me he's ready for Shelby, so I walk her down and clip her into place. My mind hasn't stopped thinking about him and the *almost-kiss*. Or at least, I could've sworn that was about to happen before I blurted out the real reason I ghosted him.

My brain says we need to stay away from each other. But my

heart says fuck that.

We shared something I've never experienced that night. If it weren't for the no fraternizing policy and him being Jase's dad, there'd be no reason we couldn't be together.

That alone makes me want him even more.

Even if the consequences could be life-changing.

Now that Miss Swift is back in her stall, I text Mallory to come over so she's not anxious while Shelby's gone. Since Mallory has only been around horses for a couple of years, we don't let her ride alone. She helps with the grooming and getting the saddle on, but I'm always a few feet away when she's on her back.

Landen arrives with the trailer, and when he and Tripp hop out, I know shit's about to get rowdy.

It always does when all four boys are together.

"Hey, sis," Landen says, coming toward me and making a show of sniffing me. "Thank God you showered. Heard you—"

"Shush your mouth before I push you in a pile of steamin' horse shit."

He snickers, elbowing my arm. "Been there, done that. No, thank you."

"You gonna come help?" Tripp asks as he approaches.

I grab Miss Swift's lead rope and enter her stall. "That's not my job. I'm doin' mine, so go do yours."

Then I bring Mallory's horse to the grooming station and clip her in so she's ready. "You can grab me her saddle, though."

"Nice try." Tripp snorts. "Where are the twins?"

Looking up and down the center aisle, I don't see any signs of them. "Hmm. They were in here a bit ago."

It's then I hear roars of laughter on the other end of the barn where Fisher's working.

Oh shit.

"Found 'em," Landen says, rushing toward the commotion.

"Goddammit." I chase after Landen and Tripp, knowing they'll add to the madness.

"What are y'all doin'?" I ask Wilder and Waylon when I find them hovering over Fisher, who's working on Shelby's hoof.

"Did ya know Jase's dad used to be a famous bull rider?" Wilder asks with amusement.

"Yes." I hold my stance, placing my hands on my hips as a pre-warning not to start anything. He already doesn't like Jase. I don't need him not liking Fisher, too.

"We're gonna take him to the Twisted Bull on Friday so he can show us his skills on their mechanical bull." Wilder's shit-eating grin is covered in mischief, and I don't like the sound of any of this.

There's also a large dance floor where couples line dance. At times, it's shoulder to shoulder with how many people are on it. The boys always get shit-faced and never fail to cause a scene.

"Wilder thinks he'll be a pro by the end of the evening." Waylon laughs.

"A pro at fallin' on his ass," Landen taunts, shaking his head.

Tripp smirks. "Should we start placin' bets now? One Benny he lasts four seconds."

"Four? I give it three before he face-plants the floor," Waylon says.

"That's a bad idea." I interrupt their bets.

Landen says six seconds, and Tripp gives him five.

My gaze meets Fisher's, and I mouth, "Sorry."

The corner of his lips tilts up in an amused grin. He's not even trying to get out of it.

"You should come, little sis." Waylon nudges me when he catches me staring at Fisher. "Bring that little boyfriend of yours."

Wilder shakes his head. "You can't invite her on guys' night. But she can be our DD." He glances at me. "We'll call ya when we're done for the night."

"You're such an asshole." I walk over and kick him in the shin. "I'll be there to make sure you don't embarrass our family in front of the whole town, aside from what you already have."

"Pfft. Too late for that," Tripp says. Wilder's had his fair share of embarrassing moments.

"So whatcha say, Mr. Farrier? I'll even buy your first round." Wilder's wide grin makes me want to sucker punch him in the gut.

"It's Mr. Underwood," I tell him, smacking his arm. "Be respectful, or Momma will have your ass."

Wilder shoves me, so Waylon steps between us. "Okay, kids. No fightin'."

Ayden walks over, scowling. "Y'all havin' a family reunion out here? If not, quit botherin' Mr. Underwood and go away."

"Tell the boys that." I scoff.

Usually, I'm the one scolding and separating the boys when they get too rowdy. But with Fisher around, I feel a sense of protectiveness, not wanting them to harass him. The last thing Fisher needs is to be stuck with my brothers in a bar with a mechanical bull and alcohol.

"Friday, ten o'clock!" Wilder shouts as Waylon pulls him away.

Fisher glances up, furrowing his brows. *"At night?"*

Landen and Tripp burst out laughing.

"Can ya handle it, old man?" Landen teases. "We work hard durin' the day but play harder on the weekends."

I roll my eyes at his cocky tone.

Fisher chuckles. "I'll be askin' y'all that by the end of the evenin'."

The boys hoot and holler as Ayden escorts them back into the barn.

"You don't have to go," I tell Fisher when we're finally alone. "My brothers are...insane. They will get wasted until they can't walk, and you'll be babysittin' them."

"I can handle a few rowdy boys. Been 'round them for most of my career. Hell, I was one."

"But you aren't anymore," I remind him.

He shrugs, bringing his focus back to Shelby's hoof. "No, but nothin' I can't handle. You worried 'bout me?"

"I worry about what they'll say to you," I answer honestly. "They aren't the biggest fans of Jase."

"Ah."

"They wouldn't like any guy I dated, so don't take that personally."

"That just means they love you."

I snort-laugh. "You just saw how we are together. Trust me, that's not why. They just like to annoy the shit outta me every chance they can. I could marry a literal saint, and they'd still manage to find somethin' wrong with him."

"I imagine that was fun growin' up in the same house together." He smirks, then drags his tool kit to Shelby's back leg.

"Ha! My parents kicked the twins out when they turned twenty-one and put them in the ranch hand quarters. I moved into my cottage a couple years ago so Mallory could take my room since Gramma Grace took the twins' room. Landen and Tripp still live there, but I wouldn't be surprised if they move out soon, too."

"Sounds like a full house."

"It always is. Gramma Grace moved in four years ago after my grandpa passed. She and my momma are always cookin' and bakin' for the ranch hands. Don't be surprised if my mom invites you for lunch or, rather, *insists* you come over. Sunday night is family supper where all five of us are required to be there, no exceptions. My brothers are usually still hungover from partyin' the night before."

"That's what they're supposed to do in their twenties. Then in their thirties they'll pay for it with achy knees and heartburn."

I bellow out a laugh at the image. "They've been workin' on the ranch for most of their lives. I'm still surprised none have broken their necks yet. They used to jump off the barn roof onto a trampoline with the rest of them waitin' to counter-jump them so they'd go flyin'."

"Christ." He shakes his head with a laugh. "Surprised your mom hasn't had a heart attack raisin' them."

"Me too."

I watch as Fisher goes through the motions of cleaning Shelby's hoof when Mallory shows up with Serena Mae—Ayden's daughter, who's two years younger than Mallory. Momma waves goodbye as the girls run toward me.

They each wrap their arms around me, and I smile. "Miss Swift's waitin' in the groomin' stall for y'all. I'll meet you there in a sec."

When Mallory first moved here, she fell in love with the quarter horse and promptly named her after her favorite singer. No one could deny her whatever she wanted after the death of her parents, so I trained her and taught Mallory how to ride.

Once they're out of earshot, I step closer toward Fisher. "I'm gonna text Jase and find out why he didn't tell me you moved here."

"Be prepared for the honest truth," he warns.

"Everyone deserves a second chance, Fisher."

"We met for breakfast this mornin', and he barely spoke to me. He didn't mind chattin' when it came to him helpin' me buy my house, but now it's like pullin' teeth to get more than a few words outta him."

"He'll come around," I say, attempting to sound reassuring, even though I'm not sure if it's true.

Jase didn't speak of his father much, so I only know the bits and pieces he shared every now and then.

"Whether or not he does, I'm not goin' anywhere." He meets my gaze, a silent promise that he's here to stay regardless. "That goes for you too, Noah. I know the circumstances make it impossible for us to be anythin' more than employees or friends, but I'm here for whatever ya need."

My heart flutters, and God, do I wish things were different. I wish I wasn't standing here with a man I wanted and fighting the urge to kiss him. The attraction we shared from the start is still there, and it's no secret Fisher feels the same.

We're so screwed.

Chapter Ten

Fisher

After Noah leaves to help Mallory and Serena with Miss Swift, I finish Shelby's hooves and continue working the rest of the day. Ruby and Trey, another ranch hand, walk the horses for me between switching them out. I don't get as many done as I'd hoped with how much extra time it takes to get into a routine. Between the Hollises and my other clients from Mr. Ryan, I'll be plenty busy this summer playing catch-up.

I only see Noah a few more times between her coming and going from the training center and corral. It's better for the sake of the *rules* and the history between her and my son that we don't see each other, but she consumes my mind either way.

Just as I'm cleaning up my rig and putting my supplies away, Mr. and Mrs. Hollis appear in their truck and walk toward me with bowls of Tupperware in their hands.

"How was your first day?" Garrett asks.

"Great. Everyone was very nice and welcomin'." I smile as Dena sets down one of her dishes.

"Noah told me you haven't stopped to eat, so I brought leftovers from supper. You can help yourself anytime to the house for food or eat at The Lodge."

"Oh, that's not necessary."

"I insist," she says.

"Either you do as she says or she'll just bring ya leftovers each night and spoon-feed you against your own free will," Garrett says, chuckling.

"There's chicken and sausage gumbo, rice, and peach cobbler for dessert."

"Mrs. Hollis, this is too much. Are ya sure?"

She pats my arm with a genuine smile. "Cookin' for my family and friends is my love language."

Grinning, I nod. "Thank you. I appreciate it."

We chat for a few more minutes, then Dena invites me to Sunday night supper. I try to get out of it, knowing it'll make things awkward with Noah, but that woman doesn't take no for an answer. She's headstrong, just like her daughter. They excuse themselves and go inside the barn. Moments later, I hear them chatting with Ayden and Trey.

Once I lock up the rig and place the leftovers in my truck, I pull out my phone.

FISHER

Thanks for sending your mom with food. It smells delicious.

I look over at the containers and smile at the first home-cooked meal I've had in years.

NOAH

Sorry for not warning you. As soon as I mentioned you didn't take a break all day, she was already putting the food in containers for you.

FISHER

So you were keeping an eye on me, huh?

NOAH

No. I just happened to notice your truck didn't leave.

I smirk because she's lying. My truck isn't in view from the training center where she spent most of her day.

FISHER

I could've packed a lunch.

NOAH

Did you?

I hop in my truck and start it, but don't pull away.

FISHER

No, I had a big breakfast.

NOAH

Just know she'll continue to bring you food now.

FISHER

She invited me to come for dinner on Sunday. Is that gonna be a problem?

NOAH

Of course she did...

I anticipate her asking me to somehow get out of it or telling me I can't go.

NOAH

It's fine with me if you think you can keep your eyes off me that long.

I chuckle, shaking my head. She's not wrong, though. I can't even deny it. Noah's breathtakingly beautiful, but it's her smart mouth and confidence that attract me to her the most.

FISHER

Says the woman who watched me all day enough to know I didn't eat.

NOAH

You're making me sound like a stalker.

FISHER

Are you?

NOAH

You wish. Here I thought you were when you showed up this morning.

FISHER

If you'd returned a text like I see you know how to do after all, you would've been prepared.

NOAH

Okay, smart-ass. Don't push your luck now that I am.

I chuckle, hearing her playful tone in my head, and all I want now is to keep her responding.

FISHER

When can I see you outside of work?

I type out the question without thinking. Hurting Jase is the last thing I want to do. Still, I can't stop myself from wanting to know more about her. Even if all we can be is friends.

NOAH

I thought we already determined that was a bad idea.

FISHER

No one said we can't hang out as friends.

Even I'm not buying my bullshit excuse, but I can't help it. Noah drives me insane. It's why I couldn't keep my eyes off her at the rodeo.

NOAH

Friends, huh?

FISHER

What's wrong with being friends?

NOAH

I dunno. Jase asked to see me Friday evening.

My stomach turns like a knife just stabbed through me, but I can't tell her that. When I asked him to hang out with me tonight, he blew me off and said maybe in a few days. Guess that won't be happening either.

FISHER

Yeah?

NOAH

After I mentioned you being the new farrier, he said he had no idea. Then he suggested we all meet for dinner. I told him I'd have to get back to him, but I'm thinking it'd be a really bad idea...

FISHER

The three of us? Shit.

Just then, my phone vibrates with a message from Jase.

JASE

I had no idea the Hollises were one of the clients you took on. My girlfriend lives there. Can you meet us for dinner Friday at six?

What the fuck? He calls her his girlfriend?

Before I respond, I send Noah another message.

FISHER

Are you sure you two aren't dating?

NOAH

Of course I'm sure. Why?

FISHER

He just texted and called you his girlfriend.

NOAH

Ugh. Probably out of habit.

Or is she clueless about my son still having feelings for her?

FISHER

I thought you said you two broke up a couple years ago?

NOAH

We did. But neither of us has dated since then, so I think he does it without realizing it.

I pinch the bridge of my nose and wonder what in the Jerry Springer have I gotten myself into.

FISHER

Should I just tell him? Get all the awkwardness out now.

NOAH

No! It was one time. No point in ruining your relationship over a one-night stand. Just act normal. He knows we've been introduced at the ranch, so we'll just talk about work and normal stuff.

I scoff at "normal stuff." Nothing about this is *normal*.

FISHER

If you say so.

I go back to Jase's message and type out my response.

FISHER

Sure. Where?

JASE

Lilian's Steakhouse, it's new.

FISHER

That works. The Hollis twins also invited me to the Twisted Bull that night. Wanna join us?

JASE

Wait. You're going to the Twisted Bull?

FISHER

Yeah. Think I can't keep up or what?

JASE

We'll see, old man. I have an early meeting Saturday.

Even though he's making fun of me and calling me old, I smile. This is the most we've ever texted.

Then I return to Noah's message.

FISHER

I invited him to go to the bar on Friday, but he says he has to get up early the next day. Are you coming?

NOAH

To watch my dumbass brothers get wasted and try to ride a mechanical bull for eight seconds? Oh, I plan to film it.

I chuckle.

FISHER

You gonna try it?

NOAH

I've done it a few times already.

My curiosity piques.

FISHER

I shouldn't even be surprised, you little AJ. You probably put your brothers to shame.

NOAH

Pretend you never saw this...

After her message comes a video.

It's a video of Noah in a pink cowboy hat, sparkly boots, and a pink skirt and tube top. She's wearing a "Birthday Girl" sash over her shoulder and riding the mechanical bull.

You can hear her brothers hooting and hollering as she clings to the horn for dear life. Whoever's recording is losing their damn mind laughing and shouting. I suspect Magnolia, but nonetheless, I can't stop smiling at how carefree and happy she looks.

She hangs on until the timer goes off, and the crowd erupts in cheers.

Then when she goes to slide off, she slips and face-plants the mat.

The videographer shuffles over to Noah, and she's laughing so hard she can hardly breathe. Her entire face is red as she struggles to get to her feet, and just when she does, Wilder storms over and knocks her over again.

That's when the clip ends, but I'm nearly pissing my pants at how funny it was.

FISHER

That was the best thing I've ever seen.

NOAH

Now you know why I don't go out with my brothers. They're ruthless and dared me to do it on my 21st birthday.

FISHER

I thought it was hilarious. Now I have to see it in person.

NOAH

Don't think so, cowboy. I was drunk off my ass, and by the sounds of it, I'm gonna have to drive my brothers home this time.

FISHER

I'll stay sober so y'all can have fun. I'll bring my other truck so everyone can fit.

NOAH

Magnolia's already on board and has a major crush on Tripp, so prepare for complete madness.

FISHER

She does? Is that weird for you?

NOAH

Nah, she's liked him forever. So now you know a secret of hers since she knows ours.

I laugh.

FISHER

Thanks.

FISHER

I better go. I'm still parked behind the barn.

NOAH

See ya tomorrow, Mr. Underwood.

FISHER

Sweet dreams, Noah.

After I get home, I shower, then grab a beer. As I sit on the couch, I look around and see the pile of boxes that still needs to be unpacked and the dishes I haven't washed. The overwhelming dread of having so much to do and no energy to do it hits me in full force. Insecurity consumes my thoughts when I think about how much I don't deserve any of this. A second chance with my son, a new life, and stability. I most definitely don't deserve a woman like Noah. I stole those moments with her, and now look where we ended up.

I can't have her.

She's not *mine*.

She's everything I can't have. After the life I gave up, one of loneliness and solitude is all I should get.

Still, I want to wrap my arms around Noah and keep her for myself.

Chapter Eleven
Noah

Focusing on my job and not glancing over at Fisher every chance I get is more challenging than I expected. Having him in such proximity will likely cause an accident because my dumbass will one hundred percent walk into a wall while gawking at him.

Watching him work and staring at his hands gave me flashbacks of him spanking my ass while I rode him reverse cowgirl. Those goddamn calloused palms did filthy things to me, and it's all I could think about when the veins in his arms popped as he worked.

As much as I try not to picture our night together, every time I close my eyes, I see the images and hear his deep growl in my ear. I squeeze my thighs as I walk to relieve the ache I remember he left there.

After our text convo a couple of nights ago, we've only said a few words to each other in passing with secret heated glances that neither of us should be doing since we agreed to be *friends*. Ruby or Trey have been walking the horses for him, and if he has a question, one of them or Ayden is around to help. I go from the corral to the training center all day with some breaks in between, so it's not feasible for us to talk without wandering ears.

When Jase mentioned meeting him at Lilian's this Friday, I panicked.

That's not a restaurant where you take a friend.

It's one of the fancier places in town with romantic dim lighting, fresh roses and candles on each table, and a fireplace in the middle of the restaurant. People dress up and drop a few hundred dollars on the wine alone.

Instead of deflecting or telling him I had plans already, I mentioned his dad. He should be the one he spends time with, not me. But that blew up in my face when he suggested the three of us go to dinner.

When I asked if that was a good idea, considering Fisher and I work together, he pushed and said it'd help him to have a buffer person since they still don't talk much. I felt too bad to say no, so I said I'd get back to him. *After I spoke to Fisher.*

I didn't tell Fisher the full truth because either way, it's a bad idea, and there's no point in making him feel worse about the situation.

Jase calling me his girlfriend to his dad already tells me this will be awkward as hell.

Knowing things are tense between them adds pressure to keep the conversation flowing.

But I'm not doing it sober.

Now I'm half dreading and half excited to see Fisher outside of work.

Until then, I'll distract myself with training.

"Ellie, you're a little slow on that second barrel. That delay could cost ya the win," I shout from the side as she finishes a run. Craig Sander's *suggestion* from the rodeo rings in my ears, and I hate that he was right. The weasel's jealous that Ellie passed on his offer to train with him and is making a name for herself with my help.

"He drags each time." She shrugs.

"Lift the reins and kick a second sooner and see if that helps."

She gets Ranger back into position, and I reset my timer.

"Go!"

I watch as she rounds the first barrel flawlessly, then does as I said for the second, making Ranger move faster toward the third and sprinting to the finish line.

"That was better!" I note her time on my clipboard, where I record them.

"I reckon he needs new shoes." She rides over to me, then hops off. "We have another competition next week, and at that point, it'll be seven weeks since his last cleaning. His feet are takin' a toll with our extra practices."

I rub my hand over his back and down his leg to take a look. There's nothing obviously wrong with it. His toe is almost to the point of being overgrown for the shoe, but he's not in the danger zone.

"Want me to have Mr. Underwood take a look? I can get him on the schedule for tomorrow."

"Yeah, would you? At least to ease my mind." Her forehead wrinkles.

"Let's go now," I offer so she won't have to wait. "I'll see if he can squeeze him in."

"Thank you." She smiles.

She leads him as we walk from the training center to the barn and down to where Fisher's set up. When he comes into view, he's in the middle of searing a shoe, and my stomach twists when he gives me his full attention.

"Hey," I say as we approach.

"Hello." His eyes meet mine in question before they shift to Ellie.

"This is Ranger. Ellie's worried somethin' might be wrong with his hooves. He's been a little slow goin' around the barrels. Would you have time to check him?"

"Yeah, no problem. I'm on Millie's last hoof now."

"Great, thanks."

Ranger boards here during their busy training months since Ellie doesn't want to move him too much. But between all the traveling and training, it's possible he could have an infected hoof.

"You're the one who won at the rodeo," Fisher says to Ellie.

My face flushes at the mention of Ground Zero.

"Yeah! You were there?" Ellie asks.

"Yep, I was in the audience when I saw Noah screamin' for ya." He smirks, and butterflies invade my stomach at how he looks at me.

Ellie laughs. "Yeah, she's a good cheerleader."

"When's the next competition?"

"Week from Saturday, so that's why I'm a little nervous. He's been jumpier and slower than usual."

"No problem. We'll get to the bottom of it." Fisher winks, and I swear a faint blush covers her cheeks.

I side-eye her giggling response. Then I mentally slap myself for reaching a new level of pathetic.

Once he's done, I take Millie back to her stall while Ellie walks Ranger so Fisher can examine his gait.

"His back leg seems to be the problem. Tie him up, and I'll start there."

Once Ranger's in position, we stand next to him as Fisher checks his hoof.

He carefully feels around and furrows his brows. "There's definitely somethin' here. I'm gonna remove his shoe and clean out the dirt so I can get a better look."

Ellie's face drops as she wraps her arms around herself. Ranger means everything to her, so if there's something wrong with him, she'll be devastated.

Fisher removes the shoe and uses his knife to remove the excess dirt. He inches closer to the hoof and carefully feels around.

"Found the problem." His voice is filled with remorse.

Ellie gets closer. "What is it?"

"Two nails are wedged near the frog, causing irritation and a possible infection. I'd get your vet out here right away."

Ellie's lips tremble. "Oh my God."

My brows pinch as frustration rolls through me. "I don't understand how this happened. He's been trainin' here since the rodeo and was doin' fine."

Fisher looks at me with a grim expression. "He likely got them from here, then."

"That's not possible," I say defensively. "His stall gets cleaned out every other day, and there'd be no reason for anyone to have nails 'round here."

The training center is only used by me or my brothers, which means no one else who isn't training is in there unless it's to watch. It'll be set up for the fundraiser in a couple of weeks, so having nails in the dirt is a big problem.

"This makes no sense..." I shake my head. "I'm gonna halt all trainin' until we look through everythin' to make sure there aren't more."

Ellie puts a hand on my arm. "Noah, it's not your fault. These things happen. He coulda stepped on them at the rodeo, and it just started botherin' him now. Doesn't mean you did anythin' wrong."

Although she's trying to make me feel better, it doesn't. I take full responsibility when something like this happens to my boarders, which is almost never because we make sure the ground stays clean. But I feel sick to my stomach that I kept pushing them to keep practicing and run faster. He couldn't tell me what was wrong and had to work in pain.

I give her a sincere look, fighting back angry tears. "I'll call the vet now and tell him it's urgent."

"I can soak his hoof in Epsom salt if you wanna grab me a bucket of water," Fisher says. "It'll relieve the pain temporarily."

"Good idea. I'll get one of the ranch hands to do it." I grab my phone and rush into the barn.

Trey's the first one I see, so I tell him what I need, and he nods.

Then I call the vet and beg him to come as soon as he can.

"What's goin' on?" Ayden asks.

"Two nails in Ranger's hoof. We need to do a full sweep in his stall and the trainin' center."

"Oh shit. Is he okay?"

"The vet's on his way over, so we'll see."

I text a couple of my brothers to help.

NOAH

SOS—training center.

LANDEN

Is this an actual emergency or like the time you needed us to bring you tampons?

TRIPP

Or the time you needed a change of underwear after drinking a 64-ounce of coffee?

LANDEN

Or when you ate too much of Momma's cheesecake and got sick from the dairy?

NOAH

You two are assholes and were dropped on your heads as babies! Now just get here and help me!

Before I lock my screen, another message pops up that includes the twins. I purposely didn't text them because they're as helpful as an umbrella during a hurricane.

TRIPP

We're placing bets on Noah's SOS. $100 she shart herself again.

Again? That lying fucker is a dead man.

LANDEN

$150 she's stuck in the bathroom stall and needs TP because no one ever restocks it.

WAYLON

$200 she ripped her jeans and is flashing her bare ass.

Oh my God. *I'm going to kill him!*

It's one thing to tease me about it in private, but now he's told my other loudmouthed brothers who don't know how to shut up about anything.

NOAH

$500 y'all are fucking idiots!

TRIPP

I'm heading over now to collect my payment.

LANDEN

Me too. Be there in 5!

WAYLON

I'm at The Lodge so bring MY payment over here.

WILDER

I'm coming to get my payment from Mr. Farrier himself.

Asshole.

NOAH

I hate y'all. Fuck off.

Then I leave the group chat.

"His stall is good," Ayden says, pushing out the wheelbarrow. "I cleaned every inch. No nails."

"That's a relief. Thank you."

I walk back to Ellie and Ranger. Fisher's working on his other hoof while the infected one soaks in a bucket.

"How's the rest of him?" I ask.

"Fine so far," Fisher says, carefully taking his time.

Ellie clings to Ranger, rubbing her hand up and down his neck.

"His stall is good to go, so I'm gonna meet my brothers at the trainin' center and look around."

"Sounds good."

"I'll let ya know if I find anythin'." I wrap an arm around her shoulders and squeeze. Then I rub my palm over Ranger's nose. "You're doin' great, buddy."

Landen and Tripp walk in at the same time I do.

"Well, you look normal," Landen teases, pretending to check over me. "What's goin' on?"

Tripp chuckles, removing his ball cap and brushing a hand over his sweaty dark hair.

I explain the situation and tell them we need to cover every inch of the center to make sure there aren't more.

"Got it." Landen gives me a firm nod. "I'll grab the rakes."

"And while y'all are here, stock up the TP in the bathrooms!" I call out, and they both laugh.

Within ten minutes, Tripp's calling out for me and shows me a few more nails he's found.

"What the fuck?" I take them. "We don't use this kind. Where are they comin' from?"

"No idea. But it looks like they were planted."

"What do ya mean? Who'd do that?" I ask, furrowing my brows.

Tripp shrugs. "Make any enemies recently?"

"No more than usual." I huff.

"Found some over here," Landen shouts from across the arena.

We rush over, and I gasp at the way they're spread out.

"It's like someone just dumped a box of them and stomped them into the ground," he says.

"This is crazy. Who could do this without being seen?"

"Coulda been in the middle of the night when we're all sleepin'," Tripp suggests.

"What about the cameras? If that's what happened, wouldn't they have caught it?" I ask.

Landen shakes his head. "Dad only installed them on the exterior, not inside."

"Shit." I clench my jaw.

"I'll check them, though," Tripp offers. "Coulda picked up someone before they entered."

"Okay, thanks. Let's get the magnetic sweeper in here. Then I want fresh dirt laid on top and leveled."

"I'll get it hooked up," Landen says.

"Reckon that means I'll get the dirt." Tripp smirks. "But I'm makin' Waylon help."

"I don't care as long as it gets done."

"What about the corral?" Landen asks.

"I was in there this mornin' and didn't see anythin' obvious, but it wouldn't hurt to sweep it to double-check." I'd rather be safe than sorry.

Most of my clients own top-level competitive show horses, so it's always been a priority to keep it clean, which is why the ranch hands sweep in here once a week. Whoever did this would've had to do it last night for me not to catch it until now.

And I'll do whatever it takes to find out who and make them pay.

Chapter Twelve

Fisher

When Noah returns to the barn, she looks pissed.

"Everythin' okay?" I ask.

She shakes her head and looks at Ellie. "Someone covered the arena in nails. This was done on purpose. I'm so sorry, El."

"Don't be. It's not your fault." Ellie reassuringly pats her back. "Who the hell would do that?"

"I'm not sure. Tripp's checkin' the outside cameras. For now, we're gettin' it swept out. Mr. Weston's on his way, so I'll be in the corral double-checkin' that too."

After Noah leaves, I continue working on Ranger, but my mind stays on her. I feel awful for both of them. Noah loves her job, and it's obvious she's one hundred percent committed to her clients. Ellie loves Ranger and takes competing seriously.

The only thing I can do is give Ranger my best care and hope for the best.

Mr. Weston shows up thirty minutes later and determines the hoof is infected. Ranger can't race until it's fully healed, which could be a couple of weeks or several months.

"Poor baby. You're gonna get all kinds of extra lovin'," Ellie says, wrapping her arms around his neck.

"How long have you been competin'?" I ask in an attempt to

distract her. I'm on his last hoof since I had to pause to let Mr. Weston look at him.

"Since I was thirteen, but Ranger was a gift for my sixteenth birthday. We've been inseparable since. I hate that we'll have to skip the fundraiser event. I was lookin' forward to beatin' Marcia Grayson's ass."

I chuckle at the competitiveness in her voice. "I know the feelin'."

"You used to race?"

"Rode bulls," I clarify. "But there'd be times I'd have to take time off to heal after fallin' or gettin' stomped on. Not an easy career."

"Oh my gosh, you're a former bull rider?" Her tone lightens. "I bet you have the *best* stories!"

I chuckle and nod because she's right. "It was many years ago. I did lots of stupid shit."

"Like what?" Her eager voice makes it hard to ignore her.

"One night after drinkin', a friend and I decided to go back into the arena and ride a bull drunk off our asses. You'd think my friend fallin' off in two seconds and gettin' stomped on woulda stopped me from doin' it, but it didn't."

She laughs, keeping her attention on me as I walk to my rig to grab another shoe.

"Broke a couple ribs and my collarbone. Nearly lost all my sponsorships, too."

"Oh my gosh. That sounds painful." She speaks with awe, but nothing is admirable about what I did in those early years of my career.

"Not the worst pain I've experienced," I mutter.

"What happened after that?"

"Took me three months to fully recover, and even when I did, I couldn't ride the same. Had to take another month off before they'd let me back on."

"What about your friend?"

"He wasn't as lucky. Broke his scapula and never came back.

His only sponsor dropped him, and he couldn't afford it on his own."

"Wow. How long did you compete?"

"From the time I was twenty-one to twenty-nine. After that, I got my farrier certification."

"Do ya miss it?"

"The lifestyle? No. The rush? Yes. But it was time to retire. I had two young kids and a wife at home always worryin' about me. It was time I acted like a family man."

"Where are your kids now?"

"Ellie, can I speak to Fisher for a minute?" Noah asks, thankfully appearing before I had to respond.

"Oh, sure! I'm gonna call my mom and let her know what's goin' on." She gives Ranger a quick peck before leaving the barn.

"How long were you standin' there?" I ask when we're alone.

"Long enough to know I'm gonna kick your ass on the mechanical bull tomorrow night."

I snort, shaking my head at her confidence. "You think the few times you've done it will be better than my decade of experience?"

"No, now I know all I gotta do is get you drunk, and I'll win, no problem."

I smirk, cleaning up my area now that Ranger's hooves are done. After his Epsom salt soak and getting checked by the vet, I bandaged it. It'll need to be soaked and cleaned daily until the wound heals.

"I'm the DD, remember?"

"You sure about that? My brothers can call an Uber or Lyft."

"And how will you get home?" I ask, knowing how easy it'd be to just take her to my house and keep her for myself.

"I'll call for my own. Unless you have a better idea?"

Her flirty tone has my dick growing hard. I live right outside of town, so a quick five-minute drive is all it'd take to bring her to my bed.

"You should let me drive you home so I know you're safe," I tell her instead of what I'm thinking.

Ellie returns before Noah can respond and takes Ranger to his stall. "I'm gonna stay with him for a little bit longer. Is that okay?"

Noah smiles. "Of course. Stay as long as ya want, and let me know if you need anythin'."

Once Ellie leads Ranger back to his stall, I grab my clipboard to check who's next.

"Are you takin' your lunch break, or should I bring the next one?" she asks.

I hesitate before answering. "Are *you* takin' one?"

She licks her lips as her gaze meets mine, a secret tell that she's thinking the same thing I am. We're not supposed to be spending time alone together.

"Probably since I can't train until everything's clean. Sweepin' the trainin' center will take my brothers at least an hour and another to level new dirt. Add in two more for their fuckin' around. What'd ya have in mind?"

"Well, turns out I still need that retreat tour."

She raises a brow. "And you want me to give it to you?"

"Who better than the ranch princess herself?"

"How'd I earn that name?"

I'd rather call her AJ or Goldie, but that'd breach our "friends only" agreement, considering it'd only make us think of our forbidden night together.

"Am I wrong? Seems you run shit 'round here."

"Only the boarders," she argues, grinning. "My brothers and parents run many other aspects of the ranch and retreat."

"If you don't wanna—"

"No, I will. But we should do it on horseback to get the true ranch experience. I can show you a couple of the popular trails, then, too."

I hadn't expected that, but I won't deny time with her.

"Sure. I'll clean up my supplies, and we can go."

"My horse is at the family barn. You can ride one of ours."

In my gut, I know this is a bad idea. The more time I spend with her, the more I want her.

But if we're going to try out this "friends" thing and spend time with each other tomorrow night at the restaurant and bar, then I need to slap on my poker face and deal with it.

Unless Jase gives me his blessing and Noah's parents lift the no employees fraternizing rule, we can't be anything more. I didn't spend years healing and overcoming mental trauma to cause more.

My dick stirs in disagreement.

Twenty minutes later, we're riding side by side toward the retreat. She points out from the ranch hand quarters, The Lodge, and the cabins. In between are the trail horse barn and pasture, the pool, fishing pond, and firepit area. People walk around and wave as we pass them. Noah leads us around and up to the trail where they give tours.

She studies the view as her shoulders relax. "This is Sunset Trail. It's a family favorite."

"Why's that?" I ask, trotting behind her.

She flashes a sly smile. "You'll see. C'mon!"

With a little kick, she takes off, and I follow. Denver's a quarter horse and one of the easiest horses I've been on. Not surprised since Noah trained him.

As we ride up the trail, I get a better view of the retreat on one side and the scenery on the other.

"It's beautiful up here," I say when I catch up.

"Just wait." Noah jumps down and grabs Donut's lead rope, and I do the same with Denver. "There's a spot up here I wanna show you."

The sun beats down on me, and sweat trickles down my neck, but I don't care. There's nowhere else I'd rather be than up here next to her.

"Here." Noah smiles at me when she glances over her shoulder. "You can see for miles."

She ties Donut to a post, so I do the same with Denver.

Once the horses are secure, I take in the view—the tops of the trees, the ranch on one side and the retreat on the other, and of course, Noah standing next to me.

"I bet this never gets old," I say.

"Never." She turns and points at something behind me. "I brought Mallory here shortly after she moved in a couple years ago. I painted those rocks with her as a way to help her grieve and have a spot to come and talk to her mom and dad."

She's mentioned Mallory moving here before, but I didn't know her parents died.

"What happened? If ya don't mind me askin'..." I admire how colorful and cheerful the rocks look.

"Car crash," Noah says in a somber tone that has my heart aching.

I know all too well what it's like to lose a loved one.

"At least they died together," she adds. "That's what helps us grieve."

Noah sits on one of the rocks, and I take the one beside her.

"Poor Mallory. So young. Did she have any siblings?"

"No. Only child." The corner of her lips tilts up slightly. "Now she has five older ones."

"That was nice y'all took her in."

"Wouldn't have had it any other way," she says, resting her hand between us. "They didn't live 'round here, so Mallory had never ridden. She wanted to learn, and I knew it'd be therapeutic for her, so I gave her lessons."

"And Miss Swift is her horse, right?" I put my hand next to hers, not quite touching but close enough to feel her warmth.

She laughs, crossing her legs and angling toward me so we're even closer. "Yeah. We couldn't talk her out of naming her Taylor Alison Swift, so we came up with a nickname when Ayden got tired of callin' her the full name after the first day."

I chuckle. "She's lucky to have y'all. I woulda never guessed what she's been through if I didn't know." My gaze finds hers as I scan her face. "Your family saved her."

"I like to think we saved each other." She breaks out into a smile as she stares out at the view. "Losin' my aunt and uncle wrecked my momma. That was her sister. My dad was distraught, too. I'd never seen him cry until the funeral."

"Grief isn't somethin' you can fully understand until you've experienced it firsthand. It's worse when it's paired with guilt and is the most painful way to live. Makes ya not wanna live at all."

She flicks her gaze to mine as if she wants to ask questions, but she places her hand on mine and squeezes it instead. My stomach flips at the skin-on-skin contact, but her expression is filled with sympathy and remorse.

"I can't even imagine what that was like for you. Jase showed me a few pics of her. She was beautiful."

My throat closes up as I give her a tight smile. "Yeah, she was. She was filled with so much heart and energy. Loved bein' outside and tryin' new things. Nothin' scared her."

"Wow, she sounds like the exact opposite of Jase." She chuckles, and I do, too, because she's right.

I wish I could explain what happened, but I can't. I've only said those words aloud once when I told my wife and the detectives. But repeating them made it real.

And I didn't want them to be true.

"Lyla woulda loved it here," I tell her instead. "She loved watchin' me work on horses and askin' a million questions about them."

I'd do anything to listen to her talk for hours again.

"Reminds me of Mallory. It's why she and Serena are good friends. They can talk each other's ears off."

"That's Ayden's daughter?"

She nods. "He and his wife, Laney, have another one comin' in a couple months. Ayden didn't even know Serena existed until last year."

"What?"

She chuckles at my expression. I wish I could bottle up the sound. It's so sweet and genuine. It makes me smile even when my heart hurts.

"It's a long story, but basically, Ayden left his hometown a decade ago to escape his abusive father. Laney didn't find out she was pregnant until he was gone, but he'd ditched his phone and all social media so she couldn't even tell him."

"Wow. So Laney raised her alone?"

"Not exactly, and that's an even longer story..." She snort-laughs. "You'll have to take Ayden out for a drink one night and get the full story because it's wild. But the short version is Laney found him on the ranch from a viral video and then flew here to tell him he had a daughter. He went to Texas to meet her, and a few weeks later, Laney and Serena moved here to be with him. They eloped, she got pregnant, and in August, they're havin' a reception."

At least someone around here got their happily ever after.

"Ayden's a lucky man to get his family back."

Her fingers intertwine with mine, and she gives me a tight-lipped smile. My gaze wanders to her mouth, desperately wishing I could close the small gap between us.

We stare at each other, neither wanting to cross the lines as the air between us grows thicker.

"Noah..."

A piercing noise echoes from her pocket, and she quickly reaches for it and silences her phone.

"Shit. I set a reminder to check on the trainin' center."

"Oh, right. I should probably get back to work."

"We still have to eat," she argues, getting to her feet, and I follow her to the horses.

"You sure there's time?"

She jumps on Donut, and when I settle on Denver, she shoots me a shit-eating grin.

"C'mon, I'll race ya to the bottom!" She kicks her heels and whistles, making Donut take off.

Christ. I wasn't expecting that.

"Let's go, Denver." My tap is lighter than Noah's. I'm not looking to fall off a cliff today nor am I as familiar with these trails as she is. There are too many trees and curves for me to confidently race her.

By the time I catch up with Noah, she's waiting with a smug expression.

"I thought you were a bull rider or, at the very least, a cowboy?"

"Ouch." I laugh. "I put all that recklessness behind me, remember?"

"Oh, right. You traded in your adrenaline junkie card for an AARP one. I'll go easy on ya next time."

It's on the tip of my goddamn tongue to remind her how she's the one who couldn't keep up with me that night, but I keep that thought to myself.

But I'll never forget I had her screaming out my name within eight seconds as she shook through her orgasm.

It's all I see when I close my eyes, and then I hear her moaning in my head when I stroke myself in the shower.

Noah leads me to The Lodge, where she introduces me to a couple of the receptionists who make it more than obvious they're flirting with me. And because I can't help messing with Noah, I eat it up and write down my number when they ask.

"Need I remind you of the no employees datin' rule?"

Her bitter tone has me smiling.

"No, thanks to you, I'm well aware of it."

We hit the buffet, where I fill my plate because everything smells so damn good, and find a table.

"Now we gotta fire them." She sits across from me, and her nostrils flare.

"Why not fire me?"

Her head snaps up as she stabs her fork into a piece of cornbread. "What?"

"Why do you automatically fire the girls and not me? I'm the one who gave them my number."

"They're the ones who asked," she bites out.

"And I coulda said no, so accordin' to your rules, shouldn't we all be fired?" I shrug, taking a bite of my chicken-fried steak.

Her chest rises and falls as if she's annoyed with me, and I choke back laughter at her frustration.

"You don't think it's rude to hand out your number in front of me?" she asks and then opens her mouth as if she wants to say something else but clamps it shut.

We both know we'd act on our feelings if we could without consequences, but considering we can't, we're stuck in this weird friend zone neither of us wants.

"I thought we were...*friends*. Like you and Jase, right?"

Ocean-blue eyes stare intently at me. Her jaw is so tense, I'm waiting for it to snap in half.

"Fine," she grinds out. "Then you can't get mad at me when I do the same tomorrow night at the bar."

The hell she will.

"Sure. I'll even be your wingman. Is that what y'all call it now?"

She scoffs as she shoves bread into her mouth.

The conversation dies, and we eat in silence. Noah acting like a jealous girlfriend is one of the hottest things I've ever seen, and I can't wait to get her alone to tell her the truth.

"We should get back to the barn," she says as she finishes eating. "Tripp and Landen have finished, so I wanna go check it out."

"Any word on the cameras?"

"Not yet. He'll probably check now that they're done."

I clear my plate and wave to the receptionists just to further mess with Noah. She turns and walks toward the exit. When I catch up to her, she acts indifferent and opens the door for me.

Neither of us speaks on the way to the Hollis family barn. Once we're inside, I lead Denver to the groomer's stall.

Once both horses are clipped in, we remove their saddles, and I follow her to the tack room.

The door whips open and nearly slams in my face when it bounces back.

"Jesus." I dodge it just in time.

"My bad," Noah singsongs without a backward glance.

That was definitely on purpose.

She sets the saddle on the stand, and after I do the same with mine, she grabs the grooming bucket. Before she can leave, I snatch her wrist and pull her toward me.

She gasps when her chest presses against mine. "W-what're ya doin'?"

I take a few steps, pushing her with me until her back is flat to the door. Her fingers release the grip on the bucket, and it falls to the floor.

Cupping her cheek, I lift her chin until her eyes meet mine. "Are you done actin' jealous?"

"I'm not!" Her racing heartbeat tells me otherwise.

My thumb brushes over her bottom lip as mine curve into a knowing grin.

I lean down until my forehead rests on hers. "I wanna kiss the fuckin' hell out of you right now, *Goldie*." My mouth moves to her ear. "And after I'd thoroughly devour you, I'd get on my knees and taste between your thighs until you came on my tongue. But I'd have to cover your mouth because I know how loud ya get."

Her breath hitches on a soft moan, and my cock jerks at the sound.

"But you—"

"Before you get upset with me for followin' the rules, just remember all the ways I'd break them for you." My mouth hovers above hers. We're less than a breath apart, and a small step is all it'd take to steal her lips.

"You did for the receptionists."

I meet her eyes and fight the urge to smile. Instead, I grab a loose strand of her golden hair and curl it behind her ear.

"And because I'm well aware of the rules, I gave them Jase's number, not mine."

Her brows rise, and I laugh.

"Figured he was single and allowed to date anyone he wants, so why not?"

And I selfishly did it to hopefully keep his mind off Noah.

Her pale cheeks change into a bright red hue.

"Now who's the one blushin'?" I ask, throwing her words from the bar that night back at her.

"But who's the hot and aroused one this time?" She lowers her gaze to my noticeable erection.

"Oh, that's definitely me." I smirk because it's not even worth trying to hide.

We stare at each other, waiting for the other to break, but before we can, someone shouts in the barn.

"Noah! You in here?"

"Shit, that's Tripp."

I move away so she can open the door, then wait a second for my dick to calm down. The last thing we need is one of her brothers getting suspicious of us when nothing is even happening.

Noah grabs the grooming bucket and goes out to speak with him. She tells him she'll meet him at the training center once we finish brushing the horses.

"Hey." I nod at Tripp when he comes into view. Then I glance at Noah. "If ya gotta run, I can finish up here and get them back in their stalls."

Tripp looks back and forth between us, and I do my best to seem normal. Not at all like I was seconds from cracking and kissing his sister.

By the way Noah looks at us, she must sense the tension coming off Tripp and reluctantly agrees.

"Sure. Thanks, Mr. Underwood."

Giving her a tight-lipped smile, I ignore Tripp's narrowed stare before grabbing the bucket and walking away before he sees right through me.

Chapter Thirteen

Noah

"Goddamn, you little hottie." Magnolia whistles after she barges through my door and sees me in my dinner outfit. "You dressin' up for Jase or Daddy Fisher?"

I roll my eyes when she waggles her brows. "What'd I say 'bout callin' him that?"

"You're tellin' me you didn't scream that when he was balls deep inside you? Because if not, that's a tragedy."

I scoff, grabbing my heels and sitting on the edge of the bed. "No, a tragedy is what this dinner is gonna end in if Jase figures out what we did."

"Speakin' of, you left me with blue ovaries after your text last night. So spill the rest of the juicy details. What happened after Tripp caught y'all?"

"He didn't *catch* anythin'. But he woulda had he come twenty seconds later..."

"I knew it!" she squeals.

I was moments away from begging Fisher to kiss me, but a part of me doesn't want to know if he would've or not. The logical side of me knows we shouldn't. It'd make everything more complicated than it already is, but the needy side of me wants his mouth and hands on me again.

When he whispered in my ear, my entire body shivered in anticipation. Over twenty-four hours later, I can still feel his warm breath tickling down my neck.

"Doesn't matter because nothin' happened or can happen again." Once my shoes are on, I stand and put in my earrings.

"Do you really think Jase would be that upset? Y'all broke up a long time ago, and it's time y'all moved on."

"You seriously think he'd be okay with me *movin' on* with his father? *Sure, yeah, go bang my dad, then let's have a therapy session about all the emotional trauma,*" I mimic in an exaggerated deep voice.

She rolls her eyes. "Oh, just tell him to shut up, or you'll make him your stepson."

I snort. "Yeah, that'll make him closer to Daddy dearest."

"To be a fly on the wall at that restaurant...are ya sure I can't be your plus-one?"

"For what? Like some weird non-double date? I'm already worried I'm gonna slip and say somethin' I'm not supposed to know."

"Like how big his dick is..."

"No! Well, yes, but more personal. He's talked about stuff I wouldn't know if we were *only* coworkers."

"Again, to be a fly on the wall..." She chuckles and motions for me to spin around so she can get the full view of me. "And you wearin' a date night dress on a non-date night is the cherry on top."

My hands rub over the ruffled fabric. "Is it too much? Should I change?"

I analyze every inch of my outfit in my floor-length mirror. I picked out a white cami dress with a ruched bust that flows just below my knees. When I pair it with navy-blue heels, it grants me a few more inches. Since we're meeting at the Twisted Bull afterward, I'm bringing my favorite cowboy boots. No way can I dance or ride the mechanical bull in three-inch shoes.

"You look perfect. I'll be waitin' at the bar to hear *all* about it."

"How will you listen if your tongue is halfway down Tripp's throat?"

"Don't give me false hope!" She scoffs when I laugh. "Nope, tonight is all about findin' me a new man. No more of these emotionally unavailable boys."

My eyes widen in surprise at the sound of her new mindset. "Finally! 'Bout goddamn time. Just don't hook up with someone you work with."

"Trust me, if there was anyone at work worth seein' me naked, you'd know about it by now. And we both know I'd quit my job if it came down to that."

Easy for Magnolia to say, but if we get caught, I won't be the one without a job. Fisher would be the unemployed one. But the ranch needs him, too. So quitting isn't an option for either of us.

"Okay, I gotta go before I'm late, but we'll talk more over margaritas!" I grab my purse and hug her.

"You got it, babe. I'll be three deep in by the time ya get there."

I shake my head, smiling. "You better wait for me. No tipsy Magnolia."

"Fine." She chuckles, walking out with me to my truck.

"Be careful," I warn when we go our separate ways.

"I should be tellin' you that." Her taunting has nervous butterflies invading my stomach. I've been dreading this for two days.

How the hell am I supposed to sit next to my ex-boyfriend and pretend I'm not thinking about his dad whispering in my ear what a good girl I am for taking his dick so well?

Lilian's Steakhouse is packed when I arrive. Nearly every

stool is taken at the bar, which means it's louder than I expected. The dining area is in the back, where it's quieter, but I'd much prefer the loudness to drown out my anxious thoughts.

"Hey." Fisher stands against the wall next to me. His eyes fixate on one of the TVs behind the bar as if he's purposely not looking at me. "Jase not here?"

"Not yet. As soon as I parked, he texted that he was runnin' late, but I let the hostess know of our reservation."

"Oh."

I steal a glance and grin at his black slacks and matching suit coat. A gray button-up is underneath but no tie. It's a different look than I've seen him wear before, but I'm not complaining. It fits him well in a professional kind of way that makes me want to slowly strip off each item.

"You look breathtakin'," he mutters so quietly I almost don't hear him.

My throat tightens when I try to thank him and reciprocate the compliment. Being alone with him feels like a date, one we never got to have, and it makes me wish even more that our circumstances were different.

"Do you wanna drink?" he asks when my silence lingers.

"Absolutely," I immediately respond. *I need one...or two.*

He finally meets my eyes, and a hint of a smile graces his scruffy face. When he brushes a hand through his hair, it messes it up in a way I wish I were the one threading my fingers through it.

"What's your poison?" he asks once we squeeze our way to the bar.

Men twice my age. And off-limits.

"I'll start with a mojito. Or wait, maybe a Long Island Iced Tea."

"A bit indecisive tonight?" He arches a brow. The corner of his lips tilts up as he waits for me to choose.

Shrugging, I take the stool next to me when it opens up. "You pick for me, then."

Once the bartender comes over, Fisher orders a Budweiser for himself, glances at me with amusement written on his face, and leans closer toward her.

"And a Screwdriver."

I furrow my brows, wondering how he came up with that one.

After she sets both drinks down, he hands her his card, and as he slides the yellow liquid-filled glass in front of me, he brings his mouth to my ear.

"Because we're both *screwed*. Enjoy." His whisper sends shivers down my spine as his free hand wraps around the back of my stool.

That's an understatement, I want to reply, but Jase approaching on my other side causes me to jump. Fisher puts a couple of inches between us and is so casual about it that you wouldn't know his tongue was practically in my ear a moment ago.

"Hey, sorry I'm late." Jase kisses my cheek. "Meetin' ran late. Can you order me a Guinness? I'll let the hostess know we're ready."

"Sure," Fisher answers, keeping his gaze locked on Jase's as his dances between us.

"Thanks."

Once Jase walks away, I inhale a sharp breath, grab my drink, and take a long sip.

"Keep these comin'."

Fisher shakes his head. "Not if you're drivin'."

I glare at him, wanting to argue, but I know he's right.

"Okay, they're ready for us." Jase grabs his beer and wraps an arm around my waist when I stand.

As we follow the hostess, Jase asks how I've been. There's an urge to shake him, but I stop myself so he won't be suspicious about my sudden refusal of his touch.

"Good, busy as usual," I tell him when he picks a seat at the square table.

Before I can do the same, Fisher pulls out my chair, and my eyes widen.

I turn and mouth, "What're ya doin'?"

He furrows his brows as if he doesn't understand the panic on my face.

"Oh shit, I shoulda done that." Jase stands, reaching the back of my chair and motioning for me to sit. Once I do, he helps push me in, then squeezes my shoulder.

"A gentleman should always pull out a woman's chair," Fisher says when he takes his own next to me.

"Thanks for the reminder, *Dad*." The way he emphasizes the word has me flinching.

Why is he being so rude?

The hostess waits until we're all situated before setting down our menus and listing the specials. Once she leaves, I open mine so I can hide my face from Jase's intense stare.

He wanted me here as a buffer, but now I'm worried he has other intentions.

"The Porterhouse sounds good," Jase says. "I bet you're gettin' your favorite type."

Why is he acting like he knows my favorite steak when the nicest restaurant he's ever taken me to had chicken nuggets on the menu?

"Actually, I'm in the mood for shrimp."

"At a steakhouse?" He scoffs, closing his menu with a smack. "Get the filet. You'll like it."

My head pounds as I think about yelling at him for being an arrogant asshole, but for the sake of keeping the peace, I stay quiet. I'll order whatever I damn well please.

Fisher must notice my annoyance because he clears his throat and grabs his beer.

"I'm thinkin' seafood, too. The crab legs sound good." He takes a sip, ignoring Jase's scowl.

Thankfully, our server appears and asks if we're ready to order.

God, yes. And bring the check before I'm tempted to run into traffic to avoid another minute of this.

"Howdy, I'm Melinda, and I'll be takin' care of y'all tonight. I see y'all have drinks, but if you need refills, let me know. Are y'all here celebratin' for a special occasion?"

Yeah, my funeral.

The brunette smiles wide, and if she feels the awkwardness radiating between us, she's not making it known by how giddy she is.

"Just a family dinner," Jase explains.

"Aw, that's precious." She directs her attention to Fisher. "Your children are so sweet to take you out. My parents are always yellin' at me to go out with them, but life gets busy, ya know?"

I grab my drink to avoid blurting out that she should shut up and just take our order. Before Jase says something hurtful about his dad or, worse, I tell her she's wrong because what we did that weekend was far from *precious*.

"I'm gonna have the grilled shrimp with a side salad," I say so we can get this over with as fast as humanly possible. I'll inhale my food without chewing if it means we can leave sooner.

When she moves to Jase and steals his attention, I glance at Fisher. He smirks, then shifts in his chair and squeezes my leg underneath the table. My heart gallops at the goose bumps his touch leaves on my skin.

Just as swiftly as he leaned over, he settles back when the server directs her attention to him next. I take small sips of my Screwdriver as we wait for her to leave.

"How was your first week workin' on the ranch?" Jase asks once she does.

"It was good. Every day is eventful." Fisher grins at me.

"What's that mean?" Jase asks in a harsh tone.

"There's a lot to do," I hurriedly answer before Fisher can. "Lots of people comin' and goin'."

"And the issue with Ranger," Fisher adds.

"What happened?" Jase asks me instead of his dad.

"Found a couple nails in his hoof," Fisher replies anyway.

"We actually found tons of nails scattered in the trainin' center arena. Tripp and Landen had to use the sweeper and level it out with more dirt. We caught the person who most likely did it on camera."

"You didn't tell me that," Fisher says at the same time Jase asks, "Who?"

Jase narrows his eyes at his dad, but Fisher ignores his scowl and stares at me.

"We dunno. They were wearin' a black hoodie and kept their head down the whole time they walked in and out."

I only saw the footage last night, or I would've told Fisher sooner.

"Whoever it was knew where the cameras were," Fisher says.

"Probably that Craig Sanders douche."

Shit, he could be right.

"Maybe. But why, after all this time, would he harass me now?"

"Who's Craig Sanders?" Fisher asks.

"A prick who needs his face rearranged. He's a jealous asshole."

"Language, Jase. We're in a restaurant," Fisher warns.

If I had a knife, I'd use it to cut the tension between them because they're only one *whose dick is bigger* argument away from getting into a fistfight.

"He's a rival trainer who's mad Ellie picked me instead of him. She's killin' it in the barrel racing scene right now, which makes sense as to why he'd cover the arena in nails. He knew she'd be trainin' with me."

Fisher's nostrils flare. "How much of a threat is this guy? Should you contact the authorities?"

"She just said they couldn't get a face on the camera. What're the cops gonna do?" Jase's cocky tone has me kicking him underneath the table with a glare.

"Creatin' a paper trail for trespassin' will help if there's another incident," Fisher explains. His clipped voice edges on annoyance at Jase's dumbass comment. Can't say I blame him.

"We shoulda reported it," I agree. "But my first gut reaction was to get it cleaned up right away and take care of Ranger. But since there's footage, I can show them what we have."

"I'll text Sheriff Wagner and tell him to swing by the ranch tomorrow," Jase says, pulling out his cell.

"I can call him myself," I say, harsher than I intended to, but his demeanor is frustrating. He never gave a shit about the ranch when we were dating, and now he's acting like he gives a damn.

With a shrug, he pockets his phone. "Alright, just thought I'd take somethin' off your plate."

He hasn't a goddamn clue what's on my plate.

"Thanks, I appreciate it. But we'll get it sorted." I give him a tight-lipped smile and nod toward Fisher so he gets the hint to make *nice* conversation with him.

"Did you get unpacked?" Jase asks him before grabbing his beer.

"About halfway. Still need to buy some furniture, but the necessities are put away."

"Where did ya buy a house?" I ask because I actually don't know where he lives.

"Five minutes outside of town on 107."

So about ten to fifteen minutes from the ranch.

"Nice, so not too far from Jase." I smile. After Jase moved out of his mom's house, he rented an apartment in town so he was closer to the office.

"I actually found a house I wanna buy." Jase grins.

I raise a brow. "Really?"

Jase was never interested in settling down or making any big plans because all he cared about was himself and doing the bare minimum. While we were dating, it wasn't that big of a deal since I still lived in my parents' house and wasn't planning on leaving for college. Now, it's nice to see him taking his life and career more seriously.

"That's why I was late. I was talkin' with my banker. Plannin' on makin' an offer tomorrow."

I reach over and squeeze his hand. "Jase, that's amazin'! Congrats!"

That's a big step for him, especially at his age. I'm genuinely proud of him and how far he's come.

"Proud of you, son," Fisher says, holding up his Budweiser and waiting for Jase to clink his back.

Jase gives him a curt nod and finally lifts his glass. "Thanks."

Taking a sip of my drink, I'm relieved the uneasiness has dwindled.

"Do you have any pictures?" I ask.

Jase whips out his phone and scrolls to the listing. "Three bedrooms and bathrooms, large backyard, dining and living rooms. Newly remodeled kitchen."

"That sounds like a dream!" I smile wide when he scrolls through the photos. "Looks beautiful."

"That's big," Fisher says. "Alotta house for one person."

"Well, sure now, but I don't wanna be single forever. Someday, there'll be a wife and kids livin' there, too." Jase gives me a look that makes my skin crawl. I'm not sure if he's gauging my reaction to him dating other women or to the idea of him settling down, but either way, he better get any thoughts of us getting back together out of his mind.

"I can't wait to see it in person," I say, keeping my voice level. Before Fisher's return, it wouldn't even be a question that he'd show me. As friends, we kept each other updated on everything. It was fun and easy. Now it's as if he's trying to show off as if to imply how well he's done without him.

"How about Sunday? I'm doin' another walk-through," Jase offers.

"Depends. I'll be workin' in the afternoon before family supper."

"I can come," Fisher says. "Before then, anyway."

Jase snaps his head toward his dad.

Oh shit.

"Wait, you're goin' to the Hollises on Sunday?"

"Dena invited me."

I keep my eyes on my drink, swirling my straw around as if it's the most interesting thing in this room.

"You're lucky. Dena's a great cook," Jase's bitter tone spits out. "Make sure to bail after dessert, or you'll get stuck scrapbookin' with them."

"Hey." I bump my foot into his shin.

He laughs, but it actually hurts my feelings. He knows how special Sunday nights are to me.

Though I shouldn't be surprised. He complained each time I stayed late, and he'd eventually leave without me.

"What's that?" Fisher asks with a sweetness in his voice.

"It's a tradition to add a page to our scrapbook each week. But we usually end up chattin' too long and doing three or four pages before we call it a night. It's old-school, but my momma loves it. Gramma Grace tells stories, and the rest of us write them down next to the photos."

"Snooze city," Jase murmurs.

"Maybe to you," I snap.

Fisher clears his throat, grabbing Jase's attention, and gives him a murderous look. It's not like he can tell him *I didn't raise you to be a little asshole* because Jase would just throw it in his face that he didn't raise him at all. But he doesn't need to say anything. One piercing look and Jase keeps his mouth shut.

The server approaches with a wide, toothy smile, oblivious to how I'm ready to pull out my hair, and delivers my salad.

"Can I get drink refills for anyone?"

"Just water for me," Fisher says.

"I'll take another Guinness. How about you?" Jase asks me.

"I'll take a water." And before she walks away, I quickly add, "Can I also get a shot of your strongest tequila?"

"Of course! Be right back with those."

I feel Fisher's heated stare, so I avoid looking at him and dig into my food instead.

"You still goin' to the Twisted Bull tonight?" Jase asks.

"I am," Fisher says before I can respond.

"Yeah, meetin' Magnolia and my brothers there."

"You'll have to record my old man fallin' on his ass when he tries to ride the bull." Jase snickers. If he's not careful, his little digs will piss off Fisher more than he already looks. Jase asked me to come as a buffer, not to help troll him.

"Why don't ya come and show me what you can do?" Fisher asks. "It's not as easy as it looks."

"Not a chance. People respect me as a real estate agent 'round here. They don't wanna see the person sellin' them a house actin' like a drunk fool on a mechanical bull."

"No one said you had to be drunk." I shrug.

"Trust me, I'd need to be to do somethin' that stupid."

"I did it," I remind him.

"Yeah, and you were plastered off your ass. Not your proudest moment, Noah."

I blink, taken aback by how he's treating me when I'm here as a favor in the first place.

Fisher's shoulder lifts slightly. "She showed me the video, and I thought she did great."

No. *No, no, no.* Why would Fisher tell him that?

Bracing myself, I wait for Jase to freak out, but he just scoffs.

"My brothers think he can't do it, so I showed him if I could do it drunk, he most definitely could," I explain.

"Except you face-planted."

"But I lasted the full eight seconds, didn't I?" I say smugly, and Fisher chokes on his beer.

Oh God. *Eight seconds.*

I resist the urge to laugh at him for choking once again at my words.

"You okay?" I ask, trying to hide my blush with my glass as I take the final sip.

He pats his chest, clearing his throat. "Just went down wrong."

Mm-hmm.

Finally, the server returns with our beverages, and I immediately shoot down the tequila. I'm tempted to tell her to bring me another, but that'd be irresponsible, so I stick with my water.

"I'll be right back with your food."

Thank God.

After the server delivers our food, we thank her, and dive in. I'm about to scarf down my shrimp like I'm aiming for the Guinness World Record and then get the hell out of here. If we weren't in a fancy restaurant, I'd chuck a piece at Jase and pray it gets caught in his throat so he'd shut up.

Just as I form my plan, someone says my name and steals my attention to the man standing next to me.

And just like that, this horrible dinner manages to get worse.

Chapter Fourteen

Fisher

Noah's expression drops when a man says her name and stands beside her. My jaw tenses as soon as he rests his hand on her shoulder. Her eyes flick to where he's touching her, and I flex my fingers to prevent me from doing something stupid.

Like ripping off his arm.

"Dylan, hi." Noah's high-pitched, nervous tone is unsettling. Whoever this guy is, she doesn't like him.

"How've ya been? It's been about a year or so. We should catch up sometime."

Noah's tight-lipped smile is met with hesitant eyes. "Yeah, it's been a while. I've been really busy with trainin' and stuff on the ranch."

"You never gave me that tour. Maybe we could do that soon?" He winks.

As I drink my water, my eyes stay glued on him over the rim. Noah's dropping obvious hints that she's not interested, but he's clueless to them.

"Not sure that's a good idea. I'm not interested in datin' right now." Noah's blunt response has me wanting to give her a high five, but that'd be awkward, so instead, I lower my gaze to my plate and hide my smirk.

"Oh, I just meant as friends, Noah. I better get back to my table, but if ya change your mind, you've got my number." He squeezes her shoulder again, and as soon as he walks away, Noah releases an audible breath.

When I glance at Jase, he's watching me with pinched brows as if he's confused about my reaction.

"Is that one of the guys you tried to date after me?"

"Jase," I say in a strict tone I'd use on him when he was a child. He's either lost his mind or his goddamn manners.

"She knows I'm kiddin'." He lifts one shoulder, but his smug expression and tone tell me otherwise.

"If y'all must know, yes, we went on a couple dates. But the sparks just weren't there, so I broke it off," Noah says.

"*Sparks*?" Jase chuckles. "You're gonna be single forever if that's what you're waitin' for, babe."

The server has impeccable timing and interrupts to bring our food. Her cheerful tone is a contrast to the uncomfortable conversation we're having.

"May I get y'all anythin' else right away?" she asks once she's placed our plates in front of us.

A stun gun with a side of Novocaine.

"This is perfect, thank you," Noah tells her.

It's hard keeping my eyes off her. She's handling this awkward dinner better than I would've. The temptation to put Jase in his place has been hard to resist at times, but Noah's quick responses have kept me from doing so.

"Thank you." I smile at the server before she leaves.

"Wait, excuse me." Jase holds up his finger to grab her attention. "I asked for extra mushrooms, and there's only like seven here. That's hardly *extra*." His loud, harsh tone almost has me speaking up to remind him of how to treat people, but Noah's red cheeks halt me. She's already embarrassed by his behavior, so I don't want to add fuel to the fire.

Noah pops a piece of shrimp in her mouth, most likely to keep herself from screaming, and I do the same with a hush puppy. We share a secret look that has us both grinning.

The server apologizes and offers to bring him more right away. Things stay quiet while we eat, and the only noise comes from me cracking the crab legs.

"So how long after we broke up did you date Dylan?" Jase asks, and I shift my eyes to glance at Noah, who's focusing on her food like it's the most interesting thing ever.

Meanwhile, I could stare at her all night because she's by far the most beautiful woman I've laid my eyes on. The only problem is that I think Jase is starting to notice how I'm looking at her.

"Noah?" Jase prompts.

"I dunno...like a year, I guess? What's it matter?"

"Just curious how long it took to get over our relationship."

Her head jerks toward him with a piece of shrimp in her hand, and I'm low-key worried she'll chuck it at his head.

"Do we have to do this now? In front of your dad?"

"Since when did you get shy?"

"I'm not, but I don't think it's appropriate for me to discuss my datin' life with you."

I clear my throat to grab his attention away from Noah. "Speakin' of, are you datin' anyone, Jase?"

"I've gone on dates. Most haven't been my type or ready to settle down."

"You're still young," I remind him. "You have plenty of time."

"You were married and had two kids when ya were my age," he says.

I nod as I continue eating. "Yeah, I did. But that doesn't mean it's for everyone."

"Not sure it was for you either."

I glance up to him staring at me as if he's daring me to argue, but he knows I won't.

"If I'm bein' honest, I wasn't ready to be a husband and a dad at twenty years old, but we got pregnant anyway. I don't regret marrying your mom because we got two beautiful children out of it. When my career took off after Lyla was born, I had to keep travelin' and doin' my job in order to make ends meet. It's not a lifestyle that works for everyone," I admit.

Jase's cold stare as he cuts into his steak has me wondering if he'll say what he's really thinking. How I neglected him, how it's my fault his sister died, or how I don't deserve a second chance to be in his life.

But he says none of those things.

Instead, he shoves a forkful of food into his mouth and gives me a hesitant nod. Either he doesn't have a comeback or he doesn't want to say it in front of Noah.

The server arrives with Jase's mushrooms, and thankfully, after that, the conversation shifts to Jase's success in his new real estate career. I'm happy he found a career he loves since I knew he wouldn't follow in my footsteps or do anything ranch work-related. Noah talks about the fundraiser and trick riding she'll be doing with Donut soon. By the time we finish eating, most of the discomfort has dissolved.

After I pay the bill, I pull Jase into a side hug and linger for a moment. "I'm proud of you for focusin' on your future. Let me know what time you're goin' on Sunday, and I'll be there."

He nods. "Thanks, Dad. Will do."

Jase hugs Noah next and kisses her head. "Thanks for comin'," he mutters softly as if he hadn't wanted me to hear.

Noah playfully sucker punches his shoulder. "Anytime, asshole."

He chuckles. "Yeah, I deserved that."

I stare at my son and hate that I see a hurt little boy who saw his father walk away when life got too hard for him. All his lashing out and poor attitude was caused by my abandoning him. We're two broken men, which means we both have to put in the effort to fix our relationship. I'm willing to take the steps to help him heal from what I did to him, but he has to put in the work, too. He's an adult now and can't use my mistakes as an excuse.

We say our final goodbyes, and when Noah and I walk out

into the parking lot, I tell her I'll follow her since she knows the way.

"You could just ride with me," she says. "Jase knows we're both goin', so it won't be like we're hidin' it."

"Think that's a good idea?" I squeeze the back of my neck, not wanting to cross any more lines even though yesterday in the tack room was a weak moment. Kissing her would've been a bad idea, but one I can't stop thinking about.

"Why not? That way, if I do drink too much, you can drive me home. Then we can figure out a way to get your truck back tomorrow."

"I thought ya weren't gonna drink that much?"

The corner of her lips curves up in a devious grin. "I reckon I lied."

Goddammit.

"Let's go, then."

The Twisted Bull is everything the name implies. Bright stage lights flicker across the dance floor as people wait in line for the mechanical bull or for alcohol at the bar. The music is loud enough to cause a migraine and has people screaming to speak over it.

I'm in hell.

Noah leads us deeper inside through the sea of people. She changed into cowboy boots before we walked in and dropped a few inches in height, so keeping tabs on her won't be easy.

"Isn't it cool?" Noah shouts over her shoulder.

Granted, if I were in my early twenties, I'd love it. I can see the appeal and why they flock here. But if one more person bumps into my shoulder and spills their beer on me, I'm hauling Noah over my shoulder and getting us the fuck out.

When we make it to the bar, her four brothers and Magnolia are sitting with a bartop full of drinks.

"Hey! Y'all finally made it!" Magnolia squeals when Noah stands next to her. "How was dinner?"

Noah shakes her head as if she doesn't want to talk about it.

Can't say I blame her.

"Fisher!" the boys shout, raising their beers.

"Ready to get in on the bet?" Tripp asks.

"What bet?" I lean against the bar, facing Noah so drunk strangers don't get any ideas.

"Who'll last the longest on the bull," he explains.

"Me, obviously."

They laugh. "If ya win, you gotta pay our tabs!"

I snort, grabbing my wallet to get Noah and me our own drinks. "Shouldn't y'all be payin' my tab if I win?"

"Don't try to speak logic to them." Noah shakes her head and waves to get the bartender's attention.

A man who looks a few years older than Noah approaches, and I already don't like the way he stares at her—like he wants to do much more than serve her drinks.

"Howdy, pretty lady. What can I getcha?"

"A strawberry margarita, a Budweiser, and a Blow Job!"

"What is that?" I murmur in her ear when the bartender busies himself.

"A blow job or a shot?"

"Yeah, Fisher. Which one's got ya confused?" Magnolia chimes in, laughing.

Shit, I forgot she knows.

I lean in closer so the boys can't eavesdrop. "Noah told me about your little crush, by the way. Which one is it again? *Tripp*?" I arch a brow, and she scowls at Noah. "Hope I don't accidentally let that slip."

"I'm gonna murder you in your sleep," she tells her. "A slow and painful death."

Laughing, I hand the bartender my card. I'm playing stupid

games, but the last thing we need besides Jase knowing is her brothers finding out. If they already don't like my son, no way they're going to like *me* sleeping with their little sister.

"Calm down, he's just messin' with you." Noah shrugs her off, then offers her the shot.

"No, babe, that's for you. Show me your best deep throat!" Magnolia's loud voice gets the attention of half the bar.

My eyes laser in on Noah bending down, wrapping her lips around the glass, and then snapping her head back as the liquid flows into her mouth. Once she's swallowed, she slams it down on the bar.

"Yes! That's my girl!" Magnolia cheers.

We stand at the bar and drink for a while before someone notices a guy they don't like. Everyone turns, and even though I don't know who they're talking about, I look too.

"Who're we starin' at?" I whisper into Noah's ear while her brothers are distracted.

She shivers against me, and I smile at how quickly her body responds to me.

"Craig Sanders," she says. "The guy we suspect is responsible for the nails. He's a jealous asshole."

"You're fuckin' kiddin' me." My jaw sets, and I grip my bottle. "Maybe I should have a chat with him."

Before Noah can stop me, I take my beer and head his way.

"Fisher, no." Her voice fades the farther I walk. This little shit's been harassing her, and I can't just stand here and do nothing. Letting my son be rude to her was hard enough, but I don't have enough willpower to stay silent with this asshole.

"Craig?" I ask when I'm behind him.

"Who's askin'?" He spins around and sizes me up. "Who're you?"

"Were you at the Sugarland Creek Ranch a few days ago?"

"I'm not sayin' a goddamn thing to you until I know who you are."

"Fisher Underwood. I'm their new *farrier*."

His face breaks out into a knowing, shit-eating grin, and it's all the confirmation I need to know he's the guy. "Okay, and what about it?"

"Were you there?"

He shrugs, taking a sip of his drink. "Don't recall."

I step closer until the tip of my boot touches his. "Think real hard, then. You put Noah and her client at risk of gettin' hurt with your little stunt. Hell, you harmed Ranger's hoof."

I stand straighter, daring him to deny it again.

"Fisher, there ya are." Wilder approaches, grabbing my arm.

"Oh, how cute. The whole Hollis clan is here tonight."

"You better watch your mouth, Sanders. Just 'cause Noah didn't invite you to the fundraiser don't mean you gotta act like a little bitch."

Oh, fucking hell.

"I wouldn't be caught dead at your stupid ranch," he spits out.

"That so? Because we got ya on camera," Wilder retorts.

"Is that so?" Craig pushes his wrists together in a cocky gesture. "Then why haven't I been arrested?"

His amused remark has me wanting to punch in his smug little boy face. Thirty-five-year-old me wouldn't have thought twice about doing it.

But I try not to be that person anymore.

The one who used violence as an outlet for my pain.

"Keep it up, and you'll wish you'd been arrested instead of what we'll do to you," Wilder threatens, and this time, I'm the one grabbing his arm and pulling him back. I see a lot of my younger self in him, which worries me. Wilder's tall, built like an MMA fighter, and could easily do some damage to Craig's lanky body.

Craig's cocky grin widens. "Have a great evening, gentlemen. Watch where you step." Then he looks around me where Noah waits and adds, "Lots of *snakes* out there."

He walks away, leaving Wilder scathing.

"He's not worth it," I tell him.

"Trust me, it would be."

He brushes past me, and I follow him back to the bar.

"What'd he say?" Noah asks.

I squeeze the neck of the beer bottle and take a drink as I glance at her over the rim. "He's definitely the one who did it. Wilder was ready to knock him out," I say, telling her word for word what happened with Craig.

"They graduated in the same year. Never got along," Noah explains. "He hates me because he thinks I steal his clients. But really, they come to me after they fire him for being incompetent."

"When you report it to Sheriff Wagner, Wilder needs to include what he said. You might wanna install more cameras and put up No Trespassing signs on that side of the ranch. That way, you can at least say you had them up if he does it again."

"Good idea. I'll have the boys do that tomorrow."

Magnolia snorts, wedging herself back into our conversation. "If they're not hungover."

"I'll do it, then. You need them up as soon as possible. Hard to tell how far he'll go, but I don't trust him."

"Join the club." Magnolia wrinkles her nose. "He wasn't always this way. Well, not as bad anyway. Not until Noah turned him down last year. Then he made it his mission to make her life a livin' hell by tryin' to steal her clients."

"I have a feelin' many girls turn him down, but he found a way to get even with you because of your shared interests," I tell Noah.

"He's made snide comments about how *it must be nice that Mommy and Daddy pay for my business*." She scoffs. "He's too dense to realize I earned it. I pleaded with my dad for five months to expand the trainin' center. Eventually, I gave a presentation on how it'd benefit the ranch with projected earnings and how I'd meet them. He finally agreed, and we expanded the arena so I could train for barrel racing. It also helped so my brothers and I could train at the same time without being on top of each other."

"And your girl smashed those earnings in half the time she promised! It brought in more clients and more trainin' hours,"

Magnolia gushes, smiling wide at Noah like a proud best friend. "Which means Mr. Hollis lets her do whatever she wants now."

Noah's cheeks tint a gorgeous color of cherry red that matches her lipstick. "Yes, but I spent years workin' my ass off for that, so Craig can fuck off."

He's gonna do a lot more than that if he doesn't leave her alone.

We finish our first round of drinks, but as soon as they call Wilder's name next in line, we move to the bull area.

He's definitely had a handful of beers by now and is rowdy as hell when he jumps on top of the mechanical bull. "Yeah, baby! Let's goooo!" He waves his ball cap in the air and grips the horn with his other hand.

The guy in charge counts down, then presses the button.

"Yeehaw!" Wilder shouts, his legs flying up and down as the bull spins, going faster and faster with each passing second.

Noah and Magnolia hold their phones and giggle as they record him.

A roar of laughter echoes when he falls off before the eight seconds are up.

He stumbles on wobbly legs before face-planting on the mat and then rolls over.

Jesus Christ.

Waylon goes out and lends him a hand, then pulls him to his feet.

"How long did I last?" Wilder asks, slurring over his words.

"Five seconds," Tripp says.

"Oof. I feel sorry for Jen," Magnolia says, earning a shove from Wilder.

"You're next," Tripp tells Noah. "I put your name on the list."

"You jerk! I've only had one drink. I can't do it sober."

I arch a brow but stay quiet. She's had two, including the one she had at the restaurant, but technically speaking, she's had four if we count the tequila and the shot. She's far from sober.

"Show us what ya got, little sis!" Tripp shouts, clapping to draw more attention.

"You owe me a drink after this!" She nudges her shoulder against Tripp as she walks into the ring.

My chest tightens as she climbs on. She adjusts her dress so it's tucked under her thighs. I don't want her to get hurt, but given the encouragement of her brothers, they're not as worried.

"Yeah, Noah! Show us whatcha got!" Magnolia cups her mouth, shouting out each word in a long drawl.

The guy counts down again, and then it starts moving. With one arm in the air, she maintains her stance, squeezing her thighs and holding the horn with a firm grip.

Her body moves naturally with the bull's as it gets faster. Ocean-blue eyes find mine for a split second before it whips around again. Golden blond locks fly around her shoulders, and as soon as the buzzer goes off, we all cheer.

"You killed it!" Magnolia jumps up and down when Noah returns, and they wrap their arms around each other.

Noah flips her hair over her shoulder. "That's what y'all get for doubtin' me." She glances in my direction. "Your turn, cowboy."

"Yeah, Fisher! Fisher, Fisher, Fisher!" As they shout my name, it grabs the attention of the rest of the bar, and soon a hundred-plus people are chanting it.

Fuck me. I'm confident I can do this, but I haven't done it in years.

I hold up my palms. "Fine. Fine."

"Wait. You're a *pro*, which means ya gotta do it with no hands!" Wilder announces.

"Yes!" Tripp agrees.

"Guys, that's not fair." Noah waves them off.

"It's totally fair! He's done this like a million times," Landen adds.

"Dude, I thought we were friends?" I quip, and they laugh.

"You goin' in or what?" the guy asks.

I suck in a breath and nod.

Giving in to the peer pressure, I walk inside and climb up. Situating myself where I can use my legs as leverage to stay in position, I ground my pelvis and then raise both arms.

The boys roar loudly, hooting and hollering even before the guy counts down.

And then it starts.

Chapter Fifteen

Noah

Fisher's focus is intense as I watch with bated breath. I can't move as the bull whirls him around, and he hangs on with just his thighs.

Thighs I want to climb on and ride like my own personal cowboy.

I don't know how he's doing it, but I'm impressed as hell.

My voice gets caught in my throat as my brothers shout and cheer him on. I focus on each movement as if it's happening in slow motion. His muscles flex with each second that passes, and for a moment, the chaos around me fades away, and it's just us.

As soon as the buzzer blasts, everyone jumps and hollers, knocking me out of my trance.

Finally, I scream and celebrate with them.

My brothers continue chanting his name as he climbs off and walks out. I smile wide at him, and he winks.

"Dude, that was awesome!" Tripp yells, smacking his shoulder.

The rest of my annoying brothers crowd him, but Fisher keeps his gaze on mine over their heads. I suck in my lower lip, wishing I could smash my mouth to his.

When they finally give him room to breathe and Waylon goes to take his turn, Fisher stands behind me.

"Want another drink?" he murmurs in my ear. His warm breath sends an electric current through my body, and I lean back to get closer.

When I turn my head, our mouths are only inches apart. "I dunno. Am I allowed to?"

"As much as I enjoy your sass, I'm holdin' on by a thread here, Goldie. So if you want one, just say the word, and I'll drive ya home later."

I like the idea of him tucking me into bed instead of him dropping me off at my car, so I tell him yes.

He squeezes my hip. "Stay here. I'll be right back."

Magnolia's too busy drooling over Tripp to notice our secret moment, but inside I'm dying.

Waylon makes it seven seconds before he's whipped to the ground. Tripp goes next, and Magnolia screams.

"I think you blew my eardrum," I tease.

She rolls her eyes and inches closer. "You gonna invite Fisher over tonight?"

Even though he's technically driving me to my house, that's not what she's referring to.

"I wish." I pout.

She waggles her brows. "I won't tell."

"You're a bad influence!" My voice is teasing as I scold her.

"Well, duh. You've been a good girl for twenty-two years. Now, it's time to live a little while you're still young and hot."

I burst out laughing. "Gee, thanks for the pep talk."

Fisher returns with a Long Island Iced Tea, and I nearly squeal at finally getting one. "Thank you!"

"Be careful. There's lots of alcohol in that," he warns in a deep baritone that has me squeezing my legs together.

"Worried ya can't handle me drunk?" I smirk around the straw as I take a drink.

Fisher leans in until his tongue swipes along my neck, and goose bumps cover my skin. "Sweetheart, I handled you just fine when I had you bent over my bed, your pussy spread wide open for my cock as you choked on your own moans. I had you comin' in *eight seconds*, remember? So no, I'm not worried."

My feet stay frozen in place as I wrap my brain around his words that have every inch of me burning hot.

Once my brothers finish, they try to get Magnolia to ride the bull, but she tells them to fuck off. I laugh as they tease her because she doesn't have an athletic bone in her body, and she wouldn't be caught dead riding one.

"I'm gettin' a drink!" she announces. "Then we dance!"

The next couple of hours includes dancing, more drinking, and Fisher glaring at me from the bar. He can't be on the dance floor with me without my brothers getting suspicious, so instead, he's drinking water and watching me like an overbearing bodyguard.

"If Tripp looked at me like that, I'd be on my knees in a heartbeat," Magnolia says as we move to the music.

"Shoulda heard what he said to me earlier." I blush when I think about it and shrug. "Too bad we can't."

"I dunno what kinda delusional universe y'all livin' in, but there's no way one of you won't crack bein' around each other every day. It's just a matter of when."

I want to argue, but she's right.

Although what we shared feels like more than just a random one-night stand, there's still so much we don't know about each other, but the more I do learn, the more I want him.

"Should we show him what he's missin' out on?" Magnolia swipes the tip of her tongue along her bottom lip. She's up to something.

Before I can argue, she grabs a nearby guy and positions him between us.

"Hey, I'm Magnolia!" she shouts over the music. "That's my friend, Noah!"

"Derik!" he responds.

"I'm givin' you full consent to touch us wherever you want as long as we can do the same to you," Magnolia tells him.

Oh my God. I want to smack her final two brain cells together, but that wouldn't stop her at this point. Either she's trying to make Fisher jealous on my behalf or hoping Tripp will take notice.

My heart thuds when I glance over Derik's shoulder and see Fisher glaring with his arms crossed over his broad chest. Dark hair strands stick to his face, almost shadowing his features in a way that makes him look like a scary mob boss.

Magnolia hits my arm, grabbing my attention.

"Don't look at him," she scolds.

I roll my eyes because I don't want to make him jealous or mad, but that shouldn't stop me from enjoying myself. I love dancing and haven't gone out in months, so I'm taking full advantage of this night, even if we're sandwiching a stranger.

When my favorite rap song starts, I go feral and lose my mind. I'm primarily a country music girly, but one artist can make me go from hoedown line dancing to jumping up and down screaming the lyrics at the top of my lungs.

As the alcohol takes over, I wave my arms above my head. Derik's hands find my hips. He moves with me as I sing along and whip my head back and forth. When his hardness presses into my back, I turn around so I can tell him to put Derik Jr. away.

But when I look up and see Fisher, my eyes widen, and a sharp gasp escapes me. I quickly scan our surroundings to make sure my brothers aren't nearby.

"They're playin' pool in the back," he says.

Glancing toward Magnolia, I can practically hear her internal squealing in my head by the *oh my God* expression on her face. But I return the same one because she's with Derik, letting him cop a feel of her ass.

"You're sure you should be touchin' me, Mr. Underwood?" I taunt, resting my palms on his chest as I continue to move my hips to the music. He removed the suit coat before we came inside, so now there's only a thin button-down shirt between us.

"I'm not sure I can stop."

His sexy bedroom eyes scan down my body as he grips my dress and pulls me closer.

My tongue peeks out between my teeth before I suck in my bottom lip, wishing he'd lean in and put me out of my misery.

"Why're ya torturin' me with that mouth I can't kiss?" He plucks my lip with his thumb, then shoves it inside. "It's bad enough I want somethin' I can't have. Even if I could, I wouldn't deserve you, anyway."

I grimace at his words because I hate that he thinks that way. The odds are stacked against us, but that doesn't mean he doesn't deserve to find love.

A new song starts playing, and our bodies continue moving together. When he buries his face in my neck, his warm breath tickles my bare skin, and I shiver. It's well over ninety degrees in here, and I'm a sweaty mess, so it's not from being cold.

"You tempt me, Goldie. I wanna slide my hand between your thighs and feel how wet you are for me. No one's ever had that effect on me before, especially in the middle of a dance floor surrounded by strangers."

And with so many people who could catch us.

My mouth breaches his ear as I wrap a hand around his neck and keep his body pressed to mine. "No one has to know, Fisher."

"You deserve more than a secret fling."

"We'd only have to keep it a secret until we're ready to tell people," I explain. "We can explore our relationship in private before decidin' what to do next and announcin' it."

With the music blasting, we're practically shouting at each other, but there's no way anyone else can hear with how close we are.

Before Fisher can respond, I'm shoved to the side and almost lose my footing before Derik catches me.

"Brother alert!" Magnolia yells, taking my place and nodding for me to follow suit as she grinds on Fisher.

I grab Derik's shoulders and form an unstable rhythm. Fisher meets my eyes as he scowls at Magnolia, who's shaking her ass.

With a smirk, I nod at him to go along with it. Hesitantly, he does and just barely touches her hip.

"Hey!" Landen comes over. "Y'all seen Wilder? We lost him."

Magnolia and I shake our heads.

"Fuck." He scrubs a hand over his face before smacking Fisher's shoulder. "She's a little young for ya, bro."

Landen laughs as he walks away, and my heart sinks at Fisher's expression.

"Whew, that was close!" Magnolia says. "Y'all need to be more *careful.*"

Once we're certain Landen's out of view, Magnolia returns to Derik, and I follow Fisher when he walks to the bar.

"What would ya like?" he asks, nodding toward the alcohol bottles.

Blinking, I stare into his defeated eyes. "You."

He swallows hard, stepping closer. "You drive me crazy. And maybe I'm going crazy because of it."

"Ignore what my brother said," I urge because I can see it's bothering him.

"How can I?"

"Kiss me, Fisher. *Please.*" I'm not above getting on my knees and begging. "Let me prove our ages don't matter."

"I'm not takin' advantage when you've been drinkin'."

I tilt my head. "I'm like sixty-nine percent sober."

A small grin forms on his face. "Although sixty-nine is a *good* number ask me when you're at zero."

"Well, that's not fair. I didn't know that'd be a barrier, or I woulda stuck with water." I pout.

"I'm glad you're havin' fun. Go ahead, order somethin'."

"Okay, fine. Order me a Buttery Nipple."

When his gaze drops to my chest, I know he's thinking about my piercings, and I smirk in victory.

"I think it'd taste even better on my skin. Should I pour it here and see?" I ask innocently, slowly sliding my strap off my shoulder.

He shakes his head as he grabs the bartender's attention, but I see the amusement in his eyes. I watch as the bartender pours Fisher his water and makes my shot.

Fisher hands it to me, and before I take it, we lock eyes. His throat flexes as he watches me shoot it down. His hand grips his glass so tight, I wouldn't be surprised if it imploded and shattered everywhere.

"Mm. That was good. Wanna taste?" I trace my top lip with my tongue.

Tempting him is dangerous, but since he's admitted how much he wants me, all I can focus on is breaking him.

Before he can reject me, Magnolia pummels between us, gasping for air. "Can I have some of that?" she asks Fisher, her eyes lasering in on his water.

Silently, he hands it over, and she gulps it down.

She releases a satisfied moan once she's chugged half of it. "Thanks. Derik invited me back to his place, so we're headin' out."

"You think that's a good idea?" Fisher asks before I can.

"Yeah, Mags. You just met him. He could be a serial killer, for all you know. Or has a murder kink."

"That's hilarious comin' from the *moral* police duo." She snorts, glancing back and forth between Fisher and me.

"At least share your location with me," I tell her. "Make it easy for me to find your body."

"Yes, *Mother*." She takes out her phone and does what I asked. "Now call me a train because I'm about to get *railed*," she singsongs and then mimics a train whistle. "Love you, bye." When she hugs me, I remind her to be careful. Then she takes Derik's hand and leaves.

"She's...somethin' else." Fisher scratches his scruffy cheek as if he's still confused about what just happened.

"At least someone's gettin' their pussy licked tonight," I mutter.

He grabs my hip and pulls me into his chest, and I suck in a breath at the quick, unexpected movement. My hand squeezes his arm to stabilize myself. People crowd the bar around us, so it wouldn't take much to fall on my ass.

"That night in the food truck with your cunt in my face plays on repeat in my head. Your scent and taste are still ingrained in my mind, so don't confuse me denyin' you with not wanting you. But if I get close enough to tongue-fuck you again, I won't be able to stop."

Then, as if on cue, his cock jerks and pushes into me. I arch a brow and smirk at his failed attempt to look unaffected.

"And why would we have to stop?"

"Because bein' together could hurt people. Before you decide you want this, you should know what you're gettin' into first."

My head spins with how the discovery of our relationship would hurt *him* more than me, yet he's asking *me* to decide.

"The risk is higher for you. Shouldn't I be askin' you to decide?"

His finger traces my jawline as he studies my features. He brushes over my cheekbone, then goes down between my eyebrows and over the arch of my nose before he rounds my other cheek and ends at my chin.

"The decision was made for me the moment we met. I didn't know who you were or why I was hell-bent on watchin' you in the crowd, but the second my heart decided, there was no goin' back for me. Even though I try like hell to ignore these feelings, the pull to be near you is too strong to ignore. If you wanna stay just friends, then I'll respect that and keep my hands off you. But if you want more, I'm all in to give this a shot."

My heart flips as butterflies invade my stomach. His touch is soft but tender, and I can't help leaning into his embrace. He's willing to take this leap with me, knowing it could blow up his life, and that has me concerned.

"Just promise you won't resent me if this goes wrong." *More specifically, he loses his son forever, and I'd be to blame for that.*

"I have a lot of regrets in my life, Noah. Lovin' you would

never be on that list. I wanna know you beyond our physical attraction."

Goose bumps cover my skin as a shiver rolls through me. His past is still somewhat of a mystery, and exploring the deeper parts of a relationship will make me fall even harder for him.

"So you wanna be hands-off while we get to know each other?"

His fingers dig into my skin as if he's fighting with his thoughts. "I want us to go…slow."

I blow out a breath because I'll take whatever I can get as long as we're on the same page.

"Alright, so we stay on the DL for now and figure out the rest as we go."

"If that means not goin' public, then yes."

I laugh because we're very much in public right now and were basically dry humping on the dance floor.

"Then you better keep your hands to yourself, Mr. Underwood." I motion with my eyes to remind him we're not alone.

"Fuck. We better go, then, because if I have to watch another man grind his dick all over you, I'll break it in half."

"Ouch." I snort. "I'll let my brothers know you're takin' me home."

"I'll go with you," he says, following before I can argue it's a bad idea. One look at Fisher's tented slacks and they're going to suspect something's up besides his boner.

"You're not very good at this *discreet* thing."

"I'm not lettin' you out of my sight in here."

"Worried someone's gonna kidnap me and make me come in *seven* seconds?" I tease as we make our way to the pool table area.

He curses under his breath, and I chuckle. When we find them, Wilder's leaning over the table with his pool stick. Guess they found him.

"Don't miss!" I shout just as he takes his shot.

"Goddammit, Noah!" He shoves me, which pushes me into Fisher. He wasn't lying about not leaving my side.

"Shit, sorry," Wilder says to Fisher.

"What 'bout me, jerk?"

"You made me miss, so no."

I roll my eyes. "You're too drunk to play anyway."

"Then why am I winnin', huh?" He leans his smug face closer to mine. "I'm up a hundred bucks."

"Wow, they must be takin' pity on ya," I taunt.

"You wanna play me next and see?"

"Nah, I just came to tell y'all we're headin' out. Y'all have rides?"

Tripp comes over, and his eyes scan above my head to Fisher standing suspiciously close to me. "I'm drivin'. I stopped drinkin' a couple hours ago."

"Where's your truck?" Landen asks me.

"At the restaurant. Figured we didn't need to both drive when we're goin' to the same place." I shrug, hoping they don't ask any more questions. It was awkward enough having to explain why I was going to a fancy restaurant with my ex and his dad in the first place.

"You never told us how dinner went with your two *dates*..." Waylon muses as if Fisher isn't here.

"Oh, because that's none of your damn business." I cross my arms, hoping they get the hint to shut the hell up.

Wilder chuckles. "Because your ex is dryer than a loaf of expired bread."

"Dude!" I smack his shoulder. "Don't be rude."

"Yeah, Wilder...*manners*," Landen singsongs in a mocking high-pitched tone meant to mimic our mother. If anyone's getting yelled at by our mother, it's always Wilder.

"Alright, I'm leavin'. Y'all bein' assholes."

"Fisher, you sober?" Tripp shoves his hands in his pockets and watches him.

"I had one drink at the restaurant hours ago and have had only water since then."

Tripp nods with approval and then asks, "Where's Magnolia?"

"Went to some dude named Derik's house."

Tripp's jaw sets as his lips tighten, and he shifts between his feet.

And because I want to see his reaction, I add, "He was hot, too. She was halfway to gettin' knocked up on the dance floor before they finally left."

Tripp turns and walks around the pool table, then grabs a pool stick. I halfway wait for him to snap it in two.

A part of me feels bad, but if he has a problem with Magnolia hooking up with guys, then he needs to finally admit he likes her.

"Ready?" Fisher asks me.

"God, yes." I wave goodbye and follow him to the exit.

"Tripp didn't look happy," he says, placing his hand on my lower back as we walk to my truck.

"I knew that'd piss him off, but he deserved it."

"So if she likes him and he seemingly likes her, why aren't they datin'?" He opens my door and helps me hop inside.

"That's the question of the century."

Once he gets into the driver's side and starts it, he takes me by surprise when he leans over.

He cups my jaw, tilting up my face until our eyes meet. It's dark inside the cab, with minimal lighting from the parking lot, but his hold on me is firm and serious. "I wanna make sure I'm clear about one thing. Just because we're takin' things slow and not tellin' anyone, doesn't mean you aren't mine." Then he brushes the pad of his thumb and leans in.

Chapter Sixteen

Fisher

I moved back to Sugarland Creek because I was ready to right my wrongs.

Years spent feeling guilt, anger, and deep grief turned me into a bitter person. A self-destructive man.

A man whose ugly past consumed him until I managed to crawl out of the darkest hole I'd ever fallen into and finally realized I was wasting my life. One Lyla didn't get to live.

I couldn't save her, and I can't change that she's gone, but I can get a second chance with Jase.

Falling for his ex-girlfriend could fuck that up, but I'm screwed either way.

Even if I deny myself happiness with Noah, there's no guarantee Jase will let me back into his life. I've learned firsthand how short life can be, and I've lived with enough regrets.

Nothing will stop me from trying like hell to be the dad he deserves, but I also want to be the man Noah deserves.

Keeping our relationship a secret may be the final nail in the coffin for Jase, but I'll tell him myself when it's time and hope he'll understand.

At my age, I'm not naive to think it won't bother him. He's an adult now too, and I need to treat him like one. He'll be upset, and I'll give him all the time he needs to figure out if he'll accept us.

Then, when Noah and I decide what we have is real and not just a fling, we'll tell people.

But I already know it's real.

It's the most real thing I've felt since the day before Lyla died.

And although I've put my adrenaline-chasing days behind me, this is one high I can't say no to.

I've officially relapsed. A feeling I haven't had in ages, and if I'm not careful, it'll send me spiraling. But it's worth the risk to give in to the first craving I've wanted in a decade.

Looking at Noah, I see the sun rising on a cool autumn day.

Fallen leaves on the ground crunching when you walk on them.

The scent of caramel pecan and pumpkin spice wafting through the air in early October.

She's my favorite time of year.

And now, she's mine.

I've resisted kissing her all night to avoid crossing that line after determining we'd be *friends*. Her getting jealous about the receptionists only cemented that our "friendship" wouldn't work.

Especially when I wanted to do more than stand up for her when Jase grilled her about Dylan.

And even more so when I saw that kid touching her.

How could I ever just be her friend when I want to be her everything?

It was then I decided even if we couldn't be together in public and had to keep it a secret, it was better than not having her at all.

I'll deal with the consequences later. Even if they ruin me.

When I help Noah into her truck, my plan is to hold her hand and drive her home. Then I'll walk her to the door, peck her cheek, and wish her sweet dreams.

But the reminder of living my life to the fullest *now* echoes in my mind, and I know I can't go another minute without tasting her lips.

So I lean over the middle console, cup her jaw, and tilt her face until her eyes lock with mine. Her surprised expression fills me with amusement because, between her body language and snarky comments, she's wanted me to kiss her all night.

Now she looks like a deer in headlights.

"I want one thing to be clear. Just because we're takin' things slow and not tellin' anyone doesn't mean you aren't mine."

Before she can respond, I brush the pad of my thumb along her lower lip, and like a magnet, my mouth breaches hers.

The instant warmth jump-starts my heart, and I snake my palm around her neck, needing more. My fingers slide up the back of her head, grabbing a fistful of hair as my free hand slides between her thighs.

My thumb finds her clit, and when I rub it over the fabric, she releases a throaty moan, and I growl at her eager whimpers. Our tongues battle for control as short, breathy gasps echo between us. Her soft lips taste like heaven, and when I take her face in both palms, I deepen our connection.

"Mm. You taste like Buttery Nipples."

She smiles against me. "Go lower to taste somethin' even sweeter."

"Fuck," I whisper, moving my mouth to her ear and pausing my movements. "We need to get outta here before we get ourselves another PDA warnin'."

I halfway expect Ian to return with his stupid flashlight and catch us a second time.

She giggles, and the sound goes straight to my already hard dick.

"At least we didn't break into anythin' this time."

"*We*? That was all you, Goldie. I was just there for the ride."

She arches a brow. "You sure didn't mind when I fell to my knees."

I swallow hard at the memory and shake my head at her deviant tone.

"Fuck no, I didn't. But your brothers could come out here any minute, and I'd have to explain why my hand is in your panties, and your lipstick is smeared all over my face."

Her little smirk makes me grin as she wipes my mouth and scruffy jawline. "There, no one would be the wiser."

I bring my thumb up and lick her sweet juices off it. "Let's get ya home."

"Are you sure you don't wanna come in?" Her taunting voice has me second-guessing my decision not to as she unlocks her front door. Her cottage is behind the main Hollis house but is hidden by trees, so there's still privacy. The only other building nearby is the barn with their personal horses.

"No, but I'm not gonna anyway." I lean against the doorframe once she opens it. She stands between my legs, and I capture her waist, pulling her closer. "If at any time you have doubts or change your mind about this, you tell me. Got it?"

"You tryin' to break up with me already?"

"No," I say with a humorless laugh. "But I don't want there to be a power imbalance between us because I'm older."

"You work for *me,* Mr. Underwood. So if there's an imbalance, it's because you're datin' your much younger boss."

I lick my lower lip, amused with her thought process. "Mr. Hollis is my boss."

"Okay, so *technically* he is...but in *actuality,* everyone works with my schedule, includin' you." Then she points her finger at my chest. "So I am, in fact, your boss, which means I get to tell ya what to do." She pokes me with each word for emphasis. "And I'm tellin' you to come inside and have your dirty way with me."

I thumb her chin, tilting her head up so I can brush her lips with mine. "You're a bad influence on me, *Noah Hollis.*"

She goes up on her tiptoes until our mouths collide. Her warmth sends a chill down my body as she fists my shirt and presses her breasts against me.

"You're bein' a stubborn mule," she murmurs when we're only an inch apart.

My hand slides down and grabs a handful of her ass, pulling up her dress with the movement and feeling her thin cotton panties. "One of us has to be rational."

"Your dick wants to stay." She wiggles her body against me, and I hold her hips firmly in place to stop her.

"Exactly, and that's the opposite of goin' slow."

She sticks out her lower lip in a faux pout, and I shake my head.

"We didn't go slow the first time," she reminds me.

"And you deserved better than a hookup in a camper, so I need to make it up to you now."

"Okay, fair enough. Wine and dine me, then fuck me against every inch of my house. Deal?"

I cough, choking on air and shock. "Deal."

She smiles, and I kiss her forehead, lingering for a moment to inhale her floral shampoo. "Sweet dreams, Goldie. I'll call ya tomorrow when I finish at the Monroes."

It takes all my willpower to walk back to her truck and not change my mind. I want nothing more than to bury myself deep inside her all night, but I've never been good at relationships. If I'm risking everything for happiness and love, I'm doing it right this time.

Chapter Seventeen

Noah

Seven o'clock comes quick when you don't fall asleep until two in the morning.

But it was worth it to be with Fisher and finally discuss the elephant in the room. We were fools to think we could just be friends after the night we shared. Though it could come back to bite us in the ass, I'm hopeful we'll be able to figure out how to tell Jase and my family.

At least for now, we can focus on getting to know each other without everyone else's commentary.

I haven't stopped smiling since I woke up, and given that I'm dealing with a feisty shit, that says a lot about how I'm feeling. Not even Craig Sanders could sour my mood today, even after everything he said last night.

"C'mon, Piper. We can do this!" I rub her neck and then adjust the reins and dig my heels. She's been a little stubborn, but we're working through it.

She takes off, jumps over the first rail, and smoothly gallops to the second, where she does another perfect leap. When we reach the third rail, the highest one, she tenses up, and I know she's going to hit it before she does.

"Alright, girl. Let's try that again." I direct her back to the second one and restart. Once she's in position, I kick and raise the reins higher right before she leaps and clears it.

"Yes!"

Piper's an Appaloosa I started jump-training a couple of weeks ago. Her owner, Harlow, is new to jumping, so we're starting easy. She's only sixteen, but her older sister, Delilah, used to date Waylon, so I offered cheap lessons to get her started. Figured it was the least I could do for their family for having to deal with my brother. Harlow comes for riding lessons a few times a week, and I work with Piper in between.

I train her for another hour, going back and correcting her jumps and finding a rhythm. Once I bring her to the barn, Ruby brushes her for me so I can go to the family barn and take Donut for a walk. With the craziness of this past week, I haven't had time, and he's getting moody.

When I check the time on my phone, a text from Jase pops up.

JASE

I'd like to get dinner with you again. Just the two of us.

I re-read his message, and my first reaction is to send the vomit emoji. Instead of offending him, I go with honesty.

NOAH

I'm pretty busy until the fundraiser.

JASE

Oh, come on. You gotta eat. Let me take you out, and we can chat like old times.

Old times? We broke up two years ago and have only hung out a few times as friends. He's living in the same de-lulu world as Magnolia who acts like she doesn't like Tripp.

But this time, I push harder.

NOAH

I don't think it's a good idea. I'm stressed with getting everything organized, plus all my training. Once things slow down, we can make plans.

I'm not being totally truthful because I don't intend to actually go to dinner with him. But at least it'll get him off my back, even if it's temporary. He never used to be this pushy, and I don't like it.

JASE

Whatever. Heard you were dancing with some rando loser at the bar. Had time for him, huh?

What the fuck?

NOAH

Are you spying on me?!

JASE

People talk in this town.

I roll my eyes at how judgy and possessive he sounds.

NOAH

I can dance with whoever I want and do whatever I please. Just because I'm busy doesn't mean you get to be an asshole.

JASE

Excuse me for thinking friends make time for each other. Now I know where I stand.

"Noah! Where're ya goin'?"

I jump when Mallory hollers from the entrance.

"To get Donut. What're ya doin'?" I ask, pocketing my phone. I'll deal with Jase later.

"I wanna ride Taylor Alison Swift! Can you help me?"

She rushes to catch up with me, and I give her an apologetic smile. "Sorry, kiddo. I have a lot of catchin' up to do. Ruby and Trey are 'round here. Can you ask them?"

"I'll just wait for you. When will ya be back?"

I look at my phone and check the time, noticing I still haven't heard from Fisher. I know he's probably never done the whole "good morning" texts because of his lack of dating, but I was still hoping I'd hear from him today.

"Gimme about forty-five minutes, okay?"

"Okay! I'll go to Serena's until you're done."

She skips ahead, and I call out to her. "Don't get in Mrs. Carson's way!"

She's nine months pregnant and could pop any day now. Though her due date isn't for a couple of weeks, she could still go into labor early.

"I won't!" she shouts as she runs out of the barn.

I hop in a four-wheeler and drive over. It's only a few minutes away, but I crank my music anyway since I didn't grab any coffee from The Lodge this morning and need a dose of caffeine to keep me awake.

The barn's dark and empty when I enter. The twins are in charge of feeding and cleaning our horses this weekend. We all take turns, but knowing them, they're probably still in bed and hungover.

"Hey, boy," I say softly when I go into Donut's stall and rub my palm up the bridge of his nose.

He nudges me with his mouth, obviously upset with me for not coming sooner.

"Yeah, I know. I'm gonna make it up to you with a nice, long ride."

After I lead him into the grooming stall and clip him into place, I grab my supplies from the tack room and brush him until he's ready for the saddle. I'll work on him more after the fundraiser since Delilah wants me to help her with trick riding. She approached me before the rodeo, but I told her I needed time to decide because my schedule was already chaotic. I haven't practiced stunts since last summer when Landen drove by on his dirt bike and spooked Donut. Rolling off in the nick of time, I got away with only a scuffed knee. My mom freaked out and demanded I have a spotter if I was going to do stunts, and since no one was willing to watch me, I stopped.

But now I'm ready to challenge myself again to see if I'd be a good fit for her. Delilah's experienced and competes regularly, but since she fired Craig, she's looking for a new trainer.

Once Donut's tacked up and I'm in position, we ride out of the barn. "Let's go visit the retreat!"

I barely have to lead him anymore because he knows the way. He enjoys seeing people and trail horses. Well, I can only assume he does, but he always seems happy to go there.

We take the trail to the retreat that brings us around the fishing pond. Guests love relaxing here and being close to their cabins. There's a hut next to it that we keep stocked with fishing gear, bait, and snacks. Next to the pond is the trail horse barn and pasture. Wilder and Waylon work there most often since they give the daily tours.

In between, across the creek are The Lodge, a gift shop, and a staff building. Since we provide a buffet style for breakfast and dinner, the cooks start early in the morning to prep for that day's meals in the staff building. It's also where housekeeping stores everything.

The gift shop just opened last fall, and when Ayden's family moved here, Laney became the manager. She had experience running her mom's boutique in Texas and was looking for a job anyway, so it was a perfect match to have her manage it.

I wave to guests as they walk by and stop a couple of times for kids to pet Donut. After I go around The Lodge, we walk past the bonfire area and pool house. Every Friday evening, we host a s'mores party for the kids and families to hang out and eat. If one of the family members can't do it, another staff member is there to help.

The pool house is open daily until nine. There's not a lifeguard on duty, but a staff member is always nearby if anyone needs assistance. I wish I had more time to enjoy it, but my work schedule keeps me busy until well after it's closed and the guests are in their cabins for the night.

There are five cabins in total. Two sleep up to twelve people, and the other three hold up to six. When fully booked, we can have upward of forty-two guests. Depending how many are staying and choosing to go on horseback rides determines how busy the twins are on their guided tours. They love making it fun with jokes and pointing out silly scenery details. Wilder likes telling girls where he had his first kiss or where he pantsed Waylon when they were teenagers. It usually gets a good laugh out of the group.

Once we pass the corral area where the charity event will be held, we ride through the ranch hand quarters cul-de-sac. The twins live in one of the duplexes, and go figure, Wilder's truck is still parked in the driveway. Waylon's is gone, though, so hopefully, he's working. There are no days off when you live here.

To get to the ranch side, we'd normally have to go back around the corral, past The Lodge, and toward the pond. But since Mallory is waiting for me to return, I take a shortcut. I guide Donut through the backwoods restricted from guests. It's the wooded area of the mountains that separates the ranch and retreat.

When we approach the barn, seeing the doors closed confuses me because I know they were left open. Looking around, I don't see anyone parked nearby. Waylon couldn't have completed all the chores in less than an hour unless he showed up right after I left. In fact, he should be here, but I don't see or hear anyone.

I drop to my feet and lead Donut to the doors. The lights are still on when I open them, but Donut's stall door is closed. I left it open so if my brothers showed up, they'd know I took him out.

"Hello?" I call out as I bring him to the grooming stall and clip him in place. "Waylon?"

The wooden floor creaks in the tack room, and my heart kicks up. I pause and listen to see if it happens again. Normally, I wouldn't be that dumb girl in a scary movie who goes down the dark basement with no flashlight or backup when a known serial killer is on the loose, but I don't think twice when it comes to my horses. Craig's already messed with me once and implied he wasn't done at the bar. I'm not about to let him get away with sneaking on the property again.

As I creep down the center aisle, another creak echoes. Someone is definitely in there. I spot a rake next to the wheelbarrow and grab it. If Craig's in there to fuck with me or plant a trap of some sort, he's about to get whacked in the head and kicked in the balls.

My stomach's in knots as I grip the rake's handle in one sweaty hand and slowly reach for the doorknob with the other. I push open the door and stab the air with the rake.

I'm met with silence as I glance around for him. One of the saddle stands tipped, knocking over some equipment, which must've been the noise I heard. Once I set the rake against the wall, I kneel and start cleaning up the mess.

When the door slams behind me, I release a strangled gasp. Boots smack against the floor, and I rush to my feet, but a hand wraps around my waist, pinning me to a hard chest. My adrenaline amps up as his hold tightens. I jab my elbow roughly in his gut, then drive my fist into his nose before he can do anything else.

He releases me with a deep grunt. "Fuck!"

I turn around with my foot ready to give him a personal vasectomy, but I'm met with long hair that is definitely not Craig's.

"Oh my God! *Fisher*?"

He stands, holding his nose, and my eyes widen at the blood dripping down his hand.

"What..." I mutter. "What're ya doin' here?"

"Didn't you get my text?"

I blink, scrambling for my phone. "No, clearly not." Once I dig it out of my pocket, I see his name on the screen.

FISHER

Meet me in the tack room when you're back.

"H-how?" I shake my head. "I thought you were at the Monroes today? Where're you parked? Why didn't ya say anythin' when I came in?" I ramble off a million questions while searching for something to help with the blood.

When I come up empty-handed, I tell him to hold tight so I can run to the restroom to grab something. By the time I get back, most of the bleeding's stopped.

I bring the paper towel to his face and clean his nose and hand.

"Well, I'm glad you can handle yourself, but Jesus Christ. I wasn't prepared for that."

"I'm *so* sorry," I enunciate slowly.

He smirks. "Noah, I'm not mad. You reacted exactly as you should've not knowin' I was in here."

"How're ya here when you told me you were workin'?"

"I finished at the Monroes early and decided I couldn't wait another minute to kiss you again, so I parked at The Lodge and walked over. I saw the four-wheeler parked here, and when I saw Donut's door open, I knew you'd gone out for a ride, so that's when I texted you. I bought some No Trespassing signs this mornin' and hung them up while waitin' for you to return. I also ordered more cameras and will install them once they arrive."

"Wow. Thank you for doin' that. I'm still tryin' to wrap my head around why you were hidin' in here."

"Well, you hadn't responded to my text, so when I heard footsteps, I hid behind the door in case it was someone else comin' in. Then when I saw you, I aimed for your neck and closed the door for privacy."

I pinch the bridge of my nose while my breathing steadies. I didn't even notice his truck when I rode past the parking lot. "Maybe you say my name next time instead of creepin' up on me?"

The corner of his mouth tilts up as he grabs my hip. "I thought you read my text and knew I was in here."

"Well, I hadn't. So when someone comes up behind me without sayin' a word, I assume it's a *murderer*!" I whisper-shout.

He twirls a strand of my hair and wraps it behind my ear. "Duly noted. Here I was, tryin' to seduce ya."

I arch a brow. "You have my attention."

He chuckles, inching closer until we're almost touching. "Kinda goes against my whole goin' slow rule. But I missed you and wanted to taste your lips."

Leaning against him, I smile now that my heart rate has gone down to normal. "That can be arranged."

Fisher cups my cheeks with both hands and crashes his mouth against mine. A whimper slips from my throat, and he sinks his tongue in deeper, causing heat to build between my legs and swim up my body. I fist his T-shirt, clinging as tightly to him as possible, and he walks us to the back of the door.

"Fuck, Goldie. This is a bad idea," he murmurs as he drags his tongue down my jawline and sucks under my ear.

"Not what a woman wants to hear when a dick is pressin' into her." I pant, exposing my neck to him.

"Trust me, I want to. But if I touch you, I won't wanna stop, and right now, we need to. I'm not fuckin' you in a barn."

I chuckle at his scowl. "I dunno. Sounds kinda hot to me."

"It won't be when we get caught." He sets his palms on the door next to my head and focuses on me. "Is anyone else workin' in here?"

"My brothers are supposed to, but Wilder's still in bed. I'm not sure where Waylon is."

He dips his mouth back to mine and softly brushes his tongue between my lips. "Tell me how wet you are."

His strained voice makes me grin at how hard he's trying to stay in control and not move too fast.

When he steps back to give me space, I spin around and press my back against his chest. Our rapid breathing is the only sound as I unbutton my jeans and slide my hand down my panties.

"Mm..." I moan, coating my finger.

He grabs my ponytail, pulls my head back, and then lowers his mouth to my ear. "Touch yourself," he growls. "Make yourself come."

It'd feel better if it were his fingers, but I can't deny his erection pressing into my back and his hot breath against my neck aren't almost as satisfying.

Short bursts of air release from my mouth as I pant through the intense sensations. His free hand grips my arm and guides my fingers while I rub circles over my clit.

"That's a good girl, Goldie. So wet for me, aren't you?"

"Mm-hmm." I bite my lip to keep myself from moaning too loudly.

"Pretend it's me touchin' you. It's me makin' you burn hot and lose yourself. Think of my mouth on your sweet cunt."

"Yes, *please,*" I beg, not caring that someone could walk in on us.

"So goddamn temptin', Noah. But I can't this time, so you're gonna have to do it for me. Slide two fingers inside your pussy."

I do as he says and then set my foot up on the grooming bucket to give myself deeper access. His whispered demands and neck kisses have me losing control within a matter of minutes.

"You're so goddamn sexy when you come."

My body goes limp against him as I rest my head on his chest and collect myself. Fisher grabs my wrist, pulls my hand from my panties, and brings my fingers to his mouth.

"Fuck me. Your sweetness is gonna taunt me for the rest of the day."

I arch my back into his erection. "I think that's the least of your problems."

He spins me around and cups the back of my neck, pulling me into his mouth and giving me a taste.

"I better go before someone sees me, but I'll call ya tonight."

"You should FaceTime me. Around eight."

He arches a brow. "Why's that?"

I adjust my body to button my jeans and fix my hair. Then I open the door and peek up and down the aisle to make sure it's clear. Once I'm certain no one is around, I turn back toward Fisher.

"Because I'll be in the tub." I wink, and he shakes his head.

"I'm already sufferin' here..." He lowers his gaze to his groin.

I close the gap separating us and give him one final kiss. "Then come over at nine. I'll leave my door unlocked."

Chapter Eighteen

Fisher

Having to bend over with a horse hoof between my legs for hours at a time with raging blue balls isn't my idea of a good time.

But when it comes to Noah Hollis, I'd suffer through anything for a chance at another taste.

So when I find myself at her door at precisely nine o'clock that night, I make sure to bring something with me that'll ensure I don't cross any lines.

Besides the ones that have me sneaking over here like I'm seventeen again.

I even parked on the retreat side again and walked half a mile to make sure no one noticed my truck. Though I didn't bring my rig this time, I'm not taking that chance.

"Is it on VHS?" she asks when I tell her I brought over a movie from the '80s.

I deadpan, and she bursts out laughing.

"Blu-ray," I defend. "Do you even know what a VHS looks like?"

"Yes, I saw it on some vintage early 2000s documentary."

I nearly stroke out at the thought of *vintage* being only two decades ago.

She finally reads the title. "We're watchin' *Overboard*?"

"I need to educate you on who Goldie Hawn and Kurt Russell are."

"Who?"

I shake my head, take out the disc, then put it into her player. "Exactly."

"Do you wanna tour beforehand? We can find some drinks and snacks, too," she says, grabbing my hand.

Since her cottage is on the smaller side, the tour takes two minutes. It's bright and quaint, exactly how I would expect a woman like Noah's place to look. Photos of her with friends, family, and horses cover the walls. There's a framed scenic watercolor photo of the ranch that looks as old as the movie we're about to watch. The sunset shining between the trees with a rustic fence in front makes for a beautiful picture.

"Who painted this?" I ask before she leads us into the kitchen.

"I'm not sure. My grandfather gifted it to my dad when he took over the ranch. It was my gift after moving out so I'd have a piece of home with me." As she stares at it, she laughs. "It's silly because I'm literally five minutes away, but we've always been close."

"None of your brothers wanted it?"

"I asked him the same thing, and he claimed they wouldn't appreciate it the way I would." She shrugs. "My brothers tease me for being a daddy's girl, but I don't really think they minded. My mom got photos printed of it so we had copies for the scrapbooks."

"Ah." The one Jase complained about. "I can't wait to see yours."

"I'm sure you will tomorrow because my mother has no boundaries when it comes to oversharing. Prepare to hear about my first period."

I scratch my cheek with amusement. Seems the whole family isn't afraid to speak their minds.

"Are you a popcorn or candy man?" she asks as she digs in her pantry. "I have both because I'm an M&Ms *in* my popcorn girly."

"That sounds good. Salty and sweet."

"Good choice. For drinks, I have sweet tea, Red Bull, or Budweiser." She turns, waiting for my response.

Arching a brow, I ask, "Why do *you* have beer?" More specifically, the exact kind I like.

She grabs a bottle for me and a Red Bull for herself. "I was hopeful you'd come tonight, so I went into town after work and stocked up. Mrs. Bridges was workin', and she's a little nosy."

I chuckle, though I don't know who that is. "What'd she say?"

"Asked who I was buyin' it for and about my plans tonight." I grin when she twists the cap before handing it to me, remembering when she'd done that at the bar the night we met.

"Thank you," I say. Then she pulls out a bottle of Jägermeister. "What's that for?"

"Me." She pops the tab of the Red Bull and then pours both liquids into her glass. "Luckily, I'm not drivin' tonight." Her little smirk has me smiling.

"I'll stick to beer. I have to walk through the woods back to my truck."

"Or you could just...stay here, and I'll give you a ride in the mornin'." She takes a sip of her concoction but stares at me over the rim.

"You tryin' to give Mrs. Bridges somethin' to talk about, ain't ya?" I walk toward her.

She nearly spits out her drink but quickly covers her mouth. "At least that'd be newsworthy."

Setting my beer on the counter, I stand between her legs, tilt up her chin, and rub my thumb along her lower lip where some of the liquid dripped. "Ya know, maybe she was just makin' conversation and being friendly."

"Oh, no. Sugarland Creek locals are gossips. It's why Gramma Grace meets up with them for Saturday brunch. They talk about *all* the town drama."

"An old ladies' club?" I grin. "That sounds hilarious."

"Not when you're the *subject,*" she counters, putting her glass down. "And trust me, if I told Mrs. Bridges I was buyin' beer for the new local farrier, who's twice my age and my ex's father, it'd be on the front page of Sunday's newspaper."

I lower my mouth, brushing my lips softly underneath her ear. "So what'd ya say when she asked?"

Noah cocks her head, wrapping her arms around my waist as I suck lightly. "Told her to mind her own damn business...in nicer words, though. I said a lady never kisses and tells."

Gripping her waist, I inhale her shampoo as I bury my face in her neck. "We wouldn't wanna give her anythin' to talk about, now would we?" I suck harder, and she giggles.

"I can cover up a hickey with the right concealer and hairstyle, but your mouth would be more useful in other places."

Chuckling, I bring my mouth to hers for a quick kiss but don't deepen it. "Let's go start the movie."

She frowns when I create distance between us. My dick's been hard all day, so if I don't, it'd only take one moment of weakness to give in to what we both want.

"Your *moralities*"—she air quotes—"are a cockblock."

Smirking, I grab my beer and her glass. "Bring the snacks."

The only TV in her house is in the bedroom area, so I set our drinks on the nightstand, and once she comes in with the popcorn and candy, I press play.

"Anythin' I need to know about this movie, or do I just dive in blind?" she asks, handing me the bowl and getting comfortable against the headboard.

"Nope, not tellin' ya anythin'. I want your raw reactions." I sit beside her so we're shoulder to shoulder, facing the TV.

"Fair enough. Prepare for honest commentary."

And not that I expect Noah to hold back, but she has a comment about everything.

The fashion, the hair, and how unrealistic it'd be that this storyline could happen in today's world with all the technology and social media. And how a woman found at sea with amnesia would be plastered all over social media and talked about in podcasts. I don't use or listen to either, so I just nod.

"Don't tell me her husband cares about her *now* when he's the one who left her at the hospital?" She sighs, rolling her eyes. "He's the worst."

I mostly keep quiet, enjoying her critiques even if it shatters my '80s-movie-loving heart.

"Oh no, the boys are gonna be heartbroken! She promised the little one she'd never leave!" She sits up and leans closer as she holds her breath.

"Then maybe I should turn it off so you aren't sad." I grab the remote as if I'm going to stop the movie.

"Don't ya dare," she scolds, reaching back and smacking my hand. "You got me hooked on this stupid film, now let me finish it."

Holding back laughter, I move behind her with the little space between her and the headboard and situate her between my legs. Then I pull her back until she's pressed against my chest.

"Should I distract you?" I tease, bringing my lips to the nape of her neck and blowing warm air on her cool skin.

"You're not playin' fair." She shivers against me as her focus stays glued on the screen. "Tryin' to seduce me now when I'm distracted."

Chuckling, I snake my arms around her waist and slide my hands between her bare thighs. She's in comfy shorts that rode up when she sat down.

"I dunno what you're talkin' about. I'm just kissin' your neck."

"Liar..." She breathes out. "And a bad one at that."

She arches as my fingers slide over the fabric covering her pussy.

"Should I stop?" I ask.

"No..." Her chest vibrates as I add more pressure.

"Keep watchin'. You gotta see this through to the end now."

"Is it gonna be a happy endin'? Because if not, then I'm turnin' 'round to get my own happy endin'."

"Noah," I laugh out her name. She's easy to rile up, and though I shouldn't be teasing her so much when I know she wants to see Annie and Dean end up together, it's amusing as hell to watch her try to resist for once.

Her hands grip my thighs as I gently rub and kiss her neck. She's trying so hard to stay focused and not crack.

"He better fight for her, goddammit." She shakes her head when Annie gets into the limo with her husband, and the kids run after it. "Oh my God. I can't take it."

"The movie or me touchin' you?"

Her head falls back against my shoulder. "*Fuck*. Both."

"Think you can come like this before their happily ever after?" I taunt, inching my fingers beneath her panties and feeling her arousal. "Goddamn, you're soakin' wet."

"You do not play fair, Mr. Underwood." She widens her legs as she squeezes my thighs. "There needs to be a 2x speed on this movie."

"Tsk tsk. No skippin' ahead. Maybe I shouldn't let ya come until after it's over and see if you can wait."

"No, no, no. I don't think I have that much willpower left in me."

Oh, sweetheart. You and me both.

"I like that idea..." I muse, slipping a finger deep inside. "No comin' until the credits roll."

With my free hand, I slide it underneath her shirt and find her pierced nipples.

Goddamn, she might not be the only one who can't hold back.

"You're evil," she grinds out, her breath erratic as she tries to keep her eyes open.

"Not yet, I'm not." My thumb finds her clit and presses hard as I continue finger-fucking her tight pussy. Her juices coat my hand, and I know it wouldn't take much to send her over the edge.

"Fisher, please. I'm not above beggin'."

"We're so close, baby. Hold on. Kurt's about to go get his woman," I tell her as he jumps off the boat and swims toward her.

"He needs to fuckin' hurry, or I swear to God," she complains when Annie jumps off her boat.

The two characters finally meet in the water and get pulled onto the deck.

"Just eight more seconds, Noah. Can ya do it?" I murmur in her ear when Dean asks Annie what he could possibly ever give her since she already has everything.

An insecurity he and I have in common.

"Seven."

Noah licks her lips as she tries to keep her orgasm from bursting.

"Six."

Annie pauses to look at the four boys making long Christmas lists and then smiles at Dean.

"Five."

And then she tells him she wants *a little girl*.

"Four. Keep your eyes on the screen, or you'll miss the final scene," I whisper, and she shudders.

I squeeze her nipple harder as the music starts playing. "Three."

Annie and Dean finally have their moment and kiss.

"Two."

The camera zooms out, showing all six of them on the boat, getting their big happily ever after.

"*One*."

And then, when I grind deeper against her pussy and circle my thumb, she shatters against me. Noah screams and bites her lip as she flies off the ledge.

"Such a good girl, Goldie." I cup her jaw and bring her mouth to mine, smelling her on my hand.

When I break our kiss, I lick one finger, then dip the other between her lips.

"Taste so good when you come, don't you?"

"That was the longest eight seconds of my life," she mutters.
I laugh. "Story of my life."

After thoroughly kissing Noah good night, I walk to my truck with blue balls *again*. She wanted to *return* the favor, but I was more than satisfied giving her what she needed. Noah will always mean more to me than our one-night stand. When the time comes to confess our relationship, whether people accept it or not, I'll know what we share isn't based on only our physical connection because each secret moment brings us closer.

Noah wanted me to stay over, but I'm meeting Jase in the morning to see the house he wants to buy. Even if I feel like shit for lying to him and keeping secrets, I still want to be the father who shows up. Maybe if I ask him questions about her, especially after our awkward dinner, I'll get a better sense of their friendship and telling him won't be as bad as I think.

Or at least, I hope.

Chapter Nineteen

Noah

FISHER

I can still smell you on me.

This man is trying to kill me with anticipation.

And he's going to pay for it.

NOAH

Then perhaps you should wash your hands.

I leave the barn and go to my truck since I need to clean up for Sunday dinner. After my usual morning chores, I did some training, checked on Ranger, replied to some emails about the charity event, and checked on Donut. I'm looking forward to working with him more once this weekend is over. I know Delilah is eager for my answer.

FISHER

You're a mood killer.

NOAH

Says the cockblocker.

FISHER

You only want me for my dick, don't you?

NOAH

No, your fingers and mouth have been very useful as well.

I giggle, knowing his reaction will be an eye roll or something equivalent. His sexting game is improving, but when I check his response as I walk in my front door, the last thing I expect is a photo snapshot of his groin. Blinking hard to make sure I'm not imagining things, I swallow down the lump in my throat and stare at *him*.

The veins in his arm and hand pop as he grips his erection through his jeans, showing me just how hard he is.

NOAH

I could take care of that if you'd let me. In case you forgot the food truck moment with me on my knees...

FISHER

I very much remember.

NOAH

I'm gonna get a complex, thinking you don't like my blow jobs.

I strip off my work clothes and turn on the shower. Dinners at my parents are always fun, but tonight I'm nervous as hell since Fisher's coming. I'm torn between acting normal and being indifferent when he's there. If anyone notices something off, they won't hesitate to mention it—especially my brothers, who almost caught us Friday night.

As I'm about to dip underneath the water, my phone rings with a FaceTime call. Deciding to answer it, I bring it in the shower with me.

"Hello, Mr. Underwood," I taunt, placing my phone on the

shelf that won't get wet. I notice he's in his truck. "I'm practicin' your name for tonight. What do ya think?"

His gaze moves up and down. "Um, I think you're naked in the shower. Why'd you pick up?"

"Don't flatter yourself, sir. I FaceTime with Magnolia in the shower, too."

He arches a brow, and I laugh.

"What? I'm a busy person. I gotta multitask." I grab the soap and lather up my arms and chest.

"Are you bein' serious?" he asks.

"Yeah, I need to get ready for supper."

"Not about that. Am I really givin' you a complex because I won't let you suck my dick?"

I bite back a laugh and nod firmly as I casually wash the rest of my body. "Yes. I'm gonna have to find some moron I meet at a bar and—"

"Noah." His deep, stressed voice cuts through the air, but I continue as I rinse off.

"And give him my best blow job. I mean, practice makes perfect, right?"

When I finally glance at the screen, his gaze is lethal. "What?"

"Your cute little tactics aren't gonna work on me."

"No idea what you're talkin' about."

Then I angle my phone down so he can see below my waist. "Hold on, I gotta put on shavin' cream."

Instead of being discreet about it, I turn away from him, bend over, and smooth it all over my legs.

"Jesus Christ."

His frustrated laughter makes me smile.

"Problem?" I ask coyly.

"Just the rock-hard boner I'm gonna have when I walk into your parents' house."

"You may wanna take care of that beforehand," I suggest innocently, then grab my razor and start shaving.

He groans. "I'm already dressed and on my way there."

"That's unfortunate for you."

"Do you have a toy in there?" He looks past me.

I spin around and notice my rose vibrator sitting on the opposite shelf.

"Yes, and she's waterproof."

"Really? Show me."

I shift the phone's position again, lifting it upright so he can only see above my chest. "You're gonna have to earn that, Mr. Underwood."

He angles his head down as if he's trying to sneak a peek beyond the screen, but his view is restricted.

His throat moves as he swallows hard. "Is your door unlocked?"

The corner of my lips tilts up. "It might be."

He shakes his head, and I hear the distinct sound of him slamming on the gas. "Don't move. I'll be right there."

I giggle when he ends the call.

Lucky for him, I still need to shave my other leg and wash my hair. If he can get here before I finish, he'll get a front-row seat with me and the vibrator.

Ten minutes later, a truck door slams from somewhere outside, then, after a moment, heavy boots echo inside and walk toward the bathroom.

I wait anxiously under the hot stream until the door flies open, and a completely naked Fisher appears.

That I was *not* expecting.

Silently, he slides open the shower door and keeps our gazes locked. I gasp when he pushes me to the wall.

Water beats over his skin as he cups my jaw and crashes his mouth to mine.

My body relaxes into him, soaking up his touch and kiss.

"On your knees, Goldie. *Now*."

I blink once at his harsh tone, but goddamn, it also turns me on.

It's gotta be all that monster smut I read before bed. *Red flags*? Nah, I'm color-blind.

I position myself in the center of the shower and get to my knees. He turns, putting his cock on full display, and when he grips it, I nearly salivate for a taste.

"I should punish you instead of givin' in to what you want." His long fingers stroke his length. "But the thought of that smart mouth near another man's junk had me speedin' over here."

My gaze finds his as I bite my lip to keep from begging like a sugar addict desperate for candy.

"Open your mouth and stick out your tongue," he orders, and I immediately comply.

Whichever side of Fisher this is, my pussy's on board with a first-class ticket.

"That's it," he praises, grabbing a fistful of my wet hair and urging me closer. He slaps his shaft over my tongue a few times before shoving himself between my lips. "Now suck my dick like a good girl."

I hollow my cheeks until they hurt and coat his thick cock with my saliva until I'm nearly gagging from how deep he goes. My hands squeeze his thighs as I use them for leverage to stay in position and move against him.

Fisher pants and groans as I push him closer to the edge. I can hardly breathe as I gasp for air and lick up his bulging vein.

"Fuckin' hell, you're so good at that, Goldie. Don't stop." His grip tightens in my hair as I suck faster. "I'm so close, baby. You want my cum down your throat?"

I dig my nails in deeper and moan a strangled response that equals to *you fucking better*!

It only takes a few more seconds of me going deeper and faster for him to groan out his release. Warm spurts land on my tongue as I swallow and lick every drop from his cock.

When I look up, he tilts his head back with a low growl. His body blocked the water before, but now it lands on me, too.

"On your feet." He holds his hand out to help me up and then cages me against the wall. "That's why I was waitin', Goldie. I knew the moment I had your hot mouth on me again, I'd fall too fast. I've never been drawn to a woman like this before, and it scares the shit outta me. I don't wanna run you off by movin' too fast, but my heart is all in, Noah. I know it's supposed to be wrong —being twice your age, Jase's dad, and the workplace policy— but when I think about you and how I feel when we're together, nothing has ever felt more right."

The vulnerability in his tone has my chest aching. The power of his words places a chokehold on me because I want nothing more than for us to be together without the secrecy.

I wrap my hands around his neck until I can touch his lips. "It feels right because it *is* right. People can get on board and support us or choose to walk away. But I'm in this with you, no matter what. Nothin' you can say will scare me off." As our foreheads rest against each other, I quickly add, "Unless you're a murderer and talk about guttin' me like a fish. That'd be enough to have me runnin'."

He chuckles softly as he moves his mouth along my jawline. "Pretty sure ya said that to me the night we met, too."

"Well, I had to ask. The one time I don't..." I mimic a throat slashing.

"You gotta stop listenin' to murder shows."

He shakes his head, and I laugh.

"We're gonna be so late now," I remind him.

"Shit, yeah. I should move my truck before someone sees it."

"Luckily, no one passes here on their way to the main house since it's behind it, but better to be safe until we tell them."

"As much as I wanna scream that you're mine so every

twentysomething boy knows you're off-limits, I kinda like keepin' this to ourselves for now."

I wrap my arms around his waist and lean my chin on his chest as I gaze up at him. "They can find out when they get our weddin' invitation in the mail."

He snorts, brushing wet strands off my face. "Your father would kill me."

I shrug. "Maybe, maybe not."

Leaning down, he takes my jaw and presses a soft, sensual kiss to my lips. The tenderness of his movements sends shivers down my spine, and if it wasn't for being late, I'd keep him in here with me all night.

"I'm gonna dry off and get dressed so I can get to the house before you."

"Good idea. It won't take me too long to finish up."

I'd planned on really fixing myself up—blow-drying my hair, lip gloss, full makeup—but now, I quickly put on tinted moisturizer and pull my hair into a ballerina bun.

As he steps out, I check out his ass before he grabs a towel. When he turns, he catches me and smirks.

"You have a nice butt, so sue me."

He chuckles, grabbing another towel to dry his hair.

"Then you'd have to sue me for doin' the same thing durin' all the times you bent over in front of me."

"We're gonna have to actively try not to be so goddamn obvious when we're around people."

His gaze falls to my breasts, then moves back to my eyes when I clear my throat. "What?"

Laughing, I shake my head. "Yeah, we're screwed."

I arrive at the house twenty minutes after Fisher leaves. Luckily, I'm only a few minutes late from the time we *actually* eat, but no one notices because two of my brothers are still missing. My dad and Fisher are having a full-on conversation about football, and I hold back a smile when I notice how uninterested Fisher is. He's trying hard to stay engaged, but as soon as our eyes lock, his expression brightens. I do a quick headshake to remind him he's not supposed to stare at me like he remembers what I look like naked.

"Sweetheart, hi." Momma walks over and pulls me in for a big hug.

I avert my gaze from Fisher and focus on her.

"Landen and Wilder are on their way, then we can sit."

"Sounds good."

Gramma Grace is icing something by the stovetop, so I make my way to her and give her a quick hug. "This smells delicious. You'll have to teach me this recipe." I dip my finger across a small piece of cake.

She whacks my wrist, and I jump.

"We have a guest tonight. He doesn't want your fingers in his dessert."

As soon as the words leave her mouth, Fisher coughs, and I turn to see him choking on his sweet tea. My cheeks heat at the thought of how I know he wouldn't mind at all, but I glance away before anyone notices my reaction.

"Goodness, Fisher. Are you okay?" My mother stands by him, softly patting his back.

"Yes, ma'am. I'm fine. Just went down wrong."

"That's because he's drinkin' that sissy shit," Tripp taunts. "I'll grab ya a beer."

Tripp stands next to me as he opens the fridge, and I nudge him. "You know Momma doesn't like drinkin' at supper."

"It's not like he's underage." He snorts, grabbing two cans of Bud Light, and hands Fisher one.

"Thanks," Fisher says and pops the tab.

"Where's Mallory?" I ask.

"With Serena at the waterpark. Told Ayden to be back by suppertime, but he texted a half hour ago and said the girls weren't ready to leave," Momma explains, shrugging.

"I'm sure they're havin' a blast," I reassure her, and she nods with a smile.

Since Mallory's parents' death, my mother has grown overprotective of her and ensures she's always involved in our family traditions.

Waylon sits and asks Fisher, "So you traveled a lot before movin' back here, right?"

"Yes, for eight years or so."

Fisher's been a farrier longer than that, and Lyla passed away ten years ago, so he didn't start traveling for his job until two years later. But Jase said he left right after his sister died. Where was he for those two years?

"Are you likin' livin' back here?" Waylon continues to ask questions.

Fisher quickly glances at me before directing his response back to my brother. "More than I thought I ever would."

"I ran into Jase at the grocery store the other day," Momma tells him, which is news to me. "Told me he was buyin' a house."

"Yes, he gave me a walk-through of it this mornin'. It's perfect for him."

"He was such a sweetheart to our Noah. We were so sad when they broke up. I coulda sworn they'd get back together, get married, and eventually have kids."

Kill me *now*.

"Not me," Tripp blurts out, and for once, I want to give him a high five for rudely interrupting.

"*Tripp*," Momma scolds. She's worried he'll offend Fisher by speaking negatively about his son, but she couldn't be more wrong in that assumption.

"She's too good for him," he defends, but what he's not saying is how much my brothers didn't like Jase out of respect for his father being here.

"Noah's too good for anyone," my dad speaks up assertively.

I roll my eyes and sigh. "Noah's right here, and she can make her own decisions on who she does or doesn't date."

"You're still young, sweetie. Jase seems to be growin' up and maturin', so ya never know. Y'all might find your way back to each other."

My mother's words make me want to throw up.

They're fixated on him because he was my only long-term boyfriend in high school. If only they knew Jase and I weren't as serious as they thought. Once he graduated, we only hung out on the weekends, and even then, it felt more like two friends hanging out. Not a couple crazy in love.

"We're just friends, Momma," I remind her. "That's all we're gonna be."

"There's a new ranch hand at the retreat who's twenty-five and single. I'll have to introduce y'all. He works with the horses," she says as if that's a requirement for me to like someone.

I liked Fisher before I even knew he was a farrier, and even though we met at a rodeo, I didn't even know why he was there at the time. I just knew there was a spark between us that I wanted to explore before the event was over.

"When did this become the Noah Dating Show? Y'all act like I'm nearin' my deathbed or somethin'."

"Don't listen to them, sweetie." Gramma Grace takes her seat next to Fisher.

Lord help him.

"You're too young to settle down anyway. Go travel the world, live your life, and only get married when you find a suitor who can handle your adventurous side. Otherwise, you're just wastin' your time on *boys*."

"A *suitor*, huh?" I muse, pouring myself a glass of sweet tea before sitting across from her and Fisher. "In that case, maybe I'll find myself an older gentleman who knows how to treat a lady," I drawl out in a deep country accent.

"That's what I did..." Gramma Grace says as she lays her napkin over her lap. "You think I married the first man who proposed? Tsk. I made your grandfather work for it."

Oh my God.

My jaw drops.

"Gramma...so scandalous," I tease.

"Mama, you sure ya wanna share that story with your grandchildren?"

"Yes!" Tripp and I say simultaneously. I'm surprised she hasn't told us already, but I'm eager to hear about it. Just as she's about to start, the front door whips open, and my other two brothers walk in.

"Finally. We're starvin'," my dad scolds, gesturing for them to find a seat.

"Don't look at me." Landen shakes his head, then points at Wilder.

No one's even shocked.

"Gramma was just about to tell us how she met Grandpa," I say as the boys grab a beer and take a chair on each side of me.

"I thought they were high school sweethearts or somethin'..." Tripp says, reaching for the food, but I quickly elbow him to wait for grace.

"Well, I was in high school when we met, but that's not when we started datin'," Gramma Grace confirms.

Once everyone's at the table, Momma says, "Let's say the blessin' first before you talk about marryin' a man fifteen years older than you."

I cover my mouth, surprised she slipped that little information in, and am disappointed that I have to wait for the story now. After we hold hands, I sneak a peek at Fisher across from me. Gramma comments on how big and strong he feels. I bite back a laugh when he blushes at her compliment.

Momma starts her usual prayer as I send my own.

Dear Jesus, thank you for this food, but please make this dinner less awkward before I do something stupid like blurt out I had sex with our new farrier and am possibly falling hard for him, too. If you could send a hurricane, tsunami, or meteor to end this dinner as soon as possible, that'd be appreciated.

And then I make the sign of the cross over my body at the same time as my mother says, "Amen."

Chapter Twenty

Fisher

Keeping my eyes off Noah when she's sitting across from me is a skill I didn't know I'd need.

It doesn't help that every time she brushes her shoe against mine, I'm quickly reminded of where we are when her grandmother inches closer.

After Mrs. Hollis said the prayer, Gramma Grace promised to tell the story of how she met their grandfather after dinner. Then she looked at me and winked.

Fortunately, the conversation switched to the fundraiser, turning their focus away from me.

"We have a busy week ahead of us to get prepared. It's all hands on deck," Garrett says, his attention pointed at the four boys.

"I like how Noah plans an event, and we all get roped into it," Wilder scoffs.

"Oh, I'm *sorry*. Is helpin' rescue horses above your morality code?" Noah's overly sweet tone has her other brothers cackling.

"That's where ya screwed up thinkin' Wilder has one of those at all." Landen nudges her.

Wilder leans back, wraps his arm behind Noah, and smacks Landen on the other side of her.

Dena cuts in. "Knock it off, y'all. We have company."

I look up from my plate as if I hadn't noticed nor am bothered by it.

"That reminds me, one of the judges can't make it, which means we're down one," Garrett says. "I was gonna email a couple on the waitlist to find a replacement. But with it bein' last minute, I'm not sure we'll fill it."

"I can do it," I blurt out after swallowing my food, and everyone's head snaps toward me. Quickly, I clear my throat. "I was hopin' to help in some way."

Noah's eyes flick from mine to her father's.

"You wanna judge?" Garrett asks.

I nod. "Yeah, sure."

"I love that idea!" Dena gushes. "You should bring your rig, too. I bet the kids would love to see how you work on hooves or mold shoes."

"That'd be pretty cool," Tripp adds. "You know how to judge?"

I grin. "I've been to enough rodeos in my lifetime. I think I can manage."

"That'd be really nice of you," Noah says, flashing me a secret smile. "I'll add your name to the brochure."

"I'm sure Jase will like that too," Dena says. "He's workin' the booth for his real estate agent's office."

"Yeah, he mentioned that to me this mornin'."

When he told me, I was a bit surprised since I know he hates being on the ranch and around horses. But it makes sense for networking purposes.

The rest of the dinner conversation goes over their plans to prepare the training center for the competitions. There's still plenty to do in five days, and I plan to help Noah however I can because she's stressing out about getting it all done on time.

"I'm available to help with anythin' extra y'all need," I say. "Put me to work."

"You're gonna regret sayin' that..." Waylon mutters, and laughter echoes from the boys.

"On Thursday, the bleachers need to be put up," Garrett tells the twins, then directs his attention to Landen and Tripp. "We need to make room for the incomin' horses, so the boarders need to be moved to either the family or retreat barn. Double up the ones that get along, but we need fifteen stalls. That doesn't include the space we need for the sheep."

"The fields behind the center need mowin' for parkin', too," Noah says.

"And what're *you* gonna be doin'?" Wilder snaps.

"You wanna list?" When she drops her fork and whips out her phone, I know she's about to put him in his place.

She clears her throat. "Get tables and chairs for booths, confirm food trucks, email the itinerary to all the sponsors and trainers, set up the silent auction at The Lodge, get horseback ridin' sign-ups posted, write my speeches, make sure the trainin' center is ready and cleaned, set up emcee's and judge's tables, confirm we'll have bathrooms arrivin' on time, oh...and all the marketin' and networkin' I organized with newspapers across the state on top of the written interviews they sent me." She shifts her eyes to Wilder with a murderous glare. "And that doesn't even include my own trainin' and talkin' to clients I'm still required to do."

The room goes silent.

"Sounds like ya need an assistant," I mutter with a grin, silently volunteering for the position. Though I'm plenty busy with my work, I'll always make time to help Noah.

"Trust me, I know." Noah scoffs and points her fork at Wilder. "Anythin' else you wanna know?"

Landen steals her fork and slowly sets it down. "Just gonna take this before you stab him."

Garrett chuckles. "Noah, don't worry. It's all gonna get done. This is the first year, so there's gonna be growin' pains as we learn what works."

She scowls. "The only *pain* is Wilder."

"Bet you're glad you only had one kid, huh?" Tripp says, and everyone's laughter halts when Noah gasps. "What?"

Poor kid's clueless.

"Actually, I have two," I tell him softly. "My daughter passed away ten years ago."

Gramma Grace finds my hand and lightly taps it. After losing her husband, I'm sure she understands. I don't want people's sympathy, though. It feels wrong.

Tripp smacks himself on the forehead, shaking his head. "Crap, I'm so sorry. I remember that now."

Noah narrows her eyes at him, and I lightly tap her foot under the table to grab her attention. When she finds my gaze, I shake my head and smile so she lets up.

"It's okay," I reassure him. "Lyla woulda loved the chaos y'all bring. She was always taggin' along to my jobs and loved meetin' new people."

"My love story ain't soundin' so bad now, is it?" Gramma Grace leans over, causing me to laugh.

"Oh, you're definitely sharin' after dessert," Noah says.

"Are ya stayin' for scrapbookin'?" Gramma Grace asks.

Smiling wide, I look at Noah. "Wouldn't miss it."

After dessert, the boys bail and claim they're goin' back to work, but judging by their mischievous looks, I'd doubt it. Dena says it's hit or miss if they stay for scrapbooking, but Noah never skips. I love how she makes an effort to spend time with her parents. They probably appreciate it more than she realizes.

"How many of these have y'all made?" I ask when Dena and Noah dump boxes of supplies and albums.

"Probably thirty or forty," Noah says. "I hired a photographer, so I plan to make a new one specifically for the event."

"I can't wait to see that." Dena grins. "Here's one ya might like." She hands me an album with a familiar cover photo.

"Oh, it's the same image as the paintin' on Noah's wall."

A sharp inhale coming from Noah makes me realize my slip.

"Yeah. How'd ya know that?" Dena asks as she spreads out colored papers and stickers.

Gramma Grace keeps her head down, but I notice the smirk playing on her lips as if she knows something she shouldn't.

Noah quickly rescues me before I can respond. "He was puttin' up those No Trespassin' signs, and I asked him about installin' a camera outside my house. After Craig showed up at the Twisted Bull and threatened me, I wanted an extra level of security."

"I was happy to assist and have already ordered them," I say truthfully. "I found a couple of good spots that'll cover the front and back of her house."

"That boy is gonna find himself on the side of a milk carton if I have anythin' to say about it," Gramma Grace grumbles.

Noah snorts as I look through the photos—pages and pages of ranch views and some of the family riding horses. I pay attention to each one, soaking in how beautiful the ranch and retreat truly are, and their history.

I hold up a photo of Noah standing bareback on a horse. "How old were ya here?"

She leans over the table and looks. "Eleven, twelve maybe?"

My brows shoot to my hairline. "You were doin' tricks that young?"

"Oh, that's nothin'. She was walkin' right up to wild horses at eight years old." Dena shakes her head, but her voice has a sense of pride. "It was like she had no sense of danger."

That's the adrenaline junkie in her.

"It wasn't so much as *tricks* as just seein' what I could get away with," Noah says, her cheeks tinting a beautiful shade of red. "I didn't have that fear around animals, so I just pushed the limits the older I got."

I smile, knowing all too well how that goes. "Either way, I'd say you have a gift."

Garrett walks in and takes a seat. "The gift of givin' her parents a heart attack."

"Not like I'm the only one." Noah scoffs as she works on a page in her book. I watch as she takes little vintage pieces and glues them around a picture.

"Well, it's different after havin' four boys and then finally gettin' my little girl. I wanted so badly to dress her up, but she wasn't havin' it," Dena says, then offers me a cup of decaf coffee.

"Sure, thank you." I take it and bring it to my lips.

"You don't allow a girl to get dirty. She'll only wanna do it more." Noah grins.

And now she has me thinking about other ways she gets dirty.

"This family photo is really nice," I say when I come across a two-page spread covered in pictures with all seven of them.

"That was our fifteen-year anniversary shoot," Dena explains. "Twins woulda been around twelve or thirteen."

Which means Noah was six or seven.

There's one of them standing in front of a barn with the main house off in the distance.

They look like the perfect Southern family.

"Are you okay?" Gramma Grace asks next to me.

I blink and realize I've been staring at the same page for a few minutes.

"Yeah, great. I'm just admirin' your beautiful family." I flip the page to more horse and ranch views.

"It's a shame what happened to your daughter. Mariah and Jase were so lost for a long time. I remember seeing them in church every Sunday." Gramma Grace covers my hand with hers, and I fight with what words to say. She's trying to comfort me, but unbeknownst to her, she doesn't know I'm the reason Lyla's dead. I don't deserve her sympathy.

I frown, looking away. "Thanks."

"Gramma, you need to share your story about Grandpa still," Noah intervenes.

I can't look at her, not right now, but I appreciate her taking the attention off me.

Dena groans as Gramma Grace shifts to look for a different album spread out in front of us.

"Here it is..." She opens it and flips a few pages before revealing their wedding photo. "Your grandfather was fifteen years older, but ya wouldn't know it because he hardly aged a day until he was seventy."

"Even then, he was pretty good-lookin'," Dena says, smirking as she digs around for more stickers and embellishment pieces.

"Where'd ya meet?" Noah asks.

I grab my coffee, wishing it were caffeinated after not getting much sleep last night.

"Well...he was the pastor at my high school."

Nearly spitting out my drink, I bring a hand to my mouth and force the liquid down, but not before Noah notices.

"Gramma!" Noah's jaw drops.

Dena shakes her head as Garrett stifles a laugh. He must know this story.

Gramma Grace shrugs with an innocent smile on her face. "We didn't date until after graduation. I started workin' as a youth leader that summer, and we grew closer."

"I can't believe you bagged a pastor."

"Noah!" Dena scolds.

Noah giggles and holds up her palm, giving each other high fives. "Good job, Gramma."

"He was a very nice gentleman, but even so, many people didn't approve. Includin' my own mother."

"So what'd ya do?" Noah asks, her attention solely focused on her as if she's hoping for answers to our current dilemma.

"What any other rebellious teenager who was told no would

do..." Gramma Grace glances up with a devious smirk. "We snuck around."

I hold back an amused grin, keeping my focus on the album so they don't notice my reaction. But *holy shit*.

Noah laughs as she rummages through more pieces and paper.

Gramma Grace might be the only one who'd accept Noah and me being together, but having her blessing would be a bonus.

"For how long?" Noah asks.

"Two years," she notes. "By that time, I no longer cared what anyone else thought because I was madly in love with him."

"You weren't a pastor's wife, though. At least not that I recall..."

"After we got married, we moved to Sugarland Creek, and he decided to go into carpentry. I became a homemaker and stay-at-home mom."

"What kind of furniture did he make?" I ask.

"Everythin'," Gramma Grace responds with pride. "Furnished most of our house as well as many other locals. He was the busiest man I knew but always made time for Sunday supper."

"It's where the tradition came from," Noah explains.

"He made most of the furniture in the guest cabins," Dena says. "Lots in here, too."

"He loved workin' with his hands and creatin' somethin' from nothin'. Couldn't get him to slow down. He passed away a few years ago from a heart attack."

The sadness in Gramma Grace's voice has me leaning over and capturing her hand. "I'm so sorry to hear that. He sounds like a wonderful man."

She places her free hand on top of mine and pats it, smiling wide. "He was. Despite our age difference, our love was real and strong. The risk to follow my heart was worth it." She winks.

The room grows somber as we go back to scrapbooking. Dena refills my mug, and I thank her.

They continue showing me other albums. Dena and Garrett's wedding album. Each of the children has their own scrapbook with memories, clippings, and photos of their lives. Several are filled with birthday celebrations, holiday festivities, and first days of school memories.

My heart aches at the family memories I took for granted. As soon as Lyla passed, I couldn't focus on what I still had but rather what I'd lost.

By the time we pack up for the evening, we'd spent another two hours talking and looking through albums. Noah shows me some of her favorites, and Dena talks about how she and Garrett started the retreat.

It's the most normal evening I've shared with others in a long time.

I just hope they still accept me when they learn the truth about their daughter and me.

Chapter Twenty-One

Noah

My heart was full after spending time with my family and Fisher on Sunday evening. It provided me with a glimpse of how things could be when we go public. Learning about my grandparents' history—where they met and how their lives turned out—gives me hope that someday we'll get our happily ever after, too.

After Fisher left, I stayed and helped clean up. He texted that he had to go home since he works early, and although I understood, I missed him.

Five days have passed, and he's spent all his free time helping me with the fundraiser. He's assisted with checking off most of my checklist. Although I'm putting my brothers to work too, Fisher's done more than all of them combined.

"That man sure knows how to work up a sweat," Magnolia whispers next to me as we watch him lead horses into the trailer so we can move them to the family barn.

I put Landen and Tripp in charge, but they conned Fisher into helping by offering him free beer.

He's not that desperate for alcohol, so I know he's only doing it for me.

We both tilt our heads as we admire his flexed arms and sculpted body.

"Could y'all be any more obvious?" Wilder sneaks up behind us, and I jump at getting caught gawking at Fisher.

"That was rude!" Magnolia smacks his arm.

"Be useful or go away," I snap.

Wilder teases Magnolia by tickling her sides, and soon, she's chasing him out of the barn. I shake my head at how he treats her like an annoying little sister, but at least he doesn't just pick on me.

Mallory and Serena walk in and head straight for Miss Swift's stall.

"Whatcha doin'?" I ask, stopping them.

Mallory lifts a baggie of veggies. "We brought her some carrots and celery."

"Lucky horse." I smile.

"I'm so excited about tomorrow!" Serena squeals.

"Me too!" Mallory grins.

"Noah, when can we have another sleepover?" Serena asks. "It's been like a month."

Every few weekends, we have a girls' night at my house. We'll stay up watching age-appropriate rom-coms and bingeing junk food. It's a tradition I enjoy having with them.

I wrap my arms around them. "Soon, I promise. Once I get through this fundraiser and some trainin' stuff, life will slow down a bit. Maybe after Ayden and Laney's weddin', we'll throw a huge slumber party!"

"Yay!" they squeal.

Fisher and I only hung out a couple of times this week when he snuck over after work, but otherwise, we've been too busy and exhausted by nighttime. During the day, we steal glances and short-lived moments in the tack room, but it's not enough.

I want him to myself for a whole weekend.

"Ex-boyfriend alert," Magnolia mutters in my ear as she

approaches from behind. "Better quit lookin' at Daddy Fisher's ass."

Rolling my eyes, I spin around and see Jase looking out of place in a snazzy suit and tie.

"Hey, there she is!" He removes his sunglasses and wraps me in an unwanted hug.

"Hi, what're ya doin' here?" I step back, putting distance between us.

He's texted every day this week, but I've yet to respond. After the way he treated me, I had no desire to talk to him.

"My boss asked me to set up our booth, and you didn't respond to any of my messages, so I wanted to see you."

What does he expect when he acts like a possessive dickhead?

I force a smile and brush loose strands off my face. "I've been busy. I told you that."

"Doesn't mean you can't spare a few minutes, Noah." He pins me with a stare.

I shove my hands in my pockets to keep myself from punching his arrogant face. "Do ya need help findin' the booths?"

We rented a huge white tent that's set up next to the training center, so it'd be impossible to miss, and each table has the companies' names. But the sooner he sets up and leaves, the better.

"Sure. I wanna talk to ya 'bout somethin'."

I grind my teeth, wishing I hadn't made the offer.

"Okay."

I find Magnolia's gaze, and she makes a gagging motion.

"Well, let's go." He grabs my hand and intertwines our fingers, then leads us down the center aisle.

As I glance over my shoulder, Magnolia shakes her head.

"Help me," I mouth.

Before I can see her reaction, Jase pulls me closer as we walk outside. I don't want to be rude or make him suspicious, but he's never this touchy-feely. He hasn't held my hand since we dated.

"Noah," he says, grabbing my attention when we stop in front of the white tent. "I wanna apologize for my behavior at the restaurant and for the way I spoke to you in our last text convo."

My brows shoot up since he's never said sorry to me before. Jase was never the remorseful type.

"I'm tryin' to make a name for myself in real estate, and I let the pressure get to me. I took my stress out on you, and that was wrong." He sandwiches my hand between his palms, looking sincere as he stares into my eyes. "I hope you know how much I value our friendship and everythin' we've been through. I've grown up a lot and didn't always treat ya right. For that, I'm sorry."

I swallow hard as my heart races, and I remove my hand from his sweaty grip. Something feels off with him.

"Wow. Um, thank you? I don't really know what to say. I'm glad we can be friends, too, Jase."

"With my dad returin', it's made me think about the importance of family. He and I have a long way to go, but you've never betrayed me. You're the only one I can see myself growin' old and buildin' a future with. You're beautiful, genuine, and wear your heart on your sleeve. And I know if I don't say somethin' now, I could lose you to someone else. No guy would ever be good enough for you, and I'm not sayin' I'd be perfect, but I'd work every day to be the man you deserve."

Usually, I'm good at deflecting and moving an awkward conversation elsewhere, but I'm one hundred percent unprepared for Jase to tell me he wants me back.

"So...what do ya think, Noah? Wanna give us another chance? I'm financially stable now. I just bought a house. I can give ya everythin' you want and more."

I wince at his little speech as my throat tightens, and I fumble for words that won't offend him. "Jase...um...where is this comin' from? We've never talked about gettin' back together in the two years since we broke up. I'm a little taken off guard here." I step back to create distance between us.

He nods and attempts to pull me closer, but I don't allow it. "I know, but I've been thinkin' about you nonstop. We were happy together. My immaturity and emotional issues are why our relationship ended. I needed to grow up and make somethin' of myself before committin' to someone. And I'm ready to do that now with *you*."

"Why *me*?"

"You're the only woman I've ever loved. Dating's been a nightmare, and after several failed attempts, I realized there was a reason for that. It's because we're supposed to be together. You're my soulmate."

Soulmate? What the hell is he talking about?

"That is very sweet, Jase. Those are words most women dream about hearin'. I-It's just, I'm afraid I'm not the right one for them."

"I don't understand." His voice goes deeper as his nostrils flare. "Is there someone else? How can you just throw away years of history?"

"You're puttin' a lot on me right now, Jase. I wasn't expectin' any of this. You gave me no signs you wanted us to get back together."

He grips my upper arm, slamming me into his chest. "Baby, we're meant to be. Just give me a second chance to prove it."

I push against him, but he squeezes harder. "You're hurtin' me."

"Say you're mine, and I'll let ya go."

"I'm not sayin' that." I slide my boot between his feet in preparation. One lift of my leg and my knee will greet his balls.

"There's someone else, ain't there?" he grinds out, his tone low and threatening.

"It doesn't matter! I'm not interested in gettin' back together," I say firmly, jerking away.

I wince when he grips my other arm, nearly shaking me.

"Who the fuck is he? Someone you met at Twisted Bull? Or someone who works at the retreat? Which loser is it?" He looks around as if he expects my mystery man to pop up, which, if Fisher witnesses his son manhandling me, could be a reality.

"Let me go!" I shout.

"Who're ya fuckin', you little whore? Let me fight him and see who really deserves you." He shoves his face in my neck and slides his tongue under my ear.

I don't give him any warning—not that he'd deserve one—before I drive my knee straight up between his legs. He releases me instantly as he falls to the ground, muttering curse words as he palms his junk.

"You fuckin' slut! What the fuck?" he squeaks out.

My heart threatens to beat out of my chest as I lean down and try to control my breathing. "I told you to let me go. You should know better than to touch me when I ask you not to."

"Goddamn psycho," he whispers, barely getting the words out.

I shrug. "Don't touch women who don't wanna be touched, and I wouldn't have had to nail ya."

Magnolia rushes over, taking my arm and pulling me back. "What the hell happened?"

"Jase learned a lesson the hard way." I'm still seething when my brothers and Fisher come over.

"Jase!" Fisher helps him to his feet, but Jase bends over his knees, still trying to catch his breath.

"Let him go, Fisher. He's our problem now." Wilder steps between me and him, cracking his knuckles.

"I'll take care of it," Fisher tells my brothers, then pats Jase's shoulder. "C'mon, I'll drive ya home."

"Get off me." Jase shakes off Fisher, and I see the hurt in his eyes as soon as he does.

"You wanna fight with the big boys, huh?" Wilder taunts, rolling up his sleeves.

"Wilder, knock it off!" I step around him to face Jase. "Walk away. Before you give my brothers a reason to hit you. *Now*."

Instead of heeding my warning, he slams me back into Wilder, making me bounce off his chest.

"You're fuckin' dead!" Landen takes the first swing, sending Jase to the ground.

"No, stop it!" I shout, but it's too late.

Tripp kicks Jase's knee when he tries to stand.

Wilder throws an uppercut to his face, and Jase stumbles backward. Blood gushes from his nose, but it still isn't enough to stop him.

"Fuckin' sissy," Jase spits.

Waylon fists his shirt and headbutts him.

Fisher tries pulling them off as I scream for them to stop. Magnolia does her best to intervene, but when my brothers get to this level of anger, they are unstoppable.

In the middle of Fisher trying to protect Jase, Landen throws a punch and hits Fisher in the nose instead.

"Oh my God, stop it! You're gonna kill him!" I yank their shirts from behind, hoping to snap them out of their rage.

It's not until blasting cold water sprays full speed at everyone do they scramble like a bunch of birds.

"The fuck?" Wilder snaps, wiping water off his face.

My dad rushes behind Magnolia, taking the hose from her and turning off the nozzle. "Get on, boys. *Now.*"

My brothers mutter curse words as they scatter. I kneel next to Jase as he holds his hands to his face, blood running down his wrists and arms. "Jesus. Are you okay?"

Fisher comes beside him, an expression I've never seen on his face before. His nose is bloody, too. I wish I could reach out and make sure he's okay.

"You need to go to the hospital. I'll take you," Fisher tells him.

"Fuck you." Jase spits more blood, leaning to his side as he tries to lift himself.

"Jase!" I scold since Fisher has done nothing to warrant his attitude. He should be thanking him for trying to stop my brothers. "Stop bein' an asshole and get checked out."

My dad approaches, lifting Jase by his shirt as if he weighs nothing. Jase groans in pain.

"You're comin' with me." Then he looks at Fisher. "Don't worry, I'm not gonna hurt him. Gramma Grace will get him cleaned up, and then we're gonna have a chat about touchin' my daughter."

Fisher looks lost, unsure if he should step in or let Jase deal with his own consequences.

"Dad, please don't be rough."

"He already got his punishment, but now he's gonna get a man-to-man talkin'-to," he says in a deep, rugged voice and gives Jase a little shake.

Looking defeated, Fisher nods as if he's giving him permission.

I see the regret written over his expression as if he knows he should have been the one to raise him properly. Jase has a history of running his mouth and acting overconfident, but he's never lashed out this badly. I could always talk him down to be reasonable, but this time, it was like he wanted to give them a reason to hurt him. I can't figure out why he'd want that, but we'll discuss it later.

Turning to Magnolia, she looks between Fisher and me.

I wrap my arms around her. "Thanks."

"Not the first time I've had to hose your brothers. Won't be the last."

I scoff. "Unfortunately."

"I'll leave y'all alone now. Might wanna get him cleaned up." She lifts her chin toward Fisher, and I nod.

"Good idea. Meet me at my house," I tell him, giving him no room to argue as I walk to my truck. My brothers can spend the afternoon finishing the rest of the chores.

"You sure it's okay for me to be here?" Fisher asks for the third time while standing in my bathroom.

"No one's payin' attention to our locations right now." Carefully, I pull off his shirt, then unbutton his jeans. "Plus, you need to wash off this blood."

I turn on the shower and strip off my clothes while waiting for it to get hot. Memories of us here just days ago still live rent-free in my head. But that's not what this time is about. Fisher's dealing with a lot more than I realized when it comes to Jase.

There's no way Jase will maturely handle the truth about his dad and me.

Fisher takes my hand and joins me under the stream as I step in. We silently wash each other, slowly moving the soap over limbs and intimate body parts.

"Talk to me," I say, breaking the silence.

"I dunno who my own kid is, and that's my fault. He's lashin' out, and there's nothin' I can do about it."

I rub my palm across his damp chest, feeling his racing heart as mine aches for him.

"Jase has always been quick to react without thinkin'. That's not your fault. He's never gotten along with my brothers, but he's never been physical like that before. I'm not sure where that came from."

"Desperation," he responds. "The thought of losin' you made him snap."

"You overheard?"

"I could read the situation pretty quickly."

"It was unexpected. I had no idea he wanted to get back together. But even if I were single, I wouldn't be interested. I tried turnin' him down as nicely as I could, but then everythin' just escalated so fast."

"He said somethin' that shoulda clued me in, but I was hopin' I was wrong."

I narrow my eyes. "What do ya mean?"

"He mentioned somethin' about gettin' a second chance at love and wantin' to do it right this time around. When he was givin' me the walk-through of his house, he talked about startin' a family and makin' memories of his own. I didn't ask him to elaborate because I thought he was implying how he didn't get those family memories growin' up. Assumed he was statin' he wanted to have them with his own wife and kids."

"Maybe you bein' here is bringin' some of those painful memories back up, and instead of talkin' with you, he's actin' out." I shrug. "Either way, it doesn't excuse his behavior today."

He frowns. "You're right, it doesn't."

"Do you mind if I ask you somethin' about Lyla?"

He brushes wet strands of hair off my cheek and slowly rubs his thumb over my jawline. "Go ahead."

"You said somethin' Sunday night that I've been wonderin' about. Jase made it sound like you disappeared within weeks of her death. You mentioned how you traveled for about eight years. But if she passed a decade ago, where were you for those two years?"

His throat shifts as he swallows hard, and I worry I've hit a nerve he won't be comfortable talking about.

"In a behavioral health facility," he finally says. "Jase doesn't know that."

"Oh..." I blink. "Why not?"

"I didn't want him to know what I'd done or tried to do. If he knew where I was, he'd ask why, and then I'd have to lie. I didn't want him to know the truth."

I tilt my head as I hear the brokenness in his voice. "Why were you in there?"

He drops his gaze as he works his jaw. "I was suicidal, Noah. Three weeks after we buried my daughter, I asked my friend to kill me."

My heart hammers as I soak in his confession and try to form the right words to say in return.

"I was in so much pain. I couldn't see the other side and just wanted to die."

"You're still here, so I'm assumin' he wouldn't do it."

"Oh, he shot me. Just not where I asked him to."

My eyes widen. "Where?"

"Shoulder." He moves his fingers to his left arm and shows me the small scar. "They removed it in surgery. Imagine my disappointment when I woke up in a hospital."

"Jase doesn't know any of this?"

"No. I didn't want him to think I wasn't strong enough to stay and be his dad. It was the lowest point of my life and one I didn't wanna explain to a fourteen-year-old. Mariah told him I was travelin' for work instead."

"What about when he got older? It might've helped him understand what you'd gone through and why you were distant."

"That doesn't matter when you're a parent. You don't leave your kids, period. It's unforgivable. I was ashamed and embarrassed. I didn't want him knowin' I chose dyin' over bein' his father."

"Grief isn't black and white, Fisher. There's that gray area, that place where we become so lost we forget about everythin' and everyone. We become so consumed with our pain it blinds us from seein' the sufferin' in those who were also left behind. I'm sure he experienced it, too, with losin' his sister."

"I can't explain why I chose to leave him when he was in pain, too."

"You woulda had to have been in unfathomable amounts of pain to reach that level. Give him a little credit. I think he could understand that now at his age."

"It wasn't just the pain. It was the guilt, too."

"She died in a hikin' accident, right?"

"I tried to catch her..." His voice breaks. "It happened so goddamn fast."

Tears break through the dam as I watch him struggle to speak. The burning sensation going down my throat has me choking.

"Her foot slipped as she reached for the next marker. She tumbled down, screamin' as she tried to grab ahold of somethin'. I was inches from catchin' her, but my foot stubbed on a big rock, and her body landed in front of me."

My God.

My voice catches in my throat as more tears roll down my cheeks.

"Her neck broke on impact."

I shake my head, wiping my face. The imagery is too much to bear. I can't respond.

"I carried her body for two miles, and when I got to my truck, I contemplated drivin' off the cliff so I could die, too. The pain was immediate and unbearable. But I knew Mariah deserved to bury her daughter, so I drove to the ER. I couldn't tell her over the phone, so I asked the sheriff to bring them to the hospital. She pounded her fists against my chest as I held her, shoutin' over and over how it was my fault her baby was gone. Jase watched as his mother broke down, and they both blamed me."

I cup his cheek, silently offering the reassurance he needs as he blows out a shaky breath. His gaze falls to our feet, and he clears his throat as if he's trying to hold back his emotions.

"My parents cut me out of their lives when I decided to make bull riding my career, so havin' close relationships with my kids was a priority. She and Jase weren't adventurous, so Lyla and me always took the day trips. I was responsible for her and blamed myself, too. I shoulda been closer or not let her go so high, but Lyla liked pushing the boundaries even when I warned her. She liked bein' brave and tryin' new things. Mariah clung to the idea that if I hadn't encouraged Lyla so much, she wouldn't have wanted to impress me by going so high. Deep down, I knew Mariah was hurtin' as much as me and needed to point the blame at someone."

I can't even imagine being in either of their shoes. Losing my aunt and uncle a couple of years ago rocked our family hard enough as it was. I couldn't fathom losing a sibling or watching my parents suffer at that level.

"I couldn't sleep, eat, or work. I don't even know what

happened during those three weeks after her funeral. I was numb and just goin' through the motions of breathing and reliving the memory each time I closed my eyes. Jase had just lost his sister, and his parents couldn't even function to ensure his needs were met."

"I'm so sorry y'all had to go through that. No parent should have to bury their child." I take his hand and intertwine our fingers. I wish I could say the right thing to take away his pain, but nothing could ever remove the ache and guilt he's felt for the past ten years.

"The only thought I had on repeat was to end my life. I never thought about dyin' before her accident, but I couldn't live in a world where Lyla didn't exist. Mariah couldn't look at me. Jase was distant from what he believed to be true. I wanted to end my sufferin' along with theirs. It was a selfish move, but I didn't care at the time."

"That's when you asked your friend to shoot you," I whisper.

He nods, squeezing my hand. "I wanted my family to at least get my life insurance. Damien was a detective, so I knew he could make it look like a robbery gone wrong or somethin'."

I blow out a breath. "Thank God he didn't listen."

"After I woke up, I'd gone back and forth on whether I hated him or was grateful he gave me a second chance."

"And after your shoulder healed, you went into a facility?"

"Yeah, he made me. He promised he'd keep the truth between us only if I'd comply in gettin' help."

"Did it work?"

"Yes and no. I spent two years goin' to therapy and grief counselin', but the pain never goes away. It simmers while the grief holds me hostage, and even when I try to remind myself it's okay to move on, the guilt pulls me back. After ten years, I was tired of the regret cripplin' me. Jase is the only family I have left, and I didn't wanna go another day without tryin' to be in his life again."

"Jase is a confused, hurt boy who had to grow up too fast. He doesn't understand why you left him. You need to tell him so he can have closure to that period of his life. He probably grew up thinkin' it was his fault you weren't around. That he wasn't good enough. Jase needs therapy to deal with his abandonment issues, and knowin' *why* you weren't around could help in his healin' process."

"I'm afraid it'll make it worse for him."

"Maybe at first. But Jase needs you more than he's willin' to admit."

"And when I tell him I'm fallin' in love with the woman he wants, how do ya think he's gonna react to that? Nothin' I tell him about the past will matter. It'll be the ultimate betrayal in his eyes, especially now that I know he has feelings for you."

My stomach twists at his words, but I don't dwell on them. "To be fair, neither of us knew he wanted to get back together with me. And I certainly didn't know who you were when we met."

"I'm afraid that won't matter to him."

And I'm afraid he's right.

Chapter Twenty-Two

Fisher

I've never shared that story with someone I cared about. The only other people who know are my therapists and my childhood friend. I haven't talked to Damien since moving here, but I check in with him every six months so he doesn't worry about me.

Admitting how badly you screwed up your life isn't an easy thing to say aloud, especially to someone you're in love with and who you want to see the best in you.

Noah's always been the exception. She makes me feel safe to reveal all the bad and ugly parts of myself. She listens and doesn't pity me. But she's the one person in this world I can't have.

Jase will never forgive me if he finds out our secret.

And if I don't choose my son, I won't be able to live with myself for screwing up a second time. Jase needs his father more than ever. He needs guidance and a role model, and most importantly, I need to be honest about why I left. I call him every night and attempt to make plans, but he constantly brushes me off.

But I didn't return to Sugarland Creek to give up that easily.

He needs to trust me again, and he never will if he finds out I've been lying to him.

After Noah and I shower, we lie in her bed, and she lets me hold her, knowing what's to come. We talk about a bit of everything except the giant elephant in the room.

Three hours pass before she shifts and faces me.

"I should go back and make sure everything's ready for tomorrow. Can we talk more after the fundraiser?"

The sadness in her tone guts me.

I trace her cheekbone, her nose, and run the length of her jawline, imprinting every inch of her face to memory. Nodding, I give her a soft smile. "Yeah. I should go check on Jase."

Once she walks me to the door, I cup her face and breach her lips with my tongue for a deep kiss.

"Can I ask you one more thing?" she asks as I place my forehead on hers.

I blow out a shaky breath. "Yeah, anythin'."

"Did you mean what you said earlier about fallin' in love with me?"

Fuck, she's not making this easy.

"Yeah, Goldie. Meant every word."

I walk up the steps to Jase's apartment and knock. After I drove to the main house, Garrett explained that Gramma Grace cleaned him up, and after they had a *chat* about respect, he went home.

"What?" Jase answers, looking as defeated as I feel with a nearly empty beer can in his hand.

I wince at his double black eyes and nose bandage. "You cooled down?"

He shrugs, then nods.

"Good. Get your shoes on."

"Where are we goin'?" he asks with hesitation as if he plans to argue.

"To visit your sister."

I haven't been to Lyla's grave since the day we buried her. I wish I could say I recall every second of that day, but I was too numb to process any of it. The only memory I have is of Mariah crying next to her mom and my parents sitting next to Jase.

My mind blocked out everything outside of that.

"Did your mom ever take you here?" I ask, driving slowly through the cemetery. A shiver runs through my body as I look out at the tombstones. I hate cemeteries.

"Each year on her birthday." Jase keeps his voice low as he looks out his window.

Once I park and we get out of my truck, I realize I don't remember where hers is. I never came again after the funeral. I knew being here would remind me of her absence and what happened in the weeks following her death, but there's no valid excuse for not visiting.

I'm a shit father.

Luckily, I don't have to ask because Jase takes the lead. The flowers they left for her last time are long dead, and I regret not bringing a fresh bouquet.

"Your mom picked out a nice tombstone."

Staring down at it, I read it for the first time.

Beloved daughter and sister
Lyla Eleanor Underwood
October 13 2001 - May 3 2013

"Grandma did. Mom couldn't hold it together long enough to decide."

"Oh." I stand with my hands in my pocket, debating how to start this conversation I never planned on having with him. "She's not the only one who couldn't."

"Honestly, I don't remember much. Only that Mom cried all day every day and you were gone a few weeks later." His somber tone drives a knife into my heart because once he hears the truth, it could change everything.

"I didn't wanna leave you, Jase. I wanted to be strong enough, but I was at war with myself."

He looks over at me, his brows pinched together. "Because they blamed you?"

"I blamed myself, too. The guilt ate me alive. The pain of losin' her consumed me." I shake my head, ashamed that it took ten years to have this talk with him. "There's somethin' ya should know about why I was gone. I dunno how much it'll matter now, but you deserve the truth."

I lower myself to the ground, flattening my palm to the fresh-cut grass and feeling closer to her than I have in years.

"I woulda died if it meant it could save her," I say, choking up at what I put my childhood friend and my family through. "I tried takin' my own life even knowin' it couldn't bring her back."

Jase steps closer, but I purposely keep my head down to avoid his gaze.

"When?"

"Three weeks after." My voice cracks as I swallow down the lump in my throat. "I felt like I couldn't exist in a world where she didn't. The pain suffocated me until I couldn't take it any longer."

He blows out a sharp breath. "Does Mom know this?"

I look at him watching me. "She does."

He frowns. "She never told me that."

"She was tryin' to protect you while livin' in her own personal hell. She needed someone to point fingers at, and I willingly accepted it because no matter what anyone told me, it was my fault."

"How'd you try to kill yourself?"

"You remember my friend Damien?"

"Yeah. He brought me gifts every year on Christmas and my birthday."

"Oh. He never told me that." Sounds like him, though.

"Braxton didn't like him comin' around. He thought Damien was one of Mom's triggers. She'd spiral for the next few days after he left. But I liked talkin' to him, so she let him stay."

"I only see him about twice a year for the same reason," I admit.

"What does he have to do with Lyla?" He sits next to me.

If I'm going to come clean, I might as well face both of my children.

"It's what I asked him to do for me. Do you wanna know the full story? I've tried to spare you the details because it's not somethin' I'm proud of, but it explains why I was gone. At least for those first two years."

He pauses briefly before nodding. "Yeah, I wanna know."

I inhale deeply, preparing my mind and heart for a deep dive into the past after already doing it with Noah. But he deserves to know just as much.

"Lyla's death felt like the lowest point in my life until three weeks later when I asked Damien to shoot me, and I realized *that* was my lowest. You and your mom blamed me, and I had nothin' to live for. I thought death was my only out."

I explain what happened that day and how I felt when I woke up in the hospital. Jase hangs onto each word, but with his flat expression, I'm not sure how he's taking it.

"You don't just get to ask someone to murder you and walk away from that. Especially to a detective." I shake my head at the irony. "Damien knew I needed help and if I didn't get it, I'd eventually succeed. The grief and pain gutted me, hollowed me out until I was nothin' but a shell, which led me to spendin' two years in a behavioral health facility. I missed you like crazy, but your mom couldn't forgive me, so we divorced. She didn't want ya to know where I was, and at the time, I agreed with that. I worried about how you'd take it. Later, I realized it left too much room for interpretation of why I was gone. Not tellin' you had you believin' I abandoned you."

"Yeah, I did. Mom said you decided to travel for work because bein' at home was a constant reminder of Lyla," he says. "I remember wonderin' why you never called or sent a postcard."

A pang of sadness hits me in full force. Each word of truth that leaves my mouth is accompanied by a dull ache in my chest.

"I had it in my mind that you'd written me off like your mother. She said y'all were better off without me, and I assumed it to be true. I thought not comin' around was makin' it easier for y'all to move on. I didn't wanna be a reminder of what happened."

"Well, it wasn't true." He takes a shuddering breath as if he's fighting his emotions, too. "I lost a sister *and* a dad within a month. Practically a mom, too. She was a mess, for years, and it wasn't until Braxton came into the picture that she was somewhat back to her normal self." There's a moment of silence as he turns his focus back onto the ground. "I really needed you." His voice is low and filled with pain as he rips up pieces of grass.

Though I don't blame Mariah for how she coped with everything, I wish she'd been honest and not made me feel like Jase didn't want me either.

"Jase." I sigh deeply and don't say another word until he peers at me again. "I have so many regrets. I spent the past eight years between therapy and grief counselin'. Every appointment or group session I went to, I talked about my goals. My number one was findin' a way back into your life. I knew I had a lot of explainin' and apologizin' to do. I'd screwed up, and I needed to find the courage to come back. I'm so sorry I let you down."

"I remember feelin' a mix of happiness and anger when you called me last year. Happy because I was overwhelmed to hear your voice. Anger because I realized how easy it woulda been for you to do that ages ago. I wanted to see you and help you get a house, but I wasn't sure if I wanted a father-son relationship."

I nod, reaching over and squeezing his shoulder. "I wish I could go back and do things differently. Trust me. I will live with that regret until the day I die. The only excuse I have is that the pain took over. Even once I left the facility, I wasn't the same man you knew as a child. But I'm here now, and I wanna be in your life if you'll let me. I'll go to family therapy with you, or we can find a grief support group. Whatever it takes. And I know ya don't owe me a goddamn thing, so if you're not ready, I'll respect that."

"It's not that easy." He lowers his head. "A part of me worries you'll leave again."

I drop my hand and rest it on my knee. "Understandable. But for the record, I'm never leavin' you again. I'm here because you're here. If you moved to the coldest place on earth, I'd follow. But please don't do that because I hate the fuckin' cold."

A small smile appears on his clean-cut face. "Noted."

There's a moment of silence as we listen to the trees blow in the wind.

"I didn't blame you, by the way," he says so quietly I almost don't hear him.

I tilt my head as another shiver rolls through me. It's eighty-five degrees, yet my bones are chilled. "What'd ya mean?"

His gaze meets mine. "For Lyla's death. You said Mom and I blamed you, but I don't."

My brows rise. "Oh. I assumed she told you about how Lyla died."

"All she said was that Lyla fell from a cliff and you didn't catch her in time. Then she said it was your fault she was out there in the first place. I didn't get the full story until Damien told me after I'd just turned sixteen."

I wince as my entire body shudders. Licking my dry lips, I lower my eyes to her tombstone. "What'd Damien say?"

Jase repeats the exact events of that day. Everything I told Noah, he also knew, and all this time, I had no idea.

"He also told me he didn't believe you were at fault," he adds. "And I don't either."

I lift my head and meet his stare. "You don't?"

"It sounds like it was a very tragic accident. But no one's to blame. Lyla couldn't be stopped. I remember how adventurous she was." He smiles as he looks up at the sky. "Always beggin' me to climb with her up the hills or bike down them. She had a thirst for that rush. Somethin' we didn't share, but I admired her for it."

Tears well in my eyes for the second time today. "You have no idea how it feels to hear you say that." I rub a palm over my eyes and nod. "And yeah, she was an adrenaline junkie like me. Didn't care how dangerous somethin' was because it just made her wanna do it more."

Jase looks back at me, his eyes narrowed. "Dad, I don't blame you for what happened to Lyla. I blame you for leavin' when *I* needed you. Years of wonderin' why I wasn't enough for you to stick around. It had me wonderin' if I'd been fun like Lyla, or outgoin' like her, then maybe ya woulda stayed." His voice cracks, and I lean over to pull him in for a hug. Tears shed down both our cheeks as we stay like this for a few minutes.

"I'm so sorry, Jase. I can't express how much. You needed me, and I let you down."

"I wanna trust you again," he admits, "but a part of me is still angry with you."

"I know." I nod, releasing my hold on him. "I want us to work through this so we can have a strong, healthy, trustworthy relationship. It's the only reason I'm here. You're my priority. I never wanna hurt you again by not being the father you need."

The guilt of falling for Noah eats at me because I know what I have to do in order to keep my promise. It'll hurt like hell, and she's going to hate me, but I must choose my son this time instead of taking the selfish route. When life got hard, I wanted to die, which meant leaving him behind. But then I didn't, and I still left.

If he has feelings for Noah, he'll never accept that I do, too.

He needs me now more than ever. I have to give him time to heal and for us to rebuild our relationship. If he finds out I lied to him and secretly dated his ex, he won't forgive me a second time.

"Do you remember when Lyla packed up her little Barbie backpack and said she was runnin' away on her bike?" Jase asks with a laugh as he stares down at her stone.

"Oh yeah. She made a peanut butter and jelly sandwich, then grabbed a bag of Doritos and two juice boxes." I chuckle at the memory. "Your mom told us to go along with it, so we made sure she packed the right clothes, tied on her shoes, and I put air in her tires."

"She was weirdly smart at nine. And sassy." Jase smirks. "Why'd she wanna run away again?"

I brush a hand through my hair as I recall that day. "She wanted a puppy and decided she was gonna find a new family who'd let her have as many dogs as she wanted."

"That's right."

"She hopped on her bike and made it to the Muellers. They had a St. Bernard who chased her around their yard and eventually wore her out. After she fell asleep on their couch, Mom and I drove over and brought her home. As I was tuckin' her in, she asked if we could get a dog like theirs."

"And then we got one four months later."

We both laugh because Lyla was nothing if not persistent about what she wanted.

"Didn't she name it Tiny?" I ask.

"Yep, Tiny the St. Bernard."

I smile because more memories of Lyla flood in that I've blocked out for years. They were too painful to remember, but I like having them now.

"He passed away a few months after you left," Jase admits. "Vet said it was a rare heart condition. Mom said he died of a broken heart because he missed Lyla just as much as we did."

I shake my head. "I'm so sorry."

Jase nods as if he's too choked up to speak.

When the wind picks up, we decide to leave, but then I ask Jase to give me a moment alone. He goes to my truck, and I stand in front of her stone, apologizing over and over for not coming sooner.

"I will always wish it were me and not you who died that day. We'll be reunited someday, and when that time comes, I will catch you and never let go. Rest in peace, baby girl."

As I walk away, I let the tears fall freely even though I hate it. I've done my best to leave my guard up, but with Noah cracking it and Jase and I coming here, it was bound to fall.

When I get in the truck, I immediately start it and roll down the windows.

"Is it stupid to think I can have a normal happy family of my own? A wife and some kids, maybe even a dog or two," Jase asks, looking outside as we drive out of the cemetery.

"No, not at all. You deserve to find someone who makes ya happy. Findin' that person you can spend the rest of your life with is a beautiful thing. And bein' a father is the greatest feelin' in the world. Holdin' you and Lyla as babies made me so proud. I know it might be hard to believe after what I did, but you two were my greatest achievements and biggest blessings."

"I reckon I really screwed up with Noah," he mutters.

My heart thuds at the sound of her name coming out of his mouth. We need to talk about her and what he'd done, but our heart-to-heart had to come first, which is why I brought him out here in the first place.

I clear my throat. "You wanna talk about it now?"

"I've never talked to her like that before. I know I overreacted, yet my temper got outta hand. She's never gonna forgive me."

"She might. What triggered this?"

"It's stupid." He shrugs, but I prompt him to tell me anyway. "Craig Sanders says he saw her makin' out with someone in her truck at Twisted Bull the night we went to Lilian's Restaurant. I guess it had me upset because I always thought we'd get back together. When I could prove I was the right guy for her, she'd see that we're a good fit. Decent job and new house. The next step is startin' a family. When she rejected me, I dunno what happened. I just saw red. The thought of her with another guy is somethin' I haven't had to worry about...until now, I guess."

My back goes ramrod straight, waiting to see if he asks me what I think he will.

Does he know we rode together in her truck? Or does he assume we drove separately?

"You were there with her brothers, right? Did you see her with anyone? When she turned me down, I asked who she was datin', but she wouldn't say."

"Um...yeah, there was one guy she was dancin' with." It's not a lie, but I still feel like fucking shit anyway. "Well, she and Magnolia. They were out there for a while."

"I shoulda known she'd find someone better."

Jase feeling down about himself is linked to his lack of confidence. Another thing I should've taught him.

"You still love her, then?" I tread lightly, hoping I'm not making myself obvious as hell.

He shrugs, and my throat goes dry.

"I thought maybe I did, but then after talkin' to Gramma Grace, she kinda helped me realize I was in love with the *idea* of her. Having a partner, wife, someone to come home to. I love her as a person, I know that much, but as far as datin', I'm not sure."

I blink a few times, confused if I should be relieved or not.

"Does that make sense?"

"Definitely."

Not.

But I don't want to give him any room to find out the truth. Not about this.

It'll be a betrayal we can't come back from.

"You need to apologize," I tell him. "To her brothers, too."

"They kicked my ass! I'm not sayin' shit to them."

I shoot him a pointed glare. "You put them in a position to protect their little sister."

"They coulda minded their own business. Noah can take care of herself." He nods to his groin, and I snort.

A warmth of pride fills me knowing that's true.

"I took a hit for you, too," I remind him, smirking.

A small smile curls over his lips. "Shouldn't have tried to protect me."

"Jase..." I say lowly. "I'll always protect you now."

Even if that means protecting him from a truth that'd hurt him.

"You wanna come in for a beer?" he asks when I park in front of his apartment.

I throw my truck into park. "Yeah, I'd love to. But I can't stay too long since I'm judgin' tomorrow."

"My boss is pissed I didn't get the booth set up. He sent someone else, but I know I won't be welcome to go now."

I follow him to his door. "Give it a few days, then apologize and smooth things over. Noah seems like the forgivin' type."

At least that's my hope.

"She is. Her brothers already hate me, so I'll never win them over."

"I don't see why not. Y'all are rowdy and like throwin' punches."

He scoffs, unlocking the door and going inside. "I reckon we need more than violence in common to stand each other. Don't exactly wanna have to dodge their fists every time I'm around."

I crack up and nod in agreement as he leads me to the kitchen, then hands me a can from the fridge. "Sounds like every other twentysomething hotheaded boy I've met. Hell, I was one, too. Y'all will eventually grow out of it and make better choices." I pop open the top. "Startin' with this cheap-ass beer."

"Hey, I have a mortgage and bills now. Gotta be responsible and all that shit."

Setting down my can, I take a few steps and pull Jase into my arms. I haven't hugged him like this since he was fourteen years old, and although he's a twenty-four-year-old man now, he'll always be a kid to me. A boy who needs his dad, no matter his age.

At first, I worry I've crossed a line, but then he shifts and wraps his arms around me, too.

And it's the best feeling in the world.

I can do this. I can be here for him while we work through the abandonment issues and surrounding grief. We can get to know each other again, and hopefully, one day, the pain I've caused will subside.

"I love you, Jase. I know I have a lot of makin' up to do, but I'm all in if you'll let me."

When I release my hold on him, Jase's eyes are bloodshot.

"I'd really like that, Dad."

It's the first time he's called me Dad with admiration in his voice.

"We've got some catchin' up to do." I smile and lean against the kitchen counter.

"What do ya wanna know first?"

"How about your first time drivin'?"

The corner of his lips tilts up, and he laughs. "Goin' right for the good stuff, eh?"

By the time I leave four hours later, my face hurts from smiling so hard. Jase and I needed this more than I wanted to admit, but it finally feels like we're making progress.

Chapter Twenty-Three

Noah

"Rise 'n' shine!" Magnolia bursts through my door with two coffees.

I stand shell-shocked with a towel wrapped around me as she smiles wide.

"Latte?" She holds it out, and I hesitantly take it.

"Who are you and what have ya done with my best friend?" I pop the lid and smell the inside before sipping it.

It's only seven in the morning, and Magnolia Sutherland is wide-eyed and bushy-tailed like she's ready to take on the world.

"Your best friend who doesn't have to work and put up with Mrs. Blanche all day."

"Mmm. This is good." I swirl it around before taking a bigger gulp. "Somethin' nutty."

"Toffee White Mocha with caramel drizzle and an extra shot."

"You made this at home?"

"If you'd ever come to my apartment, you'd see my new coffee bar setup. I bought new syrups and an expensive frother." She follows as I walk to the bathroom.

"I'm tellin' ya, you need to ditch your job and start your own business. Mrs. Blanche has nothin' on this." I smile wide at her through the mirror.

"No bank in Tennessee will give me a small business loan with my credit. I'd need a co-signer, and my parents already told me no," she says, sitting on the toilet as I grab what I need to get ready.

They're upset she didn't go to college and won't help her financially. She moved out and got a job, but she's miserable working for someone else. Magnolia would be an awesome small business owner if she could just get the chance to prove herself.

"Any idea how much you'd need?" I grab my makeup bag, then dig for my moisturizer and concealer.

"Well, no, not yet. But I was browsin' online and saw the cutest mobile café ideas. Kinda like food trucks but for coffee. Buyin' a trailer would be my biggest upfront cost, but after that, it'd be cheap overhead. I could rotate spots every few months, grow my customer base, and then who knows? Find a permanent spot and meet my future husband."

I laugh at that. "One goal at a time, Mags."

She opens her photos app and flips through the pictures she saved.

"Those western-themed ones are adorable! Oh my gosh, I love this idea!"

"Right? I'd paint the outside like a pretty rose or teal color, then have a cool sign with Magnolia's Morning Mocha or somethin' like that. Anyway, I'd need a loan to buy the trailer or truck, hire a contractor to help me gut it—unless I manage to find a used one already done, then I'd need to just fix it up. I'd have to pay for the permits and licenses, then order all my supplies and equipment. So probably upward of forty to fifty grand? Give or take."

"Okay, that's not too bad for a start-up. I bet a bank would approve you for that."

"Know of any bankers who wouldn't expect me to start payin' it back for like a year?"

"We could do a Kickstarter? They buy coffee for a year upfront, and you get your money now." I shrug, not quite sure if that'd work, but if I know Magnolia, she won't stop until she gets what she wants.

"We can brainstorm later. Today is all about you! Are you excited?"

"You mean, it's all about the charity."

She waves me off. "Yeah, them too. I need a Fisher update, too. Any word on Jase?"

After Fisher left last night, I was too emotionally exhausted to chat on the phone with her, so I just texted a summary of what happened when Fisher came to my house.

"No, just what my dad told me. Gramma Grace cleaned him up, Dad gave him a talkin'-to, then Jase went home. After Fisher left, he went to Jase's house. Haven't heard anythin' since."

I pull out my mascara and finish up my makeup routine.

"How're ya feelin' about everythin'? What does your gut say?"

I brush through my hair as I stare at my reflection. "I'd never make him choose, and even if he tried, I wouldn't let him. He came back for Jase, and it's obvious he needs his father right now. If Jase does have feelings for me, it makes this even more complicated. Regardless of me not havin' any feelings for Jase, Fisher won't risk it. He already mentioned not wanting to screw up his second chance with his son. I can't be the person to get in the way of that. He'd end up resentin' me, and that'd make all of this pointless."

"So...you're sayin' it's over, then?" She crosses her legs, staring up at me.

My heart shatters at hearing it said aloud.

"I have a tiny sliver of hope there's a way around it, but I doubt it. Fisher blamed himself for Lyla's death, then left Jase when he was only fourteen. He's not gonna make that mistake twice. I'm the threat that could take it all away for him. He'd be stupid to keep sneakin' around with me."

"That ain't fair, Noah. Jase needs to grow up and get over it."

"It's not that easy, Mags. Fisher thinks the betrayal alone would be enough to ruin their relationship. He finds out we went behind his back, Jase may never forgive him. We tell him ourselves, and Jase could make him choose. Honestly, I dunno what Jase's reaction would be, but after yesterday, I can't imagine it'd be a good one."

"So he has daddy issues. Who doesn't? He can talk to a therapist like everyone else and let his father be happy still."

I grab my blow-dryer and unravel the cord. "Now I know why you didn't pass psychology our senior year."

"It was a snoozefest with Mr. Monotone puttin' me to sleep. That ain't my fault."

"Can you find me a cute outfit while I finish up?" I ask, desperate to change the subject.

"Business cute or seduce your ex-boyfriend's dad cute?"

"Why do I ask you anythin'?" I deadpan.

She bounces to her feet and wraps her arms around me. "Because you *looooove* me."

I roll my eyes, then turn on the dryer.

It'll be hot as usual, but with local newspaper journalists coming, I want to be somewhat presentable for pictures. Instead of throwing my hair up in a messy bun like I do most days, I do a half ponytail and curl some of the strands that frame my face.

"Hot mama!" Magnolia catcalls as soon as I walk into my room.

"What'd ya find me?"

"Two sundress options—an olive-green with come-fuck-me ruffles at the bottom or a sunflower-yellow with spank-me-daddy vibes." She holds each hanger in her hands and bobs them up and down. "Which one's your favorite?"

"I shouldn't even be surprised you didn't give me a business cute option." I chuckle, then grab the olive-green one.

Once I'm dressed, I put on my favorite cowboy boots. Then I put on some jewelry, which I don't often wear with training, but I want to look nice.

"Bringin' out the big guns for Fisher, huh?" Magnolia sits on the edge of my bed, watching my every move.

"Yeah, bangles and baby hoops should entice him to ditch his son and pick me," I say dryly.

She stands and walks up behind me as I stare in my full-length mirror.

"You don't have to pretend with me, Noah. It's okay to be upset that y'all can't be together."

"I'd really like not to think about that today. At least until I have to. He'll be one of the judges, so it's not like he'll be avoidable. I'd rather live in my clueless bubble for one more day."

She rests her head on my shoulder. "Okay. Just know I'll be here when ya need me. Whoever needs a knee to their dick or hot coffee thrown at their face, you call me. But I'd rather knee them because wastin' coffee is a crime."

I lean my head on top of hers and smile. "Thanks, Mags. Glad I can always count on you for retribution."

"Day or night!"

When I get to the barn, it's all hands on deck. We borrowed ranch hands from the retreat to help with miscellaneous tasks. Sheriff Wagner and a couple of his deputies will also be present to make sure everyone stays safe and nothing gets out of hand.

Knowing I can't talk to Fisher about anything personal will weigh on me all day. Hopefully, with Magnolia and Ellie being my right-hand women, they'll talk my ears off enough to keep me distracted.

We enter the boarding stables where Ayden's already working. With today's activities, he has to get an even earlier start to clean stalls, feed, and water, and be available to help the competitors board their horses for the day.

"Mornin', ladies," Ayden greets, walking toward us with a shovel.

"How're things goin' so far? Anythin' we can do to help?"

"Don't volunteer *me* for manual labor." Magnolia elbows me.

I side-eye her, and she shrugs.

"I'll supervise," she clarifies.

After checking in with Ruby and Trey and making sure they're good to go, Magnolia and I meet up with Ellie next. Regardless of her being sad about Ranger's inability to compete today, she's in a happy mood.

The trainers and competitors start to arrive, and I welcome each one as they unload their horses. Momma and Gramma helped me make goodie bags this past week, so once they're settled, I deliver their bags and welcome them. Most of them I've informally met at other competitions or only saw their pictures in brochures, but it's nice to officially meet them.

"Thank you for not invitin' Craig Sanders. He's been the biggest nuisance of my life since I rejected his offer to work with him." Brittany MacIntire approaches with her trainer, Amelia Bradshaw.

"You and me both." I groan.

"Wait, I heard he was comin'?" Amelia looks back and forth between us. "One of his clients' sisters told me."

"He still has clients?" I snort. "Well, considerin' he's trespassed on the property and vandalized the trainin' center, he'll get a police escort if he shows his face."

"He apparently ain't so happy the Fanning sisters left him for you." Amelia shrugs. "Not that I can blame them."

There's no bitterness or jealousy in her tone, which is a welcome surprise. Harlow and Delilah Fanning deserve a trainer who can help them advance, not scream at them when they mess up. Harlow's one of my clients, so she's here to show, but since I haven't signed with Delilah yet, I wasn't able to enter her name. But she's still coming to support her sister.

We chat for a few more minutes before I welcome the next

ones. Most of the trainers are ten to fifteen years older than me while their clients are around my age. But I think that only helps me connect with them better. When it comes to horses, I have a lot of patience and understanding versus other trainers who are tense and get annoyed easily. Horses can sense that, and it often affects how they learn and perform.

"Doin' okay, sweetie?" Momma asks as we walk to the training center after getting everyone settled. She and Dad showed up early to meet everyone before we opened.

"Yeah, just nerves. But I'm glad it's finally here." I smile wide. "Couldn't have done it without y'all."

She wraps her arm around me and squeezes. "This is all you, Noah. We just assisted. You're the brains behind this. It's gonna be amazin'. You'll see."

I pat her hand resting on my shoulder. "Thanks, Momma."

Dad's playing with the microphone at the emcee table when we approach him inside. He's grinning wide and looking spiffy in dark jeans, boots, tucked in blue shirt, and cowboy hat.

"Who ya tryin' to impress, cowboy?" Momma teases, leaning in for a kiss.

"Gotta convince these people to spend their money somehow," he says, and we laugh.

"They already did if they purchased a ticket," I remind him.

"Yeah, and now I gotta get them to the silent auction." He winks.

"If you wanna raise the big bucks, auction off the twins for dates. Thirsty women will pay three to four figures." I chuckle, expecting my parents to laugh at my joke, but instead, Dad goes serious and grabs his phone.

"I was only kiddin'." I lean over as he types on his screen.

"Too late. I told Landen to add it to the list."

"Great. Well, if anyone asks, it wasn't my idea." I hold up my hands. Although they deserve the humiliation after all the shit they do to annoy me.

Ellie and Magnolia meet up with me and find a spot to sit

behind the judges' table. I'll be sitting close by with my parents and making sure everything runs smoothly while Ayden and the other ranch hands handle the horses. Landen and Tripp oversee getting the competitors lined up on time while Wilder and Waylon keep up with bringing out the barrels and jumping poles.

Gramma Grace comes in with Mallory and Serena, and they sit on the bleachers next to Momma. I wave to people finding their seats. More ranch hands walk around, helping people, and soon the arena is full to the max. My heart swells with pride, and butterflies swarm my stomach. The moment I worked on for the past six months is about to start.

Wilder walks in eating a giant cob of corn and chewing with his mouth open.

"Where'd ya get that?" I ask with my hands on my hips.

"What? The food trucks are open."

"You're supposed to be *helpin'*," I remind him.

"Relax. I can multitask. Just ask Jen." He waggles his brows, and I gag. "And I was escortin' the judges in. They're here."

My heart speeds up when I see Fisher walking at the end. My parents shake each of their hands and thank them for volunteering. Fisher's gaze meets mine, and I quickly avert my eyes before anyone notices the tension between us. When the judges sit at the table in front of us, Dad hands them a booklet of papers for each competition with all the riders' information.

"Once the charity spokesperson arrives, you can start," I tell my dad when he finishes.

I asked them to send someone so they could be a part of the event and we could present a check at the end of the day.

Magnolia pokes me in the side, grabbing my attention, then nods toward someone coming toward us.

Oh shit.

I didn't expect him to come since he lives a few hours away.

"Noah. Magnolia. Lookin' beautiful as always." He whistles, and a shudder rolls through me.

"Hi, *Ian*." I force a smile, hoping like hell he doesn't recognize

Fisher as the guy from the food truck the night he busted us at the rodeo.

"What're ya doin' here?" Magnolia asks him, purposely keeping his attention on her.

"You didn't think I'd miss the event of the summer, did ya? I knew y'all would be here and couldn't resist seein' y'all again." Instead of realizing that we don't want him here, he sits in the row behind us.

"How nice of you to support the *charity*, Ian." I emphasize the word so he knows this isn't a mingling event.

As soon as I say his name, Fisher turns around. He flicks his gaze from me to Ian, and I notice the realization on his face as soon as it hits him. I widen my eyes and shake my head to signal him to stay turned around. He flashes a look of concern before facing the arena.

Ian continues talking to Magnolia, asking why she never texted him after the rodeo and how they should hang out some weekend. She tries to turn him down, but he's not grasping the hints.

"Mags doesn't do long-distance, so unless you plan to move here, I'd say a date's pointless," I intervene when Magnolia's cheeks heat with frustration.

She whips her head toward me and whispers, "Don't give him any ideas."

"You never know. I'd move for the right person." He smirks deviously. "Speakin' of…you still with that guy I caught ya sneakin' 'round with in the food truck?"

Fuck.

"Who?"

Of course Wilder would return at the worst possible moment.

"None of your business," I mutter. "Go away."

"You just scolded me for not helpin'. Now ya want me to leave? Make up your damn mind."

"Go find the spokesperson so we can get started," I tell him. "He's probably lost."

"I'm just supposed to know what he looks like or what?"

"I know who it is. I'll go with you!" Magnolia jumps to her feet, eager to get away from Ian, but leaving me with him in the meantime.

"Those two an item?" Ian asks as he watches them walk out of the arena.

"Ew, no. She's after a different Hollis." I chuckle to myself.

"You back with Jase?"

"No," I say firmly.

"So then why can't I know who you were hookin' up with at the rodeo? Is he here?" He glances around.

I slide over and lower my voice. "It's not somethin' I want my parents to know about, so I need you to shush your mouth about it or I'm gonna ask Sheriff Wagner to escort you out. Got it?" I smile wide.

He sits up straighter and clears his throat. "Alright, sure."

Once I move back to my spot, Wilder and Magnolia return with Mr. Billings. My dad greets him, introduces him to the judges, and then I shake his hand and thank him for coming. Momma shows him where to sit and once everything's in place, Dad takes his microphone and stands between the barrels in the middle of the arena.

"Welcome to the first Hollis Fundraiser Event! We're so glad y'all are here to raise money for the Fresh Start Foundation. Every penny will go toward helping injured and rescued horses."

The crowd applauds, and my father continues his welcoming speech. He introduces each judge, makes them stand and wave, and then brings me up with him. I give a short talk and encourage everyone to have fun, buy food, and bid in the silent auction.

Once we're done, Dad talks about the different classes of barrel racers, and then it begins.

I sit between Magnolia and Ellie as we watch. I put Landen in charge of contacting me if they need anything over by the barn or waiting areas, so I keep my phone on vibrate in my pocket.

"It's weird bein' on this side of the races," Ellie whispers as we watch one of the racers fly into the arena.

I wrap an arm around her shoulder and squeeze. "I know. Not so bad out here, though. It's lots of fun cheerin' for them."

"That's true." She smiles wide.

The next competitor has a huge fan base because as soon as she runs in, two dozen people fly to their feet and scream. She rounds the first barrel and goes effortlessly around the second.

"Damn, she's fast," Ellie murmurs.

And then she barely bumps the third, but luckily it doesn't fall.

"Whew, that was close," I say.

As soon as Dad announces her time, the crowd erupts in hoots and hollers. We join in and get to our feet, applauding for the soon-to-be winner.

To Ellie's liking, the racer beat Marcia Grayson's time.

"I wanna be that fast!" Mallory turns toward me. "Can ya teach me to do that?"

I grin at the excitement in her voice. "When you're fifteen or sixteen, sure."

"Ugh, fine."

Magnolia chuckles. "I was thirteen when I started."

I give her a pointed look to keep her voice down. Mallory would have me training her on everything if I let her, but with my commitments and schedule, it's already a struggle to squeeze her in on my weekends when she asks.

An hour later, Dad announces a short break so the twins can drag the arena and bring out the jumping poles for the next competition. As they do that, Dad takes a moment to thank the sponsors who donated the cash prizes and directs people to go check out their booths between the shows.

"Go ask the judges if they'd like any beverages," Momma tells me. "I brought a cooler of water bottles, or I can get them sweet tea from the food truck."

It's on the tip of my tongue to ask her to do it, but since it's my event and I personally invited the judges, I know she won't let that slide. I wouldn't mind it if I didn't have to pretend Fisher was just another ranch worker.

I approach the table and put on a smile. "Hey, would y'all like water or sweet tea?"

They each answer, and when I get to Fisher, he's distant. "Water's fine."

Momma leaves to grab three sweet teas while I grab Fisher's water.

"Thank you," he says when I set it down in front of him. His hand wraps around mine and for a moment, we stay like that.

"You're welcome, Mr. Underwood." I grin, then release the bottle.

I take my seat, then feel my phone vibrate with a message.

FISHER

You look beautiful. I'm so proud of all your hard work. Everything's going great.

NOAH

Thanks.

Things feel weird between us, even in text, but I try to brush it off so no one notices the change in my mood.

FISHER

I'm sorry I didn't text last night. I was pretty tired by the time I got home.

NOAH

It's okay. I needed the sleep anyway. How'd things go with Jase?

FISHER

Really well. We went to Lyla's gravesite and had a long talk. I can tell you more during the next break.

NOAH

Okay. Are we still talking tonight?

As much as I want to know what Jase said, I need to know I'll see him later.

FISHER

Yeah, I'll come over once it's clear.

My dad announces the jumping competition next, and I know our time is done for now.

NOAH

Sounds good.

After I send him one last message, I pocket my phone.

I miss him so much already, and my heart aches to touch him again. Even if our hands only touched for the briefest of moments, it had my chest tightening. I'm happy for him that things are progressing with Jase, but that means our relationship suffers for that to happen.

The jumping show begins, and each one does so well, it's anyone's win at this point. Harlow's still new to it, so she's in the beginner level and managed to jump over all the poles without knocking any over. The girls and I cheer loudly for each one, getting the crowd hyped up as well.

Ian continues sitting next to us and although he stays quiet, he keeps looking over at Magnolia and me, which makes me uneasy. When he does try to engage, we pretend he doesn't exist. If he wasn't so pushy about wanting a date with her and wanting to know who I was with, it wouldn't feel so tense having him here.

Once each rider has gone through, the twins remove all the equipment as Dad announces that mutton busting is next and to stick around for a fun time. Then he brings out Mr. Billings to talk more about their charity.

"I'm grabbin' some food. Y'all wanna come?" Magnolia asks.

I shake my head. "Gonna stay here, but can you bring me back somethin'?"

"I'll go!" Ellie jumps to her feet.

They walk down the steps and more people follow suit.

When my phone vibrates, my heart races in anticipation, and I smile when I see Fisher's name. I shouldn't get my hopes up about a future between us, but I can't help it.

FISHER

Was Ian bothering you?

NOAH

Nothing I couldn't handle. How's judging going?

FISHER

If he becomes a problem, tell me.

NOAH

You just sit there and judge. We're not outing our relationship in the middle of the fundraiser.

I'm only half joking, but honestly, this would be the worst possible time for Ian to recognize Fisher and make a scene with my family and clients around.

FISHER

Doesn't mean I can't find him later and remind him how to keep his mouth shut.

I smile like a stupid lovestruck teenager at the thought of him sticking up for me, and even though it's not necessary, it's nice to know he has my back.

"Who's makin' ya this giddy?" Ian leans over, gradually scooting closer, and I quickly lock my phone.

"What do you want, Ian?"

"Talk me up to Magnolia so she'll go on a date with me."

I scoff, nearly laughing in his face. "If she were interested, she woulda told you she was."

"Maybe if you say nice things about me, she will be."

"I'm not gonna get you dates. I'm not a pimp."

"You owe me, remember? I didn't report you or call the police, and it woulda been in my job description to get you in trouble. You and your little boy toy." He arches a brow, and I'm tempted to smack it right off his smug face.

"But ya didn't, and there's nothin' you can do about it now. Is there? You have no proof and there's no cameras behind that buildin'. So nice try at blackmailin' me."

I stand, walk to my dad, and whisper in his ear to get Sheriff Wagner here.

"Everythin' alright?" he asks, calling his personal cell.

"It will be," I deadpan, then glance over my shoulder and notice Fisher staring at me intently.

If Ian being a pain in my ass isn't enough, Magnolia and Ellie rush over and pull me aside.

"Craig's here. Saw him sneakin' 'round the barn actin' really suspicious, but Ayden told him to get lost."

Goddammit. Am I an asshole magnet or something?

"Great, I just sent the sheriff here to get rid of Ian. Do ya know where he went?"

"No, but I suspect he won't leave of his own free will." Magnolia groans.

The mutton-busting event begins and we cheer for all the little kids who enter. It's cute watching them hang onto the sheep for their dear lives, but it reminds me of Craig's presence and how he could easily put so many innocent lives at risk. I'm still on edge after he scattered nails in here and can't help but be suspicious of him sneaking in today.

When Sheriff Wagner arrives with Deputy Scott, I inform him of Craig's unwanted attendance so he can keep an eye out for him, then I ask him to escort Ian out of the arena and tell him to leave.

It might be extreme, but he's making us uncomfortable and tried to blackmail me.

It's one thing to be an asshole.

It's another to do it on my own property at the event I'm hosting.

As they approach Ian, the three of us keep our backs to the bleachers. I catch a glimpse of him out of the corner of my eye as he stomps down the stairs and glares at me.

"Thank God," Magnolia mutters. "He fucked around and found out."

People come up to me and introduce themselves between events, some even asking if I have openings in my training schedule. I book a year out but tell them to email me anyway in the event a spot opens early. Others come up just to tell me how much fun they're having and enjoying the shows.

People walk in and out to grab food and drinks, and although I've been to many events since I was a teenager, I like these types the most. It's low-key but fun and exciting. Everyone is there to have a good time, eat, and socialize.

When my dad announces the next break, he reminds them to return for the showmanship event and then the awards ceremony, where I'll announce all the winners from each event.

Once the cash prizes were handed out, Landen brought over the silent auction totals so Momma could total everything. Between that, the tickets, each rider's entry fee, sponsored booths, horseback riding sign-ups, and food truck percentage donations, we handed Mr. Billings a check for one hundred and twenty-three thousand dollars.

That's over six months' worth of the charity's annual budget, which means they'll be able to continue to help a lot of horses in need with medical and physical care. My heart was so full by the time everything came to an end. Despite Craig and Ian showing up, the day was a huge success, and I hope from now on we can make it an annual thing. I'd love to be able to raise money for different charities each year.

The bonus was meeting other local trainers and their clients, seeing all the townspeople enjoy themselves, and the small businesses coming together to help make it all possible. The networking I was hoping to do was a success. I feel much better about the friendships I've made within the industry and what that'll mean moving forward.

I nearly cried at the end of my speech as I gave my thanks and appreciation. Then I made the mistake of glancing at Fisher and wanted to cry for another reason.

It's nine o'clock by the time I get home. We had a lot of cleaning to get things back in order. I helped the riders load their horses in their trailers and thanked each one of them for coming. I jump in the shower and change into comfy clothes before Fisher's expected to come over. I have a feeling I won't like what he has to tell me, but if we only have this one final night together, I'm going to make it count.

Chapter Twenty-Four

Fisher

After an eventful day at the ranch and being out in the heat, I'm exhausted. My nerves are on fire, knowing this moment was coming. Noah and I couldn't speak about anything personal with her family and everyone else around, so we resorted to texting. I'd let her know how proud I was of the hard work she put in to make this a successful fundraiser. She'd asked how things with Jase went last night, and I gave her a quick recap of visiting Lyla's gravesite and some of the things he said he went through after I left. Then she asked if she and I were still talking after the fundraiser. As much as I wish I could put this off for another few days, I can't. Noah deserves to know what's going on and not be left wondering.

I rub my sweaty palms down my jeans, take a deep breath, then knock. I didn't bother parking at The Lodge this time. Instead, I leave my truck behind her house between two trees.

When she answers, I quickly step inside, and she closes the door behind me. Her thick golden hair is tied up in a messy bun, and her face is freshly washed of the makeup she wore today. She's traded her olive-green sundress and cowboy boots for comfy sweat shorts and a tank top.

She takes my breath away.

As I inhale sharply, my heart hammers as I contemplate doing what I know I have to do.

"Hi." She smiles hesitantly.

I wrap her in my arms and push her against the door. My mouth finds hers, and I eagerly thrust my tongue between her warm lips. She fists my shirt and arches her body into mine. My cock throbs as she pleads for more.

"Noah…" I mutter her name under a pained breath. "We should talk first."

"No."

"*Goldie.*" I bury my face in her hair, wishing I could avoid the pain I'm about to bring to both of us.

"Not if what you're gonna say will break my heart. Make love to me first. Just be here with me right now. We'll worry about everythin' else after."

We haven't slept together since the rodeo, but I can't say no to her. Not this time.

She knows this is goodbye.

I cup her face and bring my mouth back to hers. Our tongues battle for more, and she moans when I tip her head back to deepen the kiss.

My hands lower to her ass, and I lift her with our lips still fused. As she wraps her legs around me, I walk us to her room, then lay her on the edge of the bed. Standing, I remove my shirt and stare at how gorgeous she is.

"Are you sure you want this?" I place my elbows on either side of her and slowly suck on her neck. "You can change your mind."

"I wouldn't stop if the world was under an alien invasion, so keep undressin,' cowboy."

Smirking against her skin, I say, "Yes, ma'am."

As I unbutton my jeans, I attempt to kick off my boots, and when I eventually remove them, I take off the rest of my clothes.

"Not a bad view from where I'm sittin'." Noah bites her bottom lip, gazing up and down my body.

"Your turn, Goldie."

I slide my fingers into the band of her shorts, but instead of yanking them off, I inch them down and kiss her bare thigh. Then another inch and kiss her other thigh.

"Sir, we're gonna be here till dawn if ya keep this up. I've waited weeks for this. I'm gonna combust at this point..." Her pleas come out in pants as I continue my sweet torture.

"Patience, *my love*. I'm not rushin' this, so you're just gonna have to deal with it."

She groans, lifting her hips as if to entice me. She's commando, so her pussy is on full display.

"Touch yourself. Get your clit ready for me."

She obliges and rubs between her legs, breathing hard as I work my way to her ankles before finally tossing her shorts.

"Look at you. Fuckin' stunnin'." I kneel between her thighs, spreading her wide for me as she continues to play with herself.

Before she can complain, I lift her left leg over my shoulder, then thrust two fingers inside her wet cunt. Her lips part into a perfect O as she arches her back and groans.

"Take off your shirt, baby. Let me see all of you."

She manages to maneuver herself just right so she can pull it above her head. I reach up and pinch one of her pierced nipples.

As I drive my fingers deep inside her, I thumb her clit and lean in closer. With her leg propped up, she's stretched open nice and wide for me.

"Goddamn, you're so close," I murmur, then wrap my mouth around her breast.

Her little whimpering noises mixed with her moaning have me rock-hard. She digs her hands into my hair, threading and pulling as I twist my wrist and sink deeper to her G-spot.

"Oh my God, right there." Her head falls back as she breathes through the anticipation.

I alternate between kissing and sucking her breasts. Selfishly, I want my marks all over her skin so that she'll never forget me, no matter what.

"You ready to come, my love?"

"Yes, please...I need to."

"You want my fingers or mouth?"

"Yes."

I chuckle as I press my lips to her heart, feeling it pound against me.

Kneeling between her legs, I slide her closer and dive into her sweet cunt. Flattening my tongue, I lick up her slit and taste her sweet juices. While I thrust two fingers deep inside, I blow warm air over her clit before sucking on it.

Her moans and hair gripping get more aggressive as I bring her closer to the edge. She begs louder and arches her back as I focus on massaging her pussy. As desperate as I am to be inside her, I want to hold on to this moment for as long as I can. The way she trusts me to please her and exposes her vulnerability to me in a way I've never had before has me eager for this to last.

She gasps and tightens around me, finally giving in to the pleasure and screaming through the high. She comes undone so beautifully, I fight the urge to sink back inside and watch her do it all over again.

"Holy shit." Her chest rises and falls as I lean over her and capture her mouth.

"You ready for me, love?" My dick jerks between her legs as she lifts her hips.

"God, yes. I've *been* ready."

I shake my head with a chuckle. "Move up the bed a little."

Once I'm between her thighs, I position myself against her opening, then slowly slide in. Noah inhales sharply as I grip her hips and watch our bodies mold together.

"Breathe, baby. Let me in."

She's tense as I fill her. Finally, she exhales and wraps her legs around me.

"You okay?" I rest my forehead on hers as she digs her nails into my skin.

"Yeah. I'm good." She sniffs, and I notice the wetness on her cheeks.

No, she's not.

Though I'm tempted to pull out and hold her in my arms, I know she needs this as much as I do. We need one more night together, just us with no outside noise. Our connection won't go away just because we can't be together.

With the pad of my thumb, I wipe under her eye and press a kiss there.

"I'm so sorry."

She nods, keeping her eyes low.

"I need you to move, please," she whispers under a pained breath. Her pussy squeezes my cock as she lifts her hips.

I'll give her anything she asks, even if it hurts.

As we move together, I tilt up her chin until she looks at me. "You feel so good, Goldie. Fuck, I can't get enough of you. You ready for more?"

"Hell yes."

I lean back on my knees, grip her hips, and slam harder until she's gasping for air. Her little whimper screams between moans have me on the brink of exploding.

Without warning, I pull out and roll her over. "On your knees and stick out your ass for me, baby."

Wild blond hair falls from her messy bun as she rests her face on the bed and parts her legs. I smack a palm against her cheek, and she yelps.

I stroke my cock as I swipe my finger through her wet slit. "If I recall, last time you said you wanted it fast, hard, deep, all-consumin', slow, painfully slow, then deep and hard again. That still apply?"

My taunting voice has her smiling as she looks at me over her shoulder. That's exactly what I was hoping it'd do.

"How do ya remember that?"

I tease my cock against her opening, covering the tip with her juices but not sliding in. She groans, pushing her hips out higher.

"I remember *everythin'* about you, Noah. There's nothin' about you I'm gonna forget. Not the way you lick your lips when you're nervous or aroused. Not the way you wrinkle your nose when you're unsure of or don't like somethin'. Not the way you cock your hip when someone's pissed you off. And definitely not the way you beg for me. So tell me what you need tonight, and I'll give it to you. *Anythin'.*"

Her cheeks tint pink as a small smile appears across her face. "Tonight, I want your all-consumin' love and passion. I want all aspects of you—from rough to sweet. Don't hold back."

I kiss the swell of her ass, then thrust inside and give her exactly what she requested.

Our bodies are slick with sweat as we slam into each other. I wrap an arm around her and squeeze her breast until she's unraveling for a second time. Between her telling me how good it feels and whispered chants of *more, more, more,* I'm nearly combusting, but if this is our last time, I'm savoring every perfect moment of being inside her.

"Let me ride you." She rolls over, and I position myself in the center of the bed.

Noah climbs over me and easily slides down my cock. She rocks against me with her palms flat on my chest as I grip her hip with one hand and rub between her legs with the other.

As I watch her, I memorize every inch of her sexy body. The swell of her breasts, the pinkness of her nipples, the tan line around her chest and shoulders from wearing tank tops outside, the smooth way her neck merges with her jawline, and her delicate ears. Every inch of her calls for me to touch, and keeping my hands off her will be torture.

She throws her head back and grinds her hips as she chases another release. Her lips part as she moans, and I reach up to pinch a nipple as she breathes through it.

Wrapping an arm around her waist, I hold her to my chest as I roll us over and pin her underneath me.

"Jesus Christ." She laughs, hooking a thigh over my waist. "I didn't ask for whiplash mode."

I chuckle, thrusting back inside until I'm seated in deep. "Keep that up, sweet girl. I'll change my mind and bring you to hell with me."

Before she can respond, I ruthlessly pound into her. Skin smacking and breathless pleas surround us in blissful harmony. I bury my nose in her hair, inhaling her sweet scent I'll miss. She claws at my arms as if she's trying to scratch her way under my skin.

"You're so perfect for me, Goldie," I whisper against her ear. "So sweet and bold. I will never stop lovin' you."

I squeeze my eyes when I hear her choke up. Then I cup her face and slam my mouth down on hers. Our bodies move in sync as I pour my soul into the kiss that feels too damn final.

"Come inside me, Fisher. *Please,*" she mutters so quietly I almost don't hear.

With one last thrust, I soar off the ledge and release everything I have into her.

She owns my heart.

My soul.

Every ounce of my love.

"Fuck, Goldie."

More tears fall down her cheeks, but I don't wipe them away this time. I lower my mouth and kiss each one.

I carry Noah to the shower so we can rinse off. We alternate between kissing and cleaning each other. Then I tell her more about Jase's and my conversation: how he interpreted me leaving and growing up without me, losing his sister, Damien visiting and telling him the truth, his reaction to my confessions, and our plan for moving forward. I explain how Jase isn't sure whether what he feels for her is real or not, and that even if he doesn't, going behind his back and lying is enough of a betrayal to lose his trust once and for all.

There's no easy way around this.

I tell my son, and he'll no longer want anything to do with me.

If I don't tell my son and he finds out about our secret relationship, he'll no longer want anything to do with me.

The only solution is to break things off now before there's a secret to find out.

I'm damned if I do and damned if I don't.

Hurting Noah is the last thing I want.

But in order to pick my son, I have to.

My heart beats out of my chest as I hold her in my arms, knowing I have to walk away from the love of my life.

"I wish I could hate you," she whispers as I spoon her under the covers. After our shower, I got dressed, but she opted to wear an oversized T-shirt. "It'd make things so much easier. Then I could blast Taylor Swift breakup songs and binge on ice cream."

"I knew you were a Swiftie," I tease against her hair, hoping to at least get a small chuckle.

"Shush. If you're gonna break up with me, at least say horrible things about me so I can feel the normal rage afterward."

"There's not one bad thing I could ever say about you."

"Oh, c'mon. You owe me this." She spins around until we're face-to-face. "What is it you said before? I'm self-absorbed. Overconfident. Too bold."

I brush a strand of her damp hair behind her ear. "I love those things about you."

"Then...somethin' else."

Dipping down, I kiss the tip of her nose. "I wish I had died that day so you woulda been spared this pain."

Her eyes bug wide. "Why would you say that?"

I shrug. "Because it's true. Stayin' alive has caused more people pain than if I had just died. Jase wouldn't have felt abandoned, Mariah wouldn't have had to divorce me, and you woulda never met me. Maybe Jase and you woulda worked out in the end after all. Who knows."

"I hope ya don't mean that. If you'd died, I woulda spent a lifetime alone, waitin' for you to show up because you're my soulmate."

"You woulda met someone else. Someone much better than me. Someone without a tragic past. Someone who could always choose you, no matter what."

Someone her own age.

She shakes her head furiously. "Not a chance in hell. Meetin' you changed my life, and even if we can't be together, you will still always be *the one* for me. I'd rather be alone than settle for second best."

"Don't say that. You deserve to be happy, and I know someone out there will do a way better job than I ever could."

"I know you want that to be true, but it just isn't."

I tighten my arms around her for one more hug. "Don't wait around for me. I need to be here for Jase. I can't get distracted or lie to him any more than I already have. Please, I need you to move on. Find someone who can give you the life ya want. Get married, have babies, build your own little ranch family. We both know I can't give you that."

She swallows hard and pushes her fists against my chest. "Now you really are pissin' me off."

Good. Then she won't hold on to hope we can somehow make this work.

"I'm twice your age, Noah. You're smart enough to know we'd never be accepted by your family or even the town. What would your clients think if they knew you were datin' your ex's dad?"

"It wouldn't be any of their damn business. And since when is our age difference an issue?"

I slide out from under the covers and grab my boots.

The longer I stay, the harder this'll be.

Fuck, it already is.

"Answer me," she hisses, sitting up on the mattress.

Once my shoes are on, and I pocket my phone, I turn and shrug. "It's always been an issue, Goldie. I just ignored it. Perhaps I shouldn't have, and things wouldn't have escalated to now."

She scoots to the edge of the bed and stomps over to me, jerking out her chin. "You're full of shit. You're tryin' to be a good dad and do the right thing, and I get that, but you don't get to devalue what we had just because you want me to move on. I love you, Fisher, and nothin' you can say or do will change that."

Those three little words wrap around my heart like a vise grip and nearly suffocate me to death.

I almost wish she hadn't said it.

So goddamn stubborn.

But hearing them is equally beautiful and painful.

I'll cherish those words until I die.

Silently, I cup her face, lower my mouth, and give her one last kiss before I walk out her door.

Chapter Twenty-Five

Noah

ONE WEEK LATER

With my arms full of photos from last weekend's fundraiser, I walk into my parents' house for Sunday supper. I'm starting my new scrapbook tonight, and it'll hopefully take my mind off Fisher for a few hours.

When I told him I loved him and he walked out the door, I was furious. And heartbroken. But mostly sad he didn't say the words back.

Even though I expected things to end, it still stung when he said I deserved better than him and brought up our age difference.

I can't even be mad at him for wanting to do the right thing, but I'm angry with myself for falling for him. As soon as I figured out who he was, I should've kept my distance. At the very least, when I knew Fisher was trying to mend their relationship, I shouldn't have pushed him to be more than friends.

Now we're both suffering.

Selfishly, I wanted one more night with him. No outside noise, no rational reasons we couldn't be together, just us making love.

It was even better than our first time, which is saying something because that night, he said dirty filthy things to me that had me losing my damn mind. But it was better because my heart was his this time. The emotions swirling through me were intense, and it meant more being with him that way.

Now, it'd only be a long-lost memory.

Before he left and I told him how I wished I could hate him, I almost did when he walked out the door. I know he only said those things because I told him to, but he sounded like he truly meant them and that hurt even more.

"Hey, sweetie!" Momma greets me in the hallway with her apron still wrapped around her waist. "You're early."

"I wanted to get here before the chaos." I smile weakly.

I wanted the distraction.

"The photographer sent me some of the files. Magnolia and Ellie also sent me some they took, so I got a good chunk printed and ready for my book," I explain as she leads me to the kitchen.

"That's great, honey. Can't wait to see them."

"Hey, Gramma." I set my stuff down and give her a side hug as she stirs white gravy on the stovetop. "Smells delicious."

Before I walk away, she nudges me. "That man of yours couldn't keep his eyes off ya last time he was here. Betta make sure y'all ain't so obvious this time."

Her voice is low, but I swear I hear her wrong.

I lean in closer. "What? Who're ya talkin' about?"

She looks around and pointedly stares at Momma before bringing her focus back to the pan in front of her. "Honey, I'd never seen a man look at a woman the way Fisher looks at you. I may be old, but I ain't blind."

My lips go dry as I comprehend what she's implying.

"How does he look at me?" I whisper.

"Like you're his whole world and he'd rather die than not exist in yours."

I gulp as my heart nearly stops beating. "You're wrong, Gramma. Nothing's goin' on."

"How come? Jase find out?"

"What? No." I shake my head. "I mean, there's nothin' to

know."

"Mm-hmm." She smirks smugly.

Before I can continue the conversation, the front door swings open, and the sound of boots aggressively pounding the floor echoes throughout the house.

And there goes the peace and quiet.

"Wow, y'all are on time. Color me shocked," I muse when all four of my brothers enter the kitchen.

"Go clean up," Momma orders.

"That means with soap, too." I grin, grabbing the plates from the counter to set the table.

"What was that? You wanna hug?" Wilder comes over in two large steps and wraps his filthy arms around me.

"No! Get away! Ugh, ew. Take a shower once in a while." I push him off with my free hand. "If I drop these, it's your ass."

"Noah, language," Momma scolds.

My other brothers manage to find the bathroom, yet he's still here bothering me.

"Then tell your alien spawn to go away."

Momma raises her brows at him and warns him without speaking a word.

"What? I was just givin' my little sis some love," he taunts, then pokes my side when Momma turns around.

"*I'm gonna murder you in your sleep,*" I whisper-hiss, then kick his shin.

"Wilder, quit annoyin' your sister and go," Dad barks as he walks into the kitchen and heads toward Momma.

"Yeah, to the next galaxy preferably."

"You're such a baby." Wilder yanks on one of my braids.

"Oh my God. How old are you? Grow up," I snap, elbowing him as I walk to the table.

"You first."

I grind my teeth. "I swear, you were dropped on your head when you came out of the womb. Killed all your damn brain cells in one shot."

"Pretty sure that's what happened to you when they let me hold ya for the first time."

"You kiss Momma with that mouth?" I snarl.

He taunts me with kissy-mouth noises, aggravating me even more.

Before I can throw a plate at him, Dad grabs his shoulder and forcefully leads him out of the kitchen. "Go wash up now."

He finally listens, and I continue setting the table.

"Momma, there's two extra plates here," I say.

I'm about to put them back when she stops me. "It's for Mr. Underwood. I invited him for supper. Jase is comin', too."

I blink hard. *What?*

My heart flatlines. It's bad enough I've had to see Fisher every day for the past week. I wasn't expecting to have to face him at family dinner.

"Why would you invite my ex-boyfriend and his dad?" Especially without telling me.

"We need to squash the tension between him and your brothers. It's time they act like men instead of talkin' with their fists."

"Why did no one warn me?" I could've prepared at least.

With a tranquilizer.

"Oh, sweetie, I didn't think you'd mind. You two are friends. Didn't y'all make up yet?"

From him calling me a whore and shoving me? That's a big fat no.

"Not really."

"Well, now y'all can smooth things over."

Oh my God.

"Do the boys know?" They're going to flip their shit.

"Know what?" Landen asks as they all return and pile at the table.

"Y'all need to listen up." Dad stands tall at the front of the table with his arms crossed. "We're having two guests at dinner. Y'all are expected to act like gentlemen and be respectful. Got it?"

"Depends. Who is it?" Tripp muses, and the three of them laugh.

As soon as Dad reveals who, they lose their minds.

Just as I knew they would.

"He ain't even apologized," Waylon says, leaning back on his chair with his hands folded behind his head.

"They're comin' to rectify that," Momma claims. "Now best behavior or *else*."

Or else she won't think twice about kicking them out to eat on the porch.

You'd think Momma was talking to a bunch of toddlers with her tone, but she knows their history. Four rowdy boys who grew up on a ranch and entertained themselves by doing reckless shit tend to act like wild horses on a good day.

"Hello," Fisher calls from the front door, and I wince at having to sit through an entire dinner with him.

And my ex-boyfriend.

I guess, technically, they're both my ex-boyfriends.

I want to throw up. *How is this happening right now?*

The last time the three of us were in the same room together, we were at Lilian's, and I was tempted to throw a piece of my shrimp at Jase's face for his rudeness.

"Hi! Come in, come in." My mother waves them in.

Gramma Grace meets my eyes with a wink before taking her seat.

What the hell is she up to?

"Sorry we're a little late," Fisher says, greeting her with a bottle of wine.

"Not at all. You're right on time," Momma reassures him. "There's two spots for y'all by Noah. I'll open this bottle, and we can say grace."

I swallow hard as I actively try to keep my focus away from the two unwanted men walking toward me. Jase takes the chair next to me, and Fisher sits next to him on the other side.

Dad and Gramma set dishes of food on the table as Momma uncorks the wine. Silence lingers as my brothers stare at Jase.

"So this ain't awkward or nothin', huh?" he whispers.

"No more than gettin' my first period during gym class in seventh grade."

He snorts, which grabs Fisher's attention. His eyes meet mine for a split second before I tear my gaze away.

Jase leans over so no one overhears. "I almost didn't come, but my dad insisted. I'm sorry for last weekend. You didn't deserve any of that."

"You coulda called or texted..." I briefly glance at him.

"I figured ya wouldn't wanna hear from me, but I really am sorry, Noah. I want us to go back to bein' friends again."

Friends? Does that mean he's *not* in love with me, then?

This time, I angle my body toward him and study his sincere expression. I avoid looking at Fisher even though he's close enough to smell his cologne.

"You're gonna have to apologize to my brothers, too," I remind him.

He winces, furrowing his brows. "They gave me two black eyes!"

Landen clears his throat from across the table, grabbing our attention.

"What?" I mouth.

My parents and Gramma sit, patiently waiting for us so we can pray.

Everyone stays quiet as we say grace, and once it's over, Momma tells us to dig in. At first, there's an awkward silence as dishes get passed around and clink together until Wilder stupidly speaks up.

"Your face healed nicely."

It's been over a week, so the swelling and bruising have already gone down.

"Yeah, thank goodness. Told my clients I walked into a metal post."

Landen snorts. "If ya consider my knuckles metal, then sure."

Dad clears his throat, glaring at Landen.

"What? I'm just sayin'." He shrugs, then directs his attention to Fisher. "Sorry 'bout hittin' ya in the midst of it."

"It's fine," Fisher says.

Jase sets down his fork. "For what it's worth, I'm sorry for my behavior. I have no excuse except I'm goin' through a lot and wasn't thinkin' straight. I assure y'all, it'll never happen again. Noah's been my friend for many years, and I hope it stays that way."

Wow. I don't think I've heard Jase speak with such sincerity before.

"That was very well said, Jase." Momma smiles at him.

"That's very sweet, Jase. Thank you," I say.

"Well, we don't accept," Tripp snaps.

Dad snarls, grabbing his attention with a warning glare.

"I think we oughta take him to Twisted Bull and see how long he can last before pukin'," Tripp suggests. "Then *maybe* we'll accept."

"I like that idea. We'll even buy you a few kegs first." Wilder laughs.

"He'll be sick for days." I scowl, shocked at myself for defending Jase after what he did, but my brothers are brutal. "Plus, he works with clients. He can't show up hungover and walkin' in circles."

"Sounds like a fair punishment to me," Waylon says.

"He apologized and gave us his word. That's enough to earn our forgiveness," Momma says.

My idiot brothers roll their eyes and groan, but they'd never take it easy on Jase since they've never liked him.

"Y'all don't need to worry. I met my therapist for the first time last week, and I'll be seein' her weekly for a while. Realized I had some past issues I need to work through," Jase explains.

"Really? I'm so proud of you!" I wrap an arm around him and gently squeeze. It takes a lot for someone to admit they need help.

"*She*, huh? She hot?" Wilder blurts out.

"If you're into older women with gray hair." Jase shrugs.

"That'll be good for Wilder's mommy issues." Landen laughs.

"Out..." Dad points at Landen and Wilder. "Take your plates and go."

"Whaddido?" Wilder asks with a mouthful. "I was just makin' conversation."

Landen's chair scrapes across the floor, and Wilder's soon follows. The room goes quiet as they walk out the door.

"Your therapist have room for another client?" I lean over and whisper so only Jase can hear me.

He chuckles. "I'll put in a referral for ya."

Smiling, I dive back into my food. It feels nice to be on good terms with him again, even if I'm at odds with his dad. The room goes back to quiet conversation as my parents talk with my brothers and Gramma. Fisher stays quiet, only speaking when he's spoken to.

"My dad went with me to a grief support group Friday night," Jase tells me a bit later.

My heart swells, knowing how badly they both need that. "That's wonderful. I mean, not that you have to go, but that—"

"I know what ya mean, Noah. It wasn't as bad as I anticipated. Free snacks." Grinning, he shrugs.

I cackle. "You could lure me to a lot of places with free snacks."

"You still trainin' with Donut this week?" Tripp asks me.

"Yep, startin' tomorrow. Gonna try to get an hour in each day so I can give Delilah an answer. Figure if he ain't killed me by Friday, I'll accept her offer."

"Dude, that's so messed up," Waylon complains. "You can't work with my ex."

"Why not? *I* didn't cheat on her."

He points his fork at me as if he's tempted to stab me in the eye. "I didn't cheat! We were on a break."

I roll my eyes at his pathetic excuse. "Doesn't every man in the history of the world say that? *We were on a break*..." I mimic in a mocking tone.

"And with Marcia Grayson, no less." Tripp's whole body shudders. "Girl talks with a lisp."

"*Tripp!*" Momma scolds.

"Yeah, but imagine her tongue skills." Waylon sticks his out, then waggles it.

"You're two seconds from eatin' on the porch with your brothers," Dad scolds.

"My apologies, Fisher. They seem to have lost their manners and minds," Momma says.

"None needed, ma'am. Reminds me a lot of the young bull riders I traveled with."

"You'd think ours were raised out with the pigs." Momma glares at Tripp and Waylon, who quickly stuff their mouths with potatoes.

"Wait till there's grandchildren," Gramma Grace speaks up with humor in her voice. "Those boys will realize soon enough to watch their mouths around toddlers."

"Ew. Don't put the image of them reproducin' in my head." I shiver.

"Oh, I cannot wait. Five grown adults and no grandchildren yet..." Momma side-eyes me, and I glance around to see who she's talking to.

"Don't look at me. The twins are almost thirty. Harass them to settle down first."

Waylon chuckles. "Wilder would get a vasectomy if the doctor would allow it."

"I hope he ends up with ten kids, all like him," I say.

"Is it dessert time?"

Speak of the devil.

Wilder charges into the house with his empty plate in hand as if he didn't get in trouble twenty minutes ago. He goes right to the counter where the pies are cooling.

"I gotta finish muckin' out at the trail barn before dark," he explains as he helps himself to a slice.

"Why wasn't that done before dinner?" Dad asks.

"I got busy," he exclaims. "And one of the fence wires needed fixin'. Slowed me down."

Landen comes through next, takes a slice for himself, then pulls Wilder back out the door.

Once the two of them are gone, Tripp and Waylon quickly finish theirs and find excuses to leave early.

"I'll help with dishes, Momma." I stand from my chair, grab my plate, and then offer to take Jase's.

"Are you done, Mr. Underwood?" I finally make eye contact with Fisher.

"Yes, thank you." His polite, formal voice is a contrast to the gravelly one he whispered in my ear last weekend.

"Jase, are y'all stayin' for scrapbookin'?" Momma asks, and my heart stops.

I barely survived dinner as it is.

"Actually, I have a client pickin' me up in about ten minutes. They wanted to view a house tonight, and I said I had plans to come here, and they offered to get me. I couldn't say no."

"I'll stay," Fisher says, and my spine goes ramrod straight.

Damn him.

"Oh, lovely! Noah brought a bunch of photos from the fundraiser. You did such a great job judgin'. I'm sure she'd love to show them to you."

Glancing over, I find Fisher staring at me with warmth in his eyes. "Can't wait."

"Fisher, how're things goin' with Jase now?" Gramma Grace asks him fifteen minutes into scrapbooking.

We cleaned up the kitchen before sprawling the supplies across the table. Fisher sat next to me so I could show him the pictures. Then he proceeded to help me decorate the pages, which felt a bit too *relationship-y*, but if so, no one else has noticed.

"It'll be a slow process, but I'm glad he agreed to get help and is talkin' to me. I told him some things from the past that he never knew, so he's also dealin' with that."

"I knew he wasn't in love with our Noah, but at least, I could see the remorse on his face when he apologized. That's a big step for anyone," Gramma says, and I blush when she brings me into the conversation.

"It is. I'm spendin' as much time with him as I can between jobs and am tryin' to be there as much as he allows it. His mom ain't my biggest fan, so I'm tacklin' that as well."

"Mariah will come 'round, especially if she wants what's best for Jase," Gramma offers.

"I hope so."

"Look at this one." Gramma holds up one of the new photos. It's me standing next to the judges' table and Fisher's sitting closest to me. "That one's a keeper. Put it in the book."

Her demanding tone has me slowly taking it from her, suspicious as to what she's up to now.

"Refill anyone?" Momma asks, grabbing the coffee pot.

"Yes, please." Fisher holds up his empty mug.

"No, thanks." I smile. "I gotta be up early to train with Donut."

"About that..." Momma puts the pot back before sitting. "You got hurt last summer when you were doing trick ridin' with him. You need a spotter this time."

"That wasn't my fault, though. Landen kept ridin' his dirt bike near the trainin' center and spooked him."

"What happened?" Fisher asks.

"Nothin' really. I rolled off and scuffed up my knees. It wasn't that bad. But Donut was shaken up after that, so I didn't continue."

"That's why you need a spotter this week if you're gonna practice."

"Momma, I don't need that. I've already warned the boys they aren't allowed to come around the center before nine o'clock. That's why I'm startin' early."

"Don't matter, sweetie. Can't risk ya gettin' hurt. You have clients countin' on you. Plus, y'all give me heart attacks with your antics as it is. I don't need you to give me a real one because you're in the hospital."

"I agree," Dad chimes in from the head of the table. He's been reading the newspaper this whole time. I didn't even think he was listening.

My shoulders slump as I fight the urge to stomp my foot like a pouting child. Have I not proven myself enough around here?

I wave out my arm and shrug. "Well, who am I supposed to ask at the last minute? The ranch hands are all busy through lunchtime. I can't sit around and wait for one of them to come and *babysit* me. I have a schedule to stick to and—"

"I'll do it," Fisher blurts out next to me.

I whip my head around toward him. "What?"

"I'll come in an hour earlier so you can have a spotter. That way, you don't have to worry about waitin' on anyone else." He shrugs and lowers his eyes down to the scrapbook as if he didn't just ruin everything.

How am I supposed to focus on training with Fisher watching my every move?

"That's a great idea!" Gramma smiles wide. "Fisher has experience handlin' bulls. I'm sure he can handle Donut just fine."

I pinch my lips together and narrow my eyes at Gramma Grace. Now I know for sure she's up to something.

"I like that idea," Dad says. "Donut's already familiar with him, too."

"Now I feel much better knowin' Fisher will be there," Momma gushes.

I exhale sharply. "Fine. Come at seven thirty."

"I'll be there," he confirms.

Chapter Twenty-Six

Fisher

I stop at The Lodge for two to-go coffees and arrive at the training center with five minutes to spare. From what I've witnessed, Noah doesn't drink it often, but considering how late we stayed up scrapbooking, I figure she'll need it this morning.

Even though she said she couldn't stay too late, we finished eight pages in her fundraising scrapbook. Her parents and Gramma had long gone to bed by the time I left. As much as I hate *only* being her friend, it was nice to sit together and just talk. She shared the designated album her mom and Gramma started after she was born. It's filled with pictures from when she was a baby, to her early school days, and years of riding. The various competitions she participated in throughout middle and high school filled at least a dozen pages. Then she brought out just one of many boxes filled with ribbons and trophies. It's no wonder horses feel comfortable and safe with her. Not only is she mostly self-taught, but she's a prodigy at her age and level of expertise.

It was nice to finish the evening on a high note after the way dinner ended. I could tell she was surprised to see Jase and me, but he needed a chance to apologize to her and smooth things over with her brothers. Jase and I may have shit to work through, but they have too much history not to make things right.

"Mornin'," I greet her inside the training center and hand her one of the coffees. "Thought you'd need a pick-me-up."

She looks adorable in her riding boots and helmet. She has her hair in a long braid with a few strands around her face, and I wish I could lean in and tuck them behind her ear.

She takes a sip, then grins. "Thanks. Didn't get much sleep, but it was worth it. I'm glad ya stayed last night."

"Me too. The most fun I've had in a while."

"I can't wait to work on it some more. Maybe next Sunday?" she asks, and I notice the flicker of hope in her eyes. It's a bad idea because the more I spend time with her, the harder it is to stay firm on my decision.

But I can't say no to her.

"Yeah, I'd love that."

Hanging out with someone I can't be with is a special kind of torture I've never experienced before. It sucks, but I also can't stay away. Seems she doesn't want to either.

"Well, ya ready to see what Donut can do?" She takes a gulp of her coffee, then sets it down out of her way.

"Yep, tell me where ya need me."

"Mostly just stay behind me so if I fall, you can grab me before I twist an ankle. Donut's pretty good at stayin' still, but he spooks easily. No matter how much I've worked on it with him, loud noises make him skittish. Probably thanks to my dumbass brother who used to ride his dirt bike 'round here."

"Don't ya think for somethin' like this, you should work on a horse who isn't?"

She strokes a soothing palm over his neck. "We have a close bond, and he trusts me. As long as there aren't any sudden loud noises, he'll be fine."

I bite my tongue, concerned she'll end up getting hurt if God forbid a car backfires nearby, but I support her nonetheless.

"Alright, I'm ready when you are." I place my coffee next to hers so I have both hands free.

"First, I'm gonna warm up and do some simple moves to jog my memory."

I don't know much about the technical terms of trick riding, but I've seen them plenty of times at rodeos. There are usually a few of them, and they perform for the audience to get them amped up. They perform in sparkly outfits and deck out the horses in glitter and matching colors. Some even do Roman riding where they stand on a pair of horses with one foot on each and then jump over poles of fire. The horses run nearly full speed while the riders hang off one side or stand on top, and honestly, it's quite dangerous. It's basically doing gymnastics on horseback.

"I've never sat in that kind of saddle before," I tell her when she swings her left leg up and around in a different way than normal. The pommel is long and straight and there are special handles on the back for various tricks. Donut also wears a collar around his neck and extra straps to secure the saddle in place with all the different movements.

"Found it last year when I decided to try this but didn't get too far before I stopped. Delilah's quite experienced already, so I'm just practicin' to be more familiar with how the moves feel, not just what they look like."

She lies across the saddle with her arms glued to her side and legs straight out, and I stand a couple of feet away so I don't get in her way, but still close enough if needed.

"What's this move?" I ask.

She turns her head and grins. "It's just a plank. Keepin' my weight distributed on both sides so he can feel the balance."

"If Delilah's already skilled at this, what does she need a trainer for?"

She sits up and walks Donut as she locks her knees and straightens her back. Then she lifts her right leg over until both are on the same side. I feel like the paparazzi watching her every move and waiting to get the best shot.

"Delilah learned under one of the best trick riders 'round here, Molly Mecca. Throughout high school, she competed and won quite a few awards. But then a few years ago, she got badly hurt and took time off to heal. After that, Molly retired, and Delilah went to Craig to help her get back to where she was. She had the skills and knowledge but lacked the confidence after being down so long."

"And now she's fired Craig and wants you?" I ask, keeping my eyes on her as she switches positions. She's not doing anything overly risky since she's warming Donut up, but I'm still on edge. I don't know what I was thinking of volunteering to do this because I'm going to stroke out before the end of her training. Every time she moves from the left to the right or spins around, I instinctively hold out my hand to catch her.

"As you can imagine, Craig was being Craig. Instead of pointin' out what she needed to work on, he just screamed at her. He'd be a good trainer if he had patience and gave guidance. But instead, he uses scare tactics and threats to get his clients to perform. That doesn't work on most people, and especially not on horses. Delilah needs someone who can tell her what she needs to improve on, help her master those things, and then she'll find that confidence again to get back to where she was. So even if I'm not a professional trick rider, I know enough to see where the disconnect is."

Noah slides onto Donut's butt as she hangs onto the handles at the back of the saddle, and my heart rate increases. One buck and she'd be on her ass.

But Donut keeps his posture as she continues riding and making him comfortable as she maneuvers.

"He seems to be okay with what you're doin'," I say.

"Yeah, I think he remembers last summer. I was worried he wouldn't."

"That doesn't mean you should go thirty miles an hour anytime soon," I warn, not mentally or physically ready for that.

"You worried 'bout me, Mr. Underwood?" She smirks as she pushes her feet up on the saddle and kneels as if she's going to stand. Luckily, though, she doesn't and puts her legs back down.

"Worried I might pass out if you don't go slow."

"You used to be a bull rider, and you're worried about *me* doin' a few baby tricks? I find that fascinatin'."

"That's for eight seconds. Granted, they're the longest eight seconds when you're on top of a two-thousand-pound animal, but I had years of trainin'."

"And I'm willin' to bet ya got hurt quite a bit."

"Yes, I did." I chuckle. "You learn quick how to tuck 'n' roll."

She laughs, moving her feet back up and down as if she's testing Donut's reaction to the quick movements.

"Sorry ahead of time for the name but wait until I try the suicide drag. I didn't get to try it last year and now that I've been watchin' more videos, I wanna see if I can do it."

I nearly swallow my tongue because I can only imagine how risky that move is. "I'd rather ya didn't."

"And why not?"

"Does the name not give it away?"

"It's actually a very common move, but yes, it can be tough at first. I didn't say I was gonna do it today, just that I wanna eventually."

"And what is it exactly?"

"Basically, it's when you hang upside down on the side of the horse as he's gallopin'. One foot goes through the saddle hole as the other hangs over your head, and you drag your hands along the dirt."

I blink a few times, trying to wrap my head around the words she just said, and start to remember seeing the riders perform that move. Their hair flies around as their arms hang over their heads, and they basically bobble across the ground. They have no control of the horse in that position, and they have to continue running without being guided. One wrong move of the horse and their neck could snap.

"Absolutely not, Noah. I don't doubt your talent, but that's too risky."

She rolls her eyes as if my concern lacks merit. "That's why you're here, remember?" She bats her eyelashes as if that'll win me over with this ludicrous idea.

Before I can respond, she jumps up on her feet and stands. Her foot slips momentarily, and I nearly jump a foot toward her but then stop myself. Donut isn't going fast, so I'm able to keep up, but knowing her, she's going to speed up at some point.

"I'm fine, just probably not wearin' the right shoes for this."

I brush a hand through my hair, already feeling my forehead line with sweat and nerves. "You should be in bubble wrap."

"Thank goodness you weren't here for the Barn Roof Trampoline tournaments. You woulda passed out." She keeps her gaze on Donut as she balances her feet firmly on the saddle, but it still makes me uneasy.

Every moment of Lyla rock climbing comes back to the surface. I was overly confident in what I knew she could do, but the moment I let my guard down, I failed her. I should've been closer, not let her go so high, and fuck me, I should've caught her.

"I probably woulda. The name alone sounds dangerous and stupid as hell."

"Wilder, being the obnoxious dumbass he is, did a cannonball and forgot to push his legs out after the first bounce. Instead of landin' on his feet, he flew right into a tree. Got himself a concussion, lots of bruisin', and a broken rib."

"Jesus Christ. I seriously don't know how your parents have survived this long."

"And the bad part is, that didn't even slow him down. A month later, he went to Blackhole Granite and jumped into the quarry. Nearly drowned when he couldn't swim back up in time. Landen and Tripp had to rush in and pull him up. Waylon gave him CPR until he finally coughed up water."

I shake my head. That boy has no fear or reality of risks. How he's survived this long is truly a mystery.

Noah sits back down, does a few easy moves, and then dismounts. My hand instinctively goes to her lower back until her feet are planted safely on the ground.

"There, that wasn't so bad, was it?" She smirks, grabbing Donut's lead rope.

"I'll let ya know when my heart rate goes back to normal."

I should be immune to taking risks and seeing people do stunts on horses, but when it comes to Noah, every little slip or bump has me on edge. I constantly remind myself how talented and skilled she is, but every morning when I meet her in the training center, I have a mini panic attack.

Each day, she gets braver and pushes herself a bit more. She even teaches me some of the stunt names she does—one-foot stand, shoulder stand, vault, the lay-up, forward fender, spin the horn, and more. Donut tolerates it all, and I appreciate how well behaved he is, so I only have to focus on her movements. After a few days, she speeds up, and Donut gallops faster. I keep as close as I can, and even though I'm a nervous wreck, I'm also impressed as hell.

Noah came into this with minimal knowledge, but she did the research ahead of time, put in the time to practice, and continued to do the moves until they felt right. She might not be an expert and wouldn't be performing anytime soon, but she's grasped the basics in just a week's time.

"Pretty soon, I'll be gettin' fit for a sparkly outfit and travelin' to rodeos!" She does a little spin around Donut, and he just stands there, unamused.

"How 'bout ya let Delilah do that, and you stay here where you belong?"

"Where I *belong*, huh? What's that supposed to mean?"

We're only a couple of feet apart, but the air between us is tense enough to slice through.

"Nothin', it's just, I prefer you on the ranch where I can still see you every day."

Her brows pinch together as if she's not sure how to take my words, but she doesn't argue or ask me to clarify.

"I'd miss bein' home anyway, but it'd be fun. Kinda jealous Delilah will get to travel to rodeos and feel all that excitement in the arena with the crowds cheerin'. I bet it's an adrenaline rush each night."

I nod along because she's not wrong. That excitement never dies no matter how many times you do it.

"When are you signin' her on?" I ask, assuming she will since she's been practicing.

"She's scheduled to come this weekend. I'll watch her and see where she's at, then I'll give her a quote, and we'll go from there. I don't suspect she'll need me more than a month or two."

"I don't doubt it. You're pretty good at this."

"*Pretty good...*" she muses with her hands on her hips.

Pulling out my phone, I check the time and see it's close to nine o'clock. That's usually when we wrap up so I can get to work, and she can get started on her training schedule. Though I enjoy every uninterrupted second I get with her. Things are no longer awkward. We're back to being friends, and no one suspects a thing.

I fucking hate it.

I want to rip off her helmet, wrap her in my arms, hold her tight, then steal all her kisses.

But I can't, so I settle for what I can get—heated glances and soft touches.

"You done for the day?" I ask.

Laney, Ayden's wife, went into labor last night and gave birth early this morning, so I know she'll want to go visit sometime today. Right as we were starting, Serena and Mallory burst in here to tell us the exciting news.

Noah looks at the time. "We've got five minutes. I wanna try the suicide drag again but faster."

It's bad enough she did it for the first time a couple of days ago, and if it wasn't for Donut being as tolerable as he is, I would've said hell no. But Noah does what she wants, so I kept up and watched her every move.

"How much faster?"

"Well, enough to drag my hands in the dirt."

Because of the position of the move, she can't wear her helmet. Riders don't during the rodeo either, but for the sake of her practicing, she's kept it on. I contemplate begging her not to do it, but I know it's no use. She won't quit until she tries, and even if she didn't, for my sake, I wouldn't put it past her to do it when I'm not around. I'd rather spot her now so she can be satisfied she accomplished it versus her doing it in private and getting hurt.

"Fine. Not too fast," I warn. "I've got old bull rider knees."

She snorts. "Puttin' that AARP medical plan to good use then, huh?"

"Very funny." I grunt.

I take a deep breath as she swings herself back up on Donut, then gets him into a steady gallop. The arena is large enough that he can gain speed and slow down when Noah needs him to and still have plenty of time before they round a corner.

They ride around one lap before she gives me a thumbs-up, and I know she's about to do it. There's no way I can keep up at their speed, so I just watch and move in a circular motion.

Noah hooks her foot, drops down his side, then hangs her other leg above her head. Her arms fall to the ground as she drags them across the dirt. It happens in less than three seconds, but she stays in that position for at least ten more.

I watch with panic and amazement. I love how quickly she caught on and how she doesn't quit when she puts her mind to something.

She pulls herself up, raises her arms, and grins wide. Smiling proudly, I clap.

When she brings Donut to a stop, she jumps down and leaps

right into my arms. I wrap mine around her, hugging her to my chest and inhaling her shampoo.

"I did it!"

"I knew ya would."

She pulls back slightly, her eyes bright and filled with excitement. A flicker of something comes over her face as she licks her lips. My throat tightens as I swallow the lump stuck there. My hand slides behind her neck, and I'm so goddamn tempted to yank her mouth to mine.

"Hey, Noah!"

At the sound of Tripp's voice, we push apart, and I quickly shove my hands in my pockets.

"You almost done so Landen and I can come in?" he asks.

"Yeah, but I gotta show ya what I just did first!"

"Wait..." I could barely breathe the last time she did it.

She explains the move, then he stands next to me as she hops on and gets Donut going.

"She's gettin' really good," I say to break the silence.

"You two were lookin' quite cozy when I walked in. Somethin' goin' on between y'all?"

When I look at him, he's studying my face as if he's daring me to lie.

"What're ya talkin' about?" Sweat lines my forehead as I try to keep my voice steady.

He pops a brow. "So you're not fuckin' my sister? Not sure how my parents would feel about that if ya were..."

Noah drops into position and shouts at Tripp to watch her. Out of the corner of my eye, I see something on the ground right in Donut's path.

"The hell is that?" I ask, moving closer.

Tripp follows, finally looking at his sister, and it's not until I see it stand up do I realize it's a snake.

"Noah, sit up!" I yell as I rush toward it.

I'm not close enough to get there before Donut sees it, and as soon as he does, he halts and rears up.

"Craig!" Tripp shouts, and I look over to see a shadow by the door.

Tripp takes off toward him as I try to grab Donut's reins, but he's spooked and takes off running with Noah still attached.

"My foot's stuck!" Noah yells as she fights to lift herself.

My heart pounds as I put my arms up and use verbal commands to get Donut to stop. I wish Tripp had stayed and gotten rid of the snake so the horse would calm the hell down. Everything's so chaotic, and I don't know how to keep Donut from bucking.

"Relax your foot!" I tell her, hoping it's enough for her to slide it out if he rears again.

Each time she attempts to reach for the pommel, he jumps, and she gets slammed back down.

I feel so goddamn helpless at how fast he's moving. The arena's too large to keep up with him.

When he rounds the next corner, I rush to get in his view and hold up my arms to hopefully get his attention to stop. He groans as his speed decreases, and I walk toward him, reaching for his reins.

Before I can grab them, Noah drops to the ground with a thud.

"Noah! Get up!"

Just as she attempts to move, the snake returns, and Donut loses his shit. He rears back, squealing, and when he goes down, his hooves land on Noah's side with a crunch.

"Fuck!"

Noah screams as she curls into a ball. She tries talking to Donut, but he's inconsolable.

I grab her wrists and drag her out of his stomping way until I can lift her. The snake is still harassing Donut, and there's no way to get him to calm down without someone removing it. But my only priority is getting Noah out of here.

She groans as I rush us outside.

"I think my ankle's fucked up," she tells me with tears in her eyes.

"I'm more worried about your ribs, baby. Pretty sure I heard a crack."

"Me too. They hurt like a motherfucker." She winces in my arms as I try to open my truck door.

Knowing she probably can't stand on her foot, I lay her down in the back seat.

"My head is throbbin'," she says painfully.

"Noah, look at me." I smack her hand a few times until she does. "Keep your eyes open, got it? I'm takin' you to the ER."

She blinks slowly as if she's fighting the urge to close them.

"Eyes. Open. You can do it, baby."

"Where y'all goin'?" Tripp asks from behind me.

I slam the door shut and resist the urge to sock him for leaving his sister behind.

"Donut got spooked and kicked the shit outta her." I hop in the front seat and roll down the window. "You need to get that snake outta there, then put Donut back. He's scared."

"Oh shit. She got hurt?" He removes his cap and rubs through his wild hair.

"Yeah, she was hangin' on the side of a horse when he bucked and reared. Her foot was stuck, and I couldn't get him to calm down. Tell your parents I'm takin' her to the ER."

I don't waste another second, resisting the urge to chew him a new one, and put my truck in drive. Glancing back, I check on her and remind her to look at me.

"Everythin' hurts."

Her little pained whimpers have my heart seizing as flashbacks surface of when I hauled Lyla into the back seat of my truck. Even though it was clear she was gone, I hung on to hope the entire walk back and drive to the hospital.

I refuse to lose Noah. She's the love of my life, and even if we can't be together, I can't go through another heartbreak. I wouldn't survive it this time.

The impact of Donut breaking her ribs could've punctured a lung or blood vessel. She could have internal bleeding into her chest cavity for all I know. The long list of possibilities terrifies me.

Reaching back, I grab her hand. "Squeeze the pain away, love. Don't let go."

Chapter Twenty-Seven

Noah

I consider myself to have a high pain tolerance, but goddamn, everything hurts like a motherfucker. The nurse was in here at some point and gave me more pain meds, but they wore off, and now I need a double dose.

My hand fumbles around as I feel for the call button. As soon as I groan, Fisher's on his feet and at my bedside.

"What do ya need, baby?" he asks.

"Pain..." I whimper, trying to hold my eyes open.

"More meds? Okay, hold on."

He presses the button and asks if I need to readjust, but the thought of it has me shaking my head. Every inch feels like a mile, and I'd rather not move unless I have to.

The nurse enters with a smile, but her eyes linger on Fisher a moment longer than necessary. Of course he's oblivious to it as he keeps all his focus on me. If I had an ounce of strength to spare, I'd tell her to keep her flirty gaze off him. But as long as she delivers what I need, I'll save scolding her for another time.

"Hi, Noah." Her voice is low but bubbly. "I have more morphine for you, but it's gonna make you drowsy."

"Good," I whisper.

"Once I'm done, I'll replace your ice packs. That should help your ribs."

I manage to nod because it's all I can do. My head pounds from the mild concussion, which is what the morphine is supposed to help with, along with every other inch of my body that's suffering.

Everything was pure chaos from the moment Fisher carried me into the ER. They put me on a stretcher and rolled me into a room for a full-body examination. I remember screaming in pain as they checked my ankle and ribs. Once an x-ray ruled out any internal bleeding from my ribs, they took me in for a CT scan and found a fracture in my ankle. Then they wrapped it until a specialist could look at it to determine whether I need surgery.

My parents arrived within an hour of my being admitted and have been talking to the doctors about a recovery plan. I already know I'm going to have to stay off my foot for six to eight weeks, but I don't want to hear it. Someone like me doesn't have time to sit around for two months.

As soon as the meds hit my system, every part of me relaxes, and I grin.

"Better?" Fisher asks, brushing his hand over my cheek.

"Yeah. Can ya tell the doctor my ankle's fine, and I won't be needin' surgery?"

"Considerin' it's black and blue, swelled up to the size of my fist, I doubt he's gonna believe that."

I frown. "Nothin' ice can't fix."

He brushes loose strands of hair around my ear and smiles weakly. "Sorry, love. Even without surgery, they're gonna tell you to stay off it. No gettin' around that."

I groan and drop it for now. "Is Donut alright? What about the snake?"

"Tripp got him to calm down and brought him back to his stall. He was shaken up, so they called the vet to give him some sedatives. The snake was found and disposed of."

It's a miracle Donut didn't hurt himself, and I'm thankful he's at least okay.

"Was there only one? Where'd it come from?"

"That's all I saw, but your brothers are searchin' the entire trainin' center and other barns to be sure. Tripp saw Craig by the barn doors. He musta released it, then waited to make sure Donut reacted."

"God, he's like a parasite that won't go away. I remember Tripp rushin' out. Did he find him?"

"No. Tripp called the sheriff, and they're on high alert for him. He wasn't at his house when they went to question him."

I groan at the thought of him still on the loose. "I didn't even do anythin' to him."

"My best guess this time is he's pissed about Delilah. He somehow knew you'd be practicin'."

"He's not gonna quit till he kills me," I say, and then my eyes get too heavy to keep them open.

"Well, the good news is you don't need surgery. The bad news is you will if you don't stay off your foot. Rest is key." The doctor looks at me, and I want to argue that I can't be off that long. But with my parents, Gramma Grace, and Fisher standing in the room, there's no fighting it.

They're going to make me stop training until I'm fully healed.

"I'll make sure she stays off it," Fisher says, and I hold my breath as I wait for my parents' reaction. "I feel responsible for what happened. The least I can do is help her through the recovery."

We haven't had more than a couple of moments alone to talk, but I see him struggling with the guilt and the reminder of what happened with his daughter. As soon as Donut reared and I felt my foot get stuck, I immediately thought about how this would affect Fisher and tried like hell to get myself out. I hadn't expected Donut to pummel me, or I would've tried harder to move faster.

Gramma grins as she looks back and forth between us, and I swear, she knows something.

"It's not your fault, Mr. Underwood," Momma tells him. "I told her trick ridin' was dangerous."

I nearly roll my eyes out of my head. "Ridin' always is when there's a snake in the arena. Wouldn't matter if I was sittin' on him regularly or hangin' off the side."

"If that were the case, you wouldn't have this many injuries." She tsks.

I don't bother arguing since I've already told her the full story.

"We'll send you home with some painkillers for the discomfort, but ultimately, time and patience are your key to healin'," the doctor says.

Two things I don't have right now.

Once the nurse brings in my discharge papers, Dad pulls around his truck, and they roll me outside in a wheelchair. They're sending me home with crutches and a boot I already want to rip off.

"Oh God." I wince, sucking in a sharp breath. Breaking three ribs on the same side is a pain I've never experienced before.

"Take it easy now," Momma says when I try to stand on my own.

Fisher's at my side, holding me up with one hand and resting his other on my back as I hunch over.

"Can you jump in?" he asks softly.

I look up at the open door. "Doubtful."

Without another word, he wraps an arm underneath my knees and lifts me. I quickly grab his shoulders as he carries me the last two feet to the truck and sets me down on the seat.

"No point in makin' ya suffer when I can help you inside

myself," he says as if to explain it aloud with my parents behind him.

"So strong, Fisher." Mom squeezes his bicep. "Don't be strainin' your back while liftin' her now."

"Gee, thanks, Momma," I deadpan, struggling to buckle myself in.

She stands next to him as Dad puts my crutches in the back. "Oh, honey. You know what I mean. You're all muscle."

I know I'm being sensitive, but I just want to go home and lie in my own bed. My mother fussed over me all day while Fisher beat himself up over me getting hurt. We all know it's not his fault, but no matter how many times I say it, he argues how he should've handled it differently.

The only thing that needs to be handled is Craig and as soon as Sheriff Wagner finds him, I'm pressing charges for trespassing and assault with intent to harm. With all the new cameras installed, we'll get a clean shot of his face this time. He's going to pay for sabotaging my career and for scaring my precious Donut. I'm going to visit him at the family barn as soon as I can so he knows I'm not mad at him.

"I'll meet ya at your house," Fisher says when Momma walks away.

"You don't have to take care of me," I say firmly. "This isn't your fault, and I'm not your burden."

His eyes darken as his jaw clenches, and I worry he's going to blurt something in front of my parents that'll cross the line.

But then he leans in close to my ear and murmurs, "You will *never* be a burden to me, Goldie. I would give up the privilege of breathin' if it meant takin' an ounce of your pain away."

It's not fair he says these sweet, caring things to me, and I can't express them back. He ended the relationship, losing his right to speak that way to me.

"You comfortable, sweetheart?" Dad asks, hopping in the driver's seat.

"Yeah, I'm fine," I lie.

Momma and Gramma get in the back seat, and Fisher helps shut their door.

"I'm gonna run to the grocery store. Figure she can't stock up her fridge, so I'll make sure she has everythin' she needs," Fisher tells my family.

"That'd be very kind, thank you," Momma says.

I stare at him, biting my tongue to tell him not to bother. The last person I want around me when I'm not feeling my best is a man I'm in love with and can't have. I have four brothers who could help. Plus, Magnolia is ready to quit her job to help me full-time. Honestly, she just wants an excuse to tell Mrs. Blanche to stick it where the sun doesn't shine, but I told her not to bother since Fisher designated himself as my personal nurse.

"Make sure you call Mallory and Serena. They've been worried sick about ya. Serena was in the ER with her grandma when Fisher brought you in," Momma says.

"She was?"

"They were just leavin' from seein' the baby. Mimi said Fisher was pale as a ghost and frazzled when he tried to explain what happened."

My heart shatters at the memory of him carrying me to his truck. I could barely keep my eyes open, and he told me to squeeze his hand until the pain went away.

I didn't let go until they brought me back into a room and told Fisher he had to wait.

Magnolia sits next to me as I lie propped up with some pillows and sulk about not being able to go to the barn to see Donut. As soon as I got in bed, I took off the boot and literally crawled under my covers.

Once Fisher showed up with bags of groceries, my parents and Gramma left so I could rest, but there's no way I can sleep soundly with him in here. I texted Mallory and FaceTimed with Serena before Magnolia came over. My brothers sent me a group text, all betting how long until I go stir-crazy.

I won at only an hour.

"He's been in there for thirty minutes cookin' ya dinner," Magnolia says. "Smells damn good, too."

"I wish he wouldn't. I don't have much of an appetite," I admit, wincing when I accidentally use my bad foot to push myself up higher.

She jumps to her feet in a panic. "What do ya need? Another pillow? More ice?"

"More meds. Fisher has them in the kitchen."

"Got it, be right back."

When she leaves, I maneuver myself to the edge of the mattress and reach for my crutches. I've never used them before, so as soon as I lift my foot, I fall back into the bed.

I can hear Magnolia talking to Fisher in the kitchen and figure I have enough time before she comes back.

Not wanting to ask for help, I readjust myself until I have them secure under my arms, then try again. I get to the hallway before I slam into the wall and knock over one of my framed photos.

"Noah!" Fisher rushes out of the kitchen with a spatula in his hand. "What're ya doin'?"

"I was just comin' back," Magnolia follows.

"I have to pee. Is that okay or am I not allowed?"

Fisher hands Magnolia the utensil before grabbing my crutches and handing those to her next.

"Hey, I need those."

Silently, he lifts me into his arms and walks me the rest of the way to the bathroom. Surely, he's not doing what I think he's doing.

"This is ridiculous," I tell him when he places me on my feet in front of the toilet.

"Can you lower your shorts or do you want me to?"

"I think I got it from here." I bite my lower lip, not wanting to admit how much it hurts to move.

"Why're you lyin' to me? Just let me help you."

"Excuse me for not wantin' to pee in front of you. I don't like bein' waited on," I admit.

"I'm not waitin' on you. You never minded me takin' off your clothes before."

I shove my fist in his chest. "You know what I mean. Can I have some privacy, please?"

"I've kissed, licked, and seen every inch of you."

A shiver runs up my spine at the memory of our last time. "Well, let's not add this to the long list of things you've seen or done."

"Noah." He cracks a smile. "Let me pull them down for you, then I'll leave."

The urge to go gets stronger, so I stop arguing and nod. "Fine. But don't look."

He chuckles as he kneels in front of me, loops his fingers in my panties and shorts, then closes his eyes.

Slowly, he lowers them down my thighs and the soft touches of his thumbs brushing my bare legs nearly have me moaning. He's careful not to touch my ankle as he stands.

"Do you wanna lean on me to sit?"

"Oh my God, no. I'd like some dignity left."

Smirking, he keeps his eyes shut. "Fine, I'll be out in the hallway. Shout when you're done."

He shuts the door behind him, but it only closes halfway. I'm too desperate to yell at him, so I don't bother. Sitting on the toilet is more painful than I expected, but I bite my lip to keep from groaning.

Once I'm finished, I manage to pull my shorts up as I stand

and balance against the counter. Then I hobble to the sink and wash my hands.

"You're done?" Fisher barges in, startling me.

"Jesus. Yes."

Without warning, he lifts me into his arms, and I settle against his chest.

"This is unnecessary. I need to learn how to use the crutches." I hug around him tighter, enjoying his warmth.

"And ya will, but it's only your first day home. You're still drowsy from the morphine and the last thing you need is to get hurt worse."

When he brings us into my bedroom, Magnolia stands from the bed and fluffs the pillows before he lays me down.

She grins at me with a brow arched as she looks back and forth between Fisher and me. I know what she's thinking, but she's wrong. Fisher and I can't be anything more than friends, and if I've accepted it, then so does she.

"I have your meds, a fresh ice pack, and I downloaded a new monster smut to your app. You're welcome." Magnolia puts everything on my nightstand while Fisher elevates my foot.

"How dare you not bring me my rose vibrator with the smut!" I mock.

"I was trynna be discreet, but fine, here ya go." She pulls it out of her bra and sets it on top of my Kindle."

I cackle, then immediately wince at the tightness it causes in my chest and side. "No more makin' me laugh."

Fisher eyes the toy, then me, and I look away. Not like I could actually use it in my condition and was only joking. I didn't think Magnolia would really bring it out here from my shower.

"I'm gonna go check on dinner." Fisher walks away, leaving Magnolia and me alone.

"That man is a goner for ya..." She shakes her head at me as if the breakup was my decision. "Shoulda heard Gramma Grace when you were knocked out. She knows about y'all."

"How?"

"She said somethin' about it being how he looks at you and how worried he is cements that she's right. Your parents weren't around, but I acted clueless, and she smirked like she knew I was playin' dumb."

"Well, she can join the club and be disappointed when she learns it's over."

"I know that's what y'all think has to happen, but I think Jase could handle it. He might be mad for a bit, but I don't see him wantin' to get in the way of your happiness."

"Two weeks ago, he got into a fistfight with my brothers when he thought I was seein' someone," I remind her.

"Yes, and then he apologized and said he wanted to be *friends*."

"It's not my decision. Fisher has to be the one to tell him. He's the one who'd be riskin' their relationship and I can't ask him to do that knowin' everythin' he's gone through to get back in his life."

"I can ask him." She stands, but I quickly grab her wrist and pull her back down.

She laughs when I scold her. "If it's meant to be, we'll find a way. Otherwise, I'd like to get over the heartbreak and move on."

She hitches a thumb over her shoulder toward my bedroom door. "With Mr. Tall, Dark, and Rugged in your kitchen makin' you a feast? Good luck, bestie. You have more willpower than I do. I'd be on my knees, beggin' him to *pick me, choose me, love me*."

Her mimicking a *Grey's Anatomy* quote has me laughing, and I scowl at her for making my ribs hurt again.

"Sorry, I can't help it. I'm just *naturally* witty."

"Mm-hmm."

"If ya don't need anythin' else from me, I'll go and let y'all have your *Lady and the Tramp* moment while he feeds you pasta." She waggles her brows as she gets to her feet.

"I can eat on my own, thank you very much."

"And I can sing like a pro, but I'd still let Justin Bieber give me singin' lessons if it meant I got to spend time with him.

Preferably naked." The corner of her lips tilts up deviously as she walks toward the door.

"Go away, home-wrecker."

"Team Selena!" she shouts as she walks down the hallway.

"Do I even wanna know what that was about?" Fisher asks, setting a large serving tray on my bed.

"Just Magnolia...being Magnolia." I dig my palms into the mattress and use all my strength to push up so I can sit. "What'd you make?"

"Parmesan chicken bowtie with garlic toast."

"Damn, that sounds so good."

He brings the plate up and grabs one of the forks.

"Smells delicious," I say, suddenly starving.

"Try it and see." He holds out a forkful, and I stare at it, wanting to argue that he doesn't need to feed me. But I'm too tired to fight, so I open my mouth and let him.

Chapter Twenty-Eight

Fisher

Noah's stubborn as shit, but after four days of me coming over, she's finally accepting my help. I've kept her fed, done her laundry, vacuumed, and dusted, all while trying to keep my emotions in check. Being just friends with the person who owns my soul is as torturous as it sounds, but I refuse to leave unless it's for work. Sleeping on her uncomfortable and too small couch is miserable as fuck, but I deal with it so she isn't alone all night.

I've cut my workdays down to five hours and start at seven in the morning so I can be here by noon. Her family and Magnolia visit while I'm gone, so she always has someone around. I know she hates it, but she needs to stay off her ankle for it to heal properly. She's gotten better at using her crutches and is down to only taking meds twice a day. All good things but all highly unlikely if she were left to her own devices.

"Can you take me to see Donut today?" she asks as I make chicken pesto wraps for lunch.

"You ready to go that far?"

"I need to get out of this house. I'm goin' stir-crazy." She throws her head back and groans. "Plus, if I so much as flinch, you'll be there to grab me."

Her smart-ass tone makes me smile. "Maybe not. Fallin' on your butt might do ya some good."

"Aww...is someone feelin' underappreciated?"

Setting her food down on the table, I bring my mouth to her ear. "You show me you do each day you allow me to stay in your life." I release my grip on the plate and step back. "I'll take ya after we eat."

I clean up the counter, then sit across from her.

"Thank you for lunch. It smells delicious." Her stomach growls when she takes a big bite, and I laugh when she gets pesto all over her mouth.

"When's the last time you ate?" I lean over and brush my thumb across her bottom lip, then lick it off.

We stare at each other, and she swallows hard. "Last night when you made dinner."

I sit back in my chair. "Gramma Grace didn't bring you breakfast this mornin'?"

"She had an appointment in town, and I told Momma I was fine by myself for a few hours."

"So no one was here?"

She smirks, taking a sip of her coffee. "Nope, and look at me, I survived."

"So I guess ya didn't hear about Craig, then?"

"What 'bout him?" She narrows her eyes, all the sass out of her tone.

"He was granted bail this mornin'." I clench my jaw at the thought of him being on the loose after only spending a night behind bars. Sheriff Wagner arrested him two days ago after finding him at his family's cabin an hour away. The judge didn't consider the charge serious enough to make the bail amount that high, so now he'll be free until his preliminary hearing.

"Great... he'll come after me when I'm down to one foot."

"The sheriff said he acted deranged when he picked him up. I told your brothers and parents on my way in, so everyone's on guard now. In fact, when your father stopped by the barn, he was carryin' his shotgun around."

"Jesus Christ." She shakes her head.

"Don't worry. I've turned on camera notifications, so if he's dumb enough to show his face 'round here, we won't miss it."

She's silent for a moment as she looks down at her food, then back at me. "Do you still carry?"

I finish chewing my food and wipe my mouth before responding. "You really want the answer to that?"

"Probably not."

Given my history with guns, Damien got rid of mine when I was in the hospital. It wasn't until years later when I was on the road a lot that I got a new one and kept it secure in my truck.

After we finish eating, I help her get dressed, all with my eyes closed as requested. Then I carry her to my truck and drive the short distance to the family barn.

"I got it," she says once she gets out, and I hand her the crutches.

It's not that she can't use them, but her ribs are still sore. One wrong move and she tumbles to the ground again. Though I wouldn't let that happen since I'm two inches away.

When I open the barn door and she goes through, I'm back at her side as she hops toward Donut's stall. As soon as he sees her, he starts whining and squealing.

Noah beams as she slowly makes her way toward him. As soon as she reaches him, she puts a hand out, and he smells it.

"I think he missed ya," I say softly.

She smiles wide. "I missed you, too, boy."

Noah pets his neck, then his nose nudges one of her crutches.

"That wasn't your fault, Donut. None of it was, okay? We're gonna get the guy who did it. I know you didn't mean to hurt me."

He leans his head against hers as she continues rubbing him. It's a sweet moment. Their bond and unconditional trust are unlike anything I've witnessed before.

I stand back as they share a few more tender moments.

"Love you, boy. I'll be back for ya as soon as I can." She kisses him, wipes her cheek, then turns and walks toward the door.

"Are you okay?" I ask as we drive back to her house.

She stares out her window and nods.

Reaching over, I squeeze her leg. "We're gonna get justice, Noah. He won't hurt you or Donut ever again."

"I wish I could believe that…" she murmurs.

She's down right now, but I'll do whatever it takes to protect her and won't rest until Craig gets what he deserves.

Once we're back in her house, she lies down and sleeps for a few hours. I rest on the couch, then get started on dinner. I stopped at the store after work and picked up more of her favorites.

She's quiet while we eat, and I don't push her to talk, but she doesn't need to for me to know she's struggling with this. Noah used to be active all day, every day, and being stuck at home with only one foot and broken ribs is a drastic change. I've gone through similar situations when I'd get hurt and have to stay away from riding for weeks at a time, sometimes months, while my body recovered.

"I'm gonna take a shower. Could you unwrap my ankle for me?" she asks after I clean up the kitchen.

"You're ready for that?"

She's been doing sponge baths to avoid standing on one foot in the shower.

"I need to wash my hair, and I feel gross overall. Just because we're on a ranch doesn't mean I wanna smell like one twenty-four seven."

"Alright, but you can't go in there alone. One slip and you'll snap your ankle."

"I won't put pressure on it," she argues. "I'll hold on to the rail and wash one-handed."

"Noah." I cross my arms and stand firm. "Just let me help you. I can do your hair."

"You bein' in there with your eyes closed sounds more dangerous than just lettin' me do it myself."

I lick my lips and rub my jawline in amusement. "I'd keep them open."

"Absolutely not." She shakes her head.

Fuck, she's so damn hardheaded. "Takin' care of you and keepin' you safe are my top priorities, Goldie. I know ya don't like it but too goddamn bad. Your parents are countin' on me, and I'm not about to let them down a second time."

She inhales sharply like she wants to argue but rolls her eyes instead. "*Fine*. But ya sneak one little peek below the neck, and I won't think twice about kneein' you."

I smirk because she's lost her mind if she thinks I can thoroughly wash her without looking. "Deal."

We go into the bathroom, and I offer to help her undress, but she swats my hand away and tells me to turn around. I comply, but I'm only a few inches away just in case. She winces, and I feel a sharp pain in my chest.

"Are you ready? Can I turn around?"

"Yeah."

I do my best to keep my eyes toward the ceiling while I take her hand and help her step inside the shower.

"Keep that foot up. Get into the middle and hold on to the rail."

I don't want her hopping around with water on the floor, so once she's settled, I turn the knob.

She jumps. "Shit, that's cold."

"Sorry, it's turned all the way to hot. Should warm up in a minute."

Stepping back onto the mat, I remove my shirt, then unbutton my jeans.

"What're ya doin'?" She holds out her palm to block her view.

"You expect me to get in there with my clothes on?"

She flickers her gaze to mine before shifting away. "I hadn't thought about that, obviously."

"Well, if I can keep my eyes above the neck, then so can you." I smirk, knowing she'll be tempted.

"Fine. But hurry up and close the door because I'm freezin'."

As soon as I'm naked, I meet her inside. We stare at each other, and I wonder if she's remembering the last time we were in here together.

A moment that'll be embedded into my memory for the rest of my life.

I wrap a hand around her good side and stabilize her. "Tilt your head back and get your hair wet."

My eyes lower to her pierced nipples as she brushes her fingers through her scalp. When she straightens, I snap my head back up. "What do ya want me to do first?"

"Um...you can start with the shampoo. It's the white bottle."

Turning around, I squeeze some into my palm, and when I return, I find her gaze was on my ass.

I arch a brow, rubbing my palms together. "You forget the rules already?"

"No. I had somethin' in my eye." She blinks a few times, and I stifle a laugh.

I massage my fingers into her scalp, and she tilts her head back with a moan. The water hits her just right, and I help rinse it out.

"Conditioner?" I ask.

"Black bottle."

I repeat the process, but this time, I take extra care slathering it into her ends before rinsing it out.

"I forgot to grab a washcloth," she says when I reach for her body wash.

"Guess you'll have to suffer with my rough hands." I grin when she groans at the harsh calluses.

Keeping eye contact, I begin with her neck and move to her chest, making sure to be as thorough as possible. Her heart races under my palm before I slide down between her breasts. The temptation to touch her the way I crave is so intense, I have to count to ten in my head to keep my dick from stabbing her.

The hot water on her back steams up the shower, and although I'm nearly freezing, I don't show it. I'd freeze to death before leaving her in here.

Next, I grab her free arm, and inch by inch, I rub my way to her ribs. It's not until I lower my eyes do I notice how big her bruise is there.

"Fuck, Noah."

"You're not supposed to be lookin'," she mouths off.

"You broke the rules first."

My focus stays on her stomach, being extra careful not to press too hard, and then I switch to her other arm.

"Hold on to me as I do this one," I tell her, taking her hand off the rail and wrapping her fingers around my bicep. Once I finish, I do the same routine on the other side.

I secure her back into position, grab more soap, then drop to my knees.

Her lips twitch as if she's eager to remind me where I shouldn't look, but as soon as I touch the inside of her thigh, she parts her lips and moans.

She's not the only one suffering.

Her sweet pussy is nearly in my face. Restraining from touching her is the worst form of self-torture, but I continue anyway. I drag my thumbs down her leg, then gently rub the soap around her ankle and foot.

She gasps, and I look up. "Shit, sorry. You okay?"

"Yeah, just tender."

"I'm movin' to your other leg. Keep this foot up," I remind her.

I start at her toes, then work my way up. When I get to her inner thigh, I dig my thumbs in deeper to massage her muscles. Her stomach tightens as I move up and carefully cover every inch of untouched skin.

Standing, I detach the showerhead and clear the soap off the front of her body.

"Doin' okay still?" I ask as she fidgets on one foot.

She nods with shallow breaths as I put the water pressure against her clit.

"How about now?" I mutter, gripping her hip.

"Oh God." Her eyes flutter closed as her head tilts.

Just because *I* can't give her an orgasm doesn't mean I can't help her get there.

"Don't fight it, my love," I whisper in her ear as I cup the back of her neck. "Give in to the pleasure."

"I thought you were worried about me fallin'."

"I've got you, baby." I tighten my hold. "Fall apart as much as you need."

She squeezes my arm as she finally surrenders, and soon, she's teetering off the edge, panting through the release.

"Thatta girl." I remove the water pressure and press a kiss to her temple. "I'm gonna wash your other side now."

Once I put up the showerhead and adjust the spray, I help her turn around so I can soap her back. As much as I want to take my time again, I know she's getting antsy having to keep her foot up.

"All done." I turn off the water, then step out to grab the towels. Once I wrap one around my waist, I help dry her hair and put another around her body.

Instead of handing her the crutches, I scoop her up and carry her out.

"I can hop," she says when I walk toward her bedroom.

"On a wet foot? No. Usin' crutches while you're soakin' wet and grippin' a towel on? Also no." I arch a brow. "You'll be back in the ER, gettin' prepped for surgery."

She grinds her teeth and groans. "This sucks."

After I set her down on the mattress, she holds the towel in place by crossing her arms and legs. She's less than amused that she can't do things on her own, and I know that struggle all too well.

"Noah." I grab her attention, then kneel so we're at eye level. "I understand being taken care of and looked after is hard. You're independent, you thrive bein' on a schedule, and you're not built to sit around and do nothin'. Those are just a few of the qualities I adore about you. When I got injured, I hated every fuckin' minute of being off work. But the one thing I've learned is that the worse attitude you have, the more miserable you'll be. So when I'm tough on you, it's because I know what happens when you don't follow instructions and fuck yourself up even more. I want you to heal as fast as possible so you can get your annoyin' ass back in the arena."

She licks her lips before sucking her bottom one between her teeth. "That's not why I'm frustrated."

"Okay, then tell me. What's goin' on?"

"You broke my heart." She pauses and lowers her gaze as if getting the words out is more painful than her ankle. "Each day you're here takin' care of me only adds to the reasons I fell for you in the first place. But I can't act on those feelings. You're off-limits, and keepin' my distance is another level of torture. I don't mean to come off as ungrateful because I'm not, but your being here is a constant reminder of what I can't have. Most girls get to go through heartbreak and cry themselves to sleep in the privacy of their own room. I can't get over it when the person who caused the pain basically lives in my house, treatin' me like a queen, and makin' me wish I didn't give up so easily. So when I say *this sucks*, it's because I wanna kiss you every second you're here. And I can't."

Her voice cracks as tears fall down her cheeks, and I swear I forget how to breathe. Her words are a dagger to my heart, and I hate myself for what I've done to her.

I should've realized how hard this would be for her and not insisted on being the one to take care of her. But I felt so damn guilty that she got hurt on my watch, and I couldn't prevent her injuries when I'd promised to protect her.

Grabbing her hand, I bring it up to my mouth and kiss her knuckles. I contemplate saying fuck it and telling Jase right now that I'm in love with Noah, but he's not the only obstacle we'd have to navigate. Her parents would have to accept their daughter with a man twice her age and hopefully not fire me.

"I'm so sorry that me being here is causin' you more heartache. If I could change the circumstances, I would. I don't wanna be the root of your pain, so if ya want, I won't stay here anymore. I'll tell everyone I have to get back to my other clients. I'm sure Magnolia would love nothin' more than to quit her job and take care of you twenty-four seven. Whatever you want, Noah."

She lowers her eyes and nods. "I think that'd be best."

"Alright. I don't wanna leave you alone tonight, but first thing tomorrow, I'll make sure someone's here."

With Craig out to get Noah, there's no way she's spending even one night alone.

"Can ya help me get dressed?" she asks after I change back into my clothes.

"Of course. What do you wanna wear?"

She points out a baggy T-shirt, and then I find her a pair of panties and get her settled into bed. I grab her an ice pack for her ribs, then prop her foot up on a pillow.

"You look cozy. All good?"

"Actually..." She fidgets, clearing her throat and sitting up higher. "Would ya mind stayin' in here and watchin' a movie with me? I know I just asked you to leave, but if this is your last night, maybe we can hang out for a couple of hours? Except this time I get to pick somethin' out since you made me watch Underboard."

I chuckle, threading my fingers through my damp hair and counting the dozens of ways this is a bad idea. "*Overboard*."

"Yeah, that." She waves me off, then pulls back the covers.

Crossing my arms, I say, "Depends. What is it?"

She grabs her Apple remote and flips through her apps until she lands on an image of Taylor Swift. I arch a brow, looking back and forth between her and the screen.

"It's time you get educated on *Miss Americana*."

We spend the next hour and a half lying side by side in her bed, and all I can think about is how I've let her down. She watches with tears in her eyes, and I can't tell if it's for the documentary or for us.

"Wasn't it so inspirin' and tragically beautiful?"

"It was really good."

I don't admit that I mostly watched her reactions out of the corner of my eye and spent ninety minutes memorizing every flawless inch of her face.

"Mallory and Serena make me watch it once a month." She giggles. "And then we blast her music and dance until the sugar high wears off."

"I thought Mallory was the Swiftie?"

"Where do ya think she learned it from?"

I laugh with her. "They're lucky to have you."

"I've been super busy this summer and haven't been around as much. I need to change that. Ayden and Laney's reception is next month, and I was helpin' them plan it."

"Well, right now, all you need to do is rest."

"I haven't even seen the new baby. Maybe I'll have Momma take me tomorrow."

My shoulders tense as I think about her leavin' the house without my help, but I can't hang on to that fear. She needs to learn how to get around and figure out what she can tolerate without me telling her.

"I think that's a great idea."

She jolts back with an amused grin. "You do?"

Lifting a shoulder, I smile. "Yeah."

Once I help her get comfortable again, I make sure she has

everything she needs, then double-check that everything's locked up.

"G'night, Noah." I stand in her doorway.

After a moment of silence, she clears her throat. "I wish I could hate you for makin' me fall in love with you, but you're the Taylor Lautner of exes."

"Am I supposed to know what that means?"

The corner of her lips curves up. "He's the favorite ex of Taylor Swift because he's unproblematic and treated her like royalty."

"Guess I'll take that as a compliment."

She smiles and nods. "Good night, Fisher."

Chapter Twenty-Nine

Fisher

I haven't seen Noah in two days unless you count parking outside her house and sleeping in my truck all night like a stalker, but I don't think it does.

That first night away from her, I couldn't stop thinking about how Craig could come onto the property to mess with her or even break into her house. It made it impossible for me to sleep at home, so I drove over at midnight and watched her house from a distance until I passed out.

I did the same thing last night, except I didn't even bother trying to go to bed. Just came over at ten and stayed until her mom and Gramma Grace showed up at eight.

"Rough night?" Landen asks.

I'm in the middle of trimming a hoof when he approaches me. When I look up, his arms are crossed, and he wears an amused grin.

"No. Why do ya ask?"

He shrugs, but amusement is written all over his face. "You look tired, is all."

"Nah, I'm fine."

He steps toward me and puts a hand on my shoulder. "I'll put a small air mattress in your truck for ya. Should fit in the back and be a helluva lot more comfortable than your front seat."

I keep my head down as I continue working, then clear my throat. There's no point denying it since he seems to know anyway. "Thanks."

"I appreciate you watchin' out for her. She's stubborn and will probably tell you she doesn't need the help."

"Yeah, I've noticed."

"And if something's goin' on between y'all, you better come clean before my parents find out on their own."

"There isn't."

I keep my focus on Ranger's hoof. Ellie asked if I'd keep an eye on the infected hoof and clean it out. I suspect he'll be ready for training again in a few weeks.

Landen chuckles. "Alright, man. Have a good one."

When he walks away, I look around to see if anyone else was listening. Luckily, we were alone. I don't blame him for not believing me, even if it is the truth, but I don't need anyone else getting suspicious.

Even though I'm not staying with Noah, I told her to let me know if she needed anything. She texted earlier asking if I'd run to the store and grab a few things. I was happy to do it for her, and it gives me an excuse to see her.

After finishing up for the day, I go home and clean up before heading into town. I look over her list and freeze when I see the word *condoms*. And if that isn't bad enough, next to it in parentheses is *the biggest size there is.*

She has to be messing with me.

Regardless, like the whipped man I am, I grab a pack of Magnum XL.

When I arrive at her house, Jase's truck is parked in front, and I contemplate returning later. But the perishables in the bags could go bad, so I suck it up and get out.

He knows I've been helping her and how guilty I felt when she got hurt on my watch, so he shouldn't suspect anything. I'll keep my distance, put her food away, then get out.

"Hey," I greet, walking in with my hands full.

Noah's on the couch, and Jase sits close next to her.

"Hey, old man. You lookin' extra nice today. You got a hot date tonight or what?" Jase's snarky tone has me grinding my teeth so I don't say anything I'll regret.

"Nah, just changed after work so I didn't come smellin' like a barn." I set the bags on the counter and start unloading stuff.

Jase continues talking to Noah about work and closing on his house next week. Then he asks if she'd help him pick out furniture and decor. She tells him about Pinterest and other websites to look at for ideas, but if he wants her to go with him, it'll have to wait until she's more physically stable.

When he goes on about other random stuff, I try to tune them out instead of eavesdropping. I know they're friends now, but I still wonder if he'll eventually want more.

Once everything's put away, sans the condoms, I head toward the door to leave. "If you need anything' else, Noah, just let me know."

"Thank you, Mr. Underwood. I appreciate it." She looks at me like she's staring into my soul.

"No problem."

"I was gonna attempt to make her supper," Jase chimes in. "You wanna stay?"

My gut tenses at the thought of another awkward dinner. "Maybe another time. I've got some errands to run. You two have fun, though."

With a forced smile, I walk out and blow out a breath.

The only *errand* I need to do is take a long-ass nap before returning tonight.

I wake up disoriented at ten o'clock with a couple of missed calls and text messages from Noah. Fearing the worst, I return the call without reading her messages first, but then it goes to voicemail.

NOAH

Why are there condoms on my kitchen counter?

NOAH

Magnum XL?!

NOAH

You must think very highly of yourself.

NOAH

Either that or you think I should be sleeping with a man of such size. But considering I needed you to carry me to the bathroom and wash my hair, I can guarantee you I'm not letting XL anything near me.

I'm confused as hell, considering it was on *her* list.

And I'm not a fan of her little dig, but I let it slide.

FISHER

I tried calling, but you must be sleeping. I don't understand. You put that on your shopping list.

When I get to my truck, I pull out the air mattress Landen left for me. Once it's blown up, I get it situated in the bed of my truck.

It's not until I park in my hiding spot does she return my text.

NOAH

What're you talking about?

Ten seconds later, she sends another one.

NOAH

Oh my God. I'm going to kill Magnolia!

NOAH

She had my phone when I was rambling off the things I needed, and she added it because she thinks she's SO funny.

I chuckle because Magnolia's car is here, which means she's spending the night. I can only imagine the way Noah's scolding her.

FISHER

Perhaps she wanted them for herself. She's after Tripp, ain't she?

NOAH

Ha! I can't believe you bought them. Didn't you think it was odd of me to have that on my list?

FISHER

Honestly, yes. But I figured it wasn't my place to ask.

NOAH

I can't even put weight on my foot, you think I'm over here taking massive dick?

I chuckle, wishing we were talking on the phone or in person because I miss hearing her snarky attitude.

FISHER

Again, wasn't my business.

NOAH

Don't do that.

FISHER

What am I doing?

NOAH

Acting like you have no right to know about my life or what I'm doing. Just because we're not together doesn't mean we can't be involved in each other's lives as friends.

FISHER

I don't want to keep hurting you, Noah.

I grab the pillows and blankets I set in the front seat and bring them to the back. As much as I love talking to her, I know it only makes it worse. Someday, she'll find someone who's right for her. When that day comes, I'll wish her the best and drown myself in a bottle of whiskey.

NOAH

I'm going back to sleep. Night.

FISHER

Good night, Noah. Sweet dreams.

I feel like I've let her down by not agreeing with her, but it's for the best. I can love her from a distance and give her room to move on.

My phone goes off just as I doze off.

A camera notification.

I look around and, in the distance, see the security light on at the family's barn.

There'd be no reason for any of Noah's brothers to be out there at two in the morning unless this is another Wilder adventure I keep hearing about.

When I look on the app, no one's in view, but I won't be able to sleep without double-checking.

I walk over, looking around for any disturbances and listening for noises. There's rustling in the bushes, and I wonder if an animal is what caused the camera to go off.

"Hello? Anyone out here?"

A clinking sound echoes from the barn. I open the door, then pull out my phone for a flashlight since it's dim lighting. The horses squeal as if they're on alert, and now I know something's off. Their intuition is never wrong.

A shadow running in the distance catches my attention. I smell the scent of gasoline as I walk toward it, and the horses continue neighing as the smell gets stronger.

"Hey, motherfucker!"

I spin around to a person in a hoodie and see a glimpse of a metal rod before he rams it into the side of my head, and I go down.

Chapter Thirty

Noah

"Noah, wake up!" Magnolia shakes me, and I squint when the light blinds me. "Something's on fire."

"W-what?" I push myself up into a sitting position, then glance around my room as I try to comprehend what she just said.

"I smelled smoke and looked around to see where it was comin' from."

"In the house?" I whip off the covers, then quickly remember I can't walk. "Can you hand me my crutches?"

She grabs them from the wall. "Outside! It's close by because the smell is strong. I think it's coming from the family barn."

Oh my God. *The horses.* A wave of panic rolls through me.

"We need to call the fire department." I grab my boot, then slip on one of my shoes.

"I did already. Also called Landen and Tripp to alert your parents."

"Okay, good." I can't stop thinking about Donut and all of our other horses. They must be so scared.

"Ready?" she asks when I stand with my crutches.

"Yeah— " The house rattles, making me fall back on the bed. I've never felt anything like that before. "Holy shit! Was that an explosion?"

Magnolia stumbles before she helps me back up. "*Fuck*. You okay? Almost felt like an earthquake."

The fear in her eyes tells me everything I need to know. Something is very wrong.

"We need to go," I say urgently.

As soon as we get outside, the smell is stronger, but it's too dark to see exactly where the smoke's coming from.

She helps me into her car, and as we drive away, I spot Fisher's truck hidden by some trees.

"What the hell is he doin' here? Can you check if he's inside?"

She parks, then quickly looks into his windows. When she hops in, she shakes her head. "It's empty, but there's pillows and blankets in the way back."

"*What*? He's sleepin' out here?" My heart pounds as I fear for his well-being. If he's not here, then where could he be?

Sirens blast as they speed up the long driveway that leads to the main house. You have to go that route to reach the barn, but I'm not waiting. I need to see what's going on now.

"Let's go." Magnolia slams on the gas, and soon we see the smoke coming from the family barn.

"Oh my God!" I can hardly breathe when I see flames coming through the window.

Magnolia parks next to Landen's truck, and we both get out. The security lights are on, but I don't see anyone. They have to be here somewhere, though.

"Landen! Tripp!" I shout.

The smoke is so strong I choke on it as I get closer. I call and text Fisher but get no response.

"Noah, look out." Magnolia points at the fire trucks, and we move back before they run us over. Three of them arrive with two ambulances.

Tripp appears from the other side of the barn to tell us Landen went inside.

"What, why?" I gasp.

He shrugs. "I told him to wait, but he doesn't listen to me."

When my parents and the twins arrive, we huddle together and wait.

The whole scene is chaotic as we watch it unfold. I feel so goddamn helpless not being able to do anything while a barn filled with my horses is on fire. Hearing them squeal and whine have me in a panic.

"*Please*!" I beg one of the firefighters. "My brother and horses are in there! Can ya get them out?"

"We'll do our best, miss. Stay back."

They're so calm, and I'm bursting into tears. The firefighters actively work on controlling the fire, but it looks like the flames are coming from the loft where extra hay is stored.

Finally, Landen appears through the smoke, dragging a body out.

"Oh my God," I shriek, grabbing everyone's attention.

Landen collapses to his knees, coughing. My parents rush over, and I go as fast as my crutches allow.

"Who is that?" I ask.

Landen shakes his head. "Can't tell."

"*Craig*?" Magnolia squeals as she takes a closer look. "His face is covered in blood, but it's definitely him."

She looks at me in horror, and given his condition, it doesn't look good.

"Is he breathing?" I ask.

Magnolia puts her ear above his mouth. "Barely."

I tell Tripp to get the medic's attention, and they follow with their supplies.

"What the hell happened?" I ask Landen as they examine Craig.

"I dunno." He coughs some more. "I went in to let out the horses, but when I saw a body lyin' on the ground unconscious, I dragged him out."

"Did you see Fisher in there? His truck is here," I ask, not even caring how suspect that sounds.

He frowns. "No, but I didn't go in all the way."

Momma tells one of the medics to check Landon, and even though he claims to be fine, they do anyway and put an oxygen mask on his face.

"Is he gonna be okay?" I ask one of the medics working on Craig. He has an oxygen mask over his mouth as they work on controlling the bleeding.

"His pulse is weak, but we still have him. We'll get him stabilized, then do a full examination and CT scan."

Even though he was an asshole and probably trying to kill my horses, I wouldn't wish death on him like this.

A moment later, horses barrel out of the barn through a cloud of smoke, bucking and squealing. Wilder and Waylon go after them, then lead them to one of the other pastures away from the flames. I count them as they run around, and my stomach knots when I don't see mine.

"We're missin' one. I don't see Donut!" I watch the barn doors, but he doesn't come out.

"I'm sure they're gonna get him, honey," Momma says, squeezing my shoulders.

Tears prick the corner of my eyes as I think about how scared he must be. I can't lose him, too.

"If Landen didn't get them out, how'd they get loose?" I ask.

"Maybe one of the firefighters managed to," Tripp suggests.

One of them comes over, and I grab his attention. "There's a horse missin'. Please, can you go back in and find him?"

"We didn't let them out, miss. It's too dangerous to go inside. We're fightin' the flames from the top because the beams become weak with that level of heat. I'm afraid they'll collapse soon."

I'm not surprised. Barns never survive fires. All that wood is a feeding ground. The best they can do is prevent it from spreading to other buildings.

"Then how..."

The moment the words leave my mouth, Donut gallops out with Fisher on his bare back. Tripp runs toward them and grabs

Donut's halter before he can take off. As soon as he comes to a stop, Fisher rolls off and collapses to the ground.

"Fisher!" I scream.

Tripp kneels beside him as another medic rushes over.

"Sweetheart, give them some room," Dad says, standing at my side.

My chest's so tight, I can't breathe. *Why was he in there?*

They flip him to his back, check his pulse, and examine his head.

"Tripp, is he okay?" I shout over the chaos.

"I dunno. He's bleedin', too."

Fisher went in there to rescue my horses and didn't leave until he got Donut.

And now he might not survive because of it.

As the realization hits me, I fall into my dad's arms and cry into his chest.

"He's critical. Get the stretcher," one of the medics directs to the other while they continue examining him.

This can't be happening. Fisher is unconscious as they secure an oxygen mask over his face.

"Is he gonna be okay?" I ask.

"We'll know more once we get him to the hospital. He may have head or lung trauma, so they'll do a full analysis to determine his injuries."

I watch as they lift him onto the stretcher, then get him into the ambulance. I'm in a daze as I try to process what's happening.

The love of my life risked his life to save my horses, and now I may never get the chance to tell him how much I love him ever again.

"Someone should go with him so he's not alone," I call out.

"I'll go," Tripp says, then gets into the back with the medics.

"We need to follow," I tell Dad.

"We will, sweetheart."

Both ambulances take off, and I struggle to understand what's happened.

Dad orders Wilder and Waylon to stick around to watch the horses. I hug Donut as tight as he allows before they take him to the pasture. Dad tells Landen to go home and take it easy. Momma kisses me before returning to the house to update Gramma Grace and Mallory.

Soon, Ayden and the other ranch hands arrive, but Dad tells them to go back home. It's unsafe for them to be here, and we can't do anything at this point.

Dad helps me into his truck, and when I look out the back window, it's surreal to see the damage. We could've lost them all, and I'm still shocked we didn't.

"It's gonna be okay, sweetheart," Dad reassures as we go down the long driveway.

"I don't understand why Craig would go this far..." I shake my head, still in disbelief. "He's already in trouble for the snake, trespassing, and intent to harm charge. Why add to it?"

"He's lashin' out, Noah. He's obviously not happy you reported him. Probably thought he could scare you into droppin' the charges, and it clearly went too far."

I shrug. "Well, he deserved it."

"I agree."

"But I'm still confused about their head injuries. Are they from the explosion, or was there a fight between them?"

"I'm curious about that, too. Also wonderin' why Fisher was here before the crack of dawn." His tone isn't harsh, but he's suspicious.

"I guess he was sleepin' in his truck. He mentioned he was worried Craig would break into my house after he made bail," I explain.

He nods, and although I can tell he wants to ask more questions, he holds back.

"You should let Jase know," he suggests.

Another person I'll have to explain to why Fisher was here.

When I call, his phone goes to voicemail, which isn't

surprising since it's after three in the morning. I send him a text so he sees it first thing when he wakes up.

As we get close to the hospital, I get a message, but it's not from Jase.

"Oh my God," I gasp when I read Landen's text.

"What is it?"

I look at him in shock. "They found a body."

Chapter Thirty-One

Noah

As soon as we get to the ER, Tripp sits with Dad and me until we get an update on Fisher's condition. Tears fall down my cheeks as a doctor explains his injuries and the process of treatment. When I ask to go back and see him, they have me wait until they move him into a room, which takes another hour.

Neither has commented on why I'm so distraught about Fisher's condition—well, more than one would be for an employee or friend. If they're suspicious, they don't voice it.

When I don't get a response from Jase, I send him another message with Fisher's room number so he can find it as soon as he arrives.

Dad drives Tripp home and returns after he checks on Landen. Between waiting, the chief of police calls, and Sheriff Wagner stops by to discuss Craig's participation and the body found. Dad gives them access to all the security camera footage so they can add it to their investigation. It's suspected whoever it is was close to the explosion and flew out of the barn. They were unrecognizable at the scene and transferred to the morgue.

Seeing Fisher with a bandage on his head and an oxygen tube across his face has me sick to my stomach with worry. They put him under anesthesia to perform a bronchoscopy to examine the level of damage in his throat and lungs since we couldn't know how long he was in the barn or if he was exposed to the explosion. After the procedure, they suctioned out secretions and debris in his throat and lungs due to smoke inhalation, but the next twenty-four hours are crucial to see if it gets worse.

Burns to his airway could become a problem, but since they're trying to be the least invasive, they'll continue monitoring before determining if more treatment is needed.

He had a CT scan to check for internal bleeding. Thankfully, there wasn't any at the time, but they're watching for possible swelling. Based on the size of the wound, whatever hit him was hard and solid.

They say he's lucky he didn't withstand any extreme burns and is only battling minor internal injuries. He'll fully recover with rest and oxygen as long as no more issues arise.

"Hey," Magnolia says softly, carrying two cups. "Brought ya some coffee. You have to be exhausted."

I take one. "Thanks."

"Any updates?" She takes the chair next to mine at Fisher's bedside. I haven't let go of his hand since they let me in here and have been quietly pleading and begging him to be okay.

"Not really. Just a waitin' game, they say."

The medication makes him drowsy as they keep him comfortable from the pain and discomfort.

"Let me take ya home for a bit so you can rest. Fisher's not goin' anywhere, and you—"

"I'm not leavin' him." I stare at his motionless body as I struggle to breathe. "He risked his life to get my horses out of that barn, and if he dies..."

"He's not gonna die," she reassures me, but I won't be convinced until I see his eyes open and hear his voice.

"His body is healin', and that takes time. You're no good just sittin' here worryin'," she adds.

"Then y'all will have to drag me outta here by my hair," I deadpan.

"Okay." She sighs and drops it.

I'm physically and mentally exhausted, my eyes are bloodshot from crying, and my body aches from sitting in this chair, but I don't care. I'm not going anywhere until he's awake.

After a moment of silence, I look at her. "He was sleepin' in the bed of his truck because I told him it was better if he didn't stay over anymore. If I hadn't done that, he woulda been in my house, *safe*. He wouldn't have gone to the barn to investigate or whatever he was doin'."

"Noah." She places her hand on my shoulder. "Ya gotta stop torturin' yourself with the what-ifs. Fisher chose to go in there. If he hadn't, all your horses woulda burned to death. If I hadn't been at your house to smell the smoke and call 911, the flames coulda caught other buildings on fire. This is not your fault for not lettin' him stay over. He chose to protect you, and knowin' Fisher, he wouldn't change a thing about that."

Though she's right, it doesn't make me feel better. He's suffering because of me.

One of the nurses enters, and we move out of her way so she can check his vitals. She tells me he's doing well considering the circumstances. She explains that once his oxygen levels stabilize and his lungs clear up more, they'll reduce his meds, and he should gradually wake up.

"Has his son arrived?" the nurse asks.

"No, I've called and texted, but it goes right to voicemail."

"When he arrives, please let us know," she says, her kind eyes trying to soothe me.

Once she leaves, Magnolia scrunches her face. "It's weird Jase is MIA, don't ya think?"

I nod. "Yeah, he was just visitin' me yesterday. We talked about house decoratin' ideas, and he made us tacos for supper. Didn't say he'd be goin' anywhere."

"Did ya call his office?"

"Yep. They said he was off today."

"Maybe one of your brothers should go to his apartment and check on him."

"Yeah, good idea. I'll ask Waylon. He's the least likely to punch him just for existin'."

She smirks because it's true.

NOAH

I can't get ahold of Jase, and he's not working today. Would ya mind going to his place to see if he's home? He has no idea about his dad.

WAYLON

Do I get to smack him around first?

I roll my eyes at his effort to be funny, but I'm too worried to laugh at his half-ass attempt.

NOAH

This is serious! Fisher's in critical condition, and his son deserves to know.

WAYLON

Fine. I'll head over and get back to ya.

NOAH

Thank you! Let him know Fisher's okay, but he really should come see him.

WAYLON

Got it.

"Okay, he's goin' there now."

"Ya ready to explain to Jase why you're so distraught over his dad?" Magnolia asks.

"Don't think this is the best time to tell him. He knows we're friends."

"Yeah, but even your father and brothers are gettin' suspicious. None of them understand why he's so protective of you...as a *friend*. Or why you refuse to leave his side. I lied for you and said you reminded him of his daughter, and you thought of him as a father figure."

I smack her leg, scrunching my face in disgust. "Magnolia! That is foul. Right to jail. Oh my God."

She bursts out laughing. "I'm *kiddin'*! Relax. That made me throw up in my mouth a little."

I shake my head, grinning. "You and me both."

"But at least I got a smile outta ya."

Twenty minutes later, Waylon finally texts me.

WAYLON

No answer. I left a note on his door just in case he comes back before checking his phone.

NOAH

Okay, thanks.

"Jase ain't home either. Where the hell could he be?"

"Maybe he has a secret girlfriend? Coulda spent the night at her place," she suggests.

"That'd explain why he's not at home but not why he's not pickin' up his phone."

"How late did he stay? When I came over, he was gone already."

"He left like fifteen minutes before ya showed up, so not that late. Around seven. Where did he go between the time he left and now?" I furrow my brows.

"I'm callin' it. He had a booty call."

I snort.

"Well, wherever he is, he better get his ass here soon."

"Hi, honey. We brought ya some dinner." Momma walks in with Gramma Grace an hour after Magnolia leaves. I knew she was getting anxious sitting here doing nothing, so I told her to go and I'd text her later.

Frowning, I look at the containers in their arms. "I don't have much of an appetite. I'm sorry."

"You need to eat and take care of yourself," Momma demands. "Fisher wouldn't want ya to starve. I brought your meds, too."

"I'm not. I'm just not hungry."

"I made your favorite. Peach cobbler." Gramma grins.

That makes me smile for a split second. "Thanks."

To appease my mother, I force-feed myself spaghetti and meatballs before eating dessert.

They tell me how the whole town's talking about the fire and what Fisher did to save our horses. There's no doubt he's a hero. I just wish I could see his warm brown eyes and hear his rugged voice.

Momma updates me on the barn and everyone at the ranch. It took the firefighters eight hours to get the blaze out completely. They've already started going through the security footage and should know more tomorrow when they begin investigating how and where it started.

"Jase hasn't shown up yet?" she asks.

"No. I'm worried about him. But I've done everythin' I can think of from callin', textin', askin' his work, and checkin' at his apartment."

"The sheriff's out lookin' for him, too. I'm sure they'll find him." Momma's kind eyes reassure me.

When I told Dad Jase wasn't answering his phone and wasn't home, he alerted Sheriff Wagner.

"I know ya don't wanna leave Fisher's side, but what about tonight? You can't sleep in that chair." Momma frowns. "I can set up the sofa for ya."

"I'll ask that hot doctor out there for some blankets and pillows," Gramma adds.

That makes me chuckle.

"Sure, but no guarantee I'll be able to sleep tonight."

Momma stands, rubs a hand over my shoulders, and pats down my messy hair, then rearranges the room.

"Can ya at least push it closer to his bed?" I ask, not wanting to even be that far away from him.

"I'll move it as close as I can. You don't wanna block the nurses' path to get to him if they need to," she says.

The nurses come in hourly, check his vitals, tell me to be patient, then leave. His doctor has only been in once, but not much can be done until he's awake. No news is good news in this instance.

As long as his stats are steady, he's healing and making progress.

When Gramma Grace goes to the nurses' station, Momma sits beside me and pats my good leg.

"I know ya love him, honey. As long as the feelings are mutual, I won't scold y'all for lyin' and keepin' it a secret." Her words are firm, but there's a hint of a smile on her face.

My foot taps nervously against the floor as my heart tries not to beat out of my chest. I hate that I had to hide it from her.

"How'd ya find out? I mean, before now..."

I'm not even trying to hide it at this point.

"Gramma." She chuckles. "Apparently, she's known for a while."

"I had a feelin' she did."

"She told me to take it easy on ya. Does Jase know?"

I shake my head. The thought of telling him after this worries me even more. "Fisher didn't want it to ruin their relationship after just returnin' in his life, so he broke things off to avoid the risk of Jase's reaction."

She crosses her legs and arches a brow. "So y'all are not even together right now?"

"No. Right after the fundraiser, he made his decision. I didn't fight it because I didn't wanna get between them. Jase was goin' through a lot, and I didn't want him to cut Fisher off because of me."

"That's very noble of you, Noah. But Jase is a big boy. He coulda handled it."

I shrug because I'm not sure how Jase would've responded. "Fisher couldn't afford to risk it. He'd already lost one child. He was tryin' to be a good dad and put Jase first."

"I can understand that," Momma agrees.

"I don't." Gramma returns with a pillow and blanket, looking suspicious as if she stole them.

"If ya were sneakin' around with someone, ya wouldn't have broken up with them if it woulda upset me?" Momma asks, placing the items on the couch for me.

"If you love me, ya woulda gotten over it. Same as Jase. I'm sure he'll feel some way about it, but eventually, he'll come around. He seems to like ya and wants his father back in his life," Gramma explains.

"Well, it wasn't my decision to make. He was afraid to lose him, and I couldn't compete with that," I say.

"He risked his life to save your horses. I doubt he's worried about that now." Gramma winks.

"I don't think Dad's gonna be as easy on me about it." I chew on my bottom lip, worried I'll disappoint or anger him.

"You let me take care of your father." She winks.

I snort. "Ew. No need to share that with the class."

"Oh, you!" She playfully swats at me, and I laugh.

"By the way, Gramma. Thanks for rattin' me out," I tease. Though I suspected she knew from what she said at our last family supper, I hadn't expected her to say anything.

"Oh, who did y'all think ya were foolin'? I knew it from the first time I saw Fisher look at ya. I'd never seen a man so in love."

My cheeks heat at her words. I can't even argue. Momma grins, and I'm relieved she's not upset. Though I'm sure the lecture will come later.

I contemplate what I'm going to do once he's awake. Will it

change anything between us? Do we go back to *just friends*? If it were up to me, we'd be together and never spend a day apart, but I can't ask him to risk his relationship with Jase after everything they've been through. He has to take that leap.

Either way, I'm here for him—as a friend or as more.

When I stand to move to the couch, Momma offers me her arm since I opted to hop on one foot instead of using my crutches. Using them requires more effort than hopping a few feet and dealing with the rib pain for a few seconds.

I rest my foot up on the chair once I get comfortable on the makeshift bed. It's been aching all day, but I've ignored it.

"Ya need ice for that?" Momma asks.

"No, the meds will kick in soon."

It's more of a discomfort than anything, but I could go without the rib pain.

"Will ya be alright if we go? I gotta get Gramma Grace to bed." Momma fusses with my pillow and pulls the blanket over me. I plan to go back to the chair and rest my head next to Fisher as soon as they leave.

"Yes, I'll be fine. His nurse comes in frequently enough that if I need anythin', they've offered to help," I tell her so they don't worry about me being here alone.

They pack up the leftovers and grab their things before giving me hugs. "Thanks for comin'."

"Of course, honey. We'll be back tomorrow with breakfast."

I chuckle, knowing nothing I say would stop them from bringing me more food.

"Okay, thanks."

After we say goodbye, I grab the blanket and drag it back to the chair next to Fisher's bed.

"Well, I guess the cat's outta the bag," I tell him, sighing with relief that their reactions weren't nearly as bad as I anticipated. I'm not sure whose response I'm more worried about—my father's or Jase's.

"You'll be glad to know Gramma absolutely adores you." I chuckle even though I have no idea if he can hear me.

As I lay my head next to our conjoined hands, my phone goes off with a text, and I hold on to hope that it's Jase.

TRIPP

I think we know who the body is. He's on camera with Craig.

NOAH

Oh my God, who is it?

He sends a still photo from the security footage, and I gasp.

Chapter Thirty-Two

Fisher

Every inch of my body is stiff and achy, but I'd rather that than burning pain. My head hurts like a motherfucker, but from what I've randomly heard from the nurse, there hasn't been any swelling or cause of concern beyond a concussion. The dumbass who hit me managed to whack me just hard enough to knock me out but not keep me down.

When I regained consciousness and realized the barn was on fire, I booked ass to open the horses' stall doors. The fire started in the loft, which gave me more time to get them loose before it engulfed the entirety of the lower floor. It's a miracle I was able to get on Donut and escape in one piece. The flames were closing in on us, and he was too spooked to go on his own. He wouldn't move until I jumped on him. By the time we barreled through the doors, I was suffocating and couldn't breathe.

Noah squeezes my hand as if she knows I can feel her. Whatever meds they're pumping through me have been slowly wearing off, and now I'm fighting for the energy to open my eyes.

"Hello?" A faint knock echoes through the room. A voice I'd recognize anywhere.

"Hi," Noah greets softly. "Who're you?"

She's about to meet the man who saved my life and changed it for the better.

"I'm Damien Lancaster. It's a pleasure to finally meet ya, Miss Hollis."

"You're Fisher's childhood friend."

"I am."

"And you know who I am?" Noah asks as if she's shocked I'd talk about her to a friend. Considering he's still a detective in the next town over, I'm not surprised he heard about what happened.

"I do." His voice is closer now, and soon, his palm rests on my arm as if he wants me to know he's here. "He called and left me a voicemail the day after y'all met and said, *'Damien, I met her. The woman I'm gonna marry someday.'*"

Although I'm not even sure I can talk, I force out the words anyway. "You bastard. Ya weren't supposed to tell her that."

"Oh my God! You're awake?" Noah squeals.

Finally, I manage to lift my eyelids halfway and smile when I see her beautiful face. "Hi, Goldie."

My throat is raw like I'd swallowed a thousand knives, and my voice is hoarse, but it's enough for her to hear me.

Noah covers her mouth as tears fall down her cheeks. "Hi."

"Are the horses okay?" I choke out. My voice is barely audible, but I need to confirm they survived. Once I opened their doors and they ran out, I wasn't sure where they ended up.

"Yes." She breaks out into sobs, nodding. "Thanks to you."

I smile weakly when she buries her head in my chest. Although my limbs feel like concrete, I manage to wrap my arm around her. I'm not wasting this moment with her.

"Hey, man. Glad to see ya alive." Damien shoots me a knowing grin.

"Yeah, we gotta stop meetin' like this."

He barks out a laugh. "Once a decade, you're right on schedule."

Between my bull riding incidents that landed me in the

hospital, the suicide attempt, and now this, Damien's seen me at all the lowest points in my life.

"How's your ankle and ribs?" I ask Noah.

I don't know how many days I've been in here, but by the looks of her disheveled hair and the dark bags under her eyes, she hasn't left this room.

"The pain ain't comparable to what it's been like waitin' for ya to wake up."

"Sorry." I grin, cupping her cheek when she leans in.

"It was worth the wait. I missed you, though. And don't think we're skatin' past the comment Damien made."

Damien laughs, and I glare at him. He's been my only family for a long time since I stopped talking to my parents years ago, but we still give each other shit.

"If I'd known that was all it'd take to wake ya up, I woulda come sooner."

"How long has it been since the fire?" I ask.

"Three days," Noah says. "They're still goin' through a lot of the rubble and doin' a full investigation. Craig's in the burn unit on life support. It's not lookin' good for him though."

"Holy shit." My heart races as I think back to who hit me. It was a tall guy who was scrawnier than Craig. "Pretty sure he had an accomplice because I saw someone on the other side of the barn before I got hit."

Before we can continue the conversation, the nurse comes in. She asks about my pain level, checks my oxygen line, then brings me water. She warns me that I'll have a scratchy throat and some coughing for a while, which is normal for having smoke inhalation. Then she tells me the doctor will be in later to discuss my treatment and when I can expect to be discharged.

"Where's Jase?" I ask once she leaves.

"Um..." Noah lowers her eyes, and Damien's lips turn into a frown as if he can sense something's wrong. "He's not comin'."

"W-what do ya mean?" I ask gruffly, then sip more water.

"I'm gonna go so y'all can talk. I'll be back tomorrow," Damien says, patting my arm. "Glad you're awake."

"Thanks for comin', man."

"Ya know I always will."

Noah's glossy eyes stare at me as she waits until we're alone. I'm not sure what's going on, but the tension makes me uneasy.

"What is it?" I ask, my heart pounding as anxious nerves settle into my veins.

"Jase was missin' for the first twenty-four hours, and no one could find him. I called, texted, contacted his work, and even had Waylon go to his place. Eventually, we gave the sheriff notice so he could keep an eye out for him, too. As far as I knew, he hadn't been located, and since he hadn't returned my calls, I hadn't expected him to barge in here when I was clingin' to you."

Shit. I exhale a deep sigh.

"I take it...he knows, then?"

"The nurses told him his dad's girlfriend hadn't left his bedside in two days, and he put it together when he saw me. He didn't even give me a chance to explain or tell him the full story. Took one look at me cryin' next to you and walked right back out."

Closing my eyes, I wish I'd been the one to tell him. Instead, he's stewing in anger and feeling betrayed.

I place her hand on my chest, longing to hold her. She looks devastated. "Fuck, I'm sorry. I shoulda told him so he didn't find out that way."

"We couldn't have known Craig and Ian were gonna torch the barn, and you'd get in the middle of it," she says.

"*Ian*?"

She nods. "Caught him on camera." Then she lowers her eyes again. "He didn't survive."

I blink a few times as if that'll change the words she just said. "*W-what*? Why would Ian work with Craig? I hadn't realized they knew each other."

"Me neither, and I dunno. My guess is they met at the

fundraiser or Ian reached out to him after I'd kicked him out. I was shocked."

Even if Craig makes it out of the hospital, he'll go to jail for arson and possibly manslaughter.

"Did ya ever find out where Jase was when no one could find him?" I ask.

"Yeah, the sheriff told me they found him at his friend's mountain cabin a few hours north. They went fishin' on the boat, and he had no cell service. He woulda had to have left town shortly after leavin' my house or early the next mornin' before I called him. Not sure it was planned because he never mentioned it to me."

"Probably a guy from work. He's talked about someone invitin' him up for a weekend, but it coulda been last minute, who knows. That's interestin' though because he never used to like fishin'."

"I've texted him all day. Even though he doesn't respond, I've sent updates on your progress, but he leaves me on read."

"He'll come around. Give him time."

"The only thing I wanna give him is an earful and chew his ass out for bein' a shithead. Ya got hurt, and he didn't even stay to hear if you're okay."

"I'm sure the nurse gave him an update," I say, hopeful I'm right.

She takes out her phone. "Ya wanna call him?"

"Do ya know where mine is?"

"I assume in your truck. You stalker," she teases, and it hits me she knows I was sleeping outside her house.

"Won't apologize for that." I wink.

"I'm gonna text him first so he knows it's you and to pick up," she explains before handing it to me. "Maybe FaceTime him?"

"Good idea."

Once Noah's message shows *read*, I call.

After five rings, he finally picks up.

"Jase?"

He stays silent as the screen points at the ceiling. If he doesn't want to talk to me or look at me, that's fine, but at least he's willing to listen.

"It hurts to talk, Jase, but I'm gonna try my best so ya can hear this from me. I met Noah at the Franklin rodeo. We connected and spent the night together. We didn't know who we were to each other in terms of you bein' the link between us. All I knew was I felt somethin' I hadn't felt in years, and I wanted to explore it. Noah realized it after she learned my last name and ghosted me. When I found out she was a Hollis, I put the pieces together that she was the family I was workin' for and tried tellin' her before I arrived, but again, she ignored my calls. I didn't know why until I showed up at the ranch, and she finally came clean."

Noah hands me my water when my voice gives out. "You want me to continue the story?" she whispers, but I shake my head. I'm not stopping until Jase gets the full truth from me.

"She knew I was here for you and how I wanted to rebuild our relationship, so we decided to be just friends. I didn't wanna risk hurtin' ya or jeopardizin' your trust."

He snorts as if my words are bullshit, but I continue anyway, even if it makes me look bad.

"At first, we tried to stay away from each other. I know that sounds cliché, but we couldn't and decided to secretly date to see how it'd go. Once it got serious, we'd tell ya and her parents. We didn't wanna announce anythin' until we knew it'd work out. But when I saw how upset ya were at the thought of her datin' someone, I knew you'd never be okay with us together, and I broke it off."

My heart aches at the way I've disappointed the two most important people in my life.

Noah holds up my water cup again, and I take a longer sip this time. My throat burns, but I keep going.

"When Noah got hurt, I blamed myself for not protectin' her, and the guilt ate at me that she got injured on my watch. So I told her parents I'd help durin' her recovery because even if we couldn't be together, I still very much cared about her."

"How'd ya end up in the barn?" Jase finally speaks.

I explained how being at her house so much was torturing her, so I opted to stop coming by so much, but I kept watch outside her house at night due to Craig making bail.

"Can't say I'm completely surprised," he says. "Maybe I shoulda noticed it earlier, but I figured I was overthinkin' things. The way you two look at each other, how you were trainin' with her and bringin' her groceries. A part of me didn't wanna see what was right in front of me."

"I tried to keep my distance, but no matter what, I couldn't help the way my eyes always found her whenever she was near," I confess. "I'm sorry for not tellin' ya."

"So y'all aren't together anymore?"

"Technically, no," I say even though it hurts to admit. "But I dunno that I can stay away after this."

I glance at Noah, who's hanging on to every word but stays silent.

Jase finally shifts the phone so his face is in view.

"Ya broke up with her? For me?"

I nod. "For our relationship. I didn't wanna lose ya."

"It'd take a lot more than datin' my ex-girlfriend to lose me, Dad. Not happy y'all lied and snuck around behind my back, but I don't want y'all miserable on my behalf. You've suffered enough. You deserve someone as great as Noah."

I choke up, not sure how to respond, but when happy, relieved tears surface, I don't fight them.

"Good luck tellin' her family, though." He barks out a laugh, and I chuckle.

Noah blushes, moving closer so he can see her face.

"Took ya long enough to come to your senses, asshat. I was about to send Landen to knock some into ya," she teases.

"I needed twenty-four hours to bleach out the images of ya two in my head," he smarts off.

Noah rolls her eyes. "You're so dramatic."

"Ya realize he's twice your age, right?" The corners of his lips curve up as he taunts her.

"You realize I'll marry him and become your stepmom just to punish you, right?"

"Ooh, naughty stepmother fantasy just entered my mind." Then he starts humming the theme song for PornHub, and I choke back a laugh. Noah has no idea where it's from, which makes Jase sing it louder.

She rolls her eyes. "This is why I'm into older men."

"You two fight like brother and sister. I dunno how y'all ever dated in the first place," I say.

"Yeah, because you're so *mature*..." Jase drawls in a mocking tone.

"Y'all need some boxin' gloves to fight it out or what?"

"He knows I'd kick his ass, bad ankle or not," Noah taunts smugly.

They banter for another minute before finally giving up. He promises to stop by tomorrow before we say goodbye. I'm relieved the air's clear between the three of us. Now all we need to do is come clean to her family.

"Oh, I should tell ya. Gramma Grace and Momma know. So that only leaves my dad and brothers," she tells me.

"Think if I tell them while I'm injured they'll take it easy on me?"

She snorts, sitting on the bed next to me. "Only one way to find out."

"Wait. I haven't officially asked ya to be my girlfriend again." I grab her hand and pull her as close as possible.

"Well, what're ya waitin' for, cowboy? Get on your knees and beg."

Her serious tone makes me cough out a laugh. "If I could get out of this bed without the risk of fallin' on my ass, I would plead with everythin' I have."

"Fair enough. I'll just pretend ya are." She smirks, and I know she's messing with me.

Smiling, I pour my heart out to her. "You've been mine since I laid eyes on you. Even when we couldn't be together, I was always yours." Then I press my lips to her knuckles. "I'm madly and desperately in love with you, Goldie. Nothin' would make me happier than you bein' mine out in the open for everyone to know you own my heart."

"Nothin' would make me happier, either." She beams, and I adore how happy she looks. "Fallin' in love with you was so damn easy and tragic at the same time. I'm ready for the world to know."

She inches closer until our mouths can finally touch. I hate that I can't kiss her the way I want to, but I'd take a peck on the cheek from her if it was all I could ever have.

"Thank you for stayin' here with me. Wakin' up to your voice and seein' your gorgeous face is the only way I ever wanna wake up again."

She smirks, then sucks in her bottom lip. "I think that can be arranged."

Chapter Thirty-Three

Noah

As soon as Fisher was discharged from the hospital and Jase drove him home, Fisher packed a couple of bags and came to my house. I was still recovering, so instead of being apart, we bunkered in my room together and rested. He made me watch more vintage movies, and I educated him on the feud that inspired Taylor Swift's *Reputation* album.

One of her best eras, if I do say so myself.

"Wow...you're stunnin'." Fisher's jaw drops when I attempt to do a spin in my bridesmaid's dress. "And I'm one lucky man."

Grinning, I hop closer, then pretend to wipe the drool from his chin. "Yes, you are."

I'm still wearing the stupid boot for my ankle, but my six-week appointment is coming up to check if it's healed enough to remove it. When moving around my house, I don't use my crutches since my ribs don't hurt as much, and I can hop without putting weight on my ankle.

It's been a long time since I've been able to work. Landen and Tripp took over most of my clients since they're already experienced, and Ayden reorganized the boarding scheduling so no new ones arrived. I've had to put a hold on the specialized ones like Delilah and Harlow. Ellie and Ranger are ready to get back to work, too. Once I'm cleared, I plan to get started again if my body can keep up.

"I was iffy about the color, but it's grown on me," I say, rubbing my palms down the silky basil-green fabric.

Fisher wraps his arms around my waist, closing the gap between us and burying his face in my neck. "It's gorgeous on you, but I think I'd like it even better on the floor."

I tilt my head as he kisses my neck and under my ear. "You're killin' me. Screw the weddin'. Fuck me instead."

He chuckles against my skin. "I'm still on rocky ground with your father and brothers. No need to give them another reason to hate me by makin' you miss the ceremony."

Fisher and I haven't gone beyond making out since we reunited, and I'm dying with anticipation for when he'll finally realize I won't break. Even though I'm no longer taking pain meds and only using an ice pack at night, he's afraid it'll be too much for me. No matter how many times I try to convince him I'm better, the fear that he'll hurt me stops him from going further.

"They don't *hate* you," I reassure him.

Fisher was back on his feet within a few days, but when it was time for Sunday supper, we came clean to the rest of my family. Landen and Tripp didn't seem as shocked by the news as the rest, which wasn't surprising since they were around us the most. Waylon and Wilder are primarily at the retreat and are too absorbed with their own lives to notice anyone else's.

My father rose to his feet, left the room, and returned with his shotgun.

Then he warned Fisher he wouldn't be afraid to use it if he dared to hurt me.

We show up every Sunday and stay to scrapbook. Fisher even started a couples album even though we only have a handful of photos together. But it gives us something to look forward to as we take more pictures.

"I dunno about that. Landen shoots me the *I'm watchin' you* finger V-sign at least once a day. I swear, he's just waitin' for me to fuck up so he can kick my ass."

I snort at his dramatics. Landen isn't as muscular as Tripp, but he knows how to fight and is quick with his movements. I've seen him wrestle my brothers since I was a young kid, and he's only gotten better and faster as he's gotten older.

"He's not gonna hurt ya," I reassure him.

"Tripp keeps tryin' to convince me to go to the Twisted Bull with them again, but then Waylon told me it was so they could get me back on the bull and see how long I'll last before I pass out. I think they're secretly hopin' to kill me."

"They won't let the bull run longer than fifteen seconds, so I wouldn't worry too much. They just want a reason to get drunk and be stupid. Not that they really need a reason..." I roll my eyes.

"I can't wait for the day Landen finds a girlfriend and I get to return the treatment."

I snort, wrapping my arms around his neck. "You'll be waitin' a while. He doesn't date. At least not since Angela broke his heart junior year. Now he just has...*flings*."

"Isn't he like twenty-six?"

"Yep. Four years older than me."

"And he's still distraught over a breakup from nearly ten years ago?"

I laugh because he's right. It's been almost a decade. "Well, after Angela was Layna, and she was the English teacher's assistant his senior year. He'd never admit it, but I'm pretty sure they had an affair. Then he graduated, and she got engaged *to* the English teacher."

His eyes widen. "Jesus. He's been traumatized."

"After those two, he's never had anythin' serious," I explain.

"Maybe I'll make it my mission to find him someone, then." He smirks as if he's pleased with himself for coming up with the idea. "Is Ellie single?"

"Oh my God, don't be playin' matchmaker with my clients.

Especially the ones I like. They don't deserve to be tortured by my brothers."

He presses his mouth to mine as he lowers his hands down my back and cups my ass. "I've never wanted to rip a dress off you as badly as I do right now." The growl in his voice and his erection poking into me nearly have me giving him the green light to do just that.

"Save that energy for later, Mr. Underwood. Are you finally ready to stop denyin' me?" I ask, adjusting the collar on his dark-green button-up. He's paired it with a nice pair of black slacks.

"I'm worried I'll crush you or re-break your ribs."

"That'd be an injury worth sufferin' for."

He gives me a pointed look. "Not funny."

"Oh, c'mon. My momentum and energy are up. If it weren't for the crutches, I'd be out ridin'." I pause with a smirk. "The horses *and* you."

"Very cute." He kisses the tip of my nose, then lifts and carries me out.

For the past month, I've visited the horses every few days so they don't forget about me when I'm back training full-time. After the fire, they were relocated between the retreat barn and boarder stables. It took a while for the family barn burn area to get cleaned up, and construction on the rebuild began shortly after.

Donut's been through so much in such a short amount of time, so I've spent extra quality time with him. I brought in an equine specialist to help monitor his behaviors so he's mentally prepared for me to ride him again without being triggered. After spending several months getting Donut at the level he was, some of what he learned has been repressed due to the trauma he suffered.

If Craig hadn't already suffered a painful death, I'd wish one upon him for nearly killing me, my horses, and Fisher.

It was a beautiful day for a wedding, and the weather didn't disappoint. Ayden and Laney renewed their vows in a small, intimate ceremony on the ranch with their families and everyone who works here. Although I couldn't walk down the aisle with one of the groomsmen, I stood with my crutches next to Serena and Mallory, and once it was over, Fisher held up my dress as I hopped to the white tent for food and drinks.

This is the first big event where Fisher and I can be openly together, and even though my brothers like to give him shit, they treat him like family and are much nicer to him than they were to Jase.

After dinner, the tables were moved to make room for dancing, and I went to the bar.

"Be careful how many you have, or I'll be carryin' your ass over my shoulder," Fisher whispers in my ear as I lean against the counter.

"I thought you liked the taste of Buttery Nipples on me?" I taunt, licking my lips.

"Mm...in that case." He pulls me into his chest. "Is it too soon to leave?"

Arching a brow, I wait for him to admit he's messing with me, but I know he's serious when he doesn't. *Finally.*

"Hell no." I down the final shot, then grab my crutches and lead us to his truck. "I can't wait to ditch these.

"Very soon. Then you'll be back to runnin' shit as usual." He smirks as he drives us to my house.

I didn't bother saying goodbye to everyone because I'll literally see them tomorrow night at Sunday supper, but I let Momma know we were taking off so she doesn't worry.

The moment I open my front door, Fisher slams it shut and

lifts me until my legs wrap around his waist. The sounds of my crutches falling mixed with my heavy panting echo throughout.

"Are you sure this is okay?" he asks, walking us to my bedroom as his erection digs into me.

"Yes, I promise. If anythin' hurts, I'll tell you. But right now, all you need to worry about is gettin' me naked and inside me as soon as possible."

"Tsk, tsk, Goldie." He carefully drops me on the mattress and hovers over me. "I've been holdin' back for over a month and ain't rushin' this now."

My head falls back on a groan, and I wish he'd put me out of my misery instead of being a gentleman just this one time.

"Don't worry, my love."

He removes my shoe and boot before planting a knee between my legs. Then he slides his hands up my bare thighs and moves my dress up. "I'll get you there in eight seconds."

"Your version of *eight seconds* is torture while you bring me to the edge and back repeatedly before finally lettin' me come."

He chuckles as he lowers his mouth above my panties and presses a kiss there. "You figured out the secret code, huh?"

"Yeah, I don't think it was that hard to break. The last time nearly had me squeezin' off your fingers."

"And with that in mind, now the question of which *eight seconds* version do you like best? My mouth..." He nuzzles his lips over the fabric covering my pussy. "Or my fingers?" His thumb brushes my clit, and my hips arch for more.

The first time Fisher had me counting was during our first night together after the rodeo, and his mouth did amazing and torturous things to me. The second time was when we watched *Overboard,* and he made me wait till the couple got their happily ever after before I could get mine.

"I should be the one makin' you count. Let's see how you like it." I pout when he moves away from where I want him and kisses up my stomach.

He shoves my dress to my chin and pulls my strapless bra

down, then focuses on my exposed breasts. His tongue flicks my pierced nipples, then he sucks them between his lips. I can tell he's being extra careful not to put his weight on my ribs, but I can handle it.

"Take off your clothes, please," I beg, ready to tear them off myself if he doesn't.

"Patience, baby."

I have zero left.

Leaning up on my elbows until I sit up, I remove my dress, then unhook my bra.

Fisher shifts back slightly to give me room, then allows me to unbutton his shirt and undo his pants. Finally, he lowers his boxers and shows me all of him.

He smirks, then licks his lips as he watches me. "By the way you're starin', I'm wonderin' if you think I'd need those Magnum XLs now?"

My cheeks heat at the memory of me chewing him out for buying condoms. "I gave them to Magnolia. Figured she'd need them before I would. But I don't want anythin' between us anyway."

He knows I'm on birth control, and until we're ready to discuss kids, I'll continue taking the pill.

"Me neither." He lowers his mouth to mine and helps me move up the bed until he's between my legs. Then he removes my panties and devours my clit until I can no longer take it.

"Oh my God. That was intense," I say between rapid breaths.

He finally positions himself between my thighs and kisses me. "Mm. I love the taste of Buttery Nipples on you."

I grin, brushing a hand through his hair and pulling his lips back to mine. "I know. It's why I ordered it."

He chuckles, burying his face in my neck as he holds himself up with his arms. "So that was your plan all along, huh? Shoulda known."

"I'm not as fragile as you think." I lower my hand between our bodies and stroke his length. "Let me prove it to you."

His eyes roll to the back of his head as I widen my legs and arch my back until he manages to slide inside me.

"Fuck, Goldie." He rests his forehead on mine as he takes one of my hands and raises it above my head. "You feel so goddamn good."

This moment is unlike any other as we connect and make love with no secrets between us. No more hiding our relationship and fearing the worst. We're free to be who we are and love whoever we want without the risk of hurting people.

The last time we slept together was emotional because I thought it'd be the last time, but now it's emotional because we have *forever*.

"I'm so obsessed with you," he whispers in my ear as he pins me underneath him. His confession has my heart soaring to the moon because the way he loves me is unlike anything I ever thought I'd have. He's one of a kind, and he's *mine*.

"Fisher, *more*. Please." I breathe out his name like a plea, desperate to come on his cock.

The rotation of his hips adds friction between us and has my clit on fire with need.

"I'm so close." I moan loudly as he pounds harder into me. "Don't stop."

He pinches my nipple as he increases his pace and sinks deeper until I feel him hitting my G-spot.

"Such a good fuckin' girl. Your cunt takes me so well, baby."

The hoarse growl in his words is all it takes to send me over the edge, moaning and screaming his name as the pleasure takes over. I squeeze his shaft as I ride the waves, and moments later, he's groaning my name as he comes inside me.

"Are you okay?" He rolls off me, then wraps me in his arms.

I turn and face him, then cup his face and press a soft kiss to his lips. "Yes. And I love you for trustin' me and not treatin' me like a porcelain doll."

His devious smirk has me wondering what's so funny until I realize what he did.

"That was you bein' careful with me, wasn't it?" I scold.

Though I'm not complaining because it was *really good* but goddammit. Now I want to experience the rough side of him.

"I didn't say a word."

"You didn't have to! I know your little tells, you liar."

"I didn't lie. I gave you exactly what you asked for."

I playfully pout as he plucks my bottom lip.

"As soon as you get the clearance for physical activity, I'll bend you over this bed and fuck your brains out. Until then...no complainin'."

I chuckle, snuggling closer. "Fine. Doesn't mean we can't shower together, though, right?"

"Noah..." His warning tone makes me smile. "You really are an AJ, aren't ya?"

"There's no adrenaline rush like sex in the shower on one foot."

He snort-laughs. "It's like you try to find ways to get hurt."

"Says the former *bull rider*. You'd be in there with me, and I know you'd keep me safe."

He gets to his feet, lifts me into his arms, then carries me to the bathroom.

"I'm gonna have you countin' until you come on my face." He sets me down in the middle of the shower, and I grab the railing. "That sweet pussy is mine."

Chapter Thirty-Four

Fisher

TEN MONTHS LATER

"Good mornin', beautiful," I whisper in Noah's ear as she sleeps beside me.

Waking up with her in my arms each day is a life I never knew possible. A year ago, I was positive I'd never find love and die alone. It was what I told myself I deserved. Until Noah jumped into my view at the rodeo and won my heart with one simple phrase—

"Happy Anniversary," I say, and her eyes pop open.

I chuckle at the panic in them as the realization hits her.

"One year ago today..."

"The rodeo."

We leave tomorrow for this year's competition, but tonight, I have plans for us.

"You know what I realized? Remember that napkin you wrote your number on? Had you given me the other one, I would've recognized Jase's and all this never woulda happened."

"Oh my God, I forgot about that. I even offered to show it to you, but you didn't wanna see it. Imagine if you had."

"How one little decision coulda changed everythin'."

"Imagine how awkward that woulda been for you to open it up to your son's number and realize who I was—besides being the family you'd be workin' for but also someone he'd dated. Had you known that night, do you think you woulda said somethin' or ignored it?"

"Honestly, I probably woulda walked out right then. But thank God I didn't know."

"No kiddin'! We wouldn't have gotten together, and Jase wouldn't have met Amelia."

"Crazy how it all turned out, huh?"

Amelia's a local trainer who came to Noah's fundraiser event last year. They followed each other on social media and started talking regularly after the fire. It wasn't until she invited Amelia to the ranch that she met Jase since he was here to watch Noah perform on Donut. She was determined to get back on him and do the same tricks she did the day she got hurt so Donut could heal from the trauma. After that, she signed Delilah, and a few months later, she joined a trick riding team. She'll be at the rodeo tomorrow for her first big show.

Once Jase and Amelia met, they hit it off and have been dating ever since.

Though Jase and I still go to our grief meetings once a month, he's still talking to his therapist, which makes me happy. Knowing everything he went through to get to this point, he's working hard each day to be the best version of himself, and that makes me proud as hell as a father.

We visit Lyla on the second Saturday of each month and take her fresh flowers. When Noah got cleared to walk on her foot again, I brought her along so I could "introduce" them. Now it's a family tradition where the three of us go and update Lyla on all the recent events and small-town gossip.

I know Lyla would love hearing about Noah's horses and all the drama we hear from Gramma Grace's old ladies' club.

"Speakin' of, I invited them to Sunday supper tonight. Your mom said it was okay, so I hope you don't mind."

"Not at all. It's always a fun time when I can tease him about datin' his dad."

I snort because they do really fight more like siblings than anything, which is hilarious, considering I want to make Noah *my wife*.

Once we added onto her cottage, there was room for me to move my stuff in so I could stop living out of a duffel bag each night I slept over. She wanted to stay on the ranch, and I wanted to be wherever she was. Jase got a nice commission after he sold my house, so it was a win-win.

I hired a contractor to expand the primary bedroom and kitchen, and add a second bathroom. We both spend hours on our feet each day and deserve a way to relax at night, so I bought the biggest whirlpool tub I could find. Our nightly tradition is to soak in it together and catch each other up on our day.

"Our breakfast is gettin' cold, so get dressed and meet me out in the dinin' room."

"You cooked?" She points her nose in the air. "Oh my God, you made bacon!"

Laughing, I help her up and hand her one of my T-shirts. "C'mon, let's feed ya. You're gonna need your energy for today."

"Don't have to convince me."

After a day of horseback riding and having a picnic lunch off Sunset Trail, we spend the afternoon downtown. Magnolia insisted she come to help Noah find a new dress for the occasion and get their nails done. They hung out at the salon while I made a pit stop at the jewelry store and then returned with their favorite coffees.

When Noah and I arrive at her parents' for supper, she's glowing in a new pink sundress and matching nails. Magnolia talked her into getting a blowout at the dry bar, so I waited while they did that. But hell, it was worth it.

Noah's gorgeous on her sickest days, but tonight, she's goddamn stunning. I can hardly keep my eyes and hands off her. I thought seeing her in a cowboy hat with braids was cute, but her all dressed up and looking happy as ever has me even more excited for tonight.

"Mrs. Hollis, you look lovely." I kiss her cheek as she greets us in the kitchen.

"You dress up nice yourself, Mr. Underwood." Her cheekiness makes me grin. She knows what's coming and has been sworn to secrecy.

We say hello to the rest of her family, and once Jase and Amelia arrive, we take our seats for supper.

Noah's mom and grandma made her favorite dish, beef baked stew with French bread, and of course, her favorite dessert, peach cobbler.

"One whole year of puttin' up with my sister. Congrats. You deserve an award." Wilder holds up his glass, and I tense because Noah won't put up with his shit.

"Hey," Noah scolds. "Why not one year of *me* puttin' up with *him*? Misogynistic much?"

"Relax." Wilder rolls his eyes as he taunts her with a devilish grin. "Anyone who can deal with you that long deserves an award."

Noah's lips curve up as she arches a brow toward him. "Oh, don't worry. I'll be *rewardin'* him all night long."

"Gross," Jase whispers next to me, and Amelia chuckles.

"What's that mean?" Mallory blurts out.

My eyes nearly pop out of my head as I look at Noah's parents. Her dad scowls at Wilder while Mrs. Hollis's cheeks flame red. Then there's Gramma Grace, who smiles wide as if she's just happy to be here.

"Nothin', sweetie." Mrs. Hollis points at her plate as a reminder to eat.

"Noah." I cough out her name in a hushed, scolding tone.

"*What*? If he can dish it out, then he can take it."

Her thick drawl has me grinning and shaking my head.

The conversation goes back to ranch and retreat work stuff, as per usual with their Sunday dinners. The closer we get to dessert, the more nervous I get. My palms are slick with sweat, but I try to act unaffected once the peach cobbler is served.

"Gramma, this is so good." Noah moans as she takes a large bite.

"It really is," I agree. I love how the hot cobbler tastes with the cold ice cream.

"When do I get the secret recipe so I can learn to make it?" Noah asks her.

"It's tradition to pass it on at one's bridal shower," Mrs. Hollis says.

"You're jokin'." Noah makes a face as if she's not happy with that answer.

"Guess that means we're never gettin' it," Landen quips, and the other boys laugh.

Mr. Hollis kicks him underneath the table. "Your wives will get it."

"So we gotta be married to get family recipes? That seems very 1950s, Momma." Noah pouts before shoving another forkful in her mouth.

"Yeah, what if she becomes a nun?" Wilder muses, and by the look on Mr. Hollis's face, I swear he's about to send him out onto the porch again.

"Shush your mouth or I'm gonna—" Noah stops when I stand.

I walk over to where I hid the scrapbook I made for her and bring it back to the table.

"What's this?" she asks when I set it down in front of her.

"I put together a little somethin' for you. Pictures of us from the past year."

She slides her plate to the side and looks at the cover where I added a recent photo of us from my birthday.

"*Our First Year Together*," she reads aloud. "Oh my gosh, Fisher! Is this what you've been workin' on?"

I lean over and kiss her temple. "I know how much you like

capturin' memories and keepsakes. Figured this was a good way to document our relationship."

She knew I started this months ago, but I stopped letting her see my progress when I came up with an idea I wanted to surprise her with.

Noah flips through the pages, touching every little greenery and floral piece, then reads where I added in details of the photos. Each new holiday we spent together, adding onto her cottage, us riding together, me trying to teach her how to clip hooves, her attempting to teach me a trick riding stunt that I gave up on, her birthday party from a few months ago, and when I officially moved in with her. So many memories and milestones from the past year that I can't even remember my life before she was in it.

"Wow, I'm speechless. This is the best gift I've ever gotten." A few tears spill down her cheeks as she looks between me and the pages. "You decorated this so cute, too."

"I might've gotten some help..." I grin up at Mrs. Hollis and Gramma Grace, who helped with the finishing touches.

When she gets to the last two pages, I dig into my pocket and clutch the velvet box.

"Oh no, I think the photo fell out of this frame." She traces it with her finger before realizing the date written on top is today's date. "Wait, what's this mean?"

As soon as I slide out of my chair, I get down on one knee and pull out the box.

She finally looks over and realizes, then covers her mouth with a loud gasp. "Oh my God. Are you just proposin' so I can get the recipe?"

I laugh, and everyone follows because that is the perfect Noah response.

"No, baby. Although, that's a happy coincidence."

I open the ring box and take her hand. "Noah, I have loved you for no less than three hundred and sixty-five days, and if you'd do me the honor of being my wife, I promise to love you for the rest of my life and all the days after. Goldie, will you marry me?"

She nods frantically before finally speaking. "Yes! Yes, I will!"

When she falls into my arms, I hug her to my chest and bury my face in her hair.

"You've made me the happiest man in the world, baby," I whisper in her ear.

"I can't believe you planned this, and then did it in front of my entire family and Jase!"

I chuckle as we pull apart.

"You're tellin' me," Jase mutters in a lighthearted tone. "I'm not callin' you Mom."

"Don't sass me or no allowance," Noah taunts in her unserious tone.

Jase shakes his head and blows out a breath. "And so it begins."

Everyone bursts out laughing, including me.

Taking Noah's left hand, I slide the diamond onto her ring finger and beam at how beautiful it looks on her. "I hope you like the one I picked out."

"It's *stunning*!" She blinks at it a few times as if she can't believe it's really hers. "But I'd wear a paper ring as long as it meant I was yours forever."

"*Taylor Swift*!" Mallory squeals at the song reference. I've gotten used to those over the past twelve months.

Noah and I lean in for a kiss.

"Okay, picture time!" Mrs. Hollis stands with her phone in her hand. She was tasked with recording the whole thing because I knew Magnolia would want to see it.

We sit side by side, smiling wide at the camera. Noah holds up her hand to show off her new ring. When Mrs. Hollis counts down and gets to one, I turn and beam at my future wife.

The perfect last photo for the final page of our first year together and the start of our forever.

Epilogue

Noah

FIVE MONTHS LATER

I never imagined I'd be married by the age of twenty-three.

I also never imagined I'd be married to a man twice my age.

I definitely never imagined I'd fall in love with my ex's dad.

But still, I couldn't be happier.

None of this was planned, and that's what makes it even better. For my whole life, I thrived on schedules and organization, and as soon as I stopped trying to figure out every piece, I met the love of my life.

It wasn't an easy or simple journey to get here, but it's one I'd do all over again if it meant I got to marry Fisher.

We had an intimate and beautiful country fall wedding at the ranch. I'd like to say it went flawlessly, but nothing rarely ever does around here with horses and changing their schedules. Still, it was the best day of our lives and one I'll remember forever.

Damien, Jase, and all four of my brothers were the groomsmen. I had Magnolia as my maid of honor and Mallory, Serena, Laney, and Ruby as my bridesmaids. The planning process was fun, but I was *mostly* looking forward to *after* the wedding.

"Home sweet home," I say as we walk through the front door of the cottage for the first time in two weeks.

Fisher brings in all our luggage and nearly collapses to the floor with how many there are. I bought too many souvenirs and had to buy an additional suitcase just to bring them home.

But it's not like I could go to a Taylor Swift concert on the way to our honeymoon and not buy merch for the girls.

Plus, I couldn't pass up on the touristy items once we flew to our actual destination. I'd never traveled out of the South before, so I wanted to explore and bring back as much as I could.

"Let me help," I say, chuckling at his attempt to carry them all in with one trip.

"I got it. You just relax."

"That's all we've been doin' for the past fourteen days. I need to get back to work."

Although we had a great time, I missed my family and the horses.

Once Fisher's hands are free, he lifts me over his shoulder and carries me to the bedroom.

"Not yet, Mrs. Underwood. I have you to myself for one more night, and I'm not wastin' one fuckin' second."

"You're gonna knock me up with that caveman behavior." I smack his ass before he drops me on the mattress and hovers above me.

"Would that be so bad?" He arches a brow.

We've talked about having a baby but not when.

"I'd like to enjoy married life for a while before gettin' pregnant," I say honestly.

"*Greedy*. I like it." He winks before burying his face in my neck and sucking under my ear.

My legs wrap around his waist, and I pull him closer. "But we can practice...*a lot*."

"Love the sound of that." He pulls back and helps me out of my clothes, then removes his.

When he kneels between my thighs, I stop him. "Wait. Before you do that, I need to shower off the plane smell and sweat."

"Don't make me tie your wrists." He pushes my hands away, then widens my legs. "I will eat this pussy like it's my last meal, and you will count to eight before I let you come on my face."

"Fuck..." I'm already panting at the thought. "Okay."

"That's my good girl. No holdin' back either."

I chuckle at the memory of when someone called guest services because they thought someone was being murdered. They asked if we had any weapons in our room, and I responded, "*Only if you count my husband's tongue*."

Apparently, that wasn't appropriate to break the ice.

The guy's face turned beet red, and he couldn't even look us in the eyes when he asked us to keep it down, or they'd have to move us.

After that, we had to get creative.

I ball my fists in the sheets as Fisher devours me with his mouth and fingers.

And for the first time ever, he gets me there in seven seconds.

"Holy shit." I pant through the words as my heart races. "That's a new record."

"I was takin' it easy on you before, my love. Now bend over and stick out that ass for me."

As soon as I get into position, he smacks it before spreading my cheeks and sliding inside. Every time he thrusts, I moan his name. The love I feel for him is unmatched by anything I've ever felt before. Even after all this time, I can't get enough of him and how he makes me feel loved and cherished.

He twists my ponytail in his hand, pulls my head back, and whispers in my ear, "Get ready, baby. Rub your clit while I fuck you and come inside your tight cunt."

God. I could explode from his words alone.

"Yes, please," I whimper.

He unabashedly slams into me, hitting my G-spot over and over as he grunts and groans. By the time I fall over the ledge, I'm flat against the bed with my thighs squeezing his shaft.

"Lift your hips for me, Goldie. I'm so goddamn close."

I do, and as soon as I meet his thrusts, he growls out his release.

My heart sputters as I catch my breath, and he collapses beside me.

"How did I ever go without you? How could I almost lose out on this?" He brushes a finger over my sweaty cheek and pushes loose strands of my hair out of my face. The somber tone in his voice has my stomach tightening at the thought of us never meeting.

"Maybe you were meant to live because *I* couldn't be without you," I say, wrapping my arm and leg over his body.

He pulls me closer, tightening his grip on me. "After all these years, I believe that wholeheartedly. Besides reunitin' with my son, you were the best thing to come out of all of this."

I bite my lower lip, contemplating my next words. "I have a confession."

He raises a brow. "What?"

"I forgot to pack my birth control, which means I haven't taken the pill in two weeks. I literally just realized it." I lower my eyes, worried he'll be disappointed or mad.

Our schedule was so messed up that I didn't remember I normally take it with my morning coffee because we weren't rolling out of bed until midday. We'd stay up late, exploring or making love, and then we'd sleep in until our stomachs growled, and we'd go for lunch.

I mentally smack myself for being so irresponsible. *This is why I thrive on routine!*

He tilts up my chin until our gazes meet and greets me with a smile. "I'd love nothin' more than to see you pregnant with my baby and start a little family with you. If that's what you're worried about, then don't be. But if you're not ready—"

"Knowin' that I could be changes things. I *do* want a baby with you. Even if it's sooner than I expected, if I am, I want this," I say with my whole chest. "I might be a little scared, but havin' you by my side makes me confident we can do this."

He brings his lips to mine, and I savor the taste. "I love you, Goldie. It's me and you *forever*. Don't forget that."

I beam as I think about how much I love him and how excited I'd be if we were pregnant.

"I never will."

"I fucked up," Magnolia says when I visit the coffee hut a few days later.

Magnolia's Morning Mocha officially opened six months ago. She saved up enough money to get started, then got approved for a business loan. She brings the trailer to the retreat twice a week to serve the guests, then parks downtown for the rest of the time. I was so proud that she finally quit her job and went after what she wanted. It's a huge success, which I love for her. She deserves it after all the work she's put into remodeling the trailer and practicing her skills to make the best drinks in the area.

I haven't seen her since I left for my honeymoon and missed her, but I was busy unpacking, doing laundry, and catching up on work.

"With what?" I ask as she makes me a coffee.

"I might've hooked up with Travis a month ago..."

I gasp, my mouth opening in shock. "Magnolia Sutherland! You did not! And why am I just now hearin' about it?"

Travis is her deadbeat ex who cheated on her and then gaslit her into thinking she was crazy.

"Because I knew that'd be your reaction."

"Well..." I shrug.

"I was drunk and horny. And very, very, *very* stupid."

"The start to every country song..." I snort but try not to laugh at her expense. "Okay, so are y'all back together now or what?"

They broke up two years ago, so their dating again would be a nightmare. I'd support her if she decided she wanted to give it another try, but I wouldn't like it.

She shudders. "God, no. I told him to lose my number and blocked him. Drunk Magnolia ain't makin' that decision again."

"*Good*. You deserve better."

She turns and faces me, handing me my cup. "I took a pregnancy test, Noah."

I hold my breath as I wait for her to tell me exactly what I know she's going to say.

Tears fall down her cheeks. "It was positive."

"Aw, sweetie." I walk around to the side and open the door, then engulf her in a hug. "I'm not sure if I should say congratulations or not but—"

"I dunno either," she admits, crying as I keep my arms wrapped around her.

She pulls back and wipes her cheeks, then fidgets with her fingers. "That's not the worst of it."

"What's worse than being knocked up by your ex?"

"I slept with someone I really like after him, and now I've ruined any chance at a relationship. He'll never want me once he finds out I'm havin' another man's baby."

"Magnolia! I leave you for a couple of weeks..." I laugh, but I'd never shame her. She's young and can have as much fun as she wants. Albeit she shouldn't have had that fun with Travis, but it's a little too late for that lecture. "You're sure he ain't the father? What happened to those Magnum XL condoms I gave you last year? Surely you didn't go through an entire pack already."

"Trust me, Travis doesn't need XL, but we did use one. It was either expired or broke." She scowls. "And yes, I'm sure. I track my period and ovulation cycles on an app. By the time I slept with the other guy, I woulda already been pregnant. I just obviously didn't know."

I'm on pins and needles as I wait for the news so I can finally share *my* news with her.

"Alright, so who is it?"

She lowers her eyes, and my heart jumpstarts with her reaction.

"It was Tripp."

And now it just flatlined.

"Wait..." I scratch my head as if my brain's trying to figure out a calculus equation. "My *brother* Tripp?"

She winces at my raised voice I didn't mean to release. Clearing my throat, I try again.

"Tripp, as in the guy you've crushed on for nearly a decade and has never shown an interest in you, Tripp?"

"Yep." She sucks in her lip as she nods. "Turns out he does kinda like me."

Fuck. This is going to crush him.

"If he truly does, he'll accept you and the baby," I tell her. "But he might not be ready for that, which you'll need to prepare yourself for that possibility."

"Oh, I am. I'm expectin' him to push me away and never speak to me again."

She sounds so defeated, and I hate that she feels that way.

"Well, I'll be here for you no matter what." I hug her again. "My little niece or nephew will be spoiled as hell."

"Thank you. I can't believe you get to sit behind me and chant *push, push, push* durin' my labor before I get to do it for you. My hot girl summer just turned into fat girl winter."

"Oh my God." I burst out laughing. "First, that was never gonna happen. Second, summer was over before your little one-night stand mishap, but if it makes you feel any better, we'll at least be fat together."

She straightens her shoulders as she lowers her gaze to my stomach. "*What*?"

I nod with a smile I can't contain. "Yeah. Just found out this mornin'."

Her jaw drops as she smashes me in a hug. "Holy shit! I never thought we'd be pregnant together!"

"Me neither. We weren't even tryin'!"

"*Damn.* Daddy Fisher sperm workin' double time." She waggles her brows, and I playfully smack her arm.

"I swear it was the water at that place. Either that or honeymoon sex works faster."

She grins wide, leaning against the counter. "What if our kids grow up and marry each other? We'd be in-laws!"

"You're nuts, you know that?"

"I do. These hormones are about to make it worse, too."

"Now we can annoy Fisher and my brothers together." I lean over to grab my coffee and taste it since I'll be switching over to decaf after this.

"About that. I need you to keep this a secret, at least until I can tell Tripp myself."

"Yeah, of course. Are you gonna tell Travis?"

She groans. "Eventually. I wish I didn't have to, but if he finds out before I tell him, he'll be even more immature about it. If it were up to me, he wouldn't exist at all."

"You know that ain't fair, though. He deserves a chance to be a father; if he chooses not to be, you can cut him out completely. Just don't let him back into *your* life, if you know what I mean."

She crosses her arms and sighs. "Yes, *Mother*. I don't wanna anyway."

"Good. Then all you need to focus on right now is eatin' healthy, stayin' stress-free, and gettin' enough sleep."

"What 'bout you? Are you still gonna ride?"

"Yes, but I won't do tricks or stunts. I'm sure Fisher will try to ban me from all trainin', but it's literally my job, so he'll just have to deal with it. But otherwise, I'm gonna make sure I don't overdo it, either. We can be accountability partners."

"I love that idea. This is much more excitin' now that you're knocked up, too." She giggles, then takes out her phone.

"Happy to have forgotten my birth control for you." I snicker.

"I downloaded this pregnancy app. You should get it, then we can track our progress and milestones. It says my baby is the size of a lentil." She holds up her hand to make a tiny circle.

Once I have it pulled up on my phone, I input the date of my last menstrual cycle, and it shows I'm four weeks along.

"Mine is the size of a poppy seed." I show her the photo on my screen. "Hm, Poppy. That's a cute name."

"Sorry, but I'm not namin' mine Lentil."

I burst out laughing at her deadpan expression. "Fair enough."

By our dates, Magnolia's two weeks ahead of me, which means we'll still go through a lot of our milestones together.

"I'm excited to go through my first pregnancy with you. Even if the circumstances aren't what you'd hoped for, you're gonna be a mom, and that's somethin' to celebrate," I tell her when she stares at her phone.

When she looks up, I notice the wetness in the corner of her eyes. "You're right."

"We'll plan a dinner and sleepover at my house this weekend. What do ya say? I'm sure Mallory and Serena would love to come for a dance party."

"Can you still have slumber parties when you're married?" she teases, wiping her cheeks when the tears fall.

"Um, duh. Fisher knows who he married. If he wasn't prepared for Taylor Swift sing-alongs and pajama nights, he shouldn't have proposed."

"You're so lucky to have each other. You won the husband lottery."

"And you will find someone equally as lucky to have you. I promise."

Before leaving, I give her one last hug, then promise to call her later after work. I haven't even told Fisher I took a pregnancy test, so I need to figure out how to announce it.

At least he's prepared for the possibility, considering we went unprotected, but I'd like to do something special like he did when he proposed.

Since he's already working in the barn, I sneak over to my parents' house and dig through the scrapbooking supplies. We've been working on a second-year-together album, and I plan to do a separate one for the wedding photos, but for now, I'll add a new page for finding out we're pregnant.

"What're you doin', sweetie?" Gramma Grace walks into the dining room with a mug in her hand.

"Just makin' somethin' to show Fisher later." I smile, closing the book before she can see the page.

There's a vintage frame in the center surrounded by little wheat clippings. On top I wrote, *Our First Ultrasound.* Once we have a picture, I'll add it inside.

She walks around the table and pats my shoulder. "You're gonna make a great mom, Noah."

"H-how?" My mouth drops open. "How do you always know stuff before anyone else?"

Gramma Grace's dimples deepen as she sits down next to me. "I'm a good observer."

"But I literally just found out, so what could you have noticed?"

Her eyes lower to my chest as she smirks. "Your breasts are swollen. That's one of the first symptoms. I saw you walkin' into the house earlier, and your hand was on your stomach. We're instinctively protective when we know we're pregnant. And finally, you're glowin'."

"I'll give you the first two, but I think you're confusin' my glow for sweat. I walked to the retreat and back."

When I went to visit Magnolia, I didn't bother driving since it's only a mile, but I didn't think about how I'd have to walk back to get to the ranch.

She raises her brow and smirks. "That *is* the pregnancy glow."

"Great." I chuckle.

She stands with her coffee and pats my cheek. "Just wait till you find out what tradition you get at your baby shower."

I furrow my brows, wondering what she could be talking about.

"Well, now I'm scared to know."

"You'll find out soon enough..." Gramma hums as she walks away, leaving me to my thoughts.

Bonus Epilogue

Fisher

"Ranger, buddy. You're snarky today." I pat his back as I move down his leg and hoist it between my thighs. "One inch to the right and you woulda nailed me in the balls. Not sure that's good for my little men."

He whines as if he doesn't give two shits about my ability to reproduce. The cold front has all the horses on edge, not that I can blame them, but it makes doing my job harder.

"You need help, cowboy?" Noah's boots come into my view before the rest of her does.

When I raise my head, I smile at her cowboy hat and braids. She's holding what looks like one of our scrapbook albums against her chest. "From a beautiful woman like you? Anytime."

She pets Ranger with her free hand and tries to comfort him. "Ellie's comin' to work with him later. Maybe that'll relax him."

"I hope so. Whatcha got there?"

"Just a little surprise I wanted to give ya. But it can wait till you're done."

"Well, gimme just a few. This is the last hoof."

She runs her fingers down his mane and helps him relax as I finish up.

"Good boy, Ranger." I pat him a few times, then Noah offers to take him back to his stall.

Once she returns, I tilt up her chin and bring my mouth to hers. "You look beautiful today."

"Well, thank you. Are you ready to see what I made?"

"Absolutely." I take off my gloves and watch as she flips through the pages of our second-year-together album.

"I made a new page. Ready?"

When she sucks in her lower lip, nerves surface at what I should expect.

"I think so."

Then she flips it, and all the blood drains from my face.

Our first ultrasound.

My eyes flick to hers, to the page with the empty space inside the frame, then back to hers again.

"You're…*we're*…pregnant?"

"Yeah, I took a test this mornin' after you left for work."

"Oh my God." I engulf her in my arms as a roller coaster of emotions hits me. "Sweetheart, that's amazin'."

My heart pounds against hers as the realization soaks in.

Before Noah, I never wanted more children.

Never thought I deserved to be a father again.

Never considered I'd meet someone as perfect as Noah and want to start over.

But she's changed all of that.

Now, I can't wait to start a family with the love of my life and watch her become a mother.

"I love you so much, Goldie. Thank you for givin' me this second chance."

She buries her face in my chest and fists my shirt as she cries in my arms.

"Baby, why're you cryin'?"

"I wanna blame it on the hormones, but I'm just so happy. I didn't even know I wanted this right now until I saw that little plus sign, and suddenly, it was all I imagined for our lives. Then I was overwhelmed with excitement and nervous I'd suck at the same time."

I pull her back slightly so I can wipe her tearstained cheeks. "You are too incredible to suck at anythin', and this is no different, my love. I cannot wait to hold our baby in my arms, but before that, I can't wait to feel their little kicks and hear the heartbeat. Every moment will be an amazin' one. You'll see."

"I know. I'm excited about all of that, too. Just worried I won't know what to do."

Leaning down, I kiss her forehead. "You won't be doin' it alone, don't worry."

"I should warn you. It's about to be double trouble because Magnolia's pregnant, too."

"Wait, what?" My brain crisscrosses in confusion. "I didn't even know she was datin' anyone."

She glances around as if she's making sure no one's in earshot, but then Ayden walks out.

"I'll tell ya later. Oh, by the way, we're hostin' a slumber party this weekend."

I raise a brow. "Your brothers are makin' me go to the Twisted Bull on Saturday."

"*Again*?"

"For my official initiation into the family now that we're married."

She barks out a laugh. "I thought they made you do that when we announced we were datin' last year."

"That was the *datin'* initiation."

"Why're you even goin' along with this? Tell them to fuck off."

I smirk. "Because as dumb as it may be, it's fun to show off and prove to them how awesome I still am. They make bets on how long I'll last on the bull, but by the end of the night, I'm up a hundred bucks, and they're too drunk to give a shit."

She sighs with an eye roll. "Better tell them we're pregnant before then so you can do the *knocked up their sister* initiation at the same time. Oh, and Gramma Grace knows even though I didn't tell her."

Grinning, I pull her closer again. "At this rate, that woman will know the gender of the baby before we do."

"You're probably right."

I cup her cheeks and stare into her soft ocean-blue eyes. "I'm so head over heels in love with you, Noah. Thank you for bein' with me, marryin' me, and havin' my baby. I couldn't ask for a better life."

We celebrated that evening by baking peach cobbler and making love. Noah started a list of baby names she likes, and Poppy stands out as my favorite if it's a girl.

If it's a boy, I'd like to name him Damien.

That weekend, Noah's brothers hyped me up as I rode the mechanical bull. I made it twelve seconds before the beer in my stomach threatened to come up if I didn't get off. When I told them they were all gonna be uncles, they made me pay their tabs.

Jase and I went to Lyla's gravesite the following week, where I shared the news that they'll have a new sibling in nine months.

When Jase gave me the biggest hug, I nearly teared up at his support. He didn't have to give me a second chance in the first place, but the fact that he did, means the world.

Hell, it changed my life.

It brought me to Sugarland Creek.

It made me want to be a better man.

And for the first time in a decade, it made me feel worthy of being a father and husband again.

Read Noah & Fisher's bonus scene by subscribing to my newsletter: https://bit.ly/BM-Bonus. You'll get an email immediately with the bonus content.

Curious about Magnolia and Tripp?
Find their story next in *Stay With Me*

If you want to read Ayden & Laney's second chance romance, grab the free prequel, *Come With Me* on any retailer!

Stay With Me

A best friend's brother stand-alone from small town romance author Brooke Montgomery about a girl who falls pregnant by the wrong man and the cowboy who takes her in...

About the Author

Brooke has been writing romance since 2013 under the *USA Today* Bestselling author pen names: Brooke Cumberland and Kennedy Fox, and now, **Brooke Montgomery**. She loves writing small town romance with big families and happily ever afters! She lives in the frozen tundra of Packer Nation with her husband, wild teenager, and four dogs. When she's not writing, you can find her reading, watching ASMR and reading vlogs on YouTube, or binge-watching a TV show she's most likely behind on. Brooke's addicted to iced coffee, leggings, and naps. She found her passion for telling stories during winter break one year in grad school—and she hasn't stopped since.

Find her on her website at
www.brookewritesromance.com
and follow her on social media:

facebook.com/brookemontgomeryauthor
instagram.com/brookewritesromance
amazon.com/author/brookemontgomery
tiktok.com/@brookewritesromance
goodreads.com/brookemontgomery
bookbub.com/authors/brooke-montgomery

Also by Brooke Montgomery

Sugarland Creek series

As Brooke Cumberland:

Pushing the Limits

The Intern Trilogy

Shouldn't Want You

Someone Like You

As Kennedy Fox:

Checkmate duet series

Roommate duet series

Lawton Ridge duet series

Only One series

Make Me series

Bishop Brothers series

Circle B Ranch series

Love in isolation series